sometimes witches
hunt their own

GRAVEBRIAR

CASEY L. BOND

ISBN: 9781087942773

Book Cover, Map and Interior Formatting designed by The Illustrated Author Design Services

Interior Illustrations by Steffani Christensen

Edited by The Girl with the Red Pen

Proofread by Kendra's Editing and Book Services

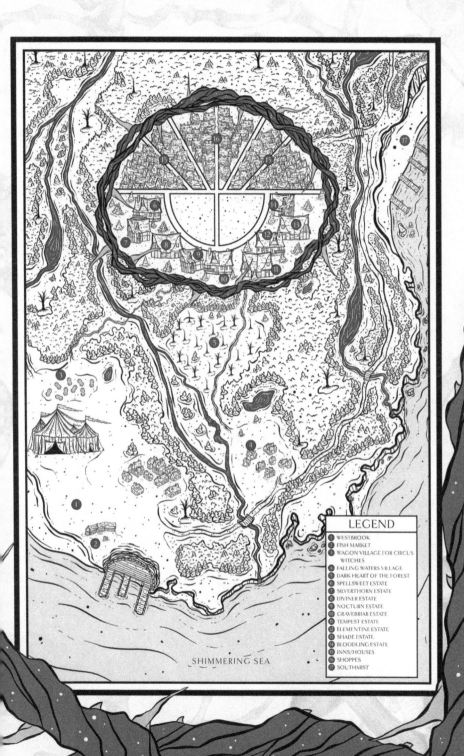

LEGEND

1. WESTBROOK
2. FISH MARKET
3. WAGON VILLAGE FOR CIRCUS WITCHES
4. FALLING WATERS VILLAGE
5. DARK HEART OF THE FOREST
6. SPELLSWEET ESTATE
7. SILVERTHORN ESTATE
8. DIVINER ESTATE
9. NOCTURN ESTATE
10. GRAVEBRIAR ESTATE
11. TEMPEST ESTATE
12. ELEMENTINE ESTATE
13. SHADE ESTATE
14. BLOODLING ESTATE
15. INNS/HOUSES
16. SHOPPES
17. SOUTHMIST

SHIMMERING SEA

Praise for Gravebriar

"Casey L. Bond weaves an enchanting world filled with magic and intrigue. Gravebriar is spellbinding and romantic, and will keep you turning the page until the end."
–USA Today bestselling author Ali Winters

"Spellbinding and rich, Gravebriar is a wildly creative, witchy journey."
–Heather Lyons, author of The Collectors' Society

"Casey L. Bond seamlessly weaves a world of magic, intrigue, betrayal, and wonder that you'll never want to leave, and characters that will become dear to your heart!"
–USA Today bestselling author C.L. Cannon

"Cracking open the pages of Gravebriar was like stepping into a world where witches roamed and magic abounded. I never wanted to leave."
–Christy Sloat, bestselling author of The Librarian Chronicles

But he, that dares not grasp the thorn,
Should never crave the rose.
~Anne Brontë

ONE

The witch city of Cauldron was touted as a lovely place to live, a place where magic of any quantity and kind was embraced and celebrated, a refuge for generations of witches living in a world that hated and hunted them.

But sometimes, witches hunted their own.

Aesthetically, Cauldron *was* pleasing, with her grand boulevard arcing in front of each of the nine Covens' Estates and her radiating pattern of cobblestone streets packed with colorful shoppes and eclectic homes. The city was governed by a Council comprised of the most powerful witch from each of the covens so that all were equally represented.

Members of the Council would advise you that their decisions were fair and impartial, and made with the consideration of the greater good of Cauldron and every witch who lived within its magical, protective hedge. But if one looked more closely or lived there long enough, they would find that the city wasn't filled with tolerance, and the Council members were too busy clamoring for power to worry themselves over something as inconsequential as fairness.

1

The once-sparkling utopian ideals had slowly leaked from Cauldron, spoiling and leaching into her soil, rendering it lifeless and brittle.

Now, Cauldron was corroded, filled with lies that were sly and handsome, sweet poison to the ear.

If *our* secrets ever spilled, everyone would discover that my coven, the Gravebriar witches, were arguably the best liars of them all...

TWO

An unease filled my bones, as dark as the long shadows stretching over Cauldron as the summer sun sank behind her steeply pitched roofs. I smiled to myself. It was my favorite time of day. Not only did the evening offer a respite from the humidity blanketing the city, and not only did the Goddess paint the sky in vibrant azure, gold, and topaz... Dusk was deceptive. She encouraged people to mentally shift their focus away from their obligations to the far more entertaining, exciting things the evening might hold.

When people were preoccupied, they forgot what – or who – stood in front of them.

My pale dress fluttered in the breeze as I walked down the uncommonly bare main avenue with a woven basket perched on my arm. It was my turn to deliver my coven's wares to an apothecary and a general witchery shoppe whose owner exclusively stocked our smudge sticks, the most potent you'd find to eradicate bad energy or unwanted spiritual house guests.

I pushed open a heavy wooden door and placed a sachet into an already-outstretched hand, wrinkled by time and hard work. The apothecary's wiry white, caterpillar brows drew together as he studied the contents of the cinched herbal packet my mother had personally grown, cultivated, measured, mixed, and sent him.

He yanked his spectacles off and brought the sachet closer, sniffing it, then tearing the pouch open and moving to his counter to pour the contents into a pristine bowl. He nodded appreciatively, not even looking up as I eased the door closed behind me and stepped from his shoppe onto the cobblestones again. The heady scent of incense lingered as I walked to my next drop-off.

Quaint wooden signs hung over each bricked shoppe, declaring its specialty in swirling, white letters.

There were Spellsweet shoppes whose shelved walls held a cacophony of glass bottles containing potions and elixirs, salts, and less savory ingredients for hexes and spells. For a price, you could purchase powerful curses or change your appearance. A Spellsweet witch could make you attractive to everyone or only one, or make people forget you existed for a time. I was very tempted to buy the latter for tonight but refrained. Mother somehow always remembered me.

Colorful Diviner tents stretched between the brick and mortars where, when they weren't empty, you could duck inside to have your fortune read. They were the source of the incense. Many a Diviner could read smoke as easily as bones or palms, cards or tea leaves.

I passed a Nocturn shoppe. Any other night, they would just be opening, keeping hours from dusk till dawn, but the Nocturn enjoyed a party as much as any other witch – perhaps more. The Nocturn's magic lay in the night. Those hailing from their coven could chart a powerful moon cycle suggesting when certain magics would be most profound, or for a greater fee, one might take you into the wood at night to show you the wonder the forest held tight to her bosom. Their shoppes were always dark, the windows covered with shutters engraved with the moon's varying phases.

Bloodlings shoppes smelled of copper, despite the doors and windows being shut. Inside, a witch of their coven could sift a single droplet of your lifeblood and tell you how long you might live or read overall health, or with a single droplet more, conjure darker magic. Their shoppes emptied midday when the witches would break to gulp the lifeblood of whatever animal they'd purchased from the Nocturn's hunt the night before, reopening after their thirst was sated.

Broad windows set the Tempest shoppes apart from the rest. Tempest witches always kept an eye on the sky. From them, one could buy clouds that would hang over a lawn long enough to water it and then dissipate or purchase gusts of wind that would blow any clouds overhead completely away so the sun might shine just where you'd like it. One could even buy a thunderstorm to sit over the house for a time of someone who'd annoyed you.

Silverthorn shoppes were simpler and tidier than all the rest. They contained neatly stacked bars and containers where slivers and shavings of all matter of metal from warm brass to cold steel were neatly arranged. Their witches didn't bother making things before someone needed them. They simply conjured what the purchaser wanted when they asked for it. Watching the Silverthorn witches contort metal, whether into simple things like utensils or tools, or complex weaponry, was always fascinating.

Not that I ever lingered long at their windows. Silverthorns weren't fond of Gravebriars and wouldn't bother to hide their disdain, regardless of the rules of decorum that the Council insisted we all follow. Whatever feud erupted between our covens had long since cooled, but just because a thing was forgiven, didn't mean it was forgotten.

I'd once believed that scars and wounds belonged to the one who earned them, but now realized they could be passed down from generation to generation.

I moved along, passing a bakerie that smelled like cinnamon bread, one of my favorites, past another Diviner tent for a palmistrist, and past an empty Elementine shoppe. Their shoppes were always empty, their witches preferring to stand outside, tempting passers-by, until they struck a deal with someone, of course. Business was conducted privately.

Their witches brought a refreshing levity to the covens. One of them might stand in the street's center juggling fiery batons or conjuring persons made of water who would walk down until there was nothing but watery stones left to testify that they'd existed. Sometimes people paid the Wind witches to startle a friend walking by an alley with a powerful gust, while the Earth witches could conjure mighty, muscled stallions from the soil packed tightly into planters, making them rear and paw the ground before crumbling into the streets.

The shoppe owners would grumble over disturbed planters and pretty plants uprooted and left clinging to life, but one word to a Gravebriar and all would be set right. We were the only coven not represented among the others in town. To buy our wares, one had to come to our Estate and speak with my mother. It was a much more personal way of doing business, she would say.

In truth, it was just a way for her to maintain control. Control over who requested and was awarded our magic, control over who spoke with any of my coven mates and about what, and control over what was conjured by her witches.

I pushed open a door and stepped into a Spellsweet shoppe that smelled strongly of burning white sage. The floorboards creaked under my feet, making the young witch snap her head toward me. Her eyes lit up. "I was hoping you'd still come today, though I'm sure your coven is busy preparing for tonight's revel. I'm burning my last bundle." I smiled and placed a fresh set of white sage smudge sticks in her outstretched hands and quietly slipped out the door. She absently locked it behind me. "Thank you," she said through the panes and wood.

With that final delivery, my basket was empty of Gravebriar wares, and I began my trek back to our Estate, though I didn't walk as quickly as I should have and lingered on the main avenue far longer than was prudent. Mother would likely panic if I wasn't back soon.

The sweeping of brooms, distant laughter, and happy chirping birds filled the air, and the sun painted the sky orange as I dutifully retraced my steps toward home, passing clothiers and shoppes for musicians. Instruments hung over every inch of their walls and could make the player deliver flawless performances. Of course, a cursed instrument would do the opposite.

I lingered in front of a gallery window for only a moment, taking in the bold, bright paint slashing one broad canvas, then beside it, a delicate pastel of a pond and its lilies. My fingers squeaked down the warm glass before I walked out of the shadowed streets and into the glow of waning sunlight toward home and the party I already wished was over.

Some would turn up their nose at tonight's revel and say that to my parents, the most beloved of the Gravebriar witches, the world was never magical enough. They would murmur about how ostentatious the place settings were, but have no difficulty tasting each perfectly portioned hors d'oeuvre and drinking their fill of the beautifully aged wine. Their costumes would be eye-catching spectacles, something at which to marvel. Something created to draw attention away from the event and our coven and refract it toward that of the wearer.

Others would drown themselves in the exquisite finery my father insisted upon and the whimsical otherworldliness my mother brought to life, never questioning why they hosted the revels in the first place. They would laugh and coo over every small detail, dance until their feet ached, and smile until their cheeks grew tired. They would enjoy an evening conjured to impress and entertain even the most magical among us.

But my coven's revels weren't just carefully crafted events orchestrated to foster a sense of witchy community; they were grand diversions. Lovely lies designed to cover unspeakable truths.

The Gravebriars were green witches, the most revered healers in Cauldron, drawing energy from all the bountiful flora nature provided. Their oils, potions, and herbal concoctions were potent, infused with heavy doses of magic only found in their lineage. And though I was the daughter of the two most powerful Gravebriars, my magic was nothing like theirs.

Tonight, if the wine flowed from the ceramic fluted fountains, spilling like dew over broad leaves, and the musicians strummed until dawn, maybe... *maybe* no one would ask about me or my disappointing magic. And my parents wouldn't have to tell their friends and Mother's peers on the Council that my magic still hadn't manifested.

The lie their tongues so easily unfurled protected me. To shield me, my parents not only endured looks of pity, they allowed the whispers of the blossoming rumor that my magic wasn't just late in showing itself, but that I might be among the magicless. That despite my impressive lineage, a void existed where magic should rest within me.

Mother, our coven's Power – the title given to the mightiest witch within it – would smile sweetly, sorrowfully, patting the backs of comforting, consoling hands, and Father would tell our friends not to worry, gently

8

reminding anyone concerned that there was a *little* magic in everyone and everything, after all, and the amount didn't matter. What mattered was how the person used the gift they were given.

Their friends agreed, of course. Who would dare insult one of the Gravebriars to their face?

The street curved as it arced in front of each of the covens' Estates. I followed the flare home, passing the dark stone that comprised the Bloodling and Shade Estates, the miasma of earthen blocks of the Elementine Estate, and the gray stone of the Tempests that matched the exact color of a clouded sky, until I came to my home.

The Gravebriar Estate was made of stacked, pale travertine and situated right in the center of the others, with four covens on either side. Its tall columns were overshadowed only by the lush flora expertly grown all around it. Some called it the jewel of Cauldron. Some called it the heart of the witch city.

I called it home.

Crossing the thick lawn, I slipped inside through a side door so I could avoid anyone who had arrived to the revel early and so Mother wouldn't know how long I'd lingered in town when she'd given strict orders to be here, dressed, and ready at least an hour ago.

As I walked down the main hall, passing rooms with great windows that faced the back lawn, it appeared no one had arrived yet. I was surprised the three eldest Diviners weren't already hovering in front of the wine fountain. I wondered what costumes they might come up with. The Diviners were never fans of the understated. They loved bold colors and rich fabrics almost as much as they loved attention.

To be admitted into the revel tonight, there were two requirements. The first was that one must have received one of Mother's paper bark birch invitations. Not that she

9

would exclude anyone. Even the Silverthorns had been sent an invitation.

The second prerequisite was that those who attended must don wings – a challenge every witch would rise to meet. The costumes would add a layer of enchantment so that revelers could fawn over one another's creativity and style.

The fact that it was another layer of distraction helped, too.

From my balcony, I watched Mother's iridescent, pink moth wings flutter as she flitted from the broad buffet tables draped with fine, white linen to the water fountain. In its middle, a melancholy travertine woman waded, holding a clay water pot on her shoulder. Her water glittered like starlight as it fell into the pool at her feet.

Mother's chestnut hair had been spelled to glisten. Her elegant dress was made of sweet-smelling fuchsia roses. Tiny buds lined the bodice. At her waist, the blooms of her gown began to open, cascading to full blossoms at her ankles. Under her feet, the thick lawn glowed in the last rays of sun.

Nine incredibly long, live-edge tables had been precisely arranged to fan out from the back terrace of our Estate, nearly reaching the tree line and mimicking the streets of our city. Each table was decorated differently; one representing each of the nine covens.

The Gravebriars' table was piled with laurel, honeysuckle, and white candles, the wicks glowing golden with calm flames. The plates were simple white squares; the flutes were clear crystal.

Black candles perched over the Shades' tabletop, the wood bearing a dark stain in their coven's preferred color. A plethora of black roses and lilies were strewn over the length of the table's center. Mother had gone as far as to conjure obsidian plates and goblets for them.

Table Nocturn harkened the night with hues of dark blue accented with solid gold plates and rimmed flutes. Even their candle wax was the color of the night sky, and the flame jumping from each taper let off an occasional spark reminiscent of tiny meteors, burning as they fell.

The Tempests' table was arranged with pale gray flowers and vines, along with matching candles and plates that looked like they were made from clouds. I wondered if they were.

The Spellsweets' was a rainbow of color from one end to the other – red to indigo and all the glorious, vibrant hues in between – but through the kaleidoscope, if one looked closely, they would see words etched into the tabletop and every plate, glass, and bowl. Their common spells graced everything they might touch, a nod to their contribution to everyone in Cauldron.

Table Elementine was an ombre of earthy brown fading to green, transforming to airy blue and white, then fiery orange and red, and finally morphing to the green-blue of mountain lakes and streams. Mother had chosen the flowers to suit each tone and somehow knitted all their magic together seamlessly, despite how different each element was from the next. Their colorful tapers hadn't been lit. Mother would allow a Fire witch to do the honors.

The Diviner table was draped with vibrant patchwork cloths reminiscent of their tents and lined with crystal balls, wreathed at their bottoms with bright ivy, freshly grown. Animal bones and crystals were strewn across the table's middle. Party favors, for none would remain by the night's end. The Diviners couldn't resist the hollow dullness or shiny chunks that hummed with power.

Table Bloodling was every hue of red from coagulated to too thin, dark to bright, and all shades between. Stained with cherry, Mother had chosen every hue of red flower she could pick to form the center's long line of twisted flora.

The dishes were crimson, as were the glasses from which they would drink. Red wax bled from candelabras, and the flame of each glowed scarlet. The Bloodlings' goblets were already filled, and the crimson liquid floating in the middles was not wine.

That left the Silverthorns, if they should deign to attend. Their plates and flutes were made of the metal after which they were named. Mother cultivated flowers in the hue, mixing them with violet and lavender sprigs. I could almost smell the lush fragrance from where I stood. Mother had crafted their candles to look like swords, alight at the tip, resting on their pommels. The Silverthorns likely wouldn't appreciate her attempt to make them feel as honored as the rest, but no Gravebriar would lose sleep over what a Silverthorn thought of them.

The entire setup was ethereal and whimsical, a tribute to the nine Covens of Cauldron, a sleight of hand in a dangerous game.

Each coven would gravitate toward their table to enjoy a meal together, and Mother's plan to keep them separated for most of the evening would succeed.

Mother sensed me at the window. She motioned with her finger for me to turn around and get ready. I slunk away from the panes but watched as witches from our coven slowly meandered onto the terrace.

At either side of our Estate were sweeping solariums. Crystal-clear glass caged by intricate iron, these greenhouses were where our coven grew the plants and herbs they needed to help the people of Cauldron. Hundreds of fireflies lit the ceilings of the solariums. More flickered through the yard.

The members of my coven spilled onto the lawn in their finery, ivy and fern and vine growing over their skin. They worked to light lanterns that would hover over the party without floating away until my mother's spell allowed it. It was a beautiful scene she'd painted, the hovering lanterns, winking fireflies, and soothing candlelight.

Father was dressed in a suit of pine bark, dark against the crisp, white undershirt he wore. His eyes darted from face to face. I knew who he was searching for when he, too, focused on my window.

I sighed. If I didn't get down there, he or Mother would come looking for me.

Leaving the window, my fingers drifted over silk curtains the very color of the forest's dark heart, the color of its shadows and secrets. I slipped further into my rooms. The canopy bed was draped and drenched in dark green and held more pillows than I could count in various fabrics and firmness that filled all but the space in which I slept.

The walls were papered with a gossamer fern print that shimmered in the light when you moved about. Beyond the bedroom was a smaller, darker room where I kept my most precious things. Letting my eyes adjust to the dimness, I stepped inside and closed the door behind me. I'd painted the bay windows black so the only light that touched this space, filtering in from the seam beneath my bedroom door, was scant.

Bog waited for me on the stout log I'd dragged in from the forest's heart, staring at me as if he knew that I needed to hurry. His soft croaking ribbit filled the air, fussing at me.

I couldn't help but run a finger down his damp back. "You're supposed to be on my side, you know. Not theirs."

His sticky toes reached out for me, but I didn't have time to hold him now. "I'll come back as soon as I can tear myself away. I promise."

I might have imagined his crestfallen expression.

I removed the pale dress I wore, pulling it over my head and letting it fall somewhere on the floor, then ran my hand over a mossy, dead trunk laying nearby and plucked a small piece of the soft, thick moss.

My chemise was strapless and clung to me from above the breast to mid-thigh. I placed the vibrant, green moss on the delicate, clingy fabric and poured my power into it. The moss spread quickly, forming a short gown that clung to me but was soft and rich and comfortable. Asking the moss to spread further, it knit into a heavy skirt that fell to the floor, complete with a small train to trail behind me.

I still needed wings...

An iridescent green beetle climbed my dress, stopping at my waist. Bog eyeballed him hungrily like he might flick his tongue out to snag a snack.

I cupped my hand and gently eased the bug into my palm. His legs tickled as he crawled over my skin. I whispered a spell and from my back, beetle wings grew, the shiny forewing and delicate but functional back wing tucked safely beneath. I spread them to see the color, a perfect copy of the little one in my hand, then tucked them again, moving back to the window. The beetle flew onto the pane and began to climb the glass.

Musicians played from a small stage nestled beneath a trio of oaks. Our first guests had arrived and like snails slowly crept over the yard, watching as the first of the platters of food appeared on the table. Steaming vegetables of every color of the rainbow, freshly baked bread loaves, cakes in every variety, and glasses of decadent mousse covered the surface while rich wine flowed over the fountains.

Mother spotted me as if she could feel me watching and waved for me to come down, this gesture more forceful than the last. She flitted from guest to guest, clasping their hands and no doubt thanking them for coming. She would tell them to make themselves at home at our Estate and enjoy the evening, gently steering them toward the wine.

A Bloodling engaged her in conversation, his membranous wings flaring, lit red from the magical blood pulsing within his veins. If I didn't recognize him and know they weren't real, I'd think he'd been born with them. They were the only parts of him, other than the center of his face, that wasn't covered in tattoos. Their coven injected ink into their skin, drawing blood to commemorate their most important moments.

Across the lawn, Father spoke with a Tempest who wore a dark gray suit accented by thunder-cloud wings, rain pouring from them as lightning forked toward his heels.

I ran a comb through my long, wavy hair and conjured mossy flats to match my gown. Locking my door, I slowly trailed down the hall and descended the staircase.

At the bottom of the steps, Arbor leaned against the railing. His suit was fitted and made from birch bark, with bits peeling and curling off his taut thighs and broad shoulders, larger peels serving as his wings. It was an obvious nod to my mother and her invitations for the evening. A smooth enough move on his part, for Mother loved to be flattered. His eyes quickly slid over me as he fussed with his suit jacket. "You look beautiful, Castor."

Father had given Arbor one job for tonight: to occupy my time and appear as though he might be falling in love with me so we could spend the evening ensconced in one another's company, affording no one else the opportunity to corner me. If they were asking about our budding relationship, they wouldn't bring up my abysmal lack of power.

Looking at Arbor, I felt nothing for him beyond bland comradery. Not even the faintest spark or glimmer of interest. And no amount of magic could ignite those feelings, much to Mother's chagrin. She'd tried her best, asking us both to consume the most powerful concoction a Spellsweet could conjure a fortnight ago. For a few days, the potion worked magnificently on Arbor, though those days were miserable for me.

I was apparently impervious to love potions, even though other elixirs seemed to work on me for a time. My theory was that my magic burned it away, and love burned hotter than other spells. Either that or love couldn't truly be conjured, but I wasn't so sure about that, given Arbor's enthusiastic reaction to the potion, and subsequently, me.

To his credit, it was Arbor who managed to convince my mother that we could pull this off without spell work. Enjoy one another genuinely – as friends – but make it appear like we might be more than that. We could pique the guests' interests *and* have a pleasant time.

"You look handsome." I smiled as I stopped at the bottom step and stood beside him.

Arbor's hair was the golden hue of honeycomb, his eyes a warm, cloudy brown, reminiscent of a puddle of mud just disturbed. He was a year older than me, one of the strongest up and coming healers in our coven, able to do almost as much as Father and Mother. Arbor was often doted upon, enjoyed high praise, and had grown confident in the past year. Confident, bordering on arrogant. But no one could say he wasn't charming. Arbor's familiar wide smile and dimple set me at ease.

He leaned in to offer his elbow. "Relax. Smile. Remember how dashing and funny I am, and we'll just go have a nice dinner and maybe dance a little."

"You make it sound so easy." I took his arm as we started walking slowly down the hall.

"It *is* easy, Castor. You just have to smile at me like I could be more than a friend and I'll handle the rest."

Arbor had a reputation for burning through amorous prospects as quickly as fire consumed parchment. Perhaps everyone would assume I was just another one of his conquests, a flash-in-the-cauldron romance that burned bright but fast. It was probably why Father chose him for this task so it would be easy to explain when tomorrow, things were over between us. Besides, with Arbor, I was perfectly safe. Comfortable.

He was a shameless flirt, but harmless. He'd never push boundaries or cross lines because he wasn't that sort. Even if he secretly was, he feared and respected my parents too much to damage his relationship with them and the future he could already see unfolding within the coven. And if he didn't fear them, he certainly feared me.

We walked down the hall, passing room after room, angling toward the back doors. All I wanted to do was run back to my dark room and stay there until it was all over. Dread coiled in my stomach. I wasn't sure why. This wasn't the first revel our coven had hosted. Mother hosted her first revel upon becoming Gravebriar Power, and they'd become seasonal events that everyone looked forward to – each more impressive than the last. Each more fantastical. Tonight's just happened to be the most elaborate, and somehow, it seemed grimmer than the previous attempts.

The dreadful feeling that settled over me earlier scuttled down my spine.

Arbor walked tall beside me. I tried to mimic his posture and reminded myself of the plan. Outside, our coven would fan out and covertly help us as well. They were told to smile at us as if we were precious, like they envied our new romance, and most importantly, to help divert anyone who approached. It was a fine web, spun by many cooperative spiders.

Arbor and I paused at the magnificent glass doors that spilled onto the terrace and from that broad, flat plain of stone, into the lush yard. Many more people had arrived. Most were chatting, already seating themselves at their respective tables with piled-high plates, marveling over Mother's careful décor.

Beside me, Arbor laughed. "Castor."

"What?" I asked, my ribs tightening like a bony corset.

He grinned and his dimple deepened. "Breathe. You look like you're about to be sick."

I raked my clammy palm over the moss I wore.

I'd suggested to my parents that we just tell the Council that my powers had recently surfaced and were... different. That being honest *almost* from the beginning would make things right.

One last lie to cover all the rest.

They would eventually find out, members of my coven – Arbor included – had argued at the coven meeting last night. But my parents were determined to keep it secret *for now*, they promised.

I pled with them privately to think about what would happen if the Council found out we'd concealed so much for so long. Father seemed to be coming around to the thought, considering the implications and consequences. But my mother was the Power of the Gravebriars and, though she always considered my father's opinion as her Second, the final decision lay with her, and she completely shut down the notion every time I broached it.

I hoped she, and we, would not live to regret it.

Arbor flashed me a smooth smile as we walked onto the terrace. It made it a little easier to smile back. Those witches who hadn't seated themselves at the tables clustered in groups dotting the lawn, laughing, drinking wine, and raving over one another's wings.

The Bloodlings were easy enough to spot. All of them wore the same membranous wings as their Power so the blood coursing through them was on full display. I wondered if they had matched their wings as a voluntary show of solidarity, or because they'd been ordered to. The Bloodling Power, Sanguine, and his Second were rumored to be strict.

Elementine witches had conjured suits and dresses with wings of their favored element. There were wings of clear, blue-green water with tiny, frothy waves rolling over them and wings with murky, still water, ornamented with tiny orange fish swimming around like the koi in our ponds. There were wings made of clay and striated rock. Wings of flame and wings of flowing and cooling lava.

My favorite so far were wings that looked like dust-filled twisters on the back of its Tempest wearer.

"People got very creative with their costuming this revel," Arbor remarked as his eyes quickly combed over everyone. He flicked a look over his shoulder and the bark peels from his shoulders elongated a little further, making his wings more dramatic. He was not one to be outdone, but with bark there was only so much a witch could do to increase their effect.

I wanted to tell him to stop fretting, but complimented him instead, drawing one of his famous smiles. Maybe tonight wouldn't be so difficult. If I smiled at him and peppered him with praise, Arbor would do anything I asked.

He and I walked down the steps to the grass and made our way across the yard. People took notice of us right away. A Diviner started our way, her fanned omen deck wings flapping behind her as she drew near. Our coven mate Laurel winked at me as she sauntered up to the Diviner and struck up an easy conversation, guiding the Diviner toward the musicians.

Arbor placed his hand on mine and leaned in to whisper in my ear. "See? Nothing to worry about."

Stars glittered overhead. Fireflies lazily blinked as they drifted from place to place.

A trio of young Spellsweets crossed the yard, passing us by. Their wings were crafted from translucent vellum with incantations scrawled across them, the words glowing golden on their arched wings. As if they could sense us watching, those appendages began to flutter, gracefully fanning the paper in and out.

"They're beautiful," I said absently, my eyes tracking their movements. One of the girls looked over her shoulder and graced me with a sweet smile, mouthing the words 'thank you.'

Arbor collected two plates from the Gravebriar table as we passed it, and together, we walked to the buffet line. He offered me one of the shining white dishes and gestured for me to go ahead of him. A Nocturn was in front of us, dressed in pale green, her wings an exact replica of a Luna moth's. She was our age and noticed Arbor behind me right away, her eyes lingering over his ensemble until she noticed me. He slid a slick hand around my waist, and her attention slid to the overflowing bounty again.

"I'm interfering with your amorous reputation," I whispered to him quietly.

"Only for the night. There's always tomorrow," he said with a wink.

I hoped he was right, and that my parents' scheme involving him would end as quickly as they'd promised. The difficult part was that I didn't trust them even a little. How could I trust such proficient liars?

We slid down the buffet line and filled our plates, then Arbor carried both to the Gravebriar table and returned with wine flutes. I accepted one, holding its long, elegant stem and collecting wine from the fountain's cascade. I crouched, pretending to fix my shoe, and took up the mushrooms from my dress, carefully cupping them in my hand. My palm glowed a milky yellow as I formed a magical, impenetrable barrier around them and nonchalantly slipped them into the fountain.

Most likely, I wouldn't even need to use them, but just in case…

Mother and Father had their plans, and I had my contingency. A little hallucinogenic mushroom wouldn't harm anyone. It would get them high and just might allow us to come out of this unscathed if something went wrong.

Arbor and I settled at the end of the Gravebriar table, where our coven mates quickly filled the seats around us, eating and chattering happily like birds at a feeder.

I was chewing on a honey-glazed carrot when Arbor tensed. "I'm surprised *they* came."

"Who?" I asked, looking around. My eyes snagged on a group of young men and women who entered the yard together, metal wings gleaming, the nearest made of cogs and cutlery. Silverthorns. Behind the first two boys, there was a trio of girls with brass, silver, and gold fairy wings, all shaped to match.

One in the back of the group walked with his head turned. His wings were made of knives, the blades resembling feathers – wings like those of an angel. He flexed them and they flared, then retracted. I couldn't stop watching to see if he would do it again.

Arbor ignored them, sawing into a bit of sweet potato sprinkled with brown sugar and oozing with butter.

"You're surprised this group showed up specifically, or just that any Silverthorns have in general?" I asked Arbor, still watching the young man with deadly angel wings.

"Because of the urgent Council meeting." The Council had called an unscheduled meeting this morning, one Mother fretted over as it cut into the time she planned to use to prepare for tonight's revel. "The Power brought his son forward this morning. It's rumored that he has an unusual power. Some were angry that they'd kept it from everyone..." Arbor's brown eyes met mine ominously.

I swallowed thickly, wiping my mouth. Perhaps that was why my parents refused to listen to reason. Maybe they were afraid the Gravebriars would be punished for doing the same thing.

Arbor leaned in, whispering in my ear. "The Shades wanted to banish the Silverthorn Power *and* his son."

My heart thundered. "And?"

"A vote was taken. The majority voted to allow them to remain, with stipulations, of course. If he breaks a single condition the Council set forth, he'll be forced to leave."

I turned to face him. "How did my mother vote?"

Arbor paused for a long moment, toying with a strand of my hair. His eyes met mine, holding them as he revealed, "She voted for banishment."

I pressed my eyes closed for a long moment.

How could she? Hypocrite! I drew in slow, steady breaths to try to calm myself. I wanted to stand up and ask for everyone's attention and free myself from the burden of lies that bound us all.

If the Silverthorns weren't banished, we likely wouldn't be either, and this entire charade could finally end. Then again, my parents had the opportunity to admit our truths or cast a merciful vote in understanding and solidarity, and they chose to ostracize. Perhaps the Council would weigh *that* betrayal against us all.

Popping the last bite of cake in his mouth, Arbor chewed quickly and washed it down with wine. Then he wiped his mouth and offered a rakish smile. "Care to dance?"

Arbor was oblivious to my inner turmoil, as he was oblivious to anything but himself.

We abandoned our seats and walked across the lawn to sway with other couples on the bedecked lawn in front of the musicians. Their notes were full of longing, heartache, and pain, but the melody was beautiful, hypnotic, and easy to get lost in. The music was likely spelled.

"I'm sorry to have mentioned the Silverthorns," Arbor said as he lay his hand on my waist, taking my other in his.

We began to sway to the rhythm. Arbor could dance. He was svelte and had many opportunities to practice. Me, on the other hand? I hadn't.

I met his eyes. "I'm glad you told me. No one else did."

He winced. "Just don't tell your parents I did."

"I won't," I promised. My words didn't erase the doubtful look on his face. He didn't trust me. None of my coven mates fully trusted me or my parents. For years, they'd been forced to lie for me, to forfeit their fun at the revels to protect the lies that shrouded me, to bend their lives, their very magic, to Mother's will.

It had to stop.

Mother refused to listen to reason, so I had to be the one to put an end to this madness once and for all.

My mind was set. I was going to the Council tomorrow. I would tell them that I hid my magic because I was afraid of it, that my parents didn't know, that none of my coven did. I would take the punishment they meted out. It was only fair.

THREE

Song after song, we danced. Couples moved around us, filtering onto the lawn and leaving it. Time seemed a slow leak. Yet the musicians played on…

Over Arbor's shoulder, the Diviner girl who tried to approach us earlier, wearing tarot card wings and with pale purple hair and eyes, hovered just outside the perimeter of the section of lawn where everyone danced. She looked more pixie than witch, her small frame and features pretty and delicate. The boy with the wings of knives passed her by, her head swiveling to keep him in sight.

Who could blame her?

Father and Mother swayed nearby, keeping keen eyes on us. When the song ended, Father peeled away from Mother, who was quickly swept up by an eager Tempest, and strode toward me and Arbor. "May I cut in?" he asked my date.

I grinned and pretended to be happy as I switched partners. The pretty Diviner who'd been lingering on the lawn found Arbor. He graciously obliged her with a dance. Her tarot card wings flittered as Arbor poured his attention over her.

But then, something shifted, and as she spoke, his confidence evaporated.

Over Father's shoulder, I watched them. His flirtatious smile was gone. She spoke, but I couldn't hear over the silky violin notes. His brows pinched together and his easy demeanor sharpened. His hand tightened on her waist.

I was twirled away so I couldn't see them anymore.

"How are things?" Father asked.

"Everything is fine," I muttered, wondering what the Diviner had said to Arbor.

"The deliveries went well?"

"They did," I confirmed.

"Arbor has done very well with his healing magic lately. He's as powerful as I am."

My attention slid to him; Arbor forgotten. "*As* powerful, or close?"

"We are equals, but he will soon succeed me. That's the only reason he isn't already considered your mother's Second. But you should know that within months, maybe weeks, Arbor will take your mother's seat as Gravebriar Power."

I knew my parents' magic would one day fade, but the thought of them not being Power and Second wasn't something I dwelled on considerably. If Arbor took the Power position, Mother would step down to Second, but how long until someone else unseated her entirely?

Arbor and the Diviner had stopped swaying. He sipped a drink he'd gotten from somewhere and his eyes darted to mine before sliding back to her.

I finally locked eyes with my father, forgetting about Arbor and his Diviner friend. "I'm sorry." I knew how much they'd enjoyed the roles they earned. How much of their lives they'd poured into them. How much time. Magic. Sacrifice.

He shrugged as if it didn't bother him, as if it was an inevitability he'd long since come to terms with, but the lines on his face betrayed his disappointment. "Magic fades with age."

I knew that, but... "You're not old," I argued.

"Your mother and I are still the most powerful, but Arbor's healing power is expanding. It has never even stalled, as sometimes happens when magic is fully tapped. He will be the most powerful healer our coven has seen since... Well, it won't be long before he supersedes us."

I knew to whom he almost referred. Mother's successor held a natural talent only Mother had exceeded, and even then, only barely. He leaned in to whisper, "If anyone knew... *You* would take your mother's place."

"I'm not more powerful than she is."

"You are. Several times over, and far more powerful than Arbor will ever be," he said lightly, smiling as if we were chatting about the warm weather, the elaborate costumes, or things to look forward to tomorrow. "Just because it's different, doesn't mean it's not stronger."

"It doesn't matter," I told him. No one knew about it, but when they found out tomorrow, they'd likely banish me.

Though... they showed the Silverthorn mercy. Maybe they would still be in a forgiving mood.

Age had settled onto Father's face. The wrinkles indenting the skin around his mossy eyes and mouth were chasms now. His skin was an ashy color instead of the sun-kissed bronze I remembered. He and Mother flitted around so much, their responsibilities for the coven and Council always keeping them busy, I hadn't noticed. I hadn't had the time to actually sit down with them and talk in... I couldn't remember when.

"Would you like to have breakfast together tomorrow morning?" I blurted. Maybe a final, simple but intimate meal with my parents would lessen the blow I planned to deal them.

He nodded with a smile. "I would love that. I know we've been terribly busy lately..."

I waved it off. "You have responsibilities."

"Our greatest is to you, though, Castor."

I swallowed thickly. They were supposed to be leading the coven, fostering the magic of those in it, and contributing to Cauldron. Instead, they spent their time concealing me.

"I'll talk to your mother about breakfast," he said as the song ended. I smiled up at him. Arbor left the Diviner to walk back to me. He deftly – mostly – wiped the heavy expression from his face, bowing to my father in respect. "I've taken enough of her time, Arbor," he said loud enough so others could hear him.

Arbor looked shaken, though he hid it well behind his handsome smile. Father paid no attention and instead left us to rejoin Mother across the yard where she was speaking with a grouping of Nocturn who sprouted wings of moths, bats, of hides from foxes, of layered bear claws...

"Do you want to go for a walk?" I suggested.

"Yeah," he absently answered, his eyes darting over my shoulder. I followed his line of sight to the Diviner whose tarot wings were fluttering as she carved a path through the tables, around the side of the Estate.

Why is she leaving?

He held my hand as we walked away from the crowd to the terrace, but it was too busy to speak freely there. "The garden?" he whispered.

I beamed up at him and smiled, kissing his cheek. "Sounds wonderful."

Arbor's hand tightened on mine. We walked through the congested terrace to a smooth, brick path that wound around the eastern solarium. He pushed open the glass and iron door, then sealed us inside.

"What's the matter?" I asked.

He put a finger to his lips before releasing my hand to scan the trees, bushes, anywhere someone might be able to hide. When he was sure we were alone, he let out a shuddering breath.

"What did the Diviner say to you?"

"Her name is Arcana," he said, raking nervous hands through his golden hair. "She said that when she saw us emerge from the Estate, she had a vision. A terrible vision."

"What did she see?"

His flustered, muddy eyes met mine. "She saw me die."

"What?" I asked, my heart caving in. I didn't want any of my coven mates hurt. "That doesn't make any sense…"

"I know." He tried to smile. "I'm a Gravebriar, surrounded by other Gravebriars. If anything happened, someone would be able to heal me."

Unless he was too far away and couldn't reach us, or someone's magic prevented him from using his. "Did she say when?"

He scrubbed a hand over his mouth. "She said events leading to my death would be set into motion tonight."

My lips parted. I searched the yard for any visible threat and found nothing amiss. Still, a sinister feeling in my bones told me that something was wrong. There was a vital clue we were overlooking. Maybe it was an entity we could not see… "I'm going to tell my parents. You should go into the Estate with some of our coven mates."

He seemed torn. "She's probably wrong, Castor. What could I possibly die from?"

"But what if she's right, Arbor?" It wasn't a risk we should take, especially after being forewarned.

He hesitated a moment before nodding decidedly. "Then let's go and do it now. I would like to escort you to them. At least allow me that. They wouldn't approve of me leaving you alone."

I didn't want to allow it. I wanted to step out, call for the nearest Gravebriar witches, and send them into the heart of our home to guard him from whatever lurked outside. I clasped Arbor's hand and tried to sense anything in his blood that might be strange, wishing I had the healing power of normal Gravebriar witches, just in case.

Sensing nothing, we set out to find our Power.

Arbor was nervous as we retraced our steps through the darkness. We didn't have to look for my parents. Mother found us when we reached the terrace. "And just where have the two of you been hiding?" she asked teasingly. Her smile fell as she took in our grave expressions. "What is it?" she said, drawing me in for a kiss on the cheek.

I leaned in to return the kiss and held her close while I told her what Arcana had divulged to Arbor. Her skin was paler as she pulled away, carefully recovering with a smile. "It's awfully humid. Perhaps you would both like to go inside and cool off?" she suggested casually, her eyes darting around us. There was no threat that I could see. "I'll speak to your father," she whispered.

She brushed an errant strand of hair off her cheek and tucked it into her chignon, then breezed across the terrace in her rose gown and walked down the steps into the yard. She found Father and caught his ear. His eyes clamped onto me, then flicked to the doors.

We were safer inside our home. The vines that grew over it hummed with protection and power.

The only coven who could take issue with ours was the Silverthorns, as far as I knew. My parents didn't confide in me, insisting I focus on myself and the lies spinning around me. They wouldn't want me to lose focus and do something to implicate myself.

Arbor and I walked hand in hand back into the large house. I broke away the moment we were clear of the door. He seemed to breathe easier within the walls and glass and shot me a smile. "It looks like our evening wasn't cut short as much as it was severed."

"It doesn't matter. It's not like we're actually courting," I scoffed.

He rolled his shoulders, watching me carefully. "We could be."

I shook my head. "No, we couldn't. I want what you can't give me, and I won't compromise."

He tilted his head to the side, gifting me with an enigmatic smile. "You can't deny the partnership we'd make."

"No, I can't. But I'd rather be alone than be with someone who doesn't love every part of me – and would *never* want anyone else. Your eye wanders, Arbor. I'm sure other parts follow."

He gave a guilty smile and laughed. "What you want is almost impossible."

I shot him a wan smile. "*Almost* isn't the same thing as *entirely*."

He tugged at his birch jacket, almost as if reassuring himself. "Your standards are high, Castor. I hope you can find someone who rises to meet them."

I inclined my head. I hoped I did, too. But I'd rather be alone than settle.

He rocked back on his heels and gave an uncharacteristically nervous laugh.

My entire body froze. The conversation I'd had with my father replayed through my mind. "Did my parents suggest you actually try to court me?"

His eyes widened. "No! No, they didn't. It's just that your father told me how powerful you've become, and I got to thinking that if we *did* seek a relationship, it might be advantageous."

"For whom?" I bristled, crossing my arms. "Not for me."

"Certainly for you," he argued. "Who better to keep you safe than the Gravebriar Power?"

I narrowed my eyes at him. "But you wouldn't be, would you? Not really. I think the best person to keep me safe is me."

He swallowed thickly and took a step away. Then another.

I tilted my head. "Do you think I'm so upset that I'd hurt you? Kill you? Arbor, I would *never* do something like that."

"I know," he said sternly, forcing himself to relax. He stood up straight and tugged at his collar. "I know you wouldn't."

Just then, Father strode through the doors, his smile evaporating when he saw us. "Are you feeling strange, Arbor?"

My fake beau shook his head, looking a little bewildered and afraid. He ran his hands over his chest and stomach. "I feel perfectly fine."

"Maybe Arcana was wrong," I suggested as Father held his palm over Arbor's heart, using his magic to see the inner workings of his body.

A faint glow erupted from Father's hand. He concentrated for several long moments. "I sense nothing amiss."

He must not have heard me... "Perhaps Arcana was wrong."

Father's eyes flicked to mine. "Arcana just today announced her intention to overtake the position of Power for the Diviners. Crystabal knows the girl is stronger now and will concede her position and take the role of Second. Arcana, though she's young, has *never* been wrong."

Arbor paled. "Never? I knew she was a strong Diviner, but... never?"

Father told him not to worry, that the future could always shift and change as he steered Arbor around and walked him further into the Estate, leaving me behind. My mind spun like a windmill in a storm. If he was indoors and tucked into his room, what could harm him there? Nothing. Father said that internally he was healthy.

Perhaps Arcana's divination *was* wrong for the first time, and she'd have to wait to claim her seat at the top of the Diviner coven.

I pivoted and stared back toward the party in full swing outside the doors. I couldn't walk out there alone. Mother would have a fit, and besides that, I didn't want to talk to anyone. Without Arbor as a buffer, I might as well invite a host of well-meaning but nosy witches to converse with me. They would begin by asking where Arbor had gone, but conversations always drifted off course and inevitably veered toward my magic or supposed lack thereof.

I walked down the westward hallway and into the solarium on the other side of our Estate. The warm, humid air felt like a thick wall when I opened the door and walked inside. A sheen of sweat beaded on my skin. From the arched windows, I watched the party among the chamomile and clover, jasmine and lilac.

Just outside the window, one of my coven mates, dressed in delicate pink cherry blossoms, stood with a Spellsweet boy. They laughed and offered one another small brushes of contact, both clearly enamored. For a second, I let myself imagine what it might feel like to have that flutter in my chest, in my stomach.

Beyond them, the fountain loomed. I could feel the resonance from the mushroom cluster. A young Tempest girl stared into the wine pooling in the fountain's basin but never reached in. Lightning forked around her head, forming a crown. It flared down her back, crackling in bright streaks that formed wings in the form of white-hot veins.

Could she sense the anomaly in the liquid? She was no Water witch. Or was she? Some covens intermingled...

She regarded the crimson pool for another moment before filling her flute and walking away.

I clapped a hand over my thundering heart. Paranoia was getting the best of me. The girl's power lay in storms, not in wine and certainly not in mushrooms. I pushed open a window to let in a bit of cool air, allowing a few fireflies to escape into the yard. My eyes lazily drifted beyond them to see monarch wings and the vibrant blue, red, and yellow of parrots.

There were wings that dripped fire, tiny flames sizzling when they hit the cool blades of grass, and there were wings carved from coal. Umbra, Power of the Shades wore wings made of souls trapped in glass, screaming and clawing at the surface. As if he could feel the weight of my stare, he turned toward the solarium. Had the souls told him I was watching?

My eyes caught on a familiar pair of wings.

I thought Arcana had left, but she stood near the musicians in a cluster of her coven mates. The Diviners in her group wore wings of arcing bones from which pendulums swung; wings formed of crystal so clear, one could see through them like they weren't even there; and wings of wax, laced with wicks that burned slowly. One even had arched bundles of lit sage that lazily wafted heady smoke into the air.

I slipped out the door and made my way to them. My coven mate Laurel noticed, her eyes flaring as she made a beeline toward me. Her dress, circlet, and wings were made from her namesake. "Castor," she said under her breath, smiling as she reached me. "Where's Arbor?"

"Inside."

"You are *also* supposed to be inside. Your mother said you were in your rooms."

"I'm not."

"Yes, I see that." She walked beside me, chattering inanely about the food and the costumes and how grand the covens had made the event with their presence. A

Nocturn boy our age approached, his spider web silk suit glistening in the moonlight and spider's legs forming wings that protruded from his shoulder blades.

Our coven mate, Lily, sharply cut between us and him and asked him to dance. He kindly obliged her, offering his arm, but kept his eyes on me and Laurel. He nodded to another of his coven. Did the Nocturn suspect what we were doing? Did every coven?

"Where are you going?" Laurel gritted.

"I have to speak to Arcana. Can you make sure no one interrupts?"

She nodded quickly, her fine brows pinching. "I'll do my best." She watched from a seat at the nearest table as I strode across the yard.

Arcana sensed me approaching and turned to face me. Her coven flanked her.

She offered a small smile. "Castor Gravebriar. You're alone. I take it your parents insisted that Arbor go inside. Not that he'll be safe there, either. Death nips at his heels... Always such a hungry dog."

"He's safe with us."

"He isn't safe anywhere. Safety is a figment of the imagination, a pretty illusion we create to comfort ourselves. As we live and breathe, we are never truly safe. And neither are the *secrets* we keep."

She knew. Her eyes glittered with the knowledge. But this wasn't about me. I'd scream my power to the rooftops, startle every nesting bird, if it would keep Arbor from harm. No one deserved to be hurt for my truth.

Arcana glanced over my shoulder toward the solarium where a shadow moved across the glass. "He waits for you..."

Who's waiting for me?

There was no way Father would allow Arbor to leave the heart of our home now, so it couldn't be Arbor in the solarium. Had someone snuck in to kill my coven mate? Or was I their true target? My blood turned cold.

I left the Diviners and quickly retraced my steps, ignoring Laurel's concerned hiss. The solarium door was cracked. I closed it behind me. The door let out a tinny snick as it sealed me in.

Stately trees flanked the right and left with ornamental potted grasses, broad-leafed tropical plants, and curling vines arranged aesthetically in front of me. It was one of my favorite places, a quiet place filled with beautiful, powerful plants and herbs all around.

I caught movement far across the expansive space. Metal wings flexed on the back of their maker. Flaring wide, then tucking in behind him. It was the handsome angel who wore wings constructed of knife blades. Every blade was different, some bright silver, some dull and tarnished, and every shade in between the two extremes. All their edges gleamed. Sharp. Deadly.

I walked around the perimeter and watched to see what he might do, hoping he wouldn't try to enter our Estate. Was he the one who wanted Arbor dead? And if he did, why?

His hair was ash brown and close-cropped, the top just slightly longer than the back and sides. He was taller than I was, his shoulders broad and his waist lean beneath the dark gray fitted suit he wore.

He turned and the warm light spilling from within the Estate illuminated his profile. He slowly unbuttoned the shirt at his neck, then stretched his head left and right. His jaw was square and strong.

I wished he'd turn toward me so I could better see his face.

The Silverthorn wasn't rushing into our home and didn't seem to care about the rooms beyond the solarium. He simply studied the plants. *Maybe he's meeting someone here?*

He outstretched his hand and let his fingers drift over the petals of a rare silver orchid. Did the familiar shade call to him?

His sharp wings flexed with his shoulder blades.

In the far corner, there was a pond with a small burbling fountain flowing in its middle, aerating the water. He moved toward it, watching the lilies dance over its black glass surface. He crouched and let his fingers slide into the water.

He would find it cool. And if he waited long enough and stayed still, he would see the shimmering scales of white and orange koi swimming beneath the broad pads.

He stood and shook the water from his skin, then turned and his eyes caught on me.

My breath trapped in my chest.

I froze.

So did he.

He tilted his head. "Hello?"

His eyes were sharper than the blades constructing his wings, slicing me. My heart pounded toward him.

I remained safely cocooned among the trees. "Why did you leave the revel?" I asked conversationally.

"I needed some space and wanted to see the famed Gravebriar solariums," he answered, staring from them to the panes of glass overhead. "And the ironwork, if I'm being honest. It's a work of art."

His perusal gave me a moment to further study him. His lips were perfect, the bottom one slightly plumper than the top with a beautiful, sharp bow in the center.

The Silverthorn was handsome. Even handsomer than Arbor.

"It *is* a work of art." I took a few steps into an area of thicker foliage so he would think I was merely here to look around, too.

His eyes tracked me, though it seemed he was trying not to let on. "My grandfather helped build them," he said.

37

"I remember him telling me how they were made, and I've seen them from afar, but never from within."

"Never during another revel?"

He shook his head. "Things changed between our coven and the Gravebriars after Grandfather died. You could say this is the first revel I've had the *opportunity* to attend, and I thought this might be my only chance to see them."

I moved toward the center walkway and stepped from behind the lush trees onto the gravel path.

He tensed when he saw my dress. He shook his head and raked his top teeth over his bottom lip, releasing it. "No wonder you asked why I was in here. You're a Gravebriar, and not just any... you're Castor Gravebriar, the Power's daughter."

My reputation preceded me. I wondered what he'd heard.

"And you're a Silverthorn in the heart of your enemy's Estate." I wasn't sure who he was or how he fit within his coven. He had me at a disadvantage.

"Not just any Silverthorn, though," he said almost playfully. "I'm the Silverthorn your Power voted to banish just this morning." My breath caught. He was the Silverthorn Power's son. Our statuses were the same. "Forge Silverthorn," he supplied.

As if his name was a hook and me a tempted fish, I walked closer until I could see the varying shades in his eyes. Warm copper around the pupils, then gold, then bright silver and dark steel at the edges. Concentric metal rings that melted one into another.

I wanted to know what his power was, what he could do with it, and why he'd hidden it from the Council. Was it his idea to keep it secret, or had his Power insisted upon it?

Was it as terrible as mine?

His gaze raked up me, stopping on my eyes and holding there. His pupils flared, then quieted again.

I used to be very self-conscious of their unusual yellow hue, but as I grew older, realized they were as much a part of me as my magic. They weren't golden, or honey, or amber. There were no striations or natural hues of blue or brown or green or gray lurking within them. My eyes were a singular, toxic shade of yellow, the same hue some creatures wore to warn off predators.

I finally spoke. "You hid your power from the Council."

He tipped his chin up proudly, defiantly. He set his jaw, but his expression wasn't angry. His lips parted, and though he spoke, I didn't hear the words because something else caught my ear.

Something unexpected and dire.

"Castor!" someone screamed from inside the house. "Castor, come quickly!"

I peeled my attention away from Forge Silverthorn and rushed down the path, pushing the doors that opened into the Estate where my father was frantically searching the hallways, poking his head into every room, shouting for me. His pine bark suit molted as he ran.

"Father?" I cried, rushing to him. *Is it Arbor? Was Forge merely a distraction while a coven mate hurt him?*

Father rushed to me and caught my elbows, his mossy green eyes searching for truth. I wondered if he'd recognize it. "Was it you?"

My brows kissed. "Was *what* me?"

He raised his voice and squeezed my arms tighter, shaking me. "You have to tell me right now, Castor. Did you poison him?"

"Who?" I asked.

"Arbor!"

What? "Of course not!" I hissed, looking around us to see if anyone was near.

Father's jaw locked. He didn't believe me. "He... What's done is done. You need to come heal him. Now."

I followed quietly as we jogged down the hall and up the sweeping staircase to the rooms on the second floor. Arbor's was the third on the left. We slipped inside where warm firelight revealed the faces of a few members of the Council.

Father cut a sharp glance at me. The Councilwitches didn't know about my magic yet, but they soon would, and he wasn't sure what would happen. Still, we had to help Arbor, and I was the only one who could, if he had truly been poisoned.

My heart clapped against my ribcage.

Mother sat on the left side of the large bed, holding her palm over Arbor's chest as a calming spell, pale green, glowed from her skin. Her magic's signature rose scent was almost overwhelming in the small space.

He lay in the bed on deep ocean sheets, his pallor ashen. Haloing him was a sweat-soaked outline of his body. His pupils were bare pinpricks. A trickle of foamy saliva slid from the corner of his mouth.

Mother looked as relieved to see me as she looked fearful. "Castor," she invited.

I sat across from her on the right side of the bed. "Arbor?" I took his clammy hand and pressed our palms together, holding his in place. His head lolled and his heart pounded. I could feel the blood rushing under his skin; tucked in the frantic swoosh was a carefully subtle but potent poison. One that unfurled like the coil of a fern leaf. No poison acted this way naturally. Someone had figured out how to cloak and conceal it, and they'd hidden it from *me*... which meant that someone knew my power.

Did my magic melt the cloak away, or did it dissolve when enough toxin slid into Arbor's veins?

Arcana, I inwardly cursed.

I called on my magic and quickly drew the substance into my skin, cleansing his blood. I recognized the toxin. Ricin. Derived from castor beans.

Mother withdrew her hand and power, numbly watching me wrench him from the poison's grip.

Arbor's heart slowed until it struck a normal rhythm. I asked for a damp rag and held my hand out, and a moment later, someone placed a clean one in my hand. I dabbed the sweat from his skin, wiped the spittle away, and watched his pupils slowly swell. Several tense minutes passed until his body acclimated to being free of the toxin, but Arbor was alert. His drowsy eyes blinked. He scanned the room, seeming to note everyone in it. His dry lips parted. "What happened?"

The Bloodling Power, Sanguine, stepped forward. His membranous wings were gone, but I could see the red and blue arteries and veins plump and rescind beneath the ashy skin of his face. His face was covered in tattooed slashes, one for each year he'd served as the head of his coven. He looked at Arbor, then to me. "That's what *we* would like to know, but it seems there is much of which we were not aware. You're a *poison* witch?"

I swallowed thickly, unable to push the affirmation around the knot in my throat.

"Castor," Mother started, running her hand over the roses along her gown. It was an unconscious habit she used to comfort herself. "Did you...?"

My jaw tightened. Father asked if I'd hurt him. Now Mother? She rose and stood with Father as he wrapped her in his arms, holding her steady as she steadied him. To say it hurt that they thought I was capable of such a thing was an understatement. It was also a betrayal. It felt like they'd driven a knife into my back and I couldn't reach the dagger's handle to pull it out no matter how I reached for it. It was lodged in a place I simply couldn't grasp any more than I could grasp how little they knew me, their only child. Because if my parents knew my heart, they would never have questioned me. My magic be damned.

I locked eyes with my mother. "I would *never* hurt Arbor. I would *never* hurt my coven or my family. I would never hurt anyone from *any* coven, or outside of them, for that matter." I stood from the bed and faced the smug Diviner Power, Crystabal. I wondered how she felt about being usurped by someone as young as Arcana. Bitterness coated her cocoa skin and coiled coral hair. "Perhaps you should question Arcana, Crystabal. She's the only other person to have spent time with him this evening."

"Your petty jealousy doesn't warrant turning anyone in *my* coven into a suspect when it's clear *you're* the one who's poisonous," she fired back. Her clear, crystal wings flitted wildly as she took a step forward.

I matched the step. "I'm *not* jealous of her. Arbor and I are just friends. Though I'm assuming your position as Power might be secured for just a little longer, given the fact that I saved Arbor. Arcana told him he would die tonight. I understand she's never been wrong – until now."

Crystabal's mouth tightened with her eyes. "You accuse Arcana, then imply *I* might have something to gain from the boy's illness? He almost died! Besides that, she didn't say he would die tonight; she told the boy a series of events that would ultimately lead to his death would spark tonight. I'd say her record is spotless." She gestured to Arbor, who watched weakly from where he lay propped on a mountain of pillows.

Wraith, the Power of the Nocturn Coven, whose ebony skin, hair, and pupils shone in the scant light provided by the flickering candles on Arbor's bedside, pushed off the wall he leaned against and leveled my parents with a scathing glare. "It seems the Silverthorns weren't the only coven hiding something disturbing, and frankly, dangerous from the Council."

"*I* asked my coven and my parents to lie for me," I told them, staring each person in the eye, "but only until

I knew what I was capable of," I regurgitated my parents' words. "I was planning to come to you tomorrow to reveal everything, as I finally have control of my magic."

Crystabal gestured to Arbor. "You call *this* having control?"

I ignored her and faced my parents.

The only thing between us was the truth. I had planned to go behind their backs and plead my case without them, hoping that by doing so I would shield them as fervently as they'd shielded me.

My mother stiffened but didn't correct my lie. Not before she saw how the Council would respond to it. Father stood silently resolute beside her.

"When did her magic emerge, Alder?" Wraith directed to my father.

Father shifted his weight and cleared his throat, but I answered them before he could speak. "There have been signs for a long while, but until this year, I didn't realize what they meant. I didn't recognize my power; I just thought my magic was nearly non-existent because I couldn't work green magic like my coven or my parents. I thought my magic was deficient. Instead, I learned it's very different from theirs."

"You poison everything you touch, don't you?" Crystabal smiled cruelly. Her words settled on my chest like a heavy stone. "And tonight, you touched Arbor and he suffered for it."

I met Arbor's gaze as he lifted his head. He looked unbearably weak, but he was strong enough to question me. "Castor?"

"I did not poison you, Arbor," I told him, looking him in the eye.

He sank back into his pillows, weak again. "Maybe you and your parents planned this together. I was almost strong enough to assume the Power position. Now, I can barely hold up my head."

Father's jaw unhinged in shock as Mother looked offended and angry. "We've sworn an oath to protect *all* of the Gravebriar witches," he defended.

"And we know how much you value honesty," Arbor spat. "How upstanding your word is."

As a violent coughing fit seized him, I tensed. Something was still wrong. "Father... check over him again."

Arbor batted Father's hand away, but another fit left him too weak to fight. Father's hand glowed over Arbor's strained body. "His lungs, heart... kidneys. They're thickly scarred."

Arbor looked at me with tears shimmering in his eyes. "Why?"

I shook my head. I could scream it at the top of my lungs and write it in my blood, but nothing would assure him I hadn't done it. I was the obvious one to blame. I was poisonous.

His tears were contagious, it seemed. Mine flooded. I fought and lost the battle to hold my lip still. It quivered traitorously.

FOUR

Arbor begrudgingly let me touch his palm again to make absolutely, doubly certain there was not so much as a trace of poison left in his system, though he wouldn't look at me and refused to speak. He just ground his teeth and endured it, pulling away as fast as he could.

My parents waited to confirm there was no trace and then put a fast plan in place so they could attend the vital Council meeting, leaving strict instructions for our coven mates to watch over Arbor and alert them if his condition deteriorated even the slightest.

To be honest, he seemed paler.

And when he spoke, his voice was weaker.

His resolve, however, was strong as mountain stone when he asked them to remove me from his room. From his sight. From the Estate and Cauldron itself.

My parents complied with the first two of his requests.

The revel was abruptly ended and everyone but the Council members were sent home. I imagined the metallic, bladed angel wings melting away from Forge's shoulders, dripping onto the ground, leaving a molten trail from our Estate to the Silverthorns'. I bet he and his friends would stride straight home to report the chaos that had unwound our status in a few fateful moments.

All the covens probably rejoiced at our fall.

The Powers gathered inside our Estate and argued until dawn, deciding what to do to help Arbor and what was to become of me.

My parents, when taking breaks, tried to use their magic to reverse the scarring. Various coven members tried. They all tried together, merging their magic in a furious attempt to reverse the poison's effects. Nothing worked.

Those who didn't have magic in their healing hands were asked to help any way they could. Laurel set about making an herbal tea to help his lungs and voice, promising to add fresh honey. Others set about concocting potions and elixirs to try to help. If they couldn't heal him now, perhaps his body would knit slowly in time. Perhaps just addressing the immediate symptoms and effects would help him for now. *For now...*

I couldn't believe Mother couldn't completely heal him. The damage must be extensive. I'd seen her erase large scars and heal wounds deep enough to leave lines on the skin, but even her magic couldn't erase what had been done. Still, there had to be something that could restore him, if not wholly then in part and more sufficiently than had already been done.

How was it possible to cloak something so potent? What toxin could be powerful enough to scar a witch's organs? Perhaps it was a concoction... or perhaps dark magic had been mixed with the poison to make it far more potent.

I planted myself in our vast library and searched for something, anything, that might help him. In grimoire after grimoire, book of shadows after book of shadows, it was re-emphasized that only one thing could cure a Gravebriar witch who was injured beyond another Gravebriar's healing magic: an actual gravebriar.

That was the answer, the remedy.

I grabbed an armful of leather-bound tomes that all echoed that singular cure and marched to the meeting room. I knocked until my knuckles turned red, until someone finally unspelled the magically sealed doors. I strode inside and laid the stack of books on the long, wooden table. The Council members turned their attention to me, anger clearly etched on their features, irritation thick in the air. But they could get over their aggravation and my intrusion. This was necessary. I had the cure.

I pointed authoritatively to one of the hefty books. "We need a gravebriar. Arbor must ingest a gravebriar to be fully healed."

My parents looked stricken. Father's mouth hung open and tears shone in Mother's eyes as she pressed delicate fingers over her lips. The Council swiveled their icy stares at them. "Do you have gravebriar to feed the boy?" Sanguine, the Bloodling Power asked, his tattooed forehead wrinkling and folding the slashed lines he bore.

Father answered for them. "We have none. No Gravebriar has been buried in quite some time...." There was a sharpness to his words, and the way he delivered them made me feel like there was a deeper, heavier meaning.

The gravebriar vine only sprouted and stretched from the soil where a Gravebriar witch was buried, just after they were interred. The vine would live for one day, then back to the dust it would go with the one who had given it a short but vital life. The last Gravebriar died just before I was born. It was Mother's duty to collect the briars, bottle them, and keep them safe, and now she was out when we needed them most? How many had she managed to pluck? What were they used for? I didn't remember any emergencies such as this growing up.

The room filled with tense silence. Wraith, Power of the Nocturn, ordered me to leave the room and I was all

but shoved out with the Elementine Power Gust's strong
wind. My hair and heavy moss dress flew backward with
me and the doors promptly slammed in my face.

I stomped to my dark room and sat. I'd been forbidden
to enter the solarium, forbidden to leave the Gravebriar
grounds, or Cauldron. So, I sat on the rotting log and let
the moss I'd borrowed and grown into a gown settle back
onto the damp bark and waited.

The minutes crept by like tiny, fledgling beetles.

Mother finally entered my room at dawn, easing the
door closed behind her and pressing her palms against it
as if someone or something on the other side might try to
knock it down. "Castor." Her voice was tired and rusted.

I didn't answer. Couldn't bring myself to. I was still so
angry at her for thinking I could possibly poison my coven
mate.

She collected herself and pushed off the door, then
walked to the doorway of the dark room I occupied, where
she paused before stepping inside. The venom on my
tongue wouldn't be kept at bay. "I won't hurt you, Mother,
if that's what gives you pause."

"I know you didn't hurt Arbor on purpose," she said
gently.

"I didn't hurt him at all, but no one believes me."

Mother pressed her eyes closed and shook her head.
The buds of her dress had begun to wilt. "Is it not *possible*
that you touched something before the revel and forgot
about it, and then while you held Arbor's hand, it just
oozed into him?"

"Magic requires intention, Mother. You taught me
that."

She nodded, weak tendrils sagging from her chestnut
chignon that now looked more like a packrat's nest than
an artful twist. "It's just that nothing about your magic
is as we expected, so I have to consider that perhaps it

behaves differently." She cleared her throat. "We will see Arbor through this tragedy, Castor. I vow it. And don't fret over Arbor's ire. He'll eventually come back around. I know your father mentioned that the two of you would make a strong couple. Together, you would be a force with which to contend. Your children would be—"

Enough of that talk. "I'm not interested in Arbor romantically. Beyond that, I'm *not* having children. We've discussed this."

"You might change your mind one day," she told me.

I shook my head in disbelief. The woman was stubborn. Refused to hear anything she didn't want to hear. She never truly listened and sought to manipulate everyone into doing what *she* wished, ignoring their wishes and desires entirely. "Open your ears, Mother. I will not have children and subject them to my magic. Look what it did to you." I gestured to her womb.

She gasped. "No, Castor. *You* didn't –"

Didn't poison her? She didn't believe that, no matter how often she said it. Neither did I.

But I *did* know I didn't poison Arbor Gravebriar, no matter how much it looked like I did. "I'm done talking about this. What did the Council decide? Should I pack my things?" I refused to look at her until she waved her hands wildly, pointing at her ear and then to the wall. Someone was listening, eavesdropping on a conversation that should just be mine and hers.

"You should ready yourself, but not for the reason you assume. You brought evidence that gravebriars might heal Arbor, and the Council wishes to give you the opportunity to go and find one. There's a very old graveyard just beyond the dark heart of the forest, a place where many of our ancestors were laid to rest. It's possible that there are gravebriars growing over their graves."

I narrowed my eyes. "Wouldn't they have been harvested by now? Wouldn't the vines have shriveled ages ago?"

She put a finger to her lips, her expression imploring me to shut my mouth. She spoke loudly as though explaining it to me, though it was directed to the person outside the door. I couldn't tell if her words were truth or lie. "The graveyard is protected by a strong and ancient magic – the magic of our bloodline. I think the gravebriar may flourish under such powerful conditions. The rules that govern its growth here wouldn't apply there with such collective magic." She walked closer, wringing her hands.

"You *think*?" I harshly whispered, supplying the part she was too ashamed to admit.

"Castor, it's the only chance we have. Many blame you for this."

"But I'm innocent!" I stood to face her.

"Innocence doesn't matter," she gritted. She crossed the room and drew my ear to her lips. "Don't you see? Arbor is injured. Someone will pay for it. As I draw breath, that someone will not be you." She stepped back and raised her voice again, willowy hands still clasping my face. "You know the forest better than anyone."

"I know the heart, but not beyond it. I've never crossed the hedge."

"It couldn't be much different," she argued loudly. "Won't you go? For Arbor?"

Ugh. She was laying the act on thick. "Of course I'll go. But I want you to do one thing for me while I'm gone."

Mother's brows gently kissed. "Anything."

"Ask Arbor if Arcana had him drink anything at the party."

She let out an exasperated sound, flicking her eyes to the wall again. I knew someone was listening, which was why I said it so they would hear and might consider the possibility that I wasn't the one who poisoned Arbor.

I hoped Crystabal was behind the wall, listening to my accusation again. "Castor."

I met her eyes. "You don't believe me when I say she had opportunity? Just ask her and watch her reaction. Whatever she used was in a Diviner fluted glass. I could probably go to the yard right now and find it."

"Like you would find your mushrooms in the wine fountain?" she sharply whispered.

If people had still been drinking, I would use them now to attempt to get out of the mess in which I found myself. "A simple hallucinogen, Mother. Everyone would have been high for an hour or so and went home happy. Those mushrooms wouldn't harm anyone and would've kept me secret, Mother. You should more than approve."

She forgot the eavesdropper and clutched her chest, looking stricken. "You aren't a secret, Castor."

"Not anymore," I said, moving about and collecting random articles of clothing I wasn't even sure I needed.

She lingered, no doubt with worse news to deliver. "The Council wants to address everyone, including you, outside."

"Now?" I asked, my stomach dropping.

She nodded. "Now."

She came to deliver their decision before I had to hear it with everyone else, allowing me a brief time to prepare what I could. A small kindness, and likely the only thing she could do for me at this point. I contemplated using the hallucinogen on everyone anyway, hoping they would wake later after a long, blissful nap and think they'd had a collective dream, but knew it wouldn't work now. We'd dug ourselves a six-foot deep hole and were standing at the bottom of the grave looking up at the onlookers. I could hear the snicks of their shovels as they dug into the rich dirt to cover us up.

51

"Thank you for trying to take the blame. I shouldn't have let you do that," she said. "I've set the Council straight on the timeline and told them that it was I who thought you should keep your power hidden away."

My lips parted. Why did she do that? They never would've known. "What will happen to you?"

"My only daughter is being sent into the wilderness," she replied bitterly.

That wasn't what I asked. My punishment, or 'opportunity,' wasn't hers. "What will happen to *you*, Mother?"

She pushed off the doorframe. "I'm to learn when they address everyone. I'll step outside so you can dress."

I nodded and swallowed thickly, knowing what the Council would likely do. Mother would be forced to step down from her position as Gravebriar Power for using her position against the covens. Father was the second most powerful witch in our coven, but they wouldn't allow him to claim the Power role because of his involvement in the concealment.

Arbor was weakened, so they might hold it for him for a time to see if he recovered, or they may instruct the next strongest witch to claim the title and say that if Arbor wanted it, he would have to rise above his current condition.

Dressing in simple dark green pants and a lightweight cream blouse, I slid on my boots and looked around my room for what I feared would be the last time. I gathered my poison frog, settling him into the cloth inside my bag, took up several types of mushrooms, a handful of tiny vials that might come in handy, and my grimoire, tucking them into the side, and met Mother outside my door. I slung the strap over my head and settled the weight across my chest as we walked silently down the hall.

Whomever had been listening to our conversation earlier was gone, or at least wasn't visible.

I looked for the telltale warbling of someone wearing an invisibility potion but didn't see distortions anywhere. They could be lingering farther away, close enough to hear but not for me to see. Or they could've abandoned us to join the others outside.

Mother's dress had gone from wilting to crumbling. She littered blossoms and petals as she walked. Outwardly, she seemed to be holding herself together, but a heart-breaking mixture of tension and tiredness settled on her face. I wanted to clasp her hand and squeeze it, to show her I understood and felt terrible it had come to this. That I wished I'd lied well enough to accept the punishment for the Gravebriars' wrong against the covens. But I wasn't sure she'd want me to touch her. She clearly thought either my power was faulty, that I was capable of poisoning Arbor by accident, or that I'd harmed him purposefully and was lying.

The petals trailing Mother shriveled, curling in on themselves by the time we reached the terrace; brittle, frag-ile remnants of what started as a lovely evening, a revel to remember.

Eighteen witches, every Council member and their Second, stood on the travertine stone our coven had laid when the Estates were established. Each set of eyes was a judge, and together, a formidable jury. Their eyes tracked us as Mother and I joined Father and our coven standing to his right. On the lawn where only hours ago we laughed and danced and ate a feast in fantastical costumes, stood the members of each of the nine Covens of Cauldron.

Parler, the Spellsweet Power, slowly stepped forward, his bowed back and legs complicating every movement. His long white hair drifted at the whim of the warm summer breeze. It ruffled his roomy, glaucous pants and matching button-up top. Parler clutched a thick book in his arthritic hands – one of the many I'd given them when I announced my findings about the gravebriar cure. I was thankful he'd read the grimoires and believed me about that, even if he believed nothing else.

His voice grated over the crowd. "As we are gathered, a Gravebriar boy lays dying. Arbor Gravebriar was poisoned last night at the revel. Castor Gravebriar stands accused of poisoning him."

My ribs tightened but I stood straight and tall, watching his blue eyes scan the crowd and feeling hundreds of pairs settle on me. I would not wilt like a petal on Mother's dress. Forge Silverthorn stood a head above most of his coven mates. His molten eyes fixed on me. I wondered if he thought it ironic that it was *me* now raising my chin proudly, defiantly, despite the situation and charges being leveled against me. I wondered if he thought I did it and was hiding away in the solarium to let the poison do what poison does...

"Let me take the opportunity to remind all that accusation is not synonymous with guilt." He paused. "There is another matter that must be addressed immediately. The Gravebriar Coven, led by their Power, have committed a grievous offense against the Council and against you all. They sought to conceal and have often lied to hide Castor's true power. The Gravebriar line, as you know, are healers; green witches. Castor, it seems, is their opposite. Her magic is deadlier. Her magic lies in poison, which is why she is the most obvious suspect regarding Arbor Gravebriar's sudden malady and condition."

Murmurs tumbled through the crowd until I could feel the eyes of every witch on me like a swarm of flies on carrion.

"Castor denies having poisoned the boy and has presented the Council with evidence of a potential cure for Arbor Gravebriar."

More whispers.

Parler Spellsweet turned to me. "*I* don't believe you are to blame for this, Castor, but many on the Council are convinced. So, we've come to a collective, though divided, decision. The majority has spoken, Castor. We will allow you to travel into the forest to search for the ancient Gravebriar burial place in pursuit of your namesake. Should you locate the gravebriar and bring it back to Arbor, and for anyone else who might need it in the future, all accusations against you will be dropped." I nodded and quietly thanked him. "If, however, you do *not* locate the gravebriar and you return empty-handed, you will bear the penalty for Arbor's injury. My advice for you – if you are unable to locate gravebriar – would be never to return, for the penalty for causing the death of a witch within our hedge is also death."

My chest felt too tight and yet hollow. I could only return if I was successful. If I stepped back into Cauldron without it, they would burn me at the stake. I could almost feel the flames licking the hem of my pant legs, warming the back of my knees, melting me inch by inch.

"I am innocent," I loudly asserted. I could almost hear Mother cringing, her petals crisping beside me. But I wanted them to hear it from me. I didn't do this. "I understand why you think I'm guilty, but I'm not. However, I appreciate the opportunity to clear my name."

"If it wasn't you, then who was it?" someone yelled from the grass.

Parler turned away from me to try to find the one who posed the question when an argument broke loose.

One of my coven mates, Holly, came to my defense, pointing to Arcana. "How about *her*? She had the opportunity."

"Why would a Diviner want to harm Arbor Gravebriar?" someone else bellowed through cupped hands.

"Why would a Gravebriar want to harm one of our own?" Spruce shouted from our coven.

"To keep him from taking her mother's position!" a Nocturn male growled, pointing at me.

"Maybe it was a Silverthorn!" a shout came from the back. "They're no doubt sour about the Council meeting yesterday. They hate the Gravebriars."

The Silverthorns bristled. "We had nothing to do with it," their Power, Sterling, blustered, his neatly trimmed silver hair shimmering in the sun. The witches of every coven became loud, chattering about who was to blame. "This is an egregious attempt to sway attention from your daughter, Rose. Something at which you've become quite adept," he said, wagging a finger toward Mother.

I'd never seen my mother truly angry until that moment. She stepped forward and her composure snapped. "I kept her hidden because of *this*! Because I knew what would happen if you knew. You don't bother to seek understanding, but would rather tear her apart for your own selfish whims! Did you consider that the Goddess chose Castor for this power because she was the only one strong enough to handle it?"

Sterling sneered, "She's only as strong as the poison she collects. Her magic is dangerous at best, and given Arbor's current state, I'd say she's a threat to us all."

"As is your son," Mother retorted venomously.

The witches turned their attention toward the Silverthorns. Flanked by his coven mates, Forge Silverthorn was so tense I thought he might splinter.

"It doesn't matter," Sterling asserted coldly. "He's being punished as well." Mother quieted along with the crowd, her anger silently building. "He's to go with Castor."

"What for?" Mother said carefully, narrowing her eyes.

"To make sure she is kept safe along the way. Collecting the gravebriar is paramount to the safety of every witch in Cauldron. The fact that you've used all of them, likely irresponsibly, is only one of the wrongs the Gravebriar Coven has made, which we will seek to right."

Mother looked to Parler, then to Gust, the Tempest Power, to Sanguine and Crystabal, Bloodling and Diviner. "Please don't do this." Her voice broke.

They turned away from her, looking over the crowd. They'd made their decision and wouldn't be swayed.

Sterling pointed at Mother and wagged his finger again. I swear if he were closer, she'd have bitten off the offending appendage. "And *you*, Rose Gravebriar, are to be replaced. If the Gravebriars are to stay in Cauldron, they will need *honorable* leadership," Sterling finished.

She scoffed, "As honorable as you have been? We are not so different, Sterling Silverthorn."

Parler managed to maintain his decorum. "Our decision has been handed down. Every witch is dismissed and should return to his or her Estate immediately. This discussion is not productive, nor will it matter as the decision is final. Castor, you must leave immediately." He pointed toward the woods.

Sterling walked to where his son was standing and looked between him and me. He clasped Forge's shoulders and looked him in the eye.

Forge's tone was sharp as chipped ice and just as frigid. "I won't do it."

He couldn't refuse to go. The Council would see their orders carried out.

"You have no choice," snapped his father, grinding his thumb into Forge's collarbone. Forge ripped his shoulder away. When they noticed me watching, Sterling escorted Forge away until the two were swallowed by fellow Silverthorn witches.

Arcana and Crystabal, the usurper and usurped, stood together whispering to themselves. I wondered how quickly the Diviners would accept Arcana and let Crystabal fall away like the dead head of a flowering plant, to wilt and wither and crumble.

I jogged down the steps of the terrace and had just started across the lawn when Mother caught me. She hugged me tight around the neck, holding me still as she whispered in my ear so that no one else could hear. "As soon as you are in the forest, run from him. Circle Cauldron and slip back into the our home at dark. We will hide you. It's not safe for you beyond the hedge."

My brows kissed. I couldn't do that. I pulled back to see her.

"The boy they're sending with you – Sterling's son, Forge... *Run. From. Him.* Go into the forest alone, Castor, then hide and come back to us at dark." I found Forge in the crowd. His bowed lips pressed into a thin line at whatever his father was still telling him.

The very thought was too dangerous to breathe, and yet she'd breathed it. "Arbor needs the gravebriar. I can't just come back without finding it. I won't burn for something I didn't do."

She looked harried. Frantic. "I will keep Arbor alive. They took my title, but not my magic. In time, and with enough resolve, I believe he will heal. But *I* will never heal if something happens to you. Run from that boy and run far and fast. Then hide. I beg you to hide and come home to me. We can conceal you until Arbor is fully healed." She brought my face before hers, her eyes boring into mine. "They will have gravebriars. What is the fastest, surest way to get them, Castor?"

My mouth fell open as her fingers tightened, her eyes blazing with anger and fear.

He was being sent to kill me, then collect the briars Arbor needed and that the Council would oversee from now on.

She kissed my cheeks and hugged me tight once more. "Slip through the crowd and don't let him catch you. Go now, before he realizes you've left."

A commotion erupted on the lawn. Mother slipped a felt hat into my hands and I quickly tucked my hair beneath it, weaving a jagged path through the witches who had been filtering through the crowd and were now trying to see what was going on. "I love you, Castor," I heard her say as I slipped away.

She'd never said those words... not that I could recall.

I knew she loved me, of course. What mother didn't care for her children? But to hear it... that was another thing.

"Rose!" Father yelled for Mother further down the terrace where he'd run to see what the fuss was about. I paused to watch as she gathered her gown of dead, crispy and flaking roses. My chest tightened as he announced, "Valerian has been stabbed."

Mother rushed to him and the crowd parted for her. They hadn't named her replacement, so for the time, she was still the Power of our coven. She was the strongest among them with or without her title.

Three of my coven mates lifted Valerian off the lawn, carrying him up the steps and onto the terrace where they laid him on a stone table.

Panting and hissing with every small movement, sweat soaked Valerian's dark hair and plastered it to his forehead. His brown skin was ashen and his cheeks puffed with each shallow breath. He sat up on his elbows, refusing to lie flat, so Mother put her hand over the wound. Blood dripped onto the table and spilled onto the terrace.

Mother worked quickly, her magic filling the air with the aromatic scent of fresh flowers. Across the lawn, Forge Silverthorn stood with his father and Nickel, who had blood on his hands and stood, staring at them, completely bewildered.

If Forge caught me in the forest and stabbed me, no one would be there to heal me. I would die and he would succeed at his macabre task. But that was only if he could find me. I rushed to the tree line, letting the forest swallow me with one gulp.

Normally when I walked through the woods, my feet barely left a sound that I noticed, but now that I needed to be quiet as a mouse, they sounded like elephant's feet, trampling and crunching everything they touched.

A rustle behind me. I turned to see if he was there but found nothing but a scampering squirrel, chewing happily on a walnut.

Hand on my chest, I calmed my breathing and hurried along, realizing that putting as much distance between myself and the Silverthorn was best. If he wanted to kill me, I had bad news for him. I wasn't going down without a fight. One touch and he'd die *with* me.

I ran as fast as my legs would push until they burned and ached, then I ran faster, leaping streams and climbing hills only to rush down their backs. Unable to forget the Silverthorn, I plunged forward heedlessly. I needed to keep my eyes open for a gravebriar bush. Finding it wouldn't erase my supposed wrongdoings, but it would be my first step in proving I could keep my word. And when I brought the gravebriar back for Arbor, maybe people would believe me when I said I didn't poison him. Maybe one day he would believe me, too.

I never wanted to lie about anything again.

Lies were viscous, and like magic, fueled with intent. The intent to deceive and conceal. I supposed that when you valued others, their opinions mattered so much that sometimes the vulnerability that came with showing them your truth was more than most were willing to chance.

Just when I thought I had put enough distance between us, another rustling sound came from somewhere behind me. Not close, but too close for comfort. I searched for someplace to hide but found nothing, so I squeezed behind a tree barely wide enough to conceal me.

Another rustle. Closer this time. Then another. And another.

I peeked around the trunk, fingertips digging into the rough bark as I scanned the forest, which was eerily still. No hares. No squirrels. Not even a bird twittered in the treetops.

There was only silence – the surest sign of danger.

I quickly searched my bag, drawn to the hum of the deadliest cluster of mushrooms I could find, and wrapped my fist around it, squeezing to release the poison and drawing it into me. I let the wrung-out husk drop to the forest floor. "I know you're tracking me. Show yourself."

Forge Silverthorn stepped out from behind a broad sycamore with his hands raised to the canopy. His demeanor was guarded, but there was an easy confidence about him, a levity I wished I possessed but never had.

His wings were gone, but I could almost see the sharpened edges gleam as I imagined him spreading them. His face bore an ash-brown shadow of hair on his jaw that made him look rugged. Dangerous. No doubt he had no time to bathe or shave before chasing after me in the forest.

I slowly backed away as he continued forward. "I'll give you one chance to walk away, Silverthorn. I have no intention of dying today." I flexed my fingers, concentrating the poison into their tips. One touch, and he would lie dead on the forest floor to be scavenged and scattered and forgotten.

He paused his steps. "You know my father's wishes, yet you haven't asked for mine."

My fingers trembled at my sides. I slid my slippery palms down my trousers. "Better for me to die than Arbor, right?"

"I have no intention of killing you, Castor."
A lie.
"Why not?" I challenged.
"Because I know you didn't poison Arbor Gravebriar."
Another lie.

I swallowed thickly, wishing that his claims were true and ready to act on my promise to end him if he lashed out at me. My heart thundered as I waited for him to produce a weapon. Valerian had just been stabbed. Likely by Nickel, but all the Silverthorns were metal mages. I could still see Valerian's sweat-soaked hair and hear his anguished pants, hisses, and groans. I could still smell the rose scent of my mother's magic pouring over him, cascading like a rush of water, spilling off the table with the coppery scent of his blood.

He stepped forward again, toe to heel, crunching leaves under his weight, hands still in the air. Sweat soaked the hair at his temples. He looked to the ground where the shriveled mushroom lay, but instead of startling, he just looked tired. As tired as I felt to the very core.

Dirt and leaves were stuck to his knees. He must have fallen.

He licked his lips. "I understand why you're afraid. You have every reason to be. The Council gave me one mandate: to travel with you and help you quickly find the graveyard. If in two days we weren't successful, they asked me to kill you, bury you, and bring the gravebriars that sprout from your grave back to them. My father said to kill you the moment we walked far enough into the forest that your screams wouldn't be heard, or sooner if I could injure you in such a way that you couldn't cry out."

"Why wouldn't you obey him and get the deed over with?" I challenged.

"I've done things I shouldn't to appease him in the past. I won't lie to you and tell you I haven't, but even *I* draw the line at killing an innocent witch, regardless of what she and her coven have concealed. Especially when I fear my coven is guilty of far worse."

I narrowed my eyes. "How do you know I'm innocent?"

He gently gestured to my face. "Because you look sick at the possibility of having to use your power on me even in self-defense. Your pallor is as green as your hair. You didn't hurt Arbor."

"Some think I did it on accident," I rasped around the knot in my throat.

He shook his head. "A witch controls the magic he or she possesses. Magic isn't accidental. Look, we're wasting time, and time is the one thing we can't control. I argued that point with both the Council and my father. Some listened, others didn't care. So, I made up my mind not to care about their wishes or orders."

His eyes caught on the shriveled mushroom laying at my feet. "I have a proposal." His metallic eyes met mine. His tongue swept over the perfect cupid's bow in his upper lip. "Put whatever poison you'd like in my body. If I do anything to make you fear me, you'll be able to use it. That way, you'll be able to relax and the two of us can move forward with the task at hand." He extended a hand to me. "I trust you, Castor. I trust that you won't hurt or kill me, just like you didn't hurt or try to kill Arbor."

He said it with such conviction that my fingers twitched. My toes stretched in my boots. I suppose I should've thought it over more thoroughly before I stepped forward, clasped his hand, and shoved the poison into his skin, then quickly wrenched my hand away and watched him. But something in me sensed the truth in him and I couldn't help but take the olive branch he extended. Especially since he offered a branch that clearly favored me.

I could feel the toxin singing as it was carried through his body, infusing every part. All it would take was one thought and he would lie dead on the plush, mossy carpet underfoot.

Forge nodded, flashing a fast smile with one hand splayed on his chest. "Thank you."

"For putting a lethal dose of poison in your bloodstream?" I asked.

He gave me an easy smile, and my toes curled a little in my boots. "For trusting me."

Was it trust or fear that led me to accept his proposal? In the end, perhaps it was both. "Please don't make me regret it."

He nodded, pursing his lips and at least showing a bit of his nervousness in the quick swipe of fingers through his hair. "Believe me, that's the *last* thing I want to do. Are you ready to begin this journey?"

I nodded. "I've never been beyond the hedge. The heart I know like the back of my hand. There's no gravebriar in it."

"I've been beyond it." He didn't elaborate. He hiked a bag up onto his shoulders, which pulled his shirt taut across his chest. "Though I admit, I don't know what gravebriar looks like. I may have snagged my pants on it more than once and had no idea what it was."

My eyes were drawn to the fine trousers he tugged on to emphasize his point. "You're still wearing your suit."

"Not the jacket," he playfully corrected, unbuttoning and rolling his sleeves to his elbows. His arms were toned and tan. Strong.

I gave him a small smile. "Not the jacket."

His bottom lip was split on one side, a couple of bloody spots fresh on his pale shirt. "I fell," he offered, pointing to the shirt, then his knees. "Bit my tongue, too." He gestured to me. "Do you want to walk together, or would you like for me to walk ahead so you can see me at all times?"

"You walk ahead."

It made me more comfortable because I could keep him in sight. I wouldn't have to be constantly looking over my shoulder. Plus, while he caught all the spider webs between branches I could admire him from behind and he would be none the wiser.

FIVE

As we quietly carved a path through the trees, the canopy became dense and the forest floor cushioned with moss turned from thin to lush. Bugs milled long-fallen logs where the sunlight couldn't reach our skin through the foliage. Croppings of delicate, feathery ferns burst from the ground. The humidity plastered my clothes to my flesh at the small of my back and chest.

I was deep in thought about all I'd read about the gravebriar. I'd hastily copied others' sketches of the plant and briars into my grimoire. According to those tomes, the gravebriar would only grow on one condition – on the fresh grave of a Gravebriar – and there was no magical graveyard that could preserve it. I'd specifically searched the other books for information on that but found nothing.

Part of me thought Mother made up the entire tale of the ancient Gravebriar graveyard just to appease the Council and give me a chance to sneak back into our Estate where she promised to protect me, while a sliver still held out hope that we would truly find it out here. But whether the graveyard existed or not didn't matter because out there somewhere, gravebriar was real. And maybe there were other instances in which it could grow. It was a shot in the dark, but it was all I had.

Forge stopped suddenly and I bumped into his back. He was quiet for a second as I peeked over his shoulders, then all around us. "What is it? Why did you stop?"

In front of my nose, his broad shoulders shook and a chuckle escaped him.

"What?" I asked, looking around him again. *What could be so funny?*

"Do you mind?" He smiled over his shoulder.

Mind what?

His brows rose. "Your hands..."

Briar gouge me. I ripped my hands off his... Well, I'd basically groped his backside. I must have tried to catch myself. The flesh of my face became an inferno, heat and embarrassment battling for supremacy over my pale skin. "I apologize."

Forge's shoulders shook again before he let out a hearty laugh. "You're red as a beet, but you're not green anymore."

"Well, at least *one* of us is amused," I grumbled under my breath.

He flashed an ornery smile over his shoulder. "Don't apologize, Gravebriar. I give you full permission to accost me whenever you'd like."

"The offer is *not* mutually extended," I quipped, moving away from him to hide my flushed, fire poker-hot face.

"Hey, where's your hat?" he called from behind me. "You could have buried your face in it," he chortled.

Ugh. My hat.

I'd gotten hot and tried to stuff it into my bag, but it didn't quite fit and must have fallen out. I sighed and was about to tell him that I lost it when I felt a plant singing to me... a most familiar song. One that had long been embedded in my heart, but that I'd never heard in such a dark, damp place as the forest's heart. My feet clumsily wandered over felled, rotten logs. The further I walked, the more the shadows lengthened, broadening as the forest's grip tightened around us.

Then the moss suddenly ended and I stood amid a broad patch of healthy castor plants. Their beans held a most deadly poison… and there was more here than I'd ever seen. Enough to kill a city of witches. Not only that, but the plants weren't here earlier in the month when I came to search for other plants and fungi. Someone had sown and grew them in a place they wouldn't naturally flourish.

I brushed my hand over one of the plant's silky leaves, feeling the hum I knew by touch. But beneath the resonance of the poison singing to me, there was another scent. The scent of a fresh-cut flower I couldn't quite place. This castor patch was grown by a green witch. It was grown with Gravebriar magic.

"Is this yours?" Forge asked, keeping clear of the plants. They wouldn't hurt him, but I was glad for the distance he kept, however small.

I shook my head. "No." He was quiet for a long moment, so I looked into his eyes and said it again. "It's not mine. I didn't grow it. I can't grow anything, not even poisonous plants. I can only use them."

"I believe you," he assured me. "I'm just not sure what to think of it. Someone's trying to get your attention, it would seem."

Get my attention, or frame me for Arbor's poisoning? "You should go back to where we left the trail and wait for me there. I'm going to get rid of the crop."

"I can cut it down," he offered, reaching into his pocket and retrieving a sliver of silver.

"No. That would still leave the beans for someone to harvest. I'll leech the poison away from them."

"You're going to take in that much poison?" he asked, his brow furrowed.

"It's not harmful to me, Forge."

He nodded slowly, clearly battling what he knew of the plant and what I was telling him, then walked out of the patch of castor plants with their pointed green leaves, egg-plant in the middles with matching veins. I walked among them, letting my palms touch each plant, squeezing the ricin from the beans, urging the leaves and stems to wilt, for the root to shrivel and recede from the soil in which it was anchored. Within minutes, the lush crop was reduced to a darkened mash of curled leaves and withered stalks.

The euphoria the ricin left in my blood was tempered by the fact that someone from my coven had been grow-ing something so toxic. The plant for which I was named. Something with which to frame me...

Forge was waiting, keeping watch like I asked. He turned to face me as I approached. "The plants are dead," I told him.

He gave a half-smile. "It must have been hard on you growing up, being different from the rest of your coven."

I shrugged. "No harder than it was for you, I suppose."

He gave me a quick, half-hearted smile that didn't reach his eyes. Forge was quiet as we walked further into the forest's dark heart where shadows were darker, the air heavier. Fresh gusts of air didn't reach this place. A heart had no need for breath.

As the forest took us into her bosom, I wondered if she would allow us to leave it or if she might hold us there, let-ting us petrify like the wood that never seemed to rot away, or be swallowed by a sea of moss so the animals under its surface might feast.

Forge remained quiet for a time. I wasn't sure if he felt the foreboding pressure or if he was using the time to think, but eventually, the tension bled from his shoulders and he began to explain the events that had the Council so flustered.

"Rumors always churn in Cauldron. My power is unique, but not opposite like yours. You've seen some of the other Silverthorns, I trust?" I nodded. "Some work brass, some steel, some gold or silver... titanium. I can work them all. My magic lies in metal – any and all metal, but that's not why my coven got in trouble with the Council. I'm not sure how much you know about me, but I'm an adept weapons master."

He walked casually and I didn't see any weapons on his person. Did he require metal to render one, or could he conjure what he wanted from thin air? And what sort of weapons? Any and all – like the metal he spun?

"The Silverthorns didn't get in trouble for conceal-ing the fact that I could make weapons, though. The Councilwitches knew of my skill." He paused. "*I* got in trouble because I armed the members of our coven..."

My brows pinched in surprise. "Against the other covens?"

He barked a laugh. "That's what your mother asked, but no. I armed them against hunters."

"Hunters?"

"Witch hunters," he elaborated. "Specifically a pack who actively seeks a way to break the hedge around Cauldron, and whom I believe are very close to doing so."

My skin prickled as I looked all around us. At the underbrush, the enormous rotting trees. The forest pro-vided innumerable places to hide. Even an army could cloak itself in her. "The Powers didn't believe you," I surmised.

He raked his lower lip with his teeth, then released it. "No, they didn't."

"Wait. How do you know all this?" I asked, watching his eyes consider me.

They glittered as he answered, "Because I hunt the hunters."

My brows slowly rose. I hadn't expected that. "Did your father sanction your actions?"

"Ah, no. He brought me before the Council himself. Asked them to banish me for what I did, but that was mostly to cover his own ass. He doesn't approve of much I do or have done. It's safe to say he wishes I was never born."

I didn't care one ounce for Sterling Silverthorn. Beyond what he'd done to his own son, there was the little matter of how he spoke to my mother as he stripped her of her position like he was gleefully tearing her heart from her chest. Then, of course, there was the personal matter of how he ordered Forge to kill me.

My parents were hardly perfect, but they wouldn't have hauled me before the Council. They would have broken their backs under a heap of lies before they did that. And they certainly wouldn't ask me to kill anyone. They've never asked any untoward thing of me, though I easily could've done it, and when I was younger, before I knew better, likely would have.

"What happened between Nickel and Valerian?" I asked, wondering if he'd seen what caused the fray between our coven mates in which Valerian was stabbed.

"From what I could tell, tension was high when accusations began flying, and Valerian and Nickel got into an argument. Valerian blew some sort of dust into Nickel's eyes, blinding him, and Nickel reacted by taking out his knife and sticking Valerian while he was still within reach."

I pressed my eyes closed. Accusations and anger weren't worth stabbing someone over, nor were they worth blinding another witch – even if only for a few moments. I knew the powder Valerian had used. We used it on one another as children, playing hiding games in the Estate so the seeker could not cheat and peek and find us. But a Silverthorn wouldn't have known it was essentially harmless and would have felt frightened. No wonder he lashed out. Valerian was a fool for using the powder, and Nickel was a fool for stabbing him. Both were wrong, but no one could see that. They would choose a side and defend it until the bitter end.

"Did you make the knife?"

He pursed his lips and shook his head. "No, it wasn't one I'd given him. Other Silverthorns form and carry their own out of the metal worked by their power. My coven mates can conjure metal items, but I infuse them with unique magic. My weapons... carry my intent. They're unique in that respect. Most work metal and that's it. I spell the weapons I create."

He was quiet for a moment, his eyes scanning our surroundings and again, my skin prickled. Did he sense a hunter nearby, or was it a habit to search for threats? His shoulders relaxed and he flicked a glance over his shoulder. "Will your mother easily be able to heal Valerian?"

I nodded. "She'll have no trouble healing him. The powder Valerian used would have dissipated in moments. Nickel's sight probably returned while Valerian was being healed. They will both be okay. They just need time to let their tempers cool."

"I'm not sure they will until we walk back into Cauldron holding the gravebriar," he somberly mused. The moment Valerian blinded Nickel and Nickel stabbed Valerian, the dormant feud between our covens erupted once more. Worse than that, because many of the covens felt betrayed by the Gravebriars for concealing my magic, it felt like a line was drawn between us and everyone now – not just the Silverthorn coven.

The worst part was that I wasn't sure returning with the gravebriar would erase any of it, but it would be a start.

"Why couldn't she heal Arbor?" he asked. "How is it that he's dying or that he needs gravebriar to fully restore him to health?"

"She and Father tried. I took the toxin from his blood, but the way some poisons work when mingled with magic…" I tried to think of the best way to explain it. "If you think of a thick scar and how tough that skin is, and then imagine layers of thick scarring, you'll get an idea of how Arbor's organs have been affected. My mother is powerful, but even she has struggled to heal the tangle left in its wake."

"You held his hand and danced with him. You didn't sense anything in his blood while you danced?"

"No, and I would've known it the moment I touched him. Poison… sings to me. Or maybe a resonance is the best way to describe it. Either way, when I danced with my father, Arcana was with him. He drank something while they spoke. It had to have been in his drink. I don't remember touching him after that. And when I took the poison away, it felt strange." I wasn't sure if I should trust him with my suspicions, but in the end, figured that telling him couldn't hurt. "I think someone cloaked it."

His lips parted. "That was quite inventive for whomever framed you."

Indeed, it was. I tilted my head. "You noticed me and Arbor the night of the revel?"

He held my gaze. "I noticed *you*, Gravebriar. He was no more than an accessory on your arm."

Butterflies flittered for the briefest of seconds before I realized that what he likely meant wasn't that I was beautiful, but that I was strange looking. Who wouldn't notice my strange yellow eyes and pale green hair? I was the sole oddity among my peers, the sharp thorn among fragrant, harmless blossoms.

He tipped my chin up with his knuckle, withdrawing his hand when my eyes locked on his. "I meant it as a compliment."

"I took it as one," I defended, lying through my teeth but holding my head high. I would not wilt for him. I would not wilt for anyone ever again.

He nodded his head toward the expanse of forest before us. "Ready to walk outside the hedge?"

I could feel the thick, churning magics ahead, but instead of feeling awe like I'd imagined I would in this moment, I felt sorrow. The hedge felt strong and weak. It felt thick and thin. It felt right and very wrong. And the wrongness stuck to me like sap on skin.

I gestured for Forge to lead us through and past the hedge, surprised when it felt comforting when I expected that wrongness to catch me up in it and not let me pass. The feeling dissipated the farther we walked from the hedge. I followed Forge as he hiked along a well-worn animal trail, only occasionally frantically tearing at spider webs that caught on his face. I tried to stifle my laughter when that happened and kept my distance so I wouldn't bump into him again.

As we left the hedge behind, the sky fractionally lightened, but the daylight didn't last. Night pushed the sun beyond the horizon and covered the land with cool shadow. We'd searched a wide swath of forest and found no cemetery, and certainly no gravebriar growing from the soil.

When twilight settled over us and a slight chill filled the air, Forge stopped. "We need to find a spot to rest for the night and build a fire. I'm starving."

I wanted to press on until we found the forsaken place, take up the bush by the root, and run home with it. But it was so dark here that we might walk by it and not know. Besides, exhausting ourselves would do more harm than good.

"Resting sounds nice right about now, but I didn't bring any food or drink," I rasped, my throat parched despite us having paused to drink from a stream several times throughout the afternoon.

Forge smiled. "Good thing you let me come along, then." He pulled the strap of his bag over his head and crouched as he rummaged through it, pulling out a tiny square of metal. He clasped it in his hand and in an instant, a dark frying pan appeared, the handle firmly grasped in his fingers.

I choked out a laugh. "That's convenient."

He winked. "Only if we have something to cook in it."

My good mood shriveled.

Forge chuckled. "Easy, Gravebriar. I don't travel into the forest without enough food to last for a couple of days. Hunting doesn't promise a bounty, you know."

"Some hunter *you* are," I teased.

He quirked a dark brow at me. I looked away, pretending to ignore him, and tried to squash the traitorous flutters erupting in my stomach. "What *is* in your bag, since you didn't pack food?" he asked.

I crouched next to him and opened the deflated canvas to reveal my frog lying within a nest of what articles of clothing I'd managed to grab. As I lifted him out, the sticky pads of each of his toes clung to my skin as he walked up my palm and gripped a finger.

Forge looked from it to me and his brows rose. "Didn't expect this little guy." He reached out to pet him.

I drew my little friend back to my chest. "Don't touch him. His skin emits a powerful poison."

"Touching him would kill me?"

I shook my head. "It would make you sick, give you cramps, and make you feel like dying was a good option, but no, unless you ate him, you wouldn't die."

Forge rubbed his palms on his pant legs. "No eating or touching the frog. Got it."

I smiled. "No eating or touching the frog. I've been considering whether I should leave him here. He belongs in the forest. I just... he's been mine since I was a little girl."

"What's his name?" he asked softly.

I groaned and looked to the heavens. He was going to make fun of me for this. "Bog."

"Bog. As in, Bog the frog?" he deadpanned.

"I was young and couldn't say frog when I found him. I called him Bog instead, and it stuck. Like him." Forge chuckled but didn't poke fun. "Other than that, I only have clothes, mushrooms, a few vials, and my grimoire."

"I bet *it's* stuffed full of poisonous things."

I smiled. "Just as you carry plenty of metal, I'm sure."

He didn't deny it, just snorted and set about plucking larger stones from the nearby stream and forming a fire ring while I collected firewood, Bog standing sentinel on my shoulder. I wondered if he would survive in the wild after being captive for so long.

While Forge fashioned a hand-drill and twisted until he sparked an ember, then lit the kindling which ignited the dead wood I'd found, I searched the stream for a rock for Bog. I found one with a small dimple, an impression just his size. I scooped water into it and sat him on the stone, bringing it back to the campsite with me. Bog put one foot into the water, stretching his toes wide when I settled his stone on the ground. His tongue flicked out to grab an iridescent beetle scuttling by, retracting back into his mouth as Bog feasted on his supper.

I flipped through my grimoire, fanning the pages over my waiting fingers. They absorbed all they touched. It never hurt to be prepared. Just in case we encountered trouble along the unmarked path we'd found. Forge mentioned hunters – hunters that wanted to bring down our hedge. It wasn't unreasonable to assume they'd be close to it. In this very forest, perhaps.

Forge's pan was perched over the flame, held up by a few taller rocks, but he was nowhere to be seen. I sat beside Bog and watched the darkness for a sign of Forge within it. It felt like forever before he reappeared with a small animal that he'd already skinned, ready for his pan. I might have made a disgusted face and he might have noticed.

"It's hare. You don't eat meat?" he asked.

I shook my head. "No."

He nodded slowly. "Good thing I swiped bread and cheese from the revel tables, then. It's in my bag." He laid the hare on the pan and it immediately smoked and sizzled, cooking fast on the hot iron.

I leaned over to reach into his bag and found the food he'd thankfully pilfered. I removed a small loaf of wheat bread crusted on the outside and soft within, along with a few chunks of tangy goat cheese. I was hungrier than I realized. And thirstier, too. After I ate, I knelt at the stream for a long time, holding my hair back to drink.

The sky overhead was black. Clouds obscured the moon and every star encircling it, and a weak, gusty breeze rustled the leaves overhead, their silver bellies shimmying.

"It could rain," I said to myself.

Forge produced a sliver of silver and formed a fork, turning his dinner over to cook the other side. He looked to the leaves. "That's not ideal…"

No, it wouldn't be ideal. Forge could fashion a shelter, but bad weather would delay our trek. Unfortunately, we weren't Tempest witches and, thus, couldn't choose the weather any more than we could our present circumstances. Or change our pasts, for that matter.

"I think it'll blow over," he muttered, studying the sky. "Gravebriar?" Forge paused, carefully looking from the pan to me. "How confident are you that you'll find this cemetery and that there will be gravebriar growing there?"

I swallowed. "Not nearly as confident as I'd like to be."

"What if I told you I know someone who might be able to help us? Would you want to go to him?"

My brows kissed. "Who is this person? And where is he?"

"The first question is easier to answer than the second, but the person is a Gravebriar exile," he said, watching me carefully. "And I hope he's closer than he could be. You could say he lives a nomadic lifestyle."

"What's his name?"

He held my gaze. "If I speak it, it never again leaves your lips. If we go to him, you speak nothing of his existence to your coven or any other. He's an ally – something I don't have many of in this world outside of Cauldron."

"I swear never to speak of him or utter his name to anyone other than you at any time," I vowed.

Seeming satisfied, his muscles relaxed and he let out a long exhale. "His name is Arum."

My lips parted, brows furrowed. "That's a strange coincidence…"

"He is who you think him to be."

I shook my head. "That's impossible. That Arum is dead."

Forge shook his head, flicked a twig into the fire, and watched the flame engulf it. His metallic eyes flicked to mine, holding them hostage. "That's just what they want you to believe."

SIX

Arum was burned at the stake just before I was born for committing a treasonous act against our coven. But if he was alive and well as Forge claimed, what else had my parents lied about?

If he were alive, she would know it.

My mother had grown up under Arum's tutelage. She'd grown more powerful because he pushed her, challenged her, never let her for one second believe she wouldn't take the Power position within our coven – a position he held and would gladly concede *if* she earned it.

Mother respected him and loved him like a father. And then, when she learned of his treachery and took the Power position from him, it was her roots that bound him to the stake so he couldn't break free, and it was she who lit the wood at the base – not a Fire witch.

"How do you know Arum?" I asked.

Perhaps the man he knew wasn't Arum at all, but an impostor who had assumed his name.

"I spend as much time outside Cauldron as I do in it, and I know a lot of things I would never report back to a soul in our city," he said, watching the juices from the hare sizzle.

"Not even your father?"

"Especially not my father," he confirmed, moving the meat around a bit. When he was satisfied that it was done cooking, he picked up a hunk with the tines of his fork and bit the steaming meat, chewing it quickly. "Our relationship would best be described as strained," he teased.

"There's more bread and cheese," I offered, trying to change to subject.

"You'll need it," he said. Forge ate quickly, and when he was finished, tossed the bones into the fire. "I was starving," he excused himself before wiping at his mouth, looking sheepish for the first time that I'd noticed. Suddenly, he went still, swiveling his head around like an owl's.

"What is it?" I whispered, tension seizing my bones.

He relaxed. "A deer. Nothing to worry about."

We hadn't come across a single witch hunter since passing through the hedge, thankfully. I didn't want to add another complication to an already impossible chore. If someone tried to kill me, I would use my power to defend myself. I knew the truth of it the moment I wrung the mushroom out and prepared to kill Forge when I realized he was close. I would've hated it. And he was right, it would've made me sick to do it, but I would have. I couldn't imagine someone blindly condemning me just because I was born with magic in my blood.

"If you're thinking I'm a liar, I'm not. There *are* hunters in the forest."

"I wasn't thinking you lied. I was thinking how fortunate we've been not to have come across anyone who wanted us dead."

He smirked. "I apologize for assuming your thoughts, Princess."

My mouth popped open. "Princess? I'm no princess."

He laughed, his molten metal eyes sparked by the firelight. At their edge was a thick band of black, the deepest

82

shade of coal. "Says the girl whose parents throw revels that are spoken of for months afterward, who spare no amount of magic or expense. Who—"

I rolled my eyes and interrupted, "And are you any less a prince? We're both the offspring of Powers. We're equals."

He reluctantly offered a, "Touché."

"Prince of Weaponry," I dubbed him. He let out a groan at that and I couldn't help but laugh. He didn't volley back with 'Princess of Poisons,' but the title echoed through my mind.

The fire was slowly dying. I would find more wood to stoke it with, but first I wanted to know more about Arum. "If we don't find the graveyard, or gravebriar, and we have to go to Arum for help, will he recognize me as a witch of his coven?" I asked, holding a strand of hair out.

"The hue of anyone's hair can be changed, so that alone wouldn't give you away. The trouble is that he was very close with your mother. If Arum sees your face, he will know your lineage immediately."

"I look that much like her?"

Forge nodded. "You do. I have a cloaking potion, if you want to use it," he offered. "Assuming you don't have a vial in your bag."

I didn't have a cloaking potion. It was one of the only things I didn't have in my rooms.

Other than my hair and eyes, I supposed I did favor Mother, I just hadn't considered it before. My lips were fuller and I had no wrinkles, but I had taken most of my features from her. My height and build, down to the curve of my cheeks and the set of my jaw. Even the smattering of freckles over the bridge of my nose matched hers. "I'll drink it if need be. I just hope we find what we need and can turn toward home instead of it coming down to asking Arum for help."

Forge scrubbed his hands down his face. "I hope so, too. Arum is—different. And he won't do anything for free."

"Not out of the kindness of his heart?" I asked just to prod.

"He'd have to possess one for that to be possible," he said, his words sharp as the edge of a blade.

I sat up straighter as my ribs tightened uncomfortably. "I assumed since we were considering asking him for help that he was an ally."

He snorted. "An ally is not the same thing as a friend."

"True," I said quietly. Every Gravebriar in my coven was an ally. Few were my friends.

"You should try to get some sleep, Gravebriar," he said, scanning the darkness lapping at us.

"What about you? Do you want to sleep in shifts?"

He shook his head. "Nah. I couldn't sleep if I wanted to."

Forge knelt in front of the stream, cupping his hands and bringing water to his face, slurping some occasionally. I stretched and sat up. He'd stomped out the fire and his bag was ready and looked far tidier than mine ever would. I combed my fingers through my hair. The motion caught his attention.

"Good morning, Gravebriar."

"Silverthorn," I rasped. I stood and smoothed my pants and blouse, giving up when the wrinkles refused to budge.

"You look beautiful as ever, Princess."

I tilted my head and gave him a scathing look that made him chuckle. I walked into the wood to tend to personal affairs and then rejoined Forge, taking Bog into my hand and hefting my bag over my shoulder. Holding Bog in my palm, I wondered if it would be better to let him go in the forest, or if he would be safer traveling with me. If something along this perilous journey went awry, I may never come back to the forest again.

His obsidian eyes flicked from me to the branches bowing over our heads.

I loved him so much. I couldn't bear to think of him not having a home with me, but maybe I wasn't being fair. Maybe I'd never been fair to him. Never considered what *he* needed, only that I needed his companionship.

He'd lived in my dark room for years, but maybe it was time for Bog to live in the daylight and step past his own hedge – *me*.

Besides, what if I didn't survive this? What if something happened and I died, or someone hurt him or took my bag and stole him away? What if they were cruel to him or killed him because they feared his yellow skin, so different than the other frogs?

His suctioning toes took hold of my finger. I knew it was just his anatomy, but somehow, I wondered if he was holding on a little tighter, if he sensed what I was about to do. If I was strong enough to do it.

"I'll miss you," I told him, stroking his back.

"You're going to leave him?" Forge gently asked from just over my shoulder. His hand ghosted down my arm.

"It's time," I croaked, my throat constricting. "I may not make it home, Silverthorn. I want *him* to survive, even if I don't."

Forge pursed his lips. "Don't say that."

"It's true." Even he couldn't insist that we would accomplish what we set out for, or that the hunters he knew of might not find us along the way, or that something else might not befall us.

Bog could survive here. It wasn't so different from the log in my room, plus there was water nearby and plenty of delicious insects for him to feast upon. It was a frog utopia here in the forest. This was where he belonged.

I gently peeled the tiny frog off my hand and held him up to a branch.

He suctioned to it and craned his neck, looking up. I didn't know if he was sizing up the branch itself or looking at the layers of the many others stretching beyond it. Perhaps he was looking at the sky and clouds. He'd spent too long in my dark corner, and while I loved him, he deserved freedom.

Still, one of the hardest things I had to do was move away from him and not pluck him off the branch and tuck him back into my bag. Sometimes letting someone go because it was best for them was the most difficult thing in the world.

Forge gave me a sympathetic look. "Are you sure about this?"

I nodded, unable to speak as a tear spilled onto my cheek. I gestured for him to lead the way.

Forge hesitated, making leaving my little friend here even harder. Then he squared his shoulders and hiked up his bag. "You sure you don't want to go first?"

I gave him a watery smile. "And miss you battling spider webs? Not a chance."

"You're heartless, Gravebriar. You and Arum – cut from the same cloth."

We didn't make it fifty paces before he was combatting a strand of silk. Through my tears, I couldn't help but chuckle.

I looked back to see Bog where he sat perched on the dull brown limb, brightly colored and still looking upward. I hoped he loved what he saw, that he somehow remembered me and that I loved him, and that his life in the forest would be full of delicious insects and lots of climbing.

Most of all, I hoped he didn't hate me for leaving him here. *I truly think it's best for him.* The feeling of dread was back, stronger now, and it said that I might be right. That my story might not have the quintessential happily ever after.

By evening, we'd found nothing.

No graveyard. No gravebriar.

Only spiked burrs that wedged in my boots and pant legs, poking at my skin uncomfortably – and spider webs. *Lots* of spider webs. The humidity pressed sweat from my pores. Though the sun was setting, it still felt like we were being baked.

Forge stopped in front of me with his hands perched on his hips. He wiped sweat from his brow and let out a deep, weary breath. "What's the call, Gravebriar: keep trudging aimlessly or seek Arum's help?"

"What are the odds Arum knows or would help us?" I countered.

"He might help us if we offer him something he wants."

"What does a man like Arum covet? What does he need?" I asked.

"A new act always helps," he mumbled, pinching his bottom lip between his thumb and forefinger.

"Act?"

Forge's molten metallic eyes slid over me and he tilted his head. "Are you a good actress, Gravebriar?"

My eyes narrowed in response. "I'm the best I know. I've acted like something I'm not most of my life."

He nodded. "True, but you've only had to fool fools. Arum is not one."

The more he warned me about Arum, the more wildly caterpillars crawled through the pit of my stomach. Forge had a cloaking potion, but if Arum was as heartless and cunning as Forge insisted, would he sense me anyway and cast us out without helping? Would this be a monumental waste of precious time that Arbor might not have?

"Tell me how I need to act."

Forge winked playfully. "It won't be too hard for you. I've seen the way you look at me."

"With disdain?" I asked innocently.

"No," he said, sauntering over to me. "Like you can barely resist me."

He reached out to clasp my waist and I swatted his hands.

"Arum needs to think we're lovers," he said, voicing exactly the thing I was afraid he was hinting at.

"Why must we convince him of such a thing?" I crossed my arms over my chest and watched his pupils dilate as he took me in. Was he acting now, or was his reaction genuine? My skin flushed at the notion.

Forge ran a knuckle over my long, green hair from my jaw over to my collarbone before easing it away. "Because he will be able to sell our act *and* our love affair to his audience to earn coppers."

"He's greedy."

Forge shook his head. "He's a survivor. Life isn't easy for a witch outside of Cauldron, and there are plenty of them. Arum gives some a way of hiding in plain sight, of thrilling others with a little magic. Even those who fear and curse it."

"What kind of an act must we provide for him? Other than selling him the story of our false love."

Forge raised a brow. "We could purchase a love potion for you if you'd like, to make it more realistic."

I scoffed. A love potion for *me*? What about *him*? "I think I can manage. Do *you* require one?"

He smirked and leaned in so his lips hovered at my ear. "I need no assistance in the art of seduction, Gravebriar." His breath puffed warm over my skin with each word and I felt goosebumps spread over my arms.

I leaned closer to show him I wasn't afraid and turned my head to face him. My lips bumped his as I asked, "And do you intend to use my name, or do you think he won't notice how you refer to me as Gravebriar?"

Forge groaned and peeled away, chuckling and relenting first. I'd won this small battle and he knew it. He scrubbed his face and tapped his chin dramatically, rolling his eyes to the sky. "You need a new name. He would recognize Castor, as well," he said, musing. His eyes calculated, the metal in them swirling like a tempest. "I'll come up with something." Forge turned toward the thinning forest, revealing the slowly sinking sun. "The last time I saw him, he was another day's walk from here. There's a creek up ahead with a deep swimming hole. I say we clean up there and head into the nearest village. A friend of mine lives there. She always keeps a room available."

What sort of friend? I wondered but didn't ask.

"What village?" I'd seen maps, of course, but hadn't stepped beyond the forest's heart. Given the sun's position, I could tell we'd traveled north, but there were several tiny villages encompassing Westbrook and I wasn't sure which was closest.

"Falls Creek. It's small, but we'll be safe there," he answered, stretching his arms over his head.

I was sticky and hot, so the mere thought of cool, fresh water sounded like an absolute dream. My steps were leaden, snapping every twig laying on the ground and trampling the undergrowth with sluggish footfalls... until I heard the creek's water rushing over rock and earth. Then, I almost shoved Forge out of the way to reach it, sliding down a small embankment and falling to my knees in the pebbles just to cup my hands and drink, drowning my face in the cold, clear perfection.

Forge laughed beside me as he bent to do the same. "I didn't know such a simple thing could win the heart of a woman. I'll have to remember this moment."

I ignored him, standing and stripping my bag off before working the buttons on my shirt. I made it to my navel before Forge spoke. Looking up, I found him staring, looking uncomfortable but not bothering to turn away. I almost rolled my eyes. If he needed no help in the art of seduction, as he claimed, then mine certainly wasn't the first female body he'd seen.

"Damn, Gravebriar," he said, swallowing thickly. "You're not shy."

"No, I'm *not* shy. I'm burning alive and sticky with sweat," I told him. "So, if *you're* shy, turn away."

Instead of turning, he began to shed his clothes, tugging at his own buttons. The muscles in his forearms flexed with every movement and every undone button revealed taut, smooth, perfectly tanned skin. He stared directly in front of him, only flicking a glance my way when I spoke.

I left my pale underthings on, mostly for his comfort as he seemed squirmy all of a sudden. "How deep is it in the middle?"

"Twelve, maybe fifteen feet?"

I smiled, climbed onto a tall boulder, and jumped into the dark pool of water where the rocky bottom was hidden. The air glided over my skin as I dove, plunging into shockingly cold water. Bubbles burst around me before I surfaced, treading water as my body acclimated.

It. Felt. Glorious.

Forge shucked off his trousers, leaving his undershorts on, and waded in from the shore.

"Afraid of heights?" I teased.

"Something like that," he answered good naturedly.

He eased into the water, lunging forward and giving himself over to the stream when it hit his navel. He swam so smoothly and gracefully I was almost envious, because I knew that no matter how often I swam, I would never have that natural fluidity. I knew how to swim, but one would never assume I belonged to the water.

A small waterfall cascaded into the creek where a deep eddy had formed. Beyond the deep hole the creek became shallow again, large boulders jutting from the water here and there to disturb the flow. I swam to the waterfall and let it tumble over my hair. I scrubbed it as best I could with my fingertips, cursing myself for not thinking of bringing basic necessities along. I'd escaped the only home I knew with whatever I could grab without a thought for how I would feed myself, bathe, or anything, really. Rational thought was difficult after the troubling conversation I'd had with Mother.

Forge floated nearby on his back with his ears submerged and water lapping at his temples, staring at the darkening sky. A few stars could already be seen in the space between where trees on one bank clawed toward those on the other. "Tell me something about you, Gravebriar."

I leaned out of the waterfall and shrugged. "You know my secret. Everyone does now."

"Ah, come on," he urged. "Everyone has more than one."

I shook my head. "There's not much to tell."

"What's your favorite color? What do you like to do in the Estate? Better yet, how often do you walk into the forest?"

"Green, but not because of a plant. I like the murky shade of green that overtakes the sky just before an electrical storm."

He righted himself in the water and met my eyes. "Didn't expect that. Go on."

"I mostly keep to myself, but I go wherever I'm told. I love to hike in the forest and sometimes sneak out at night to enjoy time in the heart alone. I don't have many true friends, but I've learned I have at least one determined enemy. I think there may be more than one. I hate that *our* covens harbor ill feelings for one another and that it's growing instead of dissipating. Insects don't frighten me. Nothing in nature does, but other witches do sometimes. And for as many lies that have swirled around me, *I'm* not a convincing liar. How about you?"

He looked up as if he was thinking about how to respond. "My favorite color is yellow-gold, like the sun in the morning as it begins to climb in the sky, though the color of your eyes is also interesting."

"What do you like to do?" I asked him.

"Other than prepare our coven for battle, you mean? Tons of things. I also enjoy walking in the woods, finding spots like this, visiting towns and villages and seeing more of the world than Cauldron can offer me."

"How did you learn of the hunters?"

He went still, fixing his eyes on me. "A good friend warned me." He didn't elaborate. I wondered if it was the same good female friend we were about to impose on. "I'm freezing," he announced before wading from the water and settling on a rock to let the water sluice from his body.

When I waded out, teeth chattering despite the warm air, he laid back on the rock and stared at the sky, respectfully allowing me privacy despite our proximity. I sat on my own boulder and tugged on a fresh set of clothes – one of the few I'd packed – and then picked up my bag and found a nearby dry rock where I could lay back and let the warm air bring feeling back into my legs. The water was more frigid than I realized.

He took up his bag, turned away from me, and began to dress himself, chuckling as I watched. "I was a gentleman while you got settled. You, on the other hand, are incorrigible, Gravebriar. Staring at me so."

"What else am I supposed to look at?" I teased.

He guffawed. "You aren't just looking because I'm all there is to see."

I shrugged a shoulder, flashing a bored smile.

He clasped the flesh over his heart. "You wound me, Gravebriar. You wound me deeply."

"I'm sure you'll recover."

He groaned and began to climb the bank.

"How far is Falls Creek?" I asked, hiking behind him. "Do I need to cloak myself before we go in?"

"We're safe in Falls Creek. Arum's eyes stay close to his assets, which I hope are still in Westbrook."

SEVEN

The village of Falls Creek was a squat grid comprised of a few dozen quaint homes, all washed in white paint, all with steeply pitched roofs and similarly bricked chimneys. A few of them leaked smoke into the air, and with the smoke rose the aroma of freshly baked bread. He told me a friend lived ahead, one who allowed him to stay when he needed it.

Forge walked to a house at the end of a small lane and knocked on the door twice. I lingered near the edge of the lawn. A young woman with long, red hair and freckles smattering her nose and cheeks answered, her stomach swollen with child. She smiled when she saw Forge. "I just knew trouble would show up on my doorstep tonight. I suppose you're in need of a room." She noticed me and her smile grew. She gave Forge a look filled with questions and excitement.

He grinned and waved me forward. "Hello, Jenny. This is a friend from Cauldron," he introduced me. "She's a Gravebriar, so that's what I call her."

Jenny laughed. "Figures. You never were creative with your flirtations."

His mouth gaped and I laughed, liking this woman already.

She invited us in and shut the door, then braced a hand on her back and gingerly walked across the floor. "Let's hope the baby doesn't decide to make her grand appearance and interrupt your beauty sleep... Silverthorn," she teased.

I tried to inconspicuously survey my surroundings. My heart warmed at what I saw. Her house was a home, and one she'd taken great care of. Her furniture was freshly painted, several knitted blankets hanging on the backs of chairs. The kitchen held a small table and plenty of workspace, and the hearth was warm. Something bubbled in the iron pot that hung over the fire, emitting a divine fragrance that reminded me how hungry I was.

"Tea?" she asked, her gaze swinging from Forge to me.

"I'd love some."

Jenny moved toward the hearth, but Forge beat her there. "I've got it. You should sit."

"I'm not helpless," she teased, already out of breath. Gratefully accepting his assistance, she moved to the table and pulled out a chair, collapsing into it. The babe in her stomach moved, bulging her skin from her left side to the right before settling again. "But I won't complain about getting a little rest right about now."

"How long do you have?" he asked, placing the kettle on a wood block in front of her, then moving to the cabinet to get three mugs, obviously very familiar with the layout of this cozy house.

"Any day now," she answered.

"Are you afraid?" I asked as Forge found tea bags.

She groaned. "Not as much as I am miserable and ready to meet my child."

Forge distributed small bags of tea amongst the cups and poured the steaming water onto them. They bobbed to the surface and from them wafted the sweet scents of chamomile, lavender, rose hips, and lemon. Beneath the natural aromas was the scent of magic.

"You got these from a Gravebriar," I said with a smile.

Jenny inclined her head. "Forge got the tea for me. It helps settle my mind a bit when I lie down to sleep." She gestured to the counter behind her. "There's bread and some leftover ham, too. The room is ready. I keep it that way just in case…"

Forge inclined his head. "Thank you." He took a couple bread slices and placed them on a cloth before me, then took a few slices of ham for himself. "And thank you for this."

She waved him off. "It's not like you haven't done plenty for me."

He shook his head sharply and Jenny sat up straighter. As we ate and sipped our hot tea, Jenny began to yawn. And she could not stop. "I'm so tired. I'm sorry," she apologized. "Would you mind locking up before you settle down?"

"I'll take care of things," Forge promised.

With a murmured, "Good night," she moved down a small hallway and closed her bedroom door behind her.

"Do you stay here often?"

"I wouldn't say often, but certainly occasionally."

I suddenly wondered who the father of Jenny's child was and whether it might be Forge. There didn't seem to be a romantic spark between them, but there was definitely *something*; a deeper familiarity that spoke to them being more than just acquaintances.

As if sensing the question tumbling through my mind, Forge quickly explained, "Jenny's my cousin."

"Oh… No wonder she teases you so." I nudged his knee with mine.

He shook his head, chuckling softly. "The two of you would no doubt get along fine."

"Is she a Silverthorn, then?"

"Jenny's not a witch, she just loved one. My cousin died just months ago."

"In Cauldron?" My parents had never mentioned an injury or malady that was deadly to one of our witches.

"No. He kept a small boat in Westbrook. A storm rose while he was out and he never returned."

"I'm so sorry."

He pursed his lips together. "Some things are out of even a Gravebriar's control. There was nothing anyone could have done in this case."

"Did he always live outside Cauldron?"

"No, he grew up in our Estate, but when he met Jenny on one of our adventures, he left the city to pursue her. They settled down together here. They planned to have a family and had just begun to see their dream bloom. I only wish he were here to see his child and raise him or her."

"Why didn't they build a house in Westbrook?"

"It's not as quiet or as safe there. He was planning to sell the boat but decided to take it out for one last sail."

A fatal mistake. My heart hurt for him, for Jenny and their unborn child. We sat in silence for several long moments. I had no idea his cousin had left Cauldron. I knew witches lived beyond the hedge. The world was vast and didn't revolve around our city, but I'd never heard of any witch giving up a life in Cauldron to live outside it, or of one courting a human.

He stretched his arms back. "If you're as tired as I am, I'd bet you're ready for several uninterrupted hours of sleep."

"I'm exhausted," I admitted. As invigorating as the swim was, I was still worn out from walking nonstop for two days. Guiltily, my mind flitted back to Arbor, and I wondered how he was doing.

Forge rinsed our cups in a basin and set them on the counter to dry. He slid a metal lock across the front door and waved for me to follow him. We walked down the small hallway to the very end and stepped into a bedroom. There was one narrow bed along the far wall, a couple of mismatched tables, and a broad, comfortable-looking chair nestled into the corner. I would take it, I decided, removing the strap of my bag.

Forge threw his into the chair before I could.

"I can sleep there," I told him. "I'm shorter than you." The chair was oversized, but if he tried to fold his taller body into it, he'd be miserable.

"That's *my* chair. I always sleep in it." I narrowed my eyes at him. "Honestly. I love it. Please, don't take it from me."

I wasn't sure if he truly wanted the chair or was being chivalrous, but I was far too tired to argue further. Still freezing, I tugged off my boots and slid under the blankets. An extra quilt lay folded at the bed's end. "Take this, at least."

He took the blanket from my hand, his cold fingers brushing mine. He laughed. "You're still freezing."

"So are you."

But the feeling in my belly was warm. Somehow, the Silverthorn wasn't afraid of me at all. He touched me and didn't recoil. Maybe it was because I'd already done so when I surged the poison into his blood.

As I settled into the bed and adjusted the pillow, I let myself believe he would have treated me the same way even if nothing dangerous was flowing through his system. I fell asleep to the sound of the soft, slow rhythm of his breath.

When I finally peeled open my eyes, sunlight illuminated the entire room. Given the brightness, I deduced it was well past dawn. I raised my head to find Forge's chair empty, the blanket he'd used folded over its back. My heart skipped a beat, but it settled once I saw his bag resting on the table next to me. I wondered if he'd laid it there so he wouldn't forget it, or to reassure me that he hadn't abandoned me before the trouble that stalked me pounced on his back, too.

The kitchen where we'd sat last night was empty, so I padded back down the hall and came upon a small door at the rear of the house.

On the back lawn, a shirtless Forge scrubbed an article of cornflower blue clothing in a metal tub that looked brand new, using an equally pristine scrubbing board that bore no rust stains. *It must be nice being a Silverthorn*, I thought, letting a small smile escape.

They spoke quietly until a board under my feet groaned. Jenny's head rose at the sound and she smiled warmly.

"Morning, Princess!" Forge greeted once more. "Or should I say, good afternoon."

I squinted upward to see the sun directly overhead and my mouth fell open. I couldn't believe I'd slept so long!

Jenny laughed. "You must have sorely needed the rest. I miss being able to sleep as long as I need."

"You'll miss it for much longer," Forge teased, to which she replied by splashing him with soapy water. "Hope you don't mind, but I'm washing our clothes," Forge said.

I was sure my sweat-soaked, grimy clothes smelled horrible. "I can wash my own."

I abandoned the doorframe and started down the steps when he held up a soapy hand. "I'm already finished with yours." He nodded to my blouse and trousers swaying on Jenny's line.

I thanked him as he dunked the blue garment into a tub of fresh water and twisted to wring it out. Jenny took it from him when he was finished and pinned it on the line

100

next to mine. "He thinks he has to do everything while he's here," she chastised, but I saw the gratefulness shimmering beneath her words.

Many witches bear babes alone, I told myself. Still, if I were in her situation, I would appreciate any and all help given.

My thoughts drifted back to Arbor, particularly how my father seemed to push me toward a partnership with him, much like the one he had with Mother. At one point, there was love kindling in their relationship, but over the years, that lit wick had burned away, leaving only a puddle of dried wax. They respected one another, worked together, and loved each other in their way, but it wasn't the kind of burning, all-consuming blaze I wanted.

I wanted something stronger than a mere wick, meant to burn away into oblivion. I wanted something all-encompassing. Something I'd never want to let go of.

I wanted something true.

Forge watched me carefully. He'd dumped the wash water from the tub and towel dried it, popping the small bubbles that remained on the side walls. "You okay, Gravebriar?"

"I'm fine."

He nodded slowly, as if he didn't quite believe me but was swallowing my answer.

A fresh stack of wood lay in a pile next to the steps I'd just descended. I turned to Forge with a question on my lips.

"Couldn't sleep," he said sheepishly.

He couldn't sleep, so he felled a tree, cut and split it, stacked the wood neatly beside his cousin's house, and then did our laundry? Jenny walked to stand next to me, hand on her stomach. "He does it every time he comes by. I always have enough to let it sit for a season and never run out, thanks to him."

She placed a hand on my shoulder, gave it a pat, and climbed the steps. "I made a fresh loaf of bread this morning. Are you hungry?"

"I am, thank you."

I followed her inside, lingering at the doorway to watch as Forge put the tubs away. He plucked up the washboard and noticed me there, giving me a small, quizzical grin.

Inside, Jenny was pulling the lid off a jar of butter. "It's sweet," she said. Removing a pale cloth from a fresh loaf of bread, she pushed the board it sat on to me. I used the small serrated knife on the board to saw a piece off the loaf, then smeared it with the sweet butter. Jenny ladled a cup of water from a basin and sat the cup in front of me. "Thank you."

Her eyes wandered down the hall. Forge hadn't stepped in yet. "Forge has never brought a girl here." I swallowed the bite of bread, waiting to see if she'd elaborate or question me. I hated questions. "You must be important to him. He doesn't let his guard down often."

Was his guard down with me? He barely knew me.

"How long –" she started, quickly going quiet when the back door opened. She smiled as if we'd almost been caught talking about him.

Forge strode down the hall and joined us. "When our clothes are dry, we should start toward Westbrook," he pointed out to me.

"But it could take hours for them to dry." *Arbor will be okay*, I told myself. *Mother won't let him die.* He was damaged, not dying.

"You can leave them and I'll have them ready when you pass back through?" Jenny offered.

"I'm not exactly sure when that will be," he told her.

She shrugged. "A day, a week, or a month, it doesn't matter. I have room to stow them. Why are you going back to Westbrook?" she asked her cousin.

His eyes sharply locked on hers, a silent warning there. "We have business with Arum."

Jenny gasped. "Whatever for? Are the two of you in some sort of trouble?"

We were, but would he tell her what sort?

"We aren't in trouble." Forge didn't explain or answer further, and his brusque tone cut the conversation short. I quickly finished my bread and thanked Jenny for feeding me, letting me stay, and for keeping my laundry.

She graciously pretended the abruptly ended conversation had never occurred, but worry wrinkled her brow. Forge retrieved our things from the room and hugged Jenny. "I'll come back as soon as I can."

Jenny nodded. "Watch yourself."

"Don't I always?" he teased.

"No," she answered. "You don't."

Falls Creek was essentially built in a large clearing. More woods lay between Falls Creek and our destination, but the traveling was easier because the path between the town and Westbrook was wide and worn. Carriage ruts had petrified in the now-dry mud road that led to our journey's end.

Nervous beetles swooped around my stomach at the thought of meeting Arum. Thoughts spiraled through my mind of what he might look like and how dangerous he might be. Jenny certainly was concerned about Forge going to him for help.

The walk to Westbrook was quiet and calm, the terrain easy. After two days of hiking, climbing over rotting, fallen trees, wobbling our ankles over rock beds, and climbing up and down hills only to trudge across streams and creeks, it was an absolute dream. I didn't even get to watch Forge's acrobatics as he swatted away spider webs... unfortunately.

The sun was just starting to set as the trees began to thin until we were able to see the town unfold beyond them.

After miles of walking, Forge finally spoke. "It's best to avoid the road when sneaking into town." A small trail, wide enough for only one of us to walk on at a time diverged from the main path. Forge peeled off it and led the way through a copse of pines. "Arum has eyes everywhere. I want you to see him and what he does before you make a decision on whether to go to him for help."

I swallowed thickly once again, wondering whether we were on the right path or if we should return to the forest to search more area for the graveyard. If Arum was as bad as he seemed, this might be the wrong way to go about finding gravebriar.

"That means we need to find Arum before dark – assuming he's still in Westbrook – and not let him find *us* first."

"What happens at dark? And what if he's no longer in Westbrook?" I asked, following closely behind.

He turned on his heel and I smacked into his chest. Forge was ready with a teasing smirk. "You love bumping into me."

"It's my life's purpose," I deadpanned.

"At dark," he paused dramatically, "Arum's show begins. We'll watch first, and then you can make your decision. But if you decide to take a chance on him, there are a few things I must insist on: the first is that you must remember to never allow him to corner you alone. Stay with me, no matter what. Don't accept food or drink from him or any of his troupe. Don't offer information to anyone, even if they try to pry it or slyly extract it from you – both of which they are quite adept at. And if you suspect he or anyone else knows who you truly are, we leave. No hesitation."

I nodded. "That sounds deceptively simple, yet remarkably complicated."

He laughed. "That it is."

It was good to hear him laugh again. Somehow, his easy demeanor settled me. Still, something was missing in his plan. If we were going to fool the unfoolable Arum, we needed to know what we were selling backward and forward. "We need a backstory."

Forge smiled. "Good thing I'm an amazing storyteller." He booped my nose and I swatted his hand. "People who are in love don't smack one another," he tsked, then his features calmed.

"If you were in love with me, you'd know never to do that again," I warned.

"In all seriousness," he began, his smirk spreading, "how do you feel about pet names?"

I chuckled darkly. "How do you feel about dying at such a young age?"

EiGHT

W e stood at the edge of the tree line where beyond, a larger town emerged, the outskirts scattered by mud-brick houses with thatched roofs. Their distorted windows glowed from firelight, and the smell of horse manure was strong in the wake of a carriage that teetered through the muddy street. Farther away, against the deepening blue sky, more intricate rooftops split the heavens.

Forge handed me a small bottle with vibrant cerulean liquid inside. A cloaking spell. "I'll still see you, Gravebriar."

"That term of endearment must be left in the forest, Forge."

He nodded. "As soon as you start swooning over me, it'll feel like you're a completely different person. The change will come naturally," he retorted. I rolled my eyes. "Seriously, though. We have to play these parts from this point forward."

The tone of his voice sent a shiver up my spine. Or maybe it was the way his eyes flicked from mine to my lips and back again. Maybe he did find me beautiful. Maybe pretending to love me wouldn't be so hard for him.

I would play this game. To help Arbor. To clear my name. And if I was being honest, it wouldn't be unpleasant. I found him handsome, his personality fun, and his quick wit exciting.

The apple in Forge's neck bobbed. "Good," he rasped. "Look at me like that. Often."

Before I talked myself out of it, I took his face in my hands, memorized the feel of his stubble, the shape of his jaw, and drew him in until his lips were a hair's breadth from mine. I pressed my lips to his. Held them there.

That single spark lit a flame in both of us, fueling a hunger I'd never experienced before. When he began to really kiss me, when our mouths moved together and he gathered me against him, my eyes fluttered closed and all I could feel was his smooth, warm lips on mine, sweetened by the swipe of his tongue. My fingers tightened on his cheeks and jaw as he wrapped me even tighter in his arms. He smelled like metal and danger and magic, and his hands felt like silk on the small of my back as he brushed a thumb back and forth, back and forth...

Moth wings scraped the inside of my stomach until he pulled away.

For a moment, he didn't speak.

Neither did I.

There were no words for what had happened. I meant to rid us both of any awkwardness created by a first kiss, but instead ignited a wildfire.

A Silverthorn would never kiss a Gravebriar like that... yet he did. *I* did. I... had no words.

"I'm not complaining in the least, but what was that for?" he breathed.

"To get it out of the way." That was the reason I'd given myself in the split-second before I acted. I didn't want Arum or anyone else witnessing our first. Plus, *I* wanted to be the one to initiate it. "Both of us will be more comfortable next time."

"Comfortable?" He darkly chuckled, throwing his head back and staring at the starlit sky. "I think your plan might have backfired, because I'm going to need a lot more kisses like that in the very near future."

He turned to me, divided the air between us, and brought his mouth close to mine. I almost let him capture it, but at the last moment, put a finger up to those pretty lips. "We're *acting*," I reminded him, but somehow the words felt half-hearted. I wondered if they sounded the same way.

Forge slid an arm around my waist and pulled me in for another quick kiss, one that made my toes curl. "I like *acting*. Acting is my new favorite pastime."

"Since when?" I laughed.

"Since I began *acting* with you."

I shook my head. "You're an incorrigible flirt. I'm sure you don't care who you're *acting* with."

His smile fell and his lips parted. He claimed another kiss, this one deeper. "I do care, and I meant what I said."

"You don't even know me," I whispered.

"I'm attracted to you, though. In many ways," he admitted.

I felt the same but refused to voice it. Pulling away from him and uncorking the tiny vial, I pressed my finger over the mouth and upturned it to sift the ingredients for poisons.

"I wouldn't hurt you," he said softly, looking downcast.

"It wasn't you I was worried about, but the Spellsweet who gave you this."

He looked troubled. "I hadn't considered that."

"Never trust anyone implicitly," I warned him. I'd learned that lesson more times than I could count. People always disappointed. People often changed their mind and their loyalties. I put the bottle to my lips and swallowed the sickeningly sweet elixir and then waited. Forge's eyes combed over me. "Did it work?"

He nodded. "I can see the spell layered over you, but through it, I still see you."

For some reason, I was happy he could still see me. I wanted him to know that I was in this with him. I wanted him to know who he was kissing and never forget it.

I tried to hide those thoughts from playing over my features and posed a question to focus him on the false cloak layered over my skin. "What do I look like to outsiders?"

"Somewhat like you, but your freckles are gone." He brushed the bridge of my nose with the pad of his thumb, then brushed my jawline. "Your jaw is more square. Your skin is olive, and your hair is dark and wavy."

"And my eyes?"

"They're all the shades of the moon. Pale silver, with splotches of darker gray."

I smiled, hoping I got a chance to see my reflection before the spell wore off. "Have you thought of a name for me?"

Forge smiled and his molten eyes glittered like the stars in the sky. "Lilith. It means darkness," Forge said. "We'll pass you off as a Shade with very little magic."

A Shade. Nothing about being a Shade fit me. Though none of the covens were a perfect fit – not even my own.

A familiar feeling of anxiety washed over me. The more lies we wove, the more I felt trapped between the threads.

He pulled a sliver of copper from his bag, a tiny shaving, and closed his fist. When he opened it again, the sliver had transformed and multiplied into a palm-full of coppers. "We need tickets, a room to sleep in, and food to fill our bellies. This will provide it."

I nodded as he tucked it into his pocket. "I'll pay you back when we get home," I promised, hating the idea of owing him anything.

"I can always make more, Gr- *Lilith*." He groaned at his mistake. "This might be harder than I thought."

"Nicknames are pesky things."

He clutched his heart again, a grin playing at his lips. "It's nothing so simple as a nickname. That's greatly offensive. Hurtful, even. Clearly, that endearment is a pet name."

I slid him a withering glance, which made a throaty laugh pour from him. His laugh was contagious and perfect, as was his entire person as far as I could tell. How could something as simple as a laugh make my knees weak?

I fought a smile so he wouldn't see it, but I think he might have felt it anyway. He nudged me playfully and gave a wink.

How could something as simple as a wink make them weaker?

This was bad. I could not develop a crush on a Silverthorn. No matter how devilishly handsome he was.

I stomped those feelings back into my stomach.

We walked to the road and kept to the drier parts as best we could. The waxing moon was bright but not yet full. Forge knew his way through the town, and he wove expertly as the houses thickened and grew taller. The noise from them grew louder as people settled in to eat their suppers. The smell of fresh-baked bread made my stomach growl. Forge noticed and apologized. "We can buy something as soon as we get our tickets. They have snacks there."

Forge straightened his clothes and raked his fingers through his short hair. Perhaps he wasn't as confident as he projected. His nervousness made mine flare. I was sure the spell made me look perfect, but still couldn't help but fidget. "What am I wearing?"

"Well, it's no ball gown made of moss, but it's a dark green dress. Simple, but it fits you well… Very well."

His eyes draped over me. I reminded myself he was only acting. We both were.

He threaded his hand through mine and though my first instinct was to pull away, I clasped his fingers and held him tight, like he was really mine. Like I didn't know the meaning of the word *pretend* and we weren't acting at all.

Forge gave an approving smile, his eyes shimmering in the moonlight.

"So this is Westbrook?" I asked after we walked past a few young men who were sharing sips from a jug of something that smelled horribly astringent. They loitered, watching horses and carriages trod and roll past. I could feel the drag of their stares on my back and Forge's hand tightened on mine.

"It's a port town. If Arum is here, he'll have his people scattered around. So remember, don't say anything here you don't want heard."

Ahead of us, where the street opened to the docks, the dark masts of many ships jutted into the inky sky. "Hey!" someone called from just behind us.

I turned to find one of the young men we'd just passed jogging to catch up with us. His eyes were glassy and greasy strands of cornstalk hair hung in his eyes. He hitched his suspenders up, wrinkling his pale shirt. "Where are the two of you headed on this fine evening?" His voice held an accent I'd never heard, stilted and harsh. I slowed my steps as Forge ignored him. "I'm talking to you, big fella," the guy said.

Forge rounded on him and eased me behind him, his broad shoulders pulled taut. "We don't want trouble," Forge said in a tone I didn't recognize.

The guy raised his hands. "Who said anything about trouble?"

The man's eyes raked over me. I couldn't see the magic overlaying my form. Was I wearing jewelry? Something that looked easy for him to steal?

He surveyed Forge and found the pouch of coppers hanging from his belt. His eyes flicked over my shoulder and caught on something. I swiveled to find his two friends standing behind me, one tall and thin, the other shorter but stout and muscular. They were all filthy. Likely hungry. And despite the threat, I couldn't help but feel a pang of sorrow for them.

The stout friend threw their empty, shared bottle on the ground. It broke with a thunk into thick chunks of hardened, orange clay at my feet. I did not step backward, didn't acknowledge his attempt at intimidation whatsoever. His eyes were glassy as well, his steps unsteady as he approached.

In an instant, Forge produced two broad, double-bladed swords.

"Don't," I warned him, pressing a hand in the valley between his shoulder blades. "Let me handle this." His brows furrowed. "Trust me," I whispered.

He nodded almost imperceptibly, transforming the swords into daggers. The drunkards didn't see the change because they focused on me as I slid around Forge and smiled sweetly at the enormous man who'd broken the jug to intimidate me. Confusion flooded his face. "What are *you* doing?" he asked as I slithered forward.

I touched his hand, fast as an adder striking, and he collapsed to the ground. When his tall friend rushed to his side, I grazed his neck.

The one who'd chased us, tasked with laying their trap, backed up and then turned to run. Forge quickly caught him, covering his mouth as he wrestled him back to me. He cursed when the young man bit him, but one touch to his arm silenced our would-be robber.

Forge eased him down gently. He should've let him fall and splatter in the mud, only to wake the next morning wondering if it was the drink that made his head pound or if he'd passed out and fallen. He might wonder if we were real or figments of his imagination. I wondered if any of the three cowards would be brave enough to bring the encounter up to their friends, or if the three would keep it to themselves and pretend it never happened. Those who lost often hated to be reminded of their failures.

Forge made his swords disappear in a blink, transforming the swords he'd conjured back into meaningless, shapeless slivers. "Are they dead?" he asked.

I shook my head. "They'll wake tomorrow – though they might wish they hadn't."

He nodded approvingly, then examined the teeth print on his hand. At least the bite didn't draw blood. "You didn't use the same poison you put in me?"

I shook my head. "In the woods, the night we stopped to eat and rest, I touched through my grimoire and gathered many kinds – just in case."

I wouldn't kill anyone unless I feared for my life, and maybe not even then. How did one know what they would do in a situation until they were in it? You could imagine, but you never knew for sure.

"Give me your coppers," I demanded, palm up and waiting.

He ticked his head back. "For them? They'll drink every penny away and then probably accost someone else once it's gone."

"You can spell weapons. Can you spell the coppers so they cannot be used for spirits or wrongdoing?"

He untied the small pouch of coin and held it, whispering a spell to limit its use. Then he slowly stretched it forward until it hit my palm. "Anyone else might have killed them. You want to feed them," he said with a confused grin.

I divided the coin among them, stuffing a third into each man's pocket. Forge could conjure more in an instant.

I returned his coin pouch and told him, "You and I are fortunate enough not to know what it's like to go truly hungry. But I know what desperation feels like now, and it's not pleasant. If we can ease it, even a little, why wouldn't we?"

He had no reply as we stood together among their bodies. I watched their chests rise and fall, wondering if Forge had checked to be sure I was being truthful. Removing a copper shaving from his bag, he used his magic to make more coin, guiding it into the pouch once again. This time, he didn't tie it to his belt, but tucked it into the pocket of his trousers.

He'd said his cousin didn't want to make a life with Jenny in Westbrook, that Falls Creek was safer. He was right.

Forge held out his hand, waiting for mine. Once I slid my palm against his, we clasped hands and walked toward the docks, striding casually as if I hadn't just incapacitated three men much larger than I. As if we were exactly what we were pretending to be: two lovers enjoying what was left of a beautiful sunset.

I looked back to the men we'd left on the muddy street. People would see them if they walked or rode by. They might also see the broken jug and assume them to be drunkards, too far gone to know when to stop or go home for the night. They might call them derelicts. Vagrants. Vagabonds.

They might think they deserve the indignity of sleeping on the ground. Perhaps they did for trying to rob us.

"That was..." Forge paused, perhaps to collect his thoughts. "I was afraid for you, but you were amazing."

"Amazing isn't the word I would use to describe my power."

His brows kissed. "How *would* you describe it?"

"A curse at worst, unfortunate at best."

"You can't believe that," he said, his easy smile back. It fell away again when I didn't match it. "Your coven loves you. You're revered."

"Reverence and fear are often confused, Forge."

He shook his head. "No, I've seen it. I saw it the night of the revel, though I didn't know exactly what was happening or why at the time. I saw them watch you. I thought they were just envious of your love affair with Arbor, but it wasn't that at all. They were all working to protect you. That's not born of fear, but of comradery."

I wanted his words to be true more than anything. Forge had noticed the well-oiled scheme working flawlessly. He didn't see how we operated day in and day out. I wasn't ostracized or hidden away. I wasn't the Gravebriar's secret. My parents – and by extension, my coven – insisted I be included in everything. If they wanted input on what to conjure for supper, they asked for my opinion. If my peers wanted to sneak out, they came and got me from my rooms. But none would get close, none confided in me or asked me to confide in them. My relationships with my coven mates were all shallow, with no depth at all. I wondered if they genuinely liked me, thought it would please my parents, or thought that by keeping me close, they could watch over me closer.

"You saw quite a lot at the revel," I noted.

Unless *I* was seeing things, the confident man before me blushed. "Yeah. It's just... I saw you at last year's Winter revel for only a moment. Some friends and I snuck over just long enough to see what your coven had conjured. Father forbade us from attending, of course, to make his feelings about the Gravebriars known. But there were icicles everywhere and perfect, white snow-covered the ground. Everyone was bundled in thick gowns and fur-lined coats... everyone but you. Your dress looked like it was spun of ice and you wore your hair long and glossy. It was as if you were spring appearing after a hard winter, the first bit of color in a frozen world, and I... I watched you. I've been out of Cauldron as much as I've been in it, so at this revel, I couldn't help but notice you again. That's when I realized spring wasn't your season at all. Summer belongs to you."

My throat clogged with emotion. "Most people who notice me at all only focus on my magic. Never me."

He shrugged. "You made an impression."

"What changed? Why did your father allow you to attend this last revel when he'd forbidden it before?"

Forge chuckled. "I didn't ask for his permission or tell him my plans."

"A wise decision," I teased.

"So... you and Arbor really aren't lovers?" he asked.

"No, we were only pretending."

He was quiet for a moment. "But not acting? Acting requires kissing."

I laughed. "No, he and I were *not* acting. I never kissed him."

"Good," he said in a satisfied tone, straightening his back a little.

The docks were wide and stretched far out into the water. Impressive ships bobbed on tiny waves, moored to heavy posts supporting the structure. Smaller boats were closest to shore, but the largest were in deeper water. Those were the ones I marveled at, stopping Forge as he turned to skirt the shore.

He smiled. "Do you want to walk along the docks for a few moments?"

"Do we have time?"

He nodded. "Some."

"Then I'd like that more than anything," I admitted.

"Come on, *Lilith*," he replied, enunciating my new fake name.

I let go of his hand and walked beside him out over the water. Some of the planks were pale and new compared to the dull, weathered boards surrounding them. The moon shone over the water, painting the crests of the small waves beyond the docks in silver light.

"There are divers here that can hold their breath beneath the water for a minute or more. They carved this harbor by hand. Breath by breath. Minute by minute. It took years, and they still dive daily to carry silt and sand away to keep the harbor from filling in again. The sea insists on dragging things to shore."

"Like shells."

He nodded. "Like shells. You'll have to find one you like to carry home with you; a keepsake of our adventure."

I'd love that.

Some of the ships' hulls were so close I could reach out and touch them, so I let my hand drift over one. The wood was wet and slippery in the spaces where barnacles didn't cling. I imagined it cutting through the water, slicing through waves so tall they crashed over the deck. I imagined a crew following their captain's orders, some climbing high into the rigging as if it were just a tree in the forest.

A young sailor watched us from the rail of the ship I'd been admiring, wearing a kind grin. "Good day, Miss. Would you like a tour?" he offered. His accent differed from the men we'd crossed. It was lazier, pleasant to the ear. His smile beamed as he waited for a reply.

I looked to Forge, who gestured to me. The decision was mine.

"We only have a few minutes."

That was apparently fine with him. His boots were silent as he made his way to the plank that lay on the dock. Forge and I met him at the bottom of it. His pants clung to his legs while his shirt was loose and comfortable, untied at the neck to expose part of his smooth chest.

With one foot on the dock and the other on the plank, he playfully greeted us. "The short tour it is, then. Have you ever been on a ship before?" the young man asked, his grey eyes glittering.

"I haven't," I answered, turning to Forge, who answered that he hadn't either.

The young man's hair was short and his jaw was cleanly shaven. His dark skin shone in the waning evening light as he extended an arm. The ballooned sleeves of his pale shirt rapped in the wind as he winked at me. "May I escort you?"

I wrapped my hand around his arm and thanked him as he led me up the plank to the ship's deck. Forge followed behind. When I threw a smile over my shoulder, I noticed a tightness to the smile he returned. If we were in too great a hurry, he should have said. Or was he worried about the sailor? Could we not trust him?

"My crew calls me Crow," the sailor said easily. "I'm at home in the nest up there," he chuckled, pointing to the crow's nest.

"I couldn't climb to that height if my life depended on it!" I teased.

"Sometimes it does," he said honestly. "But heights don't bother me. I grew up on ships. The ropes and riggings were my playground. You're new to Westbrook. What's your name?"

"Why, do you know everyone in Westbrook?" I teased.

"Not at all. But I'd never forget a face as pretty as yours," he smoothly answered.

"I'm Lilith," I answered carefully. "And this is Forge." I might have enunciated his name to make sure Crow remembered he was with me.

"What brings you here?" Crow asked.

A worried feeling settled into my belly. Why was he asking questions instead of showing us around?

I turned to Forge, noting his irritation. "We should be going. We'll be late."

Crow looked innocently, curiously between us. "Late for what?"

"To see the circus," Forge answered. "We've heard it's spectacular."

Crow's eyes lit up and he excitedly clamped his hand over mine. "If you're this enamored with the ship, wait until you see the flyers soar!"

Forge's eyes caught on Crow's lingering hand...

"Flyers?" I asked, unwrapping my hand from his proffered arm.

Our new friend saw us to the plank. "*If* they perform tonight. They always rearrange the acts to keep it fresh for repeat guests. The show will start soon. Please don't think I'm chasing you off, but if you want to find a seat for tonight's show, you should hurry. They stop selling tickets once it begins."

My heart skidded to a stop. We *had* to get in. Tonight.

"Thank you," I told Crow as we hurried down the plank.

"It was my pleasure, Lilith. I'm sorry I didn't get to give much of a tour. Come by tomorrow if you're still around and have more time," he replied.

I wasn't sure that would be an option but was grateful for even getting to step foot on the deck of the ship, to look up at her grand, folded sails and imagine them full of wind and might. "I'd like that. We'll do our best," I replied, neither a promise nor a lie.

When we were out of Crow's earshot, Forge spoke, albeit gruffly. "He *definitely* wants to see you tomorrow."

"I'm sure he was just being polite. He has better things to do than show a stranger around the ship."

Forge forced a laugh as we retraced our steps to dry land. "He wants to see you again. And he would love it if I stayed ashore..."

"Why?"

"Oh, I don't know," he answered sarcastically. "Because you're beautiful, kind, and look at the world as if it's magical?"

"It is," I retorted, raising my chin.

"Most don't look at it that way, witch or not," he argued.

I pursed my lips into a pout. "Did he make you jealous?" I teased.

"A little, yeah, if I'm being honest."

My heart skipped another beat. *He can't be serious!*

"You trusted him without a second thought as to what his intentions might be. He asked if you wanted a tour and you didn't hesitate; you just ran to him and took his arm. I just... I hope to earn your trust and for you to as easily run to me one day."

"I didn't run," I weakly argued.

He quirked a brow.

I wanted to tell him I *did* trust him but didn't want to lie. Lies had become my first instinct and I didn't like it. I wanted to become comfortable with truth. For lies to be a last resort.

The truth of the matter was that he'd been sent to execute me, and though he and I had struck a bargain, I wasn't sure if his intentions aligned with mine.

Still, maybe I could learn more from Forge by giving him a little trust...

"After the Council handed down their decision, my mother told me to run from you and hide in the forest, then circle back home once darkness fell. She promised to sneak me inside and hide me from everyone."

His lashes fluttered for a moment. "Given the warning Parler gave, I understand why you wouldn't want to return without the briar, but then again... it was your mother, your Power. Why didn't you do as she said?"

"I wish it was a simple matter of honor and I could say it was because Arbor needed gravebriar and I had the chance to find some and provide a cure. The last thing I want is to be burned at the stake, but it wasn't fear that kept me from obeying. The truth is that it's both of those things and neither of them. I don't want to be locked away. I don't want anyone to have to lie to protect me again. I just... I want a full life, and I think if I find the gravebriar, it would be the first step into it. I could show everyone how much I value Arbor's life and prove to some that I didn't hurt him."

"Do you want to reclaim your standing in the coven?"

I shook my head. "I'm not sure I do. I just want to set things right and perhaps clear my name. I don't want my entire coven ostracized or exiled because of me."

"The Council didn't threaten to exile them all."

It was my turn to quirk my brow. If he knew them at all, he knew the Council was more than capable. Their decision, once rendered, could always shift and change, like the thick sand we punched through.

Forge slid his hand through mine. "I suppose I'm also in trouble for refusing to kill you and bring back the gravebriar. For my disobedience, they'll brand me a traitor."

"Your own father?"

"Especially my father. He'll be the first to shout the accusation, the first to point out my iniquities. Strained relationship, remember?"

"I'm sorry." An idea occurred to me. "You know, you could go back now and tell them that no gravebriar grew from the ground when you buried me. You could tell them I poisoned the ground and everything around my grave died. Even the trees."

"That's not what would happen," he argued.

I clutched his arm. "But they would *believe* you. My mother would believe you. My father would. My entire coven would accept your claim. The Council would follow suit. Even your father."

"You're not poisonous, Cas—"

I silenced him with a finger to his lips, then leaned in and whispered into his ear, "Lilith." The apple in his throat bobbed. "Everyone in Cauldron believes I am. You could use that against them and go home. Explain that once you realized I wouldn't produce a plant, you went searching for the graveyard on your own, just in case."

"What about Arbor?"

"I'll keep searching and will eventually find the gravebriar for him."

"You think your coven can keep him alive indefinitely?"

I told him what Arcana had prophesied, that a series of events had been set in motion that would lead to his death. "I feel desperate right now. As desperate as the three men we left back in town. Desperate to find this cure, to see what becomes of my parents and my coven, to see what my future might hold there – if anything – and if nothing, desperate to make something of it despite everything that's come before."

"Asking Arum for such information will prove to be dangerous."

"There are other means of eliciting information from a person," I hedged.

His eyes locked on mine. "What ways?"

NiNE

The sand thinned beneath our feet, packing tightly into a harder crust where stubborn tufts of grass took advantage, rooting where they could. We crested a small knoll and entered a gentle valley where three black and white striped tents were nestled, the center of the trio much larger than the two that flanked it. The tents glowed from the placement of flickering lights placed at regular intervals around their circumferences. Like hives of honeybees, the tents hummed with the din of excited chatter.

A small ticket booth sat outside the largest tent. It, too, was striped, but up close, I realized the stripes weren't black and white at all; neither were the ones on the tent. They were green; dark and pale in alternating swoops. In Cauldron, Arum was born a Gravebriar and he hadn't forgotten the coven's signature color. In fact, he flaunted it.

Perched on a tall stool inside the ticket booth was a woman with hair the color of fresh blood and circles painted on her cheeks to match. She'd drawn large freckles on her nose and fake brows over her boldly lined eyes. Her lips were forest green and her thinly striped dress matched the tents looming over us. "Five coppers each," she said, perking up as she took in Forge. Her gaze slid down him until the small counter in front of her blocked her view.

He was oblivious to her perusal as he withdrew the pouch of coppers from his pocket. The girl sat up straighter in the tall stool she occupied, now enamored with his coin. I wasn't sure which she wanted more. He plucked out ten coppers and laid them on the counter, sliding them through a small hole in the clear window that separated us from her.

The girl gathered them in her palm, then dumped the coins into a container at her feet. The sound of metal hitting metal told me she'd sold plenty of tickets tonight. She turned and took up two tickets, letting her fingers linger on the tickets for him and watching me for a reaction.

I obliged her by jerking the tickets from under her fingertips. She huffed but didn't say anything; I didn't bother turning around to gloat. After all, I was going to the show with him and all she would have was a view of him walking away... not that it was a bad view, by any means.

Forge chuckled as we walked toward the tent. He tucked the rest of his coins away and shot me an approving grin. "That was perfect."

"She was rude."

"*Now* who's feeling a little jealous?" he quipped as we approached two unusually tall men standing by the tent flaps.

When we got closer, I saw they weren't two separate men at all, but a man with two conjoined torsos peeling from his lower half. Their features were identical despite the different designs of paint circling their eyes and mouths, which had the desired effect of leaving them looking menacing instead of fun or friendly.

"Tickets," the frowning man on the left demanded, his palm opened expectantly.

His friendlier brother on the right tipped his head to my friend. "Forge. Didn't think we'd see you again while we were in Westbrook."

"I described your entertainment to this enchanting creature and she just had to come and see it for herself." He grinned, taking my hand and kissing the back of it. His lip print cooled on my skin as he lowered it again.

The man softened. "I still need your tickets."

I handed the tattered paper tickets to him. He tore them in half and returned one side to me as the sour twin held open the tent's flap for us to walk inside. When we did... my mouth fell open at the grandeur.

From the knoll, the tent looked small. Standing at the ticket box, it looked much larger, but I never would have dreamt that inside it would appear so vast. An enormous pole pushed the top center of the tent far into the air. Torches were lit all around the ring, casting a warm glow that made everything appear golden and enchanted. Sawdust coated the ground, leaving a lingering woodsy scent that mingled with the aromas of sugar and butter that wafted from the food vendors. Movement seemed to erupt from every nook as spectators jostled for seating that would provide the best view of the show.

Overhead, a taut rope was stretched from one side of the tent to another, a dangling rope ladder draped down from either end. A svelte, petite girl who barely looked to be in her teens stood on the rope. She balanced on the thread, dressed in a tiny glittering leotard the same shade of blue as the night sky we'd just left outside, a hue she wore streaked through her pale blonde hair and even on her lips. Her skin shimmered, reminding me of moonlight dancing over waves.

She raised one arm, lifted her chin and gave a bow, then turned and bowed to the other side of the tent. The length of her foot bent around the braided strand, gripping it tightly. She began walking on the thin rope, stopping here and there to swoop one of her legs precariously over the edge. She stooped to sit on the tight line, waving to the happy crowd, but as she stood again, the rope swayed and she lost her balance.

There was nothing beneath her but packed, dry earth.

The crowd collectively gasped.

I covered my mouth and nose. Held my breath.

The girl recovered her balance and stood to regain her composure, flashing a smile and bowing to each side of the arena before taking off, running across the rope like it was nothing more than earth and grass beneath her feet, the rope and sheer will propelling her. She launched herself into a series of jumps and cartwheels, coming to a stop at the opposite ladder with a proud smile that glittered like her outfit, then raised both hands in triumph.

Forge clapped with everyone and leaned to whisper in my ear. "Her name is Zephyr. She's an Elementine. Wind..."

My lips parted. Forge had said that Arum hid witches in plain sight, but this was quite a creative way to do it. In his circus, they showcased their magic in the form of incredible feats instead of hiding it away.

"We should find seats." Bleachers curved around the entire tent, packed full all around us, but on the other side at the very top were a few empty seats. Forge and I carved our way beneath the metal stands and emerged on the other side of the tent, climbing up steps that carved between the rows of patrons to reach the seats we'd spotted.

The stands were crammed with men, women, and children, young and old, people from every social class and facet of humanity, and they were all excited. Giddy laughter erupted from every side, echoing over the tent walls as though they were solid. No sooner had we sat down before everyone craned their necks to watch as two horses and their rider entered the ring beneath the tightrope walker who was still descending her ladder.

The rider's fiery orange hair trailed behind her as she stood astride two horses, a foot on the back of each enormous stallion. Her glittering bodysuit was the color of a burning flame, blue at her ankles, rising to orange and then yellow, and at her neck, white. The horses obeyed her every whim, rearing when she ordered, then prancing and galloping at a short click of her tongue. She would leap from one to the other and the horses were always there where she wanted them, when she needed them.

"She's a Shade," I whispered to Forge, who grinned and nodded. Shades were witches whose power was linked to spirit, and spirit resided in everything living and dead.

The witch and her horses had an amazing, unbreakable bond that was visible for all to witness, but the people of Westbrook thought she was just skilled with her ability to break them. The witch had never broken anything, spirit or will. She'd just asked, and the animals chose to obey. They loved her. There was no other explanation for their devotion. They worried for her and strove to make her proud. Sought her approving smile, the strokes she brushed down their manes when they delighted her, and thus delighted everyone watching.

The Shade soaked in the applause, the cheers, the gasps, oohs and aahs. And when her horses began to tire and her tricks came further and further apart, she rode out the same door she'd ridden in, the flaps closing tightly behind her. Shadows appeared in the light beneath the door flaps as performers prepared for whatever spectacle was next.

A small army of women and men in garish green outfits entered the stands, selling sloshing drinks and packets of popped corn and salted nuts. When our vendor reached us, the box he held had been ransacked of goods, but Forge used his coppers to buy one of every food the vendor had left, urging me to taste it all. He also purchased a drink for us to share, as there was only one left.

"Dinner doesn't get better than this," he teased.

I realized he might be right when I took a sip of ale and the swirl of flavors hit my tongue. The beverage was frothy and cold and tasted of wheat, while the salty, buttery puffed corn crunched softly between my teeth. Taking a bite of an apple that appeared to be shellacked in crimson sugar, I groaned as the tart apple crunched in my mouth, juices dripping down the wooden stick I held. The combination of sweet, salty, and savory was something I'd never experienced before; it cemented my love for the wonderment that comprised the circus.

When everyone had been served, the vendors disappeared and everyone in the stands slowly took note of the man standing quietly in the center of the ring. Waiting.

The crowd went silent, like birdsong when a predator was near.

He wasn't exceedingly tall or short, but his height was the only thing about him that seemed average. His tailed waistcoat glittered in the torchlight that flickered all around the tent, the fabric the same dark evergreen of the forest. His vest was the green of slick, bright green frogs perched at the edge of a freshwater pond, and he wore a matching top hat and trousers that disappeared into shiny black boots.

I wished I could see his face up close. He wore a mustache that curled at the ends, but I couldn't see his hair or eyes. "Arum?" I guessed.

Forge sat up straighter, rubbing his palms on his trousers. "That's him."

Arum addressed the crowd, his gravelly voice capturing every ear. Even the children kept still. In the heavy humidity, I smelled the magic of his spell fill the air. I could almost see it unfurl like smoky ribbons, see the people around me

130

take it into their lungs and hold it there just to cling to the feeling a little longer.

He asked if we'd enjoyed the acts so far and when everyone applauded, informed us that we hadn't seen anything yet. He called himself the ringmaster and indeed he was. While I knew Arum hailed from the Gravebriar line, I wondered if he wasn't part Spellsweet.

The eloquent words he spoke were vital, as thick and sweet and golden as honey, reducing everyone in his presence to nothing more than greedy flies. The Shade with her horses and the tightrope walker Elementine whet our appetites, each entertaining the crowd while the last tickets were sold.

Now, the true show would begin.

"Welcome one. Welcome all," he said, sweeping his hands toward each side of the tent.

The audience roared. He waited until they settled again. And then, he entranced them…

"Come with me on a journey, to a land where faeries roam," he invited with a friendly wave. "Where a tiny pinch of pixie dust, can make a man forget his home."

Overhead, the flyers began, and I realized why Crow mentioned only them. Swinging from one trapeze to the other, the male flyer caught the lovely female flyer and they swung together, dressed as fairies with tiny gossamer wings fluttering at their backs.

The crowd gasped with every twist, every switch from one trapeze to the other, every fold and bend and spiral flip. I could've watched them all day, but the flyers weren't meant to be the center of the story; they were just there to pique our interest…

On the ground beneath them, a lovely dancer entered the ring with Arum, plucking flowers from the ground that everyone assumed were fake. I knew better. I could smell their freshness and sense the Gravebriar magic that conjured them.

She wore a pale pink leotard with a matching sheer skirt trailing from the backside to her ankles.

The ringmaster's voice boomed out across the tent.

"A princess of the northern lands roamed in a field of flowers.

She knit them into a fine-spun crown and placed it upon her brow.

The faery prince of the southern isles smelled her fragrant blooms,

And abandoned his flying faery ship when he took in her sweet perfume."

A handsome young man with dark hair and bronze skin entered the ring wearing a fine suit trimmed in silver, circling the girl who'd deftly twisted her flowers into a circlet and eased it onto her head. His silver crown was as sharp and ethereal as his expression.

He smiled at the girl and a moment later, she mimicked his grin. He held his hand out and she slipped her tiny one into his. They danced as musicians played softly, a poignant tune meant just for them.

"He wooed the princess of the north and begged her for her hand," Arum continued in his spellbinding voice, weaving a poem with a sing-song cadence.

"She gave it to him willingly, forsaking her own land."

The lithe dancer and the boy ran away together, disappearing through a tent flap.

A large man entered the ring wearing a cape of fine red cloth with white fur ringing his neck. With a hand over his brow, he pretended to search for something, finding nothing but the boy's silver crown laying forgotten in the dirt. He ran to it, picked it up, and studied its unique design. His grimace soured into hate.

"The northern king woke up to find, his precious daughter gone.

On the ground, he discovered a crown, and knew that she'd been conned.

He vowed revenge on the southern prince, on his pretty isle gray.

And promised his wife he would find their child, and her captor he would slay."

A great army of performers marched through the tent in taut lines, precision guiding their steps from north to south; all Elementines armed with bows and arrows that burned in their hands. Those at the front of the procession breathed fire or spun it while keeping step to an orchestra I hadn't realized was there at first, too dazzled by the spectacle of it all.

"And when the horde of the king of the north came to the stormy sea,

He ordered his army to fly across, to where his sweet daughter be."

The fiery army left the ring, slipping away in the dark as Tempest witches unfurled from thick, storm-cloud silk ribbons that flowed from the tent's ceilings, the ribbons turning into flapping flags in their wake as they churned around and around. It looked like they were flying.

Tiny lightning bursts filled the tent and when people looked, the tent flaps were waving in the wind and lightning split the sky, despite there being no clouds hanging above. No one seemed to notice that finer point.

The fiery army returned, regaining the spectators' attention as they battled the aerial artists, many of whom unraveled from their silks until they lay prostrate on the ground with their eyes facing the heavens as Arum continued his tale.

"The faery prince of the southern isles, he saw the swarm close in.

He ordered his army to fight the threat, the battle they must win.

The king of the north, and prince of the south, they fought within the fray.

And many a faery lay bloodied and still, when the sun arose next day."

A shudder ran up my spine when Arum moved to the side, revealing the two lovers lying on the ground, wrapped in one another's arms. The faery princess's blossom crown lay askew on her head.

The crowd went silent and the only thing I could hear was the throbbing pulse of my heart in my ears.

Forge shifted beside me. "Arum's shows are always shocking. He wants everyone to remember them."

He was gifted, because I knew I would never forget what I'd seen. I didn't know why it struck such a chord within me, but I felt that chord in my chest still thrumming. Resonating. Not like the feel of poison, but of something far worse.

TEN

After a brief intermission where the circus's vendors circulated sweet treats and more mugs of frothy ale, Forge slid closer and we conversed secretly amid hundreds. Between bites of a red candy-coated apple, he warned, "The rest of the show will be much like the opening acts. Have you decided whether you want to press forward to speak with him, or would you like to leave now? We can slip out before he's able to come ask why we're here."

My head ticked back in surprise. "Are you saying he knows we're here?"

"He knew the moment our tickets were torn." He took a sip of ale. "Likely before we approached the ticket booth."

"I want to speak with him."

He nodded resolutely. "Then after the show ends, we'll request an audience." Worry shone in his eyes and it made me want to soothe it away.

"I'm not afraid of him. Whatever blood sings through me, also sings through him."

He leaned forward and looked at me intently. "I know I've teased you about it, but you're nothing like him."

"You don't know me well enough to make that judgment," I said, straightening my back.

He tilted his head so his mouth was near the corner of mine and grinned. "I'm glad we met in the solarium before all this mess began."

"Why?" I breathed.

"Because those few minutes showed me your heart, and every moment since has reinforced what I learned of you then." He brought his hand up and brushed his thumb over the corner of my mouth. "Candy."

The fluttering in my stomach had nothing to do with the fact that the show had resumed, though I turned my attention to the Bloodlings with tattoos all over their bodies who leaped and sprang all over the floor in difficult acrobatic feats. In Cauldron, their tattoos were illustrations of the trials of their lives and how they'd overcome them. It was a beautiful tapestry of pride and triumph if one looked closely enough.

Bloodlings would almost reach a euphoric state during tattooing, not because of the blood that rose from their flesh during the inking, but because the ink freed them as they claimed their truths. Theirs was one of the most tightly-knit covens in Cauldron because everyone knew everyone's past. Nothing was hidden.

I wasn't sure if these Bloodlings carried on the same traditions or had formed their own, but their tattoos were obviously important to them as each and every Bloodling witch performing proudly displayed them.

I wondered about their blood magic. While I'd asked Mother about it many times, she always changed the subject. Perhaps she didn't know much about it herself, or perhaps she knew and didn't think I should.

Forge watched their performance, but every so often, his focus drifted to me and it made me aware of myself in a way I wasn't used to. At home, I never liked to be the center of attention. My power was the root of all the lies my coven kept, sure, but *I* was never the focus. The focus lay on the intricate story woven with lies, not in the root of that story. Roots weren't meant to be seen.

The Shade who'd ridden the stallions returned carrying a hollow golden ring twice as tall as she. Behind her trailed a lion that roared so loudly, I jumped and tucked into Forge a little.

When he laughed and slid his arm around my back, I didn't shrug him off. The raw power in the tawny beast was thrilling. Almost as thrilling as pretending to be wanted.

The Shade asked the enormous cat to jump through her ring a few times as she prowled all around the circumference, showing him off. The muscles in the lion's flanks flexed and relaxed, propelling him just where she asked. When she lit the ring on fire, he jumped unflinchingly, trusting her not to hurt him or put him in harm's way. He leapt through the fire again and again, and each time, every spectator held a collective breath until the pads of his large feet hit the ground again, until we were sure no smoke rolled from his thick mane.

When the Shade and her beast completed their act, she extinguished the flaming ring and she and the lion bowed together in all directions before exiting.

The conjoined men who had manned the tent's entrance and taken our tickets before allowing us through the flaps entered the ring and juggled a trio of daggers. They slowly added more blades until dozens were slicing through the air and being caught and flung back up again. "Silverthorns," I whispered into Forge's ear.

His fingers tightened on my side and he scooted closer to me so our sides were flush. We watched a third Silverthorn join them. She was close to my mother's age, still clinging to youth but showing the earliest signs of aging. Her once-dark hair was gray at her temples; some of her wrinkles were visible even as her face was relaxed.

Dressed completely in chain mail, she sharply withdrew a sword from her hip and proceeded to swallow it.

I couldn't help but think of how perfect a Silverthorn girl would be for Forge. The respect shining in his eyes for the performance and performers was enough to make me wish, for just a second, that my magic was different. That our circumstances were different and that the night of the revel had ended with us talking until the party ended, then parting ways afterward and perhaps finding one another the next day in town, sitting together on a tea house patio and learning one another sip by sip.

"You okay?" he asked, watching me carefully.

I nodded and gave a smile. "Yeah. Just thinking."

"Copper for your thoughts?" he gently teased.

I shook my head.

He placed a small dagger in my hand. "Made you this," he said. Its blade was thin and sharpened to a fine point. The handle fit my hand perfectly, my fingers molding around it.

"First your coven. Now you're arming your enemy?"

"You aren't my enemy," he volleyed softly.

"Does your father feel the same way?"

"I don't care what my father or coven think. Beyond that, in this place and with these people, if you don't carry a weapon, they'll assume you are one." He took up his own curved blade and showed me how to test the weight with my finger, letting the weapon teeter until it became still, completely horizontal and perfectly balanced. "Until we leave here, it has to be you and me on guard against them all."

"I'm with you," I told him, studying how the torchlight flickered in his steely eyes.

"No matter what happens or what is revealed," he emphasized. He'd said it before, but the way he said it now made me wonder if he knew more than he was willing to admit in this moment. Like he could see the cliff we were approaching, even though we weren't sure our conjured wings would carry us.

Still... Arbor lay dying. There was no other choice but to leap. "I'm with you, Forge. Completely."

"And I'm with you, Princess. I swear it."

I didn't like the conviction in his voice. A promise like that was destined to be broken.

Forge described Arum as being heartless, but the man had heart. Perhaps it was calloused or maybe even barbed, but it beat in his chest as fervently as mine. Even from afar, I could see there was no void in him. He was filled with hunger, like the look an emaciated mutt gave when it spotted someone with food, knowing the means to ease his pangs for a time lie within the stranger's curled hand. Part plea, part threat. He was starving and willing to ask for your castoffs, but if you refused him, he was more than willing to bite.

Arum didn't leave Cauldron with a successful show. He left with nothing but his magic, and I wasn't even sure how he'd managed that. Instead of cowering, this cast-out mutt toughened himself and scrounged for everything he could until he became strong enough to take from other mutts, strong enough to consume *them* if they crossed him.

All the spectators gradually bled away into the night, walking back to town, to their homes – permanent or temporary – while some trailed toward the dock and their ships.

The performers began the arduous task of cleaning up. The conjoined men, who'd already wiped off most of their makeup onto their sleeves, swept popped corn and other crumbs from the metal stands close to us. Their attention oscillated between their task and shooting us equally distrustful and curious glances.

Forge asked for an audience with Arum, so the friendlier twin shouted the request down to someone else, who yelled it to another, who hollered to someone in the back I couldn't see.

The men worked around us, even though we moved so they could clean where we'd been sitting. In the ring, the tightrope walker held a shovel. A young boy hurried after her with a large bucket as she scooped animal droppings from the floor. I wasn't sure where the beast was housed, but still heard the rumble of the lion as it lazily padded away.

Heavy footsteps on the stairs drew my attention. Arum climbed to us, his glittering jacket discarded and the sleeves of his shirt rolled up to his elbows. His thick, dark hair was turning the slightest bit silver at his temples. There was no way this man could be old enough to have taught my mother.

His eyes were fastened, not on Forge whom he addressed, but on me. "To what do I owe the pleasure, Forge Silverthorn?" he questioned, flicking a glance from me to Forge.

Forge cut to the heart of the matter. "I need information that only you might have."

Arum's dark eyes narrowed. "Why is that my problem?"

"Because I'm willing to bargain to get that information," Forge teased.

Arum crossed his arms. "I'm listening."

"One show. One night only. An act with the two of us."

I grinned up at Forge, hoping the excited expression I wore didn't look like the fear and nervousness I actually felt.

Arum squinted at me. Was it possible that he could see the spell painted over me, or even if he could sense my toxicity lurking beneath it? "What is your name, my dear, and why are you wasting your time on the likes of this one?" He grinned, hooking a thumb at Forge. There was a challenge in his tone, playful as it was.

I laughed but slid my arm around Forge's back. He repaid the gesture and drew me close. "I'm Lilith."

While Arum had some wrinkles settling into his forehead and around his mouth when he smiled, he barely looked older than me. He tore his moustache off and flung it over his shoulder, where the broom of one of the tall men caught it immediately. Without the thick, curled band of hair decorating his top lip, he looked even younger. I had so many questions but knew I couldn't ask them without him learning who I was. "It's terribly itchy," he supplied. He stared at me until I was sure he would need to blink. He never did. "What do you want to know?"

"We need to know where to find a gravebriar bush," I told him. When Forge's hand tightened on my waist, I realized he must have preferred to ease into the question, but I didn't think there was a way to do that. Arum was like that frigid pool mid-stream. The quickest way to know his depths was to plunge in quickly.

Arum choked a laugh. His brows rose for a second until he composed himself. "And what would a witch of any other coven need with gravebriar?"

Forge answered, "One of my coven mates was injured in a fight he foolishly instigated against a Gravebriar witch. The Gravebriars refuse to heal him, so we seek the thing that would heal his wound without their magic."

"Oh, if anyone is to be healed, it'll be with their magic," Arum corrected. "The very source of it." Arum was quiet for a long moment.

Forge spoke up. "Time is something we don't have to waste, Arum. Will you help us?"

The ringmaster finally blinked, then made a counteroffer. "That sort of information would require *three* nights of entertainment."

Forge shook his head. "We don't have that much time. The boy is wasting away. Surely you can show some kindness, which I'll be happy to repay one day. One night only. Think of the publicity."

"*Two* nights, and I'll tell you what I know about gravebriar. But only because I'm feeling generous tonight."

He called that generous?

"If you plan to tell us to plant a Gravebriar witch in the ground to get the bush to grow, you can save your advice," I spoke up. "Do you *have* gravebriar, or know where to find it?"

Arum's demeanor turned downright frigid as his dark orbs locked on me. "What magic do you possess?"

"I'm a Shade, though I have very little magic." Another bitter, pretty lie.

"A Shade?" Arum sized me up, searching for a hint of soul-binding magic or evidence of our lie. "I reserve the right to alter the acts you create," he said. Forge and I nodded our assent. "After two performances, on two back-to-back nights, beginning tomorrow evening, I'll give you my answer – which does *not* include burying a Gravebriar witch – and you'll each get an equal share of the evening's profits as if you're a full-fledged member of my troupe. Otherwise, you can see yourselves out of my tent."

He'd doubled down.

Forge looked at me. I nodded imperceptibly. Arum knew where to find gravebriar; I could see it in the shining slice of his eye. He knew. Besides that, he might already have some. We just had to perform twice, gather the information, and run like hell back to Cauldron and hope Arbor was still alive, that Mother was able to keep her promise to preserve him.

Arum extended his hand to me. I shook his firmly, solidifying our agreement, and then Forge solidified his word as well. Arum looked us over. "Where are you staying? The inns are full, from what I've heard."

Forge sighed. "We haven't gotten that far yet. The show was about to begin when we reached the outskirts. We'll figure something out."

"There is an empty wagon out back you're welcome to use. You are members of my troupe for the next two days, and I take care of my own," Arum offered.

Forge sharply thanked him and we watched as he nimbly jogged down the steps and disappeared like a phantom. I still couldn't wrap my mind around his age, but maybe this man was named for Arum, potentially his father or grandfather. It would make much more sense if he was the offspring of the Arum my mother had known.

A kitschy village comprised of garishly painted wooden wagons draped with thick canvas were arranged in rows behind the tents.

The canvas covers of the Elementines' tents were easy to spot, painted with flame, mountains, swirls of blue to mimic the wind, and curled, frothy waves. They congregated in the lawns in front of their homes, laughing and sipping ale, going quiet as we passed them by. The petite Wind witch who nearly fell from the tightrope huddled amongst them, standing with the two flyers. She'd changed into more comfortable clothes that hung off her small frame. Her eyes tracked us even after the others returned to their conversations, keeping their tones quiet to guard their words.

The Bloodling tents were next and like the shoppes in Cauldron, they were steeped in the familiar copper scent. The Bloodlings stretched out in hammocks, relaxed on the grass, or lounged on rocks and stumps of trees they'd pulled into their yard. They were keyed up, animatedly chattering about the show and the looks on the patrons' faces.

One was pouring glasses of blood for his coven mates. Did they consider themselves a small coven, or part of a larger one at which Arum sat at the head?

Their tattoos were on full display, bolder and more colorfully vivid than the witches in Cauldron donned. The artist among them was talented. I wished we could trail closer to study more of their stories, but the hard looks they shot us assured that we weren't welcome.

The conjoined men and the woman who swallowed her sword argued from their respective porches, their silver wagons gleaming in the moonlight. They obviously didn't share the same level of comradery the others did.

We never saw the lion or the Shade witch, but the community of wagons stretched far beyond the only one that sat empty. It was perched in the center of them all, the slats dark with no light escaping from inside. It was the only one that was still as death itself.

What made goosebumps rise on my flesh was that it was painted in varying shades of green, painted vines stretching over the canopy. Circling the base of the wagon were blossoms in every color.

The wagon had once belonged to a Gravebriar witch.

I wondered where the witch had gone or if it might have once belonged to Arum. It seemed older than the rest. Worn and weathered in ways those neighboring it weren't.

While pondering the fate of my coven mate, it occurred to me that we were surrounded by Arum and his troupe, and the image of an archer's target entered my mind. If Arum was the archer, we were positioned in the bullseye.

Thunder rumbled in the distance as we took in our temporary lodging, though the clouds overhead were wispy and sheer. "Heat lightning," Forge said.

I walked up the steps and used my forearm to lift the heavy door flap, letting my eyes adjust to the darkness. To our right, Forge found a candle on a simple silver stick, along with a box of matches lying beside it. He struck one, the sharp snick then whoosh of flame filling the space just before the flame's light cast shadows. There was a humble single bed in the back of the wagon, freshly made, as if Arum had been expecting someone.

We'd walked into a trap. I could feel it and sense the tension pouring from Forge like smoke curling from the candle he'd lit. It melted atop a square table, painted in more vining patterns with a few colorful blooms stretching from it. Among the roses and chamomile were delicate, belled buttercups and pale blue morning glories. Many plants that held healing properties could also be poisonous.

Two chairs wearing bright poppies and stalks of foxglove were pushed beneath it. To the left there was a long, narrow wooden table with a copper pitcher and basin, along with two stacked cups and two plates. Forge removed his bag and placed it on the bed. Over our heads, the vines painted onto the canvas outside could be seen within, shadows of the plants our shelter wore.

I eased the strap of my bag over my head and let the bulk swiftly settle on the floor. Despite the fact it wasn't that heavy, I felt a twinge of relief.

Forge took the pitcher and promised to return with water. I sat on the side of the small bed, thankful for a moment alone. A moment to breathe.

I scrubbed my hands over my face and hoped my parents were okay, wondering who the Gravebriar Power was now. They hadn't mentioned my mother's replacement while handing down their decisions. For a few fateful moments, events spiraled and chaos reigned instead of the Council.

My thoughts slid to Arum. He was so… strange and intense and in his eyes was an eerie awareness. Most people who spoke to you barely listened when you spoke in return. Arum soaked in every word and committed them to memory. I wondered if he would use my hastily spoken words against me.

I couldn't muster the strength or will to sit up straight when Forge came back inside. Exhaustion to the soul was hard to conceal.

The copper pitcher was full. He poured me a cup and I sipped on it. "You look how I feel," he offered as he poured himself a cup and sat beside me. The curve of his spine matched mine. A tired fold of bone.

"Why do I feel like we're worms in the beak of a mother bird soaring toward the mouths of her babes?" I asked.

The hand raising his cup to his lips paused just shy of it. "Because we are."

I nodded. At least my instinct was right. "How powerful is he?"

"He'd still be Power if he lived in Cauldron." His tone was careful.

"He can't be my mother's mentor. He's older than us, but certainly not older than her," I argued.

Forge turned his head to the side, elbows on his knees now. "There is only one Arum, and he had no sons. His Spellsweet must be gifted to make such intense youth potions. My father said that after he 'died'," he emphasized with air quotes, "a host of witches left Cauldron as a protest of sorts. He said they didn't want to live in a place where the innocent burned."

The comment rubbed me the wrong way. Would my mother knowingly burn an innocent man, or did she believe him to be guilty?

I wished things were different and that I could simply sit down with Arum and ask him all the questions rushing through my mind to determine what his version of the truth was. Didn't everyone have their own?

"So your father knows he's alive?"

"I'm not sure. He's spoken of Arum and the witches who left after he was punished, but hasn't given me any indication that he knew."

"And you knew but didn't tell him?"

He shrugged. "Strained, remember?" Forge unlaced his boots and toed them off, placing them neatly in the corner. "You can take the bed."

"And where will you sleep?"

"There's room on the floor," he answered. I had no doubt that he'd sleep there, bone tired as he was.

"There's room for us both here."

He let out a breath of relief. "Are you sure?"

I nodded. "I promise to refrain from groping you."

He laughed. "If you're sure, Gr— Lilith." He'd caught himself again. I knew the little term of endearment that so quickly formed in his mind would be a difficult habit to shake. I chalked it up to exhaustion and knew he'd berate himself enough, so I didn't mention the gaffe. He hitched a thumb over his shoulder, gesturing toward the door. "I'll step outside and give you some privacy."

I thanked him and watched as he slipped through the canvas. Rifling through my bag, I was reminded I hadn't considered what articles of clothing I was grabbing when I took them from my room. I had one more change of pants, a short blouse and a long one, and a single change of underwear. No more socks. Nothing to sleep in.

I hadn't exactly expected to have company. Did my subconscious assume I'd fail, or that Forge would kill me before I changed clothes?

I pressed my eyes closed, then remembered the basin and turned my head to it. Perhaps we could borrow some soap and scrub what we were wearing. The wind whipped outside, rattling the canvas. I slipped my trousers and shirt off and slid the long button-up shirt over my head. It was pale gray, one of the many subtle metallic shades trapped in Forge's eyes.

Sliding into the white bed sheets, I considered calling out to him but remembered we were surrounded by Arum's troupe, his eyes and ears. If we were lovers as we were pretending to be, he wouldn't bother stepping outside to let me dress and I wouldn't need to call out to him when I was decent. Instead, I settled into the mattress and studied the canopy art. Forge slipped in moments later.

He tugged his shirt over his head. The warm glow of the candle painted his muscles with orange light as shadows settled into the concave places. My face heated as I watched him pour a little water into the basin and scoop it onto his face and into his hair. He held the table as it dripped from him and I watched his chest expand and contract, noticed a trail of hair form at his belly button and descend. "Is it okay if I sleep without the shirt? It's filthy and I get hot when I sleep."

I grinned. "I don't mind in the least. As long as you don't mind that I'm sleeping without trousers."

He groaned. "And now I'm picturing you without pants. I'll never sleep now."

A chuckle bubbled from my chest. "I had no idea you were so affected by me."

"You have no idea." He scrubbed his hands down his face one last time before turning around and walking slowly toward the bed.

My entire body heated for him. I lay on my side, facing the door. In case anything happened, I wanted the exit in my sight. He lay on his side facing me, his back to the door. There was only one pillow. I edged it toward him, but he stilled my hands by gently wrapping his hand around my wrist.

"You keep it." Bending his arm, he used it as his pillow.

"Should we sleep in shifts?" I whispered.

He shook his head. "We need to rest. I'm an extremely light sleeper. I'll wake if I hear the slightest noise."

I wondered if he'd always been a light sleeper or if something had happened to make him one.

"When you said there were other ways to elicit information from a person..." he said in a low tone, "what ways did you mean?"

"I could use a hallucinogen."

"Get them high and ask questions." He grinned appreciatively.

"I slipped hallucinogenic mushrooms into the wine fountain the night of the revel," I admitted.

"Why didn't you use them to get out of trouble?"

"Because I wanted the lies to end. Plus, I didn't want to do anything else that might make someone think I had hurt Arbor and was trying to cover my deed."

"Why did you agree to Arum's terms, then? Or did you just say it to get us close to him so you can use your magic?"

I shook my head. "I wasn't lying. I don't *like* using my power that way. If he'll give us the information for two shows, I'd rather work for it." I also wanted to experience life – however briefly – outside Cauldron and its demands.

"Do you fear your magic?" he asked carefully, his lips pursing ever so slightly.

"Sometimes."

"But you're so careful with it."

"I am, but even the most cautious person in the world can make a mistake, Forge."

He squirmed until he found a more comfortable position, then admitted, "I don't worry about you using it because I know that you fear it. I worry what someone else would do if they knew what you were capable of and tried to force you to use your power for evil."

I'd had vivid nightmares of the same.

It would be nice to say it could never happen, that I would be strong enough to resist anyone who tried, but until a person was in a situation, they never knew what they would do.

I watched his molten eyes swirl beneath the dark slashes of his brows until I couldn't hold my eyes open any longer. They drifted shut once. Twice. And then darkness shrouded me.

ELEVEN

The first thing I noticed when I woke was how warm I was. The second was the large, calloused hand splayed across my hip. Forge was still asleep on his side, pressed against my back, his other arm still folded beneath his head. It had to be numb. His lashes fanned his tanned cheeks and he breathed slowly, deeply. It was the most peaceful I'd seen him.

I had a feeling that the easy smile Forge wore was like a layer of ice on a lake. Beneath that ice the water churned, trying to weaken and break what held it in. Something under his surface seemed perpetually unsettled. But every so often in moments like these, that ice cracked and allowed the frigid water to escape through the break.

A loud cackle came from outside and his eyes cracked open, suddenly awake. He stretched the hand on my hip and then went still, his breath trapped in his chest and his eyes widening until they couldn't anymore.

"Who's groping who now?" I teased.

He moved his hand away and rolled onto his back, staring at the ceiling. Then he winced. "My arm is asleep." I couldn't help but giggle. He raised his head and gave me

151

an incredulous look. "I was gallant and gave you the pillow and *now* you poke fun at me?" he guffawed.

I buried my face in the thin pillow and laughed heartily into the stuffing. "Yep," I answered.

"You're cruel, C—Lilith."

Both of us froze. Forge raked top teeth over his plump bottom lip and let out an almost silent curse. His head fell back onto the downy mattress. We had to be careful – so, so careful. A slip like that in front of Arum and we would be in deep trouble.

"Should we leave now before I screw this up for both of us?" he whispered.

I shook my head, sliding my eyes down the canvas walls. They weren't thick enough for my liking and certainly weren't soundproof. Not to mention, if Arum had a talented Spellsweet, he could ask for a potion that would allow the walls to absorb our words for him.

"What do you want to do today?" he asked, changing the subject. "We have some time to see the town before we need to help set up tonight."

"That would be nice." A thought settled into my mind and I leaned up onto one elbow. "Forge, what is our act going to be?"

Forge sat up on the edge of the bed with his back to me as he rubbed the back of his neck. "You're not going to like it."

Forge promised we'd discuss our act over breakfast, which made my stomach rejoice. While I'd expected it to be bigger than Falling Waters, Westbrook was much larger than I realized. The town, a hundred times larger than Jenny's small village, was divided into gridded, rectangular blocks where homes and inns were planted.

A large group of twenty or so worked at one end of the muddy streets, planting layers of brick into the earth to form a sturdy road. In the distance, Forge pointed to a thick trail of smoke that rolled into the air. "That smoke is from the brickyard. It looks like they're working hard to get the streets lined before the weather turns cold. They've been talking about it for years, so it's good to see they're finally doing it."

We walked past the working men and women toward the shoppes, inns, and restaurants clustered at the end of the road farthest from the sea, but close enough that the tang of salt air still lingered. Mingling with the briny scent of the ocean was something sugary and warm, freshly-baked and mouthwatering.

Forge smiled. "Guess I know where we're going first."

He threaded his fingers through mine and tugged me toward the smell. Despite having all but gorged on treats at the circus last night, it felt like I hadn't eaten in years. I unthreaded our fingers and stepped inside a bakerie while he hovered behind me.

An older man and woman worked behind the counter, fussing at one another. She told him he was going to burn the loaves if he didn't hurry and get them out of the oven, and he told her to mind what she was doing before she ruined the dough, to which she let out a hearty guffaw. They bickered back and forth until Forge cleared his throat, then their heads snapped up at the same time.

The gray-headed man pushed a set of thick, round spectacles up onto the bridge of his nose, deftly eased a large tray of fresh bread out of the brick oven and set it on a long table, and smiled as he removed his mitts. "What can I do for you?"

There was a small display of various breads, some drizzled in honey, some with butter coated in cinnamon, some with strawberries stuffed into the middles, as well as golden apple tarts and small cakes.

"We'll take one of each," Forge replied.

The woman's eyes lit up. "One of... everything?"

"Please," he confirmed.

She glanced over her shoulder at her husband, who quickly moved forward to extract one of each pastry and bread and cake from the display, filling up two plain white platters. "Of course, sir," he muttered.

"What drinks are available this morning?" asked Forge.

The man handed each of us a platter. "We have fresh milk, water, fresh squeezed orange juice..."

Forge pivoted to me with raised brows.

"I'd love some juice," I told him.

"I'll take the same, please," Forge said.

The man told us to sit and he'd bring our drinks to us. We sat beside each other, facing the window, which overlooked the street. Forge removed more than enough coppers from his bag to pay for twice what we'd bought. The man hurried to us carrying two small glasses of orange juice.

He thanked us profusely when Forge paid him after insisting we were being too generous, but took the coppers, gratefully patting his breast pocket as he walked away. His wife gave a relieved sigh and smiled at her husband as he passed her behind the counter. She rolled the pin across her dough gentler, the tension in her fingers gone.

Forge raised his glass, so I raised mine to meet it, waiting to hear his toast. "To the greatest act at the circus tonight."

I swilled my juice, waiting for him to tell me more. "Which is...?"

"If we go with my idea, we'll need a different one for tomorrow. Arum likely won't want the same show twice in two nights."

154

He was deflecting. Again. Which meant he really thought I wouldn't like his proposed act. "What's your idea for tonight, Forge? You're dancing around it. Plant your feet."

"You would be strapped to the Wheel of Death while I throw knives at you," he said before taking a bite of apple tart.

I abruptly stopped chewing a clump of honey bread, remembered it was there, and chewed it quickly before wiping my mouth and taking a sip of juice to wash it down. Then I sat back and stared at him. "You want to throw knives at me?"

"Yes."

"Have you done this before?" I asked.

He winced. "No, I haven't. But my magic is just as precise as yours."

A calculating gleam entered my eye. "And since you're trusting me, you want me to afford you the same respect?"

He gave a steady nod. "I would never hurt you."

I swallowed thickly, the seeds of doubt taking root in my mind. "Or you could use this to stage an unfortunate accident, bury me, wait for the gravebriar to sprout, and go back home, hailed a hero."

If he thought I wouldn't have time to activate the poison singing through his veins before he killed me, he'd better think again. I would have ample time before I took my last breath. I wiped my mouth roughly and tossed my napkin on the table.

He leaned forward. "I don't give a damn about being considered heroic, especially by anyone in Cauldron. And what kind of hero would one be if he slaughtered an innocent to attain the glory?"

"Most would say it doesn't matter how you get to the finish line as long as you cross it before everyone else," I argued, palms flat on the sticky table.

"Good thing I'm not like most people, then. I *do* care. And I've been completely honest with you from the moment I met you in the solarium. I don't mean you any harm." He gently took hold of my hand and brushed his thumb over the back of it. "How can I prove it?"

"You can start by not skewering me. And know that if you do, I'll have plenty of time to activate the poison in your blood and drag you into the afterlife with me." I pulled my hand away and tucked it beneath the table, feeling the warmth from his thumb leaching away.

"I won't hurt you. I swear it." His brows pinched. "We could come up with something else if you're too uncomfortable."

"What?" I asked. "I've come up with no ideas whatsoever." Beyond that, I *wanted* to trust him. I wanted to believe him when he said he would never hurt me. The only way to tell if he was being honest was to give him a chance to prove he was a man of his word, or a liar. "The wheel is a good idea. Arum will love it."

"He will," Forge agreed. "And I meant what I said. I'll be careful."

Why would he come this far and risk so much, only to kill me now?

After demolishing the pastries and breads on both platters, Forge gathered the crumbs into his hand and brought the plates back up to the counter. After leaving the bakerie, he showed me around Westbrook. Each street looked much like the previous one with thatched roofs, quaint homes, larger inns, and shoppes. The buildings were so different than those at home. Not only in their architecture, which obviously wasn't meant to stand the test of time but would serve them well enough for the time being, but in what they carried. The fashions in the windows were plain and functional. The fruits and vegetables weren't nearly as vibrant as what I was used to seeing, and much of the produce was partially spoiled.

There was a storefront with hats worn by carved wooden busts with hollow eyes that peeked from beneath the brims. Again, the styles were functional and not outlandish in the least. Arum certainly hadn't gotten his fantastic top hat there.

The farther we walked, the more I realized what else was missing... There were no galleries with beautiful paintings, no instrument shoppes, nothing fun or soul-stirring. Only necessities, and bare ones at that.

We in Cauldron were fortunate to be able to appreciate such things and keep them. My guess was that there were painters and craftsmen within this town, but that their labors sailed away with the ships docked in the harbor to be sold in other more vibrant towns and cities.

We passed a butcher with haunches of meat hanging from his ceiling, the smell of rawness pouring from his doorway, past several small bakeries that smelled divine, a cobbler with a mountainous supply of plain shoes and boots, and a carpenter who made everything from tool handles to children's toys and furniture.

Near the brickyard, where rectangular red bricks dried in the sun, was a tannery that smelled horribly foul and a blacksmith whose hammer strikes seemed to somehow echo the pulse of the place. And the docks? If the blacksmith was Westbrook's pulse, the harbor was its heart.

We were rushed last night and the fish market was empty, so I'd barely given it a second thought. I didn't see the women, men, girls, and boys haggle over pricing and the quality of filets. I didn't see the smiles, the salt wind lifting tendrils and tufts of hair, and the lingering hints of sunburn on necks and cheeks and chests.

I didn't hear the laughter last night, but this morning it filled the air, louder than the cries of gulls walking along the land or soaring overhead.

Forge smiled. "Open your hands."

I opened my palms.

"Cup them."

He poured the crumbs he'd collected from breakfast into my waiting hands. "The gulls love crumbs," he explained.

I tossed a few on the ground and several saw the motion, landing and pecking the crumbs off the soil. They flapped their wings and rushed to find another. I kept scattering and feeding them until my hands were empty.

I smiled at Forge. "Thank you."

He inclined his head, his hands stuffed in his pockets. It was only the second time I'd ever seen him look sheepish.

Seeing the mighty ships moored in bobbing rows in full daylight was even more thrilling than it was last evening. Forge and I took our time strolling down each long row and taking in the differences of the ships. Forge explained how some were meant for trade and pointed out others that were outfitted with canon and meant for war.

The warships scared and thrilled me. What would it be like to be on the ship, firing at another? What would it be like to be on the receiving end of such deadly ire?

True to his word, Crow was on his trade ship, sitting on a new pile of crates, peeling an apple with a small pocketknife when he caught sight of us. "Lilith!" he shouted, beaming a smile down to me. "You missed me!"

I laughed. "Of course we did!"

Forge whispered in my ear, "He wasn't talking about both of us. He was hoping *you* missed *him*." When I looked at Forge beside me, he wore a smug expression. "He looked forward to your visit, like a man weary of the night awaits the dawn."

I swatted his chest. "You're terrible at dramatics."

Forge quirked a brow as Crow tucked his knife away and jogged down to meet us. "Would either of you like an apple?" he asked.

"We just ate breakfast at a bakerie in town, but thank you for offering," I replied.

"The ship's owner is aboard. Would you like to meet him?" our new friend asked, taking a crisp bite from the flesh of his fruit.

"We'd love to."

Crow's sleeves were rolled up to his elbows, his shirt unbuttoned to mid-stomach, the pale fabric flapping in the warm summer breeze. He offered me his arm as he had last night. His smile was as wide and contagious today as it was yesterday.

Forge followed me and Crow onto the ship's deck wearing a self-satisfied grin. I ignored him... mostly.

Beneath us, the sea churned in small but determined, choppy waves where yesterday it felt calm. My full stomach turned a little, but I wanted to meet the ship's owner and see more of the great vessel.

Crow led us to a cabin where two double doors were open to let in the salty breezes. The windows were sparkling clean. I'd expected them to be coated in salt, but the ship was well-cared for. Through the window, I spotted some of the crew working in the sails and riggings while others swabbed the deck, dragging their thick mops over the planks. Nestled into a nook farther into the room was a single messy bunk, and between us and it sat a desk with books and maps splayed all over the top, partially obscured by the person bent over a ledger.

Crow cleared his throat. "Excuse me, sir," he began, but I recognized the man before he swiveled around.

His shoulders weren't neatly tucked into a finely tailored, glittering jacket, but Arum wore his plain shirt as if it was exactly that. He turned to face us with flourish, spinning on his heels. His eyes caught my hand wrapped around the arm of his crew member and narrowed. "Lilith," he greeted, then peered over my shoulder without addressing Forge by name. Instead, he looked to Crow. "To what do I owe this pleasure?"

"I wasn't aware you knew my new friends, sir," Crow beamed.

"Actually, the three of us came to quite an interesting arrangement last night. Forge and Lilith have agreed to perform in my show for the next two nights."

Crow's brows shot up in surprise and his pale brown eyes sparkled. "What magic do you…"

"Mind your tongue," Arum snapped.

"Aye, sir." For the first time, Crow's happy demeanor burned away like fog from the morning sun. He studied me and I knew he was trying to guess what sort of witch I was.

"Those closest to me – those I *trust* – know what my circus really holds, Lilith. But they are the only ones who know. If word got out, my people would be shunned. Worse than that, they would be hunted. Their livelihood depends on the success of this circus. It is my responsibility to keep the hunters from stepping foot within the tents."

"I understand."

He chuckled darkly, his eyes full of mirth. "I don't think you do, but you will. One particularly deadly pack has had their sights on Cauldron for quite a while. I believe they might finally be close to cracking that worthless pot."

Forge tensed beside me.

"I'm sure you've told her everything, as she's so important to you," he said, a teasing grin tugging at the corner of his lips. I kept my expression stony so he wouldn't know how much the jab smarted. Arum folded his arms over his chest. "I came to speak to you two this morning but found you'd already left the wagon. I trust you found it comfortable?"

"We did," Forge answered. "Thank you."

Arum relaxed and leaned against the desk. "I have a great favor to ask you, Lilith."

Me? "What favor?"

"I've recently come to possess a rather large, constricting serpent. Shadow – the woman you saw perform with the horses and lion – has her hands full with those animals. I was hoping you could show off our most recent addition. You would only have to walk around with the snake draped over your neck. Spectators would fear her, but at the same time be completely enamored with her."

Forge stepped forward, his words low and sharp. "She has very little magic. Wouldn't that be dangerous?"

Crow looked uneasy. "Sir, that snake —"

Arum's dark eyes cut to Crow and severed his words. "Is harmless," he finished. "A constricting serpent squeezes its prey. It carries no venom." Arum gestured to me. "Besides, the decision is neither of yours. It is Lilith's. So... do you think you can handle it?"

This was a test; a trial I was afraid I might not pass. But what choice did we have? Serpents didn't scare me, and I only had to parade it around. "I can."

He smiled. "Then it's settled."

"We had another act planned," Forge tempted.

Arum took the bait. "Oh? What's that?"

"The Wheel of Death."

Arum's eyes glittered greedily. "We haven't used that in quite some time. The other Silverthorns aren't as sharp as you, and the last time it was used, well, let's just say there was spurting blood and screaming and..." he rolled his hand, "you get the idea."

I didn't want to be skewered, but Arum had admitted to Forge's power and control. If he let us do this, given the past show's accident, it would mean he trusted Forge to do it well.

Arum wore a satisfied grin. "The Wheel of Death it is, then. As it's rare, I'll allow it for both nights."

"We agreed to two shows," Forge said. "You just asked her to show off your serpent, which is outside the boundaries of our bargain. It's either the serpent or the Wheel of Death, Arum. Not both."

"Actually, I asked Lilith for a favor, to which she agreed without amending our original agreement, Forge."

Forge just barely contained his anger. The muscle in his jaw ticked as if he were chewing Arum up and was preparing to spit him out again.

"We will advertise it as an exclusive, two-nights only act. If it's enticing enough, they'll beg to see it again. I may set up a booth to pre-sell tickets for tomorrow on the way out."

"Your other acts are incredible. I'm not sure we can top them," I complimented, meaning every word.

Arum curled his fingers over the wooden desktop's rim. "We alter the other acts so they are thrilling – the lion will swat at his Shade if she asks him, roar at her if she pleads, or the Elementine girl who walks the rope will pretend to nearly fall to elicit a guttural reaction – but at the end of the day, many acts are predictable. Make sure yours isn't." His voice was sharp as a blade, sharpened with warning. "Shadow will find you to let you borrow one of her outfits, Lilith."

The Shade Shadow was tiny. There was no way I'd fit in anything she owned. He was sizing up my cloaked appearance, not me.

"Crow?" Arum said in a slick, authoritative tone.

My new friend stood up taller beside me. "Sir?"

"Thank you for all your hard work preparing the ship for its next journey." He produced a striped, golden token.

"Give this to the men at the door and they will let you and a friend into the show tonight."

"Thank you, sir!" he said emphatically, clutching the token in his free hand. "I appreciate that."

"I appreciate your *discretion* in all matters," Arum replied carefully. He turned to me and Forge. "I'm afraid we have business to discuss. See that you're ready early and at the tent by sundown."

Crow saw us down the ramp to the docks and promised to be there tonight to watch. The fact that I was a witch didn't seem to matter to him. Maybe because he was well-acquainted with Arum and his secrets. Perhaps he was one and wouldn't dare defy Arum's order to keep quiet.

There was a refreshing genuineness to Crow. He was just as enthusiastic about seeing me tonight as he was last night at the possibility of seeing me today. And though I wasn't sure his enthusiasm rose from attraction, as Forge believed, it was nice for someone to perk up about my presence and not just tolerate or include me because they were expected to.

As Forge and I left him behind trailing slowly back to the tents and wagons, I wondered about the hunters. Specifically, who they were and why they feared witches.

"Forge... who hunts us?" I asked quietly as we kept to a sandy section of shore that was empty save for us and the gulls who caught the wind overhead.

The sun glistened over the sand as if it was made of diamonds, the glimmering beams striking the sea and making it look like it was filled with churning shards of glass. Rolling waves pushed themselves ashore only to slip back into the water.

Forge stopped and turned to me, then cupped my elbows and leaned into my ear. "There are many who don't understand that everyone possesses a modicum of magic, even if it's been diluted over generations. That many farmers have the touch of Gravebriar blood that allows them to cultivate beautiful crops, or that the blacksmith hammering in the distance, beating steel into a sword is part Silverthorn, or the sailors part Elementine or Tempest.

"The witches who used to live in places like Westbrook and openly practiced magic weren't always good. They were greedy, some taking money for curses and elixirs that would ruin. People began to see them as evil, and then as dangerous." He stared at the sea. "That fear never abated and is the reason why some still hunt witches. But the hunter with his eyes on Cauldron... I've been told he seeks to right some sort of grievance. I don't know the specifics yet, but I'm working on it."

"How well do you know him?" I dared ask.

"I don't. I know one man who does. He is my only connection to the hunter, and he could've fed me a lie about the hunter's motivations."

"The witches in Cauldron haven't done anything to anyone outside the protective hedge," I defended. "Why would any witch help him hunt other witches?"

"There's a lot you don't know about the Council and Cauldron's past," he breathed against my neck, his lips grazing my skin and igniting a fire beneath it.

My fingers tightened on his shoulder blades. "Then enlighten me."

"I'm shocked your parents don't involve you..." he challenged, taking his lips away so he could watch my reaction.

"They never wanted me to know what was going on, and keeping up with the host of lies I clothed myself with took up all my time. As much as they were using the revels to distract everyone from my power, they were using the lies to distract *me*. I see that now."

"Why would they want that?" He tipped his chin up a tick.

"Because I could take away everything they've so carefully crafted. I'm the most powerful in my coven and they, and everyone else, know it."

He nodded as if he knew. I could almost see thoughts race through his mind, the implications of the healing Gravebriar coven being led by a girl whose magic led to illness and death.

The fact that we weren't made aware of the threat looming outside the hedge was bigger than Arbor's poisoning and my implication in it. This was dire news for every witch in Cauldron if Forge and Arum were right. There was still so much I didn't know; things Forge could reveal if I asked the right questions and garnered enough trust. I bet I'd barely grazed the tip of the berg lying under the water's surface, still as death.

Who led this pack? Why was the witch trying to tear us apart? What did we do to him or her? Hatred that vicious wasn't arbitrarily grown. It was sown and cultivated, nurtured until it became the fruit of the vine. Delicious retribution...

"Enough of this heavy conversation," he said, steering me away from the leaden thoughts swirling through my mind. His eyes suddenly glittered. He drew me toward the water until the cool swell swallowed my feet, soaking my boots. I couldn't help but laugh, then tore away from him and kicked the surface of the next wave so seawater sprayed him in an arc that stretched from knee to shoulder. His mouth gaped before his expression turned feral. "Turnabout's fair play."

He didn't kick water at me; he lunged, clasping his hands around my waist and hauling me deeper. I thrashed and laughed and tried to break free, scooping at the water's surface, but Forge was strong. My foot punched into the sand and knocked him off kilter, toppling us together into the water. Bubbles rose all around us, but he was upright and hauling me out of the water before I could enjoy them.

Laughter bubbled from my chest as I wiped the saltwater from my eyes.

"Are you okay?" he asked, worry creasing his brow as he looked me over. His chest rose and fell sharply. Water sluiced from his skin, separating and then falling from his dark lashes.

"Of course I am," I answered playfully. "I'm not as graceful a swimmer as you, but I do well enough."

He let out a sharp exhalation.

His hands settled on either side of my face. His metal eyes sliced into mine.

The knot in his throat dipped.

"Kiss me?" he rasped.

This was not just acting. It wasn't a playful means of ridding ourselves of awkwardness. This was something else entirely and he and I both knew it.

We were standing atop a boulder, staring at a deep pool. He wanted to jump in, but also wanted me to take his hand and jump with him. He wanted me to trust him.

Trusting him with my life was one thing. The poison singing through his blood was a safety net. Trusting him with my heart took far more courage. She walked a rope with nothing beneath her, and if she fell... she would shatter. If I gave my heart to him, shattered or not, he would own every piece.

I clasped his forearms.

Pushing up onto my tippy toes, I pressed my lips to his and let them peel away.

Yes, my lips said without a word.

A rumble of a growl resonated in his chest. He wrapped his arms around my lower back and lifted my feet off the ground. They swished through the water as he walked us deeper.

With every step into the sea, the waves covered us more and his kiss became something else. Warm. Wanting. Wicked.

As our lips searched, his hands memorized my arms, my sides, my back and neck. His thumbs traced my jawline.

Mine raked over his shoulder blades, right where his glorious wings had been perched the night of the revel. They traced his back and ribs, sliding up his chest.

We parted moments later, chest deep in the swells, panting, our eyes locked and still clinging to one another. My hands were fisted in his shirt. I wondered if the emotions swelling my chest and clouding my judgment were rushing through him, too. If I wore the same awestruck, terrified expression he did.

Gulls flew into the wind, soaring without having to flap their wings, crying to one another with a shrill, plaintive sound. The breeze tugged a feather from one and sent it to the sand. It tumbled until I trapped it against the earth with my foot and bent to pick it up. Forge and I were enjoying the sea, and I was searching for the perfect shell to take home with me. I wanted a reminder of this day, of this exact moment once I was back in Westbrook.

Forge's feet left larger prints than mine, but we left parallel tracks as we meandered along the shore. He picked up a cockle shell and held it out for me to see. It was beautiful – white with purplish hues – but it wasn't the one. I shook my head.

He chucked it over his shoulder as he had all the others I'd rejected.

"Are you worried?" I asked, the anxious feeling refusing to be kept at bay any longer.

"About Arum?" he asked as though nothing ever bothered him.

"For your family and coven. Are you worried they won't be prepared to fight back if the hedge is breached?"

"The covens' magic, if used together, could combat any threat."

"But they're so divided right now. It would be the perfect time for someone to strike."

He scuffed his foot in the sand. "Only if the hunters are aware of that."

"Do you worry about returning home? How you'll be treated when you go back? How your father will react?" I watched him carefully, but his expression didn't change. He craned his head back and looked up at the sky.

"Let's just say I'm fully aware that Sterling Silverthorn won't be happy to see me. However, I'm not worried about returning or of his reaction, and I'm not worried about my coven mates' support. I'll stand alone if I must."

"You won't have to stand alone. I'll stand with you."

He gave me a half-hearted smile. "Thanks, Gravebriar."

"You shouldn't thank me. I'm the one who dragged you into this mess."

He shook his head. "This mess was not your doing. Though I hope when we return, you will set things right, once and for all."

Ahead, something glimmered in the sun, nestled in the powdery sand. I followed its sunshine wink to the perfect shell, small enough to keep in a pocket, a shiny coral-peach with a small hole in the top. I beamed up at Forge.

"That's the one?" he asked.

I smiled. "That's the one."

TWELVE

Shadow, Arum's Shade witch, was waiting for me on the steps of our wagon, looking bored and completely put-out by the chore Arum had assigned her. She wore a simple cotton dress and her bare feet were crossed at the ankles. Dark circles rimmed her eyes and her hair was frizzy and wild.

Our boots squelched as we approached her, completely drenched, my hand wrapped in Forge's larger one. She stood and rolled her eyes, muttering something about the folly of lovebirds. "You need a proper bath. I smell the sea on you from here."

She trudged down the wagon's two steps to the trodden path that stretched and connected each wagon like earthen arteries, then marched down the small road to her own wagon, which was much more ornate than ours. Draped with wide swaths of black fabric that billowed in the light breeze, dark stepstones led to her door.

I left Forge behind and followed, then stayed on the porch and timidly peered inside as a puddle of seawater collected beneath my boots.

"You can come in as long as you sop up the water after your bath," she called. "Unless you'd prefer to undress outside."

I quickly stepped inside. A few feet away sat an empty tub, soap, and a cloth with which to dry off. Shadow's wagon held a small bed with dark blankets, a matching armoire, and a small table strewn with makeup. Vibrant wigs perched on each of her four bedposts while sparkling crystals dangled from the ceiling, refracting any light they caught.

A thin wisp of a girl with pale white hair, skin, and eyes ducked inside, slipping past me to reach the tub. Wordlessly, she stuck her hand in and began to fill it with water. With magic.

"Warm or cold?" Shadow asked as she rifled through the dark armoire where garments glittered and ruffles flowed.

"Warm, please."

The girl mutely acknowledged the request and several moments later it was filled halfway. Tendrils of steam slid from the water's rippled surface as she removed her hand and scurried away.

Shadow shrugged. "Her name is Brook. She's not the most socially adept, but she's kind and can produce hot or cold water, so she's useful." She walked past me to the steps and plopped down on them.

I peeled off my wet clothes and sat in the tub, quickly working the soap bar through my salty hair, washing the sea from my skin and replacing it with the scents of rosemary and cinnamon.

"Arum says you have little magic," she said conversationally.

I'd told Arum I was a Shade witch. As a young girl, I often wished I was.

Shade witches dealt with souls. Of the dead, but also the living. Their coven allowed for witches to soul-bind to one another, and many soul-bound couples stayed monogamous to one another for life, as some humans did.

There was no marriage ceremony or promises made. A soul-binding was much more intimate than that; evident in the way they looked at one another and the way they went out of their way to care for the other's comfort and safety. Bound souls didn't need words or jewelry to proclaim their status… they just were. It was a beautiful thing to behold.

When I was little, I often watched soul-bound couples. They would gravitate toward one another, share knowing glances, find reasons to innocently touch one another like contact was something they both needed and craved, but also was as natural as a climbing vine.

If what I'd felt in the sea kissing Forge was an inkling of what being soul-bound was, I couldn't imagine what Shade witches felt.

"Unfortunately, that's true," I agreed as I toweled off. "I have no discernable Shade magic."

"I guess it doesn't matter with the beast you'll be handling. I'm powerful enough to soul-bind to a lion, but this serpent has no soul. None that *I* can discern, at least," she added.

That did not comfort me in the least.

"It took four exceptionally strong men to uncoil the beast from around my neck the last time I held it. My face was purple and my lips were blue, and I saw the spirits of the dead all around before *they* pushed me back into my body."

My body went rigid and my heart stuttered in my chest. "You died?"

She shrugged, her dark hair moving with her shoulder. "Only for a moment." I clutched the cloth around me as she stood and ducked back inside the shady interior. "Our ancestors will restore you if you slip away prematurely," she chirped, pulling something out of the armoire. "This would be perfect for you."

I tried to tamp down the feeling of terror bolting through my veins. Her Shade ancestors restored her, but my Gravebriar ancestors certainly wouldn't be able to restore me if the beast strangled me.

The more immediate issue was what she held in her hand...

Dangling from the hanger was the skimpiest bodysuit I'd ever seen. "That is *not* going to fit me."

She waved away my concerns. "Sure it will."

She threw a sack at me. From it, I withdrew a pair of plain underwear and stockings. "Arum sent me shopping for you. The costume is a corset, so you won't need a separate one."

Joy.

I quickly tugged on the panties and dragged the stockings as high as they'd go on my waist. Then she handed me the metallic outfit. My cheeks heated as I wondered what Forge would think of the color and its scandalously revealing cut.

I shimmied to pull it up into place and was shocked that it curved to fit my hips. I held the fabric to my stomach and chest while Shadow laced it, jerking each strand tightly as the silken ladder climbed up my back. She knotted it tightly and stepped away with one brow raised.

"Perfect." I let go of the beaded corset and she grinned. "You look positively uncomfortable, though it fits you perfectly. I have a little bustle if you'd like to cover your backside."

"Definitely," I said.

"There's a mirror back here. You'll need makeup. I can do it for you if you want."

Shadow's makeup was rather...*theatrical* last evening, and I preferred a subtler look. No doubt she'd disapprove, but I'd be more comfortable with less on. "I can apply it."

I walked toward the small vanity and in the oval mirror saw myself as Shadow and the others did. Dark, wavy hair, a different face, and as Forge said, pretty, moonlit eyes. I looked like a woman who knew exactly what she was capable of, a woman who wouldn't allow a serpent to tighten its body around her throat and squeeze, a woman who would bare *her* fangs to any threat.

"You'll have to put your hair up," Shadow warned. "The serpent feels like it weighs as much as a lion."

She found the bustle and fastened it at each hip. A small cascade of matching dark silver ruffles covered my derriere, but beyond that, they looked amazing. I sat in front of her mirror and brushed my hair, gathering it into sections and braiding it in a swirl that started at the base of my head and coiled around and around until I pinned it carefully in the center.

"I've never been able to braid."

"I can show you if you'd like."

"I'd like that. Right now, I'm so tired I can barely function, but I'll take you up on that offer tomorrow, if there's time." Shadow pointed to a small tub of vibrant red, an undercurrent of blue pulsing beneath the fiery shade. "Men love red lips on a woman."

I wondered what Forge would think of the rose-petal shade, and if seeing it on my lips would entice him to kiss me the way he had this afternoon in the sea.

Shadow shoved a pair of shoes at me. Their heels were taller than most of mine at home, but they matched the outfit she'd loaned me perfectly, the same dark gray of glittering steel. They reminded me of *him*. The whole outfit did.

"I should find Forge," I told her. "Thank you for loaning me the outfit, for the bath, and the makeup." I slid my feet into the shoes, which fit me perfectly. How fortunate that Shadow's feet and mine were the same size, and that I'd been able to squeeze into her costume.

She shook her head as a husky chuckle erupted from her chest. "You're about to take on the first beast I've ever loathed. I'm the one who should be thanking you. Arum was insistent we use the reptile, but thus far, I've managed to sway his longings by pushing my lion to new, ferocious heights." She nodded to the door. "Speaking of Arum – he wants a word with you. Alone."

My bones tightened. Forge had warned me against allowing him to corner me.

Shadow noticed. "Nothing untoward. Just a question, I believe. Arum's one of the few good men I've met. All in our troupe are trustworthy, Lilith. The only question is: are you?"

No, I inwardly breathed. *No, I'm not.*

"Thank you again." I bent to collect my soggy things, preparing to sop up the wet mess I'd left on her floor.

"Don't. You'll ruin yourself. I'll bring them over before I bathe. There's a line from your wagon to the next. I'll tie it, hang them, and they'll be dry in the morning."

I thanked her again and stepped outside.

Arum waited in the largest of the three tents, dressed and ready in a suit made of chartreuse sequins with a top hat to match. Red and black ribbons ran down the outside seams of his pant legs and lined the hat's brim. He stood in front of a large wheel propped against one of the tent's poles, his hands folded behind his back as he watched the conjoined twins wash dust from the wooden monstrosity. Stripes in alternating shades of dark and bright green swirled from the wheel's center in a dizzying pattern. There were two metal foot pedestals protruding where my feet would sit, and two handles to wrap my hands around. Thick, but worn leather buckles dangled from the wheel, used to cinch my wrists and ankles to keep me from falling on my head when it spun around.

Arum slowly turned. Kohl rimmed his dark, fathomless eyes and he wore another fake moustache, this one thicker than last night's and uncurled at the ends. His skin pulled up beneath it, contorting into a sinister-looking smile. "Lilith." He gestured to the wheel. "What do you think?"

"It's lovely."

He quickly glanced over me. "Shadow chose your costume well. Has she introduced you to our stubborn serpent yet?"

"Not yet. She said you had a question for me."

"I do, indeed," he said. His mood was strange. He was almost giddy, but beneath the manic lay a hint of danger. "Tell me, how are things in Cauldron?"

My jaw locked. Why was he asking me this?

He smiled. "Forge said that things are relatively comfortable for the moment, other than the little tiff between the Silverthorns and Gravebriars – which he intends to mend with our arrangement. Not that the Silverthorns and Gravebriars have gotten along in some time. Do you concur with him about the state of things within the great witch city?"

"I've seen no other unrest."

He nodded. "Yet, unrest snaps at the heels of every witch living within its borders."

"Then it must also be snapping at the heels of every witch living outside them," I pointed out. "Not that you seem troubled."

"On the contrary. Things in Westbrook have been peaceful for far too long, which means it's time for trouble to descend. As such, we will be packing up and leaving after the show tomorrow night."

He was leaving after the show we agreed to finish? We couldn't let him weasel away without the information he promised. "If you believe trouble prowls so close you need to flee, why wait?"

He gestured to the stands. "First and foremost, I am a businessman, and my business is to feed and keep safe those in my troupe. For the next two nights, that generosity will extend to you."

"And afterward?"

"Afterward, you should carefully make your way home and advise your ridiculous Council that the hunters are working on a powerful spell to melt their precious, protective hedge."

I huffed a laugh. "Those hedges have stood since Cauldron was founded."

He leveled a harsh glare at me. "Girl, all things built will one day be broken. Only a fool thinks himself invincible. Unfortunately for you and coven Shade, your Council is comprised of nothing but."

"Then why should I go back?"

"Do you value anyone inside the borders?" I swallowed thickly and nodded once. "Then warn *them*, at least."

He watched me closely and I fought the urge to squirm.

"Your Council has ignored many a warning in the past. Perhaps they would hear *you* out on the matter."

My corset felt tighter. "They won't listen to me. I'm no one important."

He shook his head and chuckled. "Lilith," he drawled. "I don't know who or what you are, but I *do* know you aren't powerless. Some witches can sense these things and I am one of the fortunate ones... The flaming depths of your magic could consume this tent in the blink of an eye."

He was testing me...

176

"I'm not Elementine."

"Are you still claiming to be a Shade?"

I stood straighter. "I *am* a Shade."

"Then prove it. Master the serpent and *perhaps* I'll believe you."

I tipped my chin up. "You believe Shadow, though she can't tame him."

"My dear, you are not Shadow. Shadow does not lie to me." He turned away, his suit coat drawing tightly against his shoulders as he crossed his arms.

Just as I turned to leave, he called out to me. "Lilith, a word of friendly, but sage, advice?"

I stopped and turned to face him.

"Be careful in whom you place your trust. Sometimes betrayal cuts to the bone. Other times it cleaves the bone in two."

Shaken, I pushed through the tent's flaps, unsure where to go. My mother had warned me away from Forge. She begged me to run – far and fast. Now Arum, a complete stranger, was doing the same. *Was* he duplicitous? Should I run? What if he wasn't talking about Forge at all? If not, to whom could he be referring?

Shadow was outside, her voluminous dark hair expertly tucked into a bright purple wig, wearing a tight bodysuit the color of a plum's dark skin. The fabric was silken and the cut flattered her well. "Lilith? Are you okay?" she asked, drawing closer.

"I'm fine," I tried to reassure her, and myself. "I'm just nervous, I guess."

She gave a knowing nod. "Performance jitters. They get even the most seasoned of us at times, and this is your first show, right?"

"The first of two. Tomorrow will be the last," I replied shakily. My fingers trembled as I checked my hair for the thirteen thousandth time.

She waved me over. "Do you want to see the snake?"

Why she thought that might settle my nerves, I wasn't sure.

I didn't normally fear snakes, but knowing it had tried to strangle her – a talented Shade – gave me pause.

Still, I'd like to see what I was dealing with. "We should probably get acquainted before the show."

"The stands will be teeming with people within the hour. Not to add to your anxiety," she added hastily. "Look, I'm terrible with apologies, but I'm sorry I was rude earlier. It's a poor excuse, but I was just tired. My mother was Shade, my father Nocturn, and while my power favors hers, I'm afraid I took my sleeping habits from him. I usually sleep until just before the show, but…"

I wondered if she took anything else from her father. The Nocturn consumed blood and survived on little else. They were the quietest among the covens, but I wondered if that was true or if we just slept during their boisterous hours. The Nocturn preferred darkness and sought out the shadiest places and darkest of corners while visiting. I wondered if the light hurt their eyes. They seemed most at home in the heart of night.

A few years ago, a young Elementine went missing in the wood near dark. The Nocturn fanned out and covered the forest. One found her huddled beneath a tree, cold from the chill of autumn the night, and brought her home safely.

Arum woke Shadow – during her sleeping hours – so she could help me get ready. "I'm sorry. I didn't mean to disturb your rest."

Shadow shrugged, her sleek wig bopping with the motion. She led me past a large open-air trailer lined with steel bars. In the corner, curled into a ball like an enormous house cat was her lion. His lids were folded tightly, but he flicked both eyes open and focused on Shadow immediately. He purred, the rumble vibrating his pen and the earth under our feet. I could feel it reverberating in my heart's bony cage.

"This is Sarabi," Shadow said as he rose and shook out his mane. He padded to us, his muscles flexing under his shorn fur, the pen floor groaning under his feet. If he wanted to be free, there was no way this rickety cage would hold him. Yet, he seemed content there. Content with her. She held out her hand and petted his head. He closed his eyes and leaned into her touch. "Good evening, friend. Are you ready for tonight?" she asked.

He yawned and Shadow laughed. "You're as cranky as I've been. That won't do." I smiled as she waved me forward. "Would you like to pet him?"

I wanted to say no, but when would I get another chance to pet Sarabi, or any other lion, for that matter? Besides, a Shade would not shrink away, I reminded myself. I put my hand into the bars. The giant cat's paw slit the air as he swatted, almost catching me with his razor-sharp claws. His back tightened as he spread his feet apart and roared in my face.

I stepped back, putting distance between us, unsure if the bars would hold him if he wanted through them.

Shadow scolded Sarabi for his rudeness and then used her magic to calm him. He plodded back to his hay-strewn corner and laid back down to finish his nap. He closed his eyes again and let out a grumpy huff.

Satisfied that he was settled, she turned to me. "Let's hope the serpent is more agreeable." She looked me over. "You really have *no* discernable Shade magic, do you?"

"No, I don't." I wasn't lying about that.

We walked past a paddock where her horses grazed with a score of others. The fence panels that enclosed them were easy to put up, easy to tear down. After tomorrow night, this entire area would sit empty, the only evidence of Arum's circus and his troupe occupying the land would be the trodden paths and ruts made by his wagons' wheels.

Did Shadow know she was about to be uprooted? Would she mind? Persons living a nomadic lifestyle had to assume they wouldn't stay in one place long enough to become beholden to it. I wondered what it would be like to roam where I liked, when I liked. To see the world beyond Cauldron. Beyond Westbrook.

Westbrook was unique, and while I was sure many cities would look like it on the surface, I imagined each had its own flavor, architecture, and atmosphere.

Beyond the horse pen on a small rolling cart whose brake was firmly set was a rectangular box made of thick glass. The box's lid was made of metal mesh, thin enough that only a gnat could pass through its tiny openings. The box itself wasn't tall. I could probably reach down into it and touch the leaves and dirt that littered the bottom, or pluck up the twisted limbs someone had placed inside. Over one particular twist of gnarled wood lay the tail of an enormous serpent cloaked in an elegant pattern of brown, black, and white scales.

The constrictor glided across the ground and lifted her head to see us better. Her slitted pupils dilated, then contracted. Her tongue flicked out, sliding side to side to taste our scent. "What's her name?" I asked.

"At least you can sense that she's female," Shadow teased. "She won't tell me what she's called, and every time I attempt to name her, she tries to eat me."

The constrictor didn't have hypodermic fangs. She didn't need them. Her manner of killing was much more personal than a quick, fatal strike. She got to know her victims, intimately entwined herself around them, and then tightened and squeezed until she hugged them so tightly their blood stopped flowing, their breath stilled, their lungs unable to expand. Then the rows of sharp, hooked teeth would draw her meal in as she swallowed them whole, stretching her body around the prey until they became part of her nourishment.

Her girth was impressive. Neither Arum nor Shadow had mentioned that the creature was large enough to take in and digest a human.

"When did she last eat?" I asked nonchalantly as the snake brought her head toward the glass.

"A week ago." Shadow placed her hand on the glass. "She's probably hungry by now." The snake lunged toward her, stopping just short of the glass and flicking her tongue side to side. "She prefers the taste of hare, but takes great pleasure in hunting anything that fears her." Shadow removed her hand. "The key to surviving is to never show your terror."

She stepped back and something behind me caught her eye. "Uh… I need to go do something… in the tent," she said abruptly, then hurried to one of the smaller tents, quickly finding a split in the fabric I couldn't see from where I stood. I wasn't sure I'd see it if I was standing in front of it.

The sky was a muted, cornflower blue as the first of a few stars salted the sky, appearing as tiny glittering jewels. Laughter rose from the opposite side of the tents. Arum must have opened the ticket booth. Shadow said the stands would fill within the hour. Members of the troupe scurried in every direction.

Maybe that was why I didn't recognize Forge at first glance, or maybe it was his outfit.

He was dressed like a sailor, like Crow, but more dangerous than a storm at sea. His pale shirt was unbuttoned

181

at the top and loosely tucked into snug black trousers. A pair of black leather boots swallowed the bottoms of his legs and wrapped themselves just below the knee. Lining a blood red belt around his waist and two harnesses that crossed his chest were small, sharp knives.

Forge didn't recognize me at first either, but the moment he did made my pulse flutter. His lips parted and he blinked once. Twice. He snapped his mouth closed and the dark slashes above his eyes sharpened. I stood tall and proud, waiting for him with my shoulders back, spine straight, and my head held high. He stopped in front of me, then clamped both of his hands on my waist and held me tight, as if afraid I might float away to become one of those glittering stars and he was my only anchor to the earth.

A long moment passed and still, he was silent.

Musicians formed a circle nearby, tuning their instruments and plucking chords. One soundly beat his drum. Forge didn't look away from me to watch them. His eyes combed over my face and slid down my throat. Lower. He held me away from him a little, his gaze sliding down my legs to the tips of my toes, which curled in the pointed tips of my heels at his perusal.

Forge let out an agonizing, "Damn, Gravebriar."

"What's the matter?" I asked.

"I want to kiss you, but your crimson lips would smear and Arum wants us inside."

I smirked. "That *is* a conundrum."

"Quite a quandary," he said, his lips not turning upward into their usual confident grin.

"A dilemma, to be sure," I teased, smiling.

"You are being cruel, *Lilith*," he emphasized. Somehow, I knew that inwardly, he'd used my true name. Could feel his husky voice curl around each syllable.

"If you truly want to kiss me, sir, I'm sure you won't be deterred. My crimson lips aren't the only kissable place I possess."

He let out a throaty chuckle and pressed his lips to my jaw, along my neck where my pulse leaped for him, down to my collarbone. I didn't notice anyone near us until someone cleared their throat – loudly.

Forge peeled his lips from my skin.

We turned to find Arum standing behind us with an annoyed look on his face. "Forge, go help inside."

"With what?"

Arum's dark gaze cut to him. "Find *something* to make yourself useful."

I thought he'd been making himself quite useful. For a moment, I forgot the world and its worries and had just… felt. The warmth of his body near mine, the softness of his lips, the passion of his kiss, his strong, steady hands on my waist. For a moment Forge wanted me, and if he was acting, he was damn good at it.

Forge shot me a look that read: *be careful*, then left Arum and me alone. The flap sealed him in with a snap.

"You've seen the serpent?" he asked.

"I have."

"Are you still willing to handle her?" His brow quirked.

I put a hand on my hip. "I'm not afraid, if that's what you're asking."

"Good," he retorted. "Because you're one of two acts in the pre-show and you need to get ready. You're in the ring in ten minutes." He waved at a stocky gentleman who rolled the serpent's glass cage toward us. The snake did not appreciate the movement and struck toward the man, stopping short of the invisible wall again.

She was smart. She could sense her boundaries.

"Like nature's most vicious and efficient predators, she rules by intimidation," Arum explained.

"Have you held her?"

Arum chuckled, "I'm not a fan of serpents, and *this* constrictor would be the last I would deign to hold."

"Where did you find her?"

"She came from an ocean away. Shadow went with me to port one day when a strange ship arrived. A sailor urged us to come and see the animals they'd brought from distant lands; strange, wonderful beasts, he called them. Shadow bound her soul to the lion right away. It was an instant bond. The merchant insisted we take the serpent and didn't charge a single copper for her. I should've known then to refuse, but she is beautiful. Is she not?" He leaned down to better see her and her slitted eyes honed in on him.

She was beautiful. A lovely, deadly thing.

The musicians, satisfied with their instruments, moved inside. The hustling troupe made their way in after them, filtering into the two smaller side tents.

He stared at his tent as though he could see through it, to a spot in the curved stands. "It's almost time."

The gentleman at the snake's cage slowly removed the lid. "Easy, girl," he coaxed as she swiveled her head toward him, flicking her tongue to taste his fear. It wafted off him in waves, like heat over baked earth in summer.

"I'll get her," I offered. The faster I touched her, the quicker the sedative I intended to feed into her would work.

Arum's helper flicked a glance to him. He nodded, then ticked his head to the tent and the man ducked inside.

"Is the Elementine on the tightrope?" I asked.

"She's climbing the ladder now. Her show will differ from last night's, though. You will enter when I introduce you, and then you will begin the story I plan to weave tonight."

"How do you come up with those tales?"

He smiled. "I either find inspiration, or it finds me." He held the flap open and peeked inside where the torchlight seemed brighter than it had last night. "Show time."

THIRTEEN

I slipped my hand into the serpent's cage. She took a few seconds to acquaint herself with my scent before slithering her heavy body up my arm. Arum's brow furrowed. "Perhaps you *do* have a touch of Shade magic. Shadow never managed that."

Her muscles and scales propelled her up my arm, and she draped herself over my shoulders. I let a mixture of calming chamomile and red mushrooms slide through my palms as I laid my hands on either side of her body at my shoulders. She tightened her grip on me, curling her head and tail beneath either of my arms and holding me tight.

I pushed more of the calming mixture into her and waited for her to relax. She did, fractionally. I hoped it was enough, but in case it wasn't, kept feeding a steady dose into her scales.

Arum waved me inside where the Elementine girl was climbing down the ladder at the end of her tightrope. Her canary yellow outfit drifted on a slight breeze that reached no one but her. Not even the flames on the wall nearest her flickered.

Crow was seated in the front row. I could see him to the left, just over Arum's shoulder as he settled into the center of the ring with a flourish, the light somehow hitting his suit and making him sparkle like a firefly. He bowed in each direction and the crowd roared with excitement. He waited until they calmed themselves, until not even a whisper slid over the tent walls. "The direst stories are those of opposing wills," he began, waving me forward. "Because in the end, only one can triumph, and the other… must die."

My eyes darted to the ringmaster. *Die?*

The serpent, now calmer, removed her head from the pit of my arm and flicked her tongue toward the crowd. I wondered if the varying scents overwhelmed her or if she sifted through them like sand to find one she craved.

Arum had given me no direction as to how his story would go, so I just held my head up confidently and circled the ring, showing off the beautiful creature draped over me. She began to slowly move, creeping higher on my neck as she laced herself around my torso.

"There once was a girl, whose tongue was forked, breathing beautiful lies.

She came upon a snake one day, much to her surprise."

My eyes flicked to Arum, who shot me a meaningful gaze.

I didn't know if the Spellsweet cloaking elixir and spell was fading or how he knew… but he *knew* I wasn't who I claimed to be. I was the lying girl he spoke of… and that meant we were in trouble. I looked for Forge, forgetting the snake for a moment, terrified about what this would mean for him, for me. For the deal we'd struck. But he wasn't at ringside in any place I looked.

A moment of inattention.

An uptick in my pulse.

The smell of fear.

That was all the constrictor needed.

She quickly coiled her long body around my ribs and shoulders. I held her skin tightly, pouring a more potent poison into her. I didn't want to kill her. I just wanted her to *stop... squeezing... me.*

My ribs creaked under her pressure.

I took a breath and held it so she couldn't tighten further, so there would be room the next time I took a rushed breath, and kept walking, presenting her to the crowd. I kept my features schooled, though my heart thundered. I knew the serpent could feel its pulse, but I couldn't calm it.

Crow stood from his seat and slowly sank back down when the man behind him shouted that he couldn't see.

"*The snake, she tricked the poor young lass, into taking her back home,*

Then made herself comfortable among her things, deciding no more to roam."

The constrictor waited, holding me tight until I needed that breath. When I released it to take another, she squeezed fast, tightening around me and gripping hard until one of my ribs cracked. Fiery pain shot through my middle as the crowd gasped. Had they heard it?

"*The snake waited many days and nights, for the girl to warm to her,*

When she finally fitted the beast 'round her neck, the serpent all but purred."

She squeezed tighter. I gritted a scream, surging a paralytic into the serpent as a last-ditch effort to subdue her.

"*The snake, she killed the* lying *girl, and left her lying prone..."*

I fell to the ground, the constrictor tightening as the crowd hushed. I knew their reactions. Some would suck in shocked breaths. Some would cover their mouths and noses. None would rush to help me. They would assume it was part of the show, and I supposed in a macabre way it was.

My eyes sought Forge and fell on Crow's worried expression. He jogged toward the ring's entrance, calling my name, but two Bloodlings caught him and kept him from entering Arum's domain.

I blinked, trying desperately to tear the constrictor away.

I needed her... off me.

Needed a... breath.

My fingernails dug into her scales, slicing the skin beneath.

Arum's voice filled the tent once more. Calm and serene. Ever the storyteller, as I lay dying.

"The snake coiled on the girl's soft bed, after swallowing flesh and bone."

I will not be consumed.

I poured every deadly thing I could into the scales, forcing it beyond them, into flesh, muscle, and hollow bone.

The snake finally loosened its grip.

I was finally able to take several breaths as I lay on the ground, each inhalation sparking a fire in my bottom left rib. Tears pricked at my eyes.

Arum's eyes widened when he saw me. He motioned to someone lurking within the small tent and the torches went cold, leaving everyone and everything drenched in darkness. The snake's limp bodyweight fell from my flesh onto the ground as someone helped me sit up. My eyes adjusted as Arum crouched before me. He leaned into my ear. "Are you injured?"

"Yes."

"I will heal you when we are free from the audience's eyes."

I nodded once, trying not to move. Breathe. Speak.

He hooked an arm over my shoulder and helped me stand, then rushed me from the ring. Every step sent fire racing across my ribs. Each was worse than the last.

My mouth gaped in a silent scream.

Someone ran up behind us and took the limp constrictor out of the ring, rushing back into the smaller tent with its body. I'd killed it. I didn't want to, but I sensed that she wanted to wring out my bones and I couldn't let her do it. She was more than capable.

I held the ribs on my left side, wincing as Arum all but dragged me over the dusty earth.

"You'll be fine soon enough," he said sternly.

Forge met us, frantic and worried. "Tell me you're okay," he pleaded.

I cried out from the movement, the pain lancing through my bones, even as I stopped and only stood. Only breathed. "I'm fine," I lied as a sheen of cold sweat formed on my brow. "Where were you?"

"I heard your bone splinter," he said. "I know you're not fine. The only reason I was delayed was because of the conjoined goons you employ, Arum. I intend to have a serious talk with them later."

Arum rushed ahead and held the large tent flap up, and Forge helped me outside, where the sky had turned to the deepest shade of midnight blue and all the stars slowly crawled across the sky.

"Firstly," Arum began, "she knew the serpent would constrict, and my story was nearly over when it did. That's why I kept it short. Secondly, I thought she was only acting. And thirdly, when she needed it most, I *did* help."

My trembling legs supported my weight and my breathing evened out. I held my ribs, but the pain quickly shrank away to nothing. *That's strange*, I thought to myself. *Maybe the rib didn't crack; it just popped out of place.*

Arum watched, rapt with something he saw on my person or in my expression. "The pain is easing?" he carefully asked.

"Not easing. Vanishing." I laughed, still surprised. "I think I'm fine."

Arum gave a mirthless laugh. "Among the witches I suspected you might be, I never imagined you were *her*. There is only *one* witch who can heal herself, and I only saw it a handful of times before I left Cauldron. Every other Gravebriar requires the magic of a coven mate or a gravebriar itself to be restored, but not you…"

I warily watched as he reached into his fine jacket's pocket, removed a pouch, and blew dust at me. The spell I was cloaked in vanished like a dust cloud dragged by a stiff, magical wind.

"Castor Gravebriar," he said in a tone that made me feel like he was the true serpent, and I the hare he'd been hunting. He removed a small vial from his inner jacket pocket. "Drink this immediately and your cloak will return."

"Why would you conceal me?" I asked as he shoved the vial into my fingers. The glass was warm from his hands.

"Because no one else can know you're here."

Even though I'd lied to him, he was protecting me. Or perhaps he was protecting himself and his troupe. I couldn't be sure. His eyes darted around us nervously, watching for signs of anyone who might be eavesdropping.

I uncapped the vial and drank the sweet liquid. Forge nodded. "The cloak is back."

"How could it possibly be identical?"

"Because it's a copy cloak," Arum answered, staring at me.

"That means *you* can see through it now," I guessed. If a Spellsweet made it for him specifically, it meant he was now master over it.

He nodded once. "A word of advice, Castor: don't ever lie to me again." A shiver scuttled up my spine as he turned to walk away. "There are nine acts before yours. Take a moment to compose yourselves. And Forge?" Forge turned his attention to Arum. "That doesn't require your lips on her skin." Forge's brows knitted. "And as badly as you want to 'have a talk' with my 'goons,' Forge, I wish to speak to *you* later. We'll have a very interesting conversation, I'm sure." He left us standing outside as he ducked back under the flap.

Inwardly, I was panicking. Uncharacteristically, Forge was, too. Forge ran his hands through his short hair and brought them down to scrub his face. I couldn't bring myself to move even my smallest finger. I was frozen to the soil as I sifted through the memory of what had just transpired.

"This complicates things," he rasped.

"Forge?" I said calmly, though beneath my placid surface deadly currents churned. He turned to me. "I just healed myself."

Arum knew the moment it happened before he even saw through the cloaking spell. Removing the spell just allowed him to confirm it.

"I know. I don't understand how, but I know." He raked nervous hands through his hair again. "Have you ever healed yourself before?"

"I can't recall ever being hurt."

"Never?"

I shook my head. I didn't remember ever suffering an injury, especially not a broken bone. The pain was so sharp; I certainly would have remembered that.

"He knew from the beginning that I was cloaked and lying. He just didn't know who I was."

Forge nodded gravely. "I told you he was no fool. Do you want to leave now?" he asked.

"I can't," I told him. "I can't go back to Cauldron without the gravebriar."

He raked his teeth over his bottom lip. "Then the only thing to do is to get through this performance, then talk to Arum. He didn't seem like he wanted anyone in his troupe to know you were here. Maybe he'll give us what we need and tell us to go," Forge said easily, but we both knew our complications had just multiplied. I wondered how things were in Cauldron, how Arbor was doing, and if Mother, Father, and our coven were keeping him stable. Were things quieter there, or had they taken a turn for the worse?

"I'm torn," I admitted. "I need the gravebriar, but don't want to endanger you or anyone else to get it. Besides, you said at the first sign of trouble…"

"We've been in trouble since the moment we approached the ticket booth," Forge said wryly. "Likely since we emerged from the forest's edge."

"Well, let's go, then." I tugged on his arm but he didn't budge an inch.

"Arum might tell you now that he knows who you are. He's your coven mate," Forge argued.

"He just threatened you."

Forge growled and began to pace, battling with himself over what our next move should be. We needed information. I could take it from Arum and then we could leave, but I couldn't make a move while the show was going on.

Inside the tent, the musicians played a frolicking melody. The crowd collectively laughed, gasped, startled, and made sounds of awe. The hooves of Shadow's horses pounded the ground as she performed. She was the second act of nine.

Seven more to go.

Forge's eyes glittered with indecision in the cool moonlight. "If we're staying, I'd like to turn your costume into silver, but in the end, it's your decision. If you want to leave, we run now."

My brows furrowed. "Go where, though?"

He shrugged. "Wherever we choose."

But not back to Cauldron. And we wouldn't find the cure for Arbor. And everyone would think me a murderer. Perhaps then I would be hunted by those I considered friends, family.

"Why do you want to transform my costume?"

He pinched his lips together and set them free again. "I can sense metal. My aim will be surer."

"I thought you were confident in your abilities not to skewer me!" I tried to laugh, but it came out forced as all of Arum's warnings about Forge, along with my misgivings about him and the paranoia and doubt crept over me like the legs of a thousand centipedes.

His knuckle brushed mine and he let his pinky intertwine with mine. No one was watching. No one was there but us. Was he still pretending? It didn't feel like it. It felt so real it made my chest ache. Or maybe that was just the ache of a heart that desperately wanted to trust another, to believe that someone might want her just because. "I would never hurt you, Castor."

I nodded nervously, unable to keep tears from pricking at my eyes. "Change it. Let's go to Arum after the show."

"You're sure?"

"No, but yes," I answered.

He pulled out a sliver of silver and held it to the shimmering costume fabric at my waist, the other hand holding another piece. The last time he held me like this, his grip was steely. Now, it felt gentle, cautious as his power flowed warmly into me. The heat was more like what radiated from a cozy fire instead of the inferno his namesake evoked.

Slowly, the metal spread from his hands, coating every shimmering inch of Shadow's costume. I wondered if she would love it more or consider it ruined. Though silver was lighter than lead or iron, the garment felt heavy. The apple of his throat bobbed as he stepped back and took his hands away.

"It's almost time," he said. "Do you want to leave or go to the wheel? I'm with you, no matter your choice."

The wheel of death.

My heart skipped, frightened and ready to flee.

"Trust me," he breathed. "I'm more powerful than my father."

My eyes flicked to his, searching. "Why haven't you claimed the Power position?"

"For the same reason you haven't. I don't want it."

I opened my mouth to protest but he was right. I could have claimed it and there was nothing my parents could have done to stop me, but I didn't want the role. I wasn't sure I was prepared for his answer but voiced the question that took root in my mind. "What *do* you want?"

His brows slanted. "I thought I knew. Now, I'm not so sure."

"What changed?"

He laughed, but it wasn't carefree. It was rough and full of confusion. I felt it to my marrow, because I felt the same. "My life changed the moment you walked into the solarium, Castor."

His life? "My life was predictable until you entered the forest, and now it's one crisis after another!" I countered.

He gave a teasing smile. "Adventure, you mean…"

A tired laugh bubbled out of my chest. "It's certainly that."

Shadow poked her head out of the tent and waved us inside. "Lovebirds, you're up next!"

FOURTEEN

The conjoined men rolled and guided the wheel into the large tent and two silly boys dressed as clowns with bulbous, red noses and exaggerated lips ran to add support in the form of legs that attached and braced the back of it so it wouldn't fall or roll away. They took turns standing where I would, pretending to be caught with the knife and dramatically folding over and collapsing to the ground. One spun the wheel and flopped onto his backside, his expression baffled.

The crowd laughed at their antics. I looked away and took a deep breath.

"I'll escort you to the wheel and help you up onto it, then bind your wrists and ankles," Forge said just before Arum waved to us. The ringmaster's hat glistened in the firelight, a sickening shade of green.

We walked into the ring, the firelight dancing over my costume. The noisy crowd went still as they watched us walk, my arm around Forge's. He likely felt I was part constrictor, I held him so tightly. Forge clasped my hand and twirled me around once, winking when we began forward again.

"*Once there was a silver moth who fluttered 'round a flame,*" Arum lyrically announced as he waved to us.

When they realized who I was – the girl killed by the snake – whispers slid over the tent walls and rose to the pointed top.

She wasn't dead, she was only acting.

The snake is fine and so is she.

None of their reassurances were true.

Forge and I approached the wheel as Arum continued. Despite the cleaning, its paint was dull and the evidence of prior knicks and gashes littered the surface.

"*So taken by the light it threw, she never saw him aim.*"

Forge's hand found mine and he gestured toward the wheel. I stepped up onto the foot ledges and gripped the hand pegs as he strapped my calves and biceps onto the wood with metal clamps that locked tightly. "Trust me... I've got you. I already know you by heart."

My heart skipped, then raced away until Arum's boisterous voice sliced the ribbon unfurling between me and Forge.

"*He plucked her from her flight divine, and pinned her silver wings.*

To a piece of broad red oak where still she lays, but no more sings..."

The crowd looked on in fascination and horror, their mouths agape in awe as Forge took his position a few feet away. The fate of Arum's last story in which I was the actress had been realized. Would this one be, too? Would I be pinned to the wood?

Arum chuckled and gestured between us. "I have never thrown a knife, sir, but even *I* could avoid striking her from that distance." The crowd cheered as he goaded, delivering a pushing motion aimed toward Forge's chest, "Move back."

Forge smiled warily and shrugged, moving several more feet away. He pulled a knife from the harness crossing his chest and tested its weight as the musicians played chilling music. He gripped the knife's blade, raised his arm, and flung it.

I didn't look away or close my eyes, but startled when I felt cool metal against the side of my foot, followed by the reverberating wave rippling through the wooden wheel.

"A true marksman, it seems... That was much too simple," Arum challenged. "Can you throw two knives at once?"

Forge laughed, drawing two blades. He flung them before I could draw and hold my breath. Each blade embedded into the wheel beneath my elbows.

"Three?" Arum teased.

Forge launched a trio, his movements blurring, but his aim was true. One landed at my waist, the second impaled the wood at my collar bone. The third pinned just shy of the bustled skirt just outside my thigh.

I breathed easier until the conjoined duo emerged from the small tent nearest me. Forge nodded to them and they gave the wheel a spin. I'd known what to expect, but not being able to see Forge well made my stomach churn more than the spiraling motion. The packed crowd, combined with flickering firelight and Arum's glittering ensemble morphed into a kaleidoscope of colors and shapes.

Wood splintered beside my temple, my neck, my wrist, my ankle, inner thigh, and beside the rib the constrictor had splintered. Forge never ran out of knives because he could make more in an instant.

The wheel stopped and my vision cleared after what felt like a long moment. I almost wished it hadn't when Arum tied a thick, green swath of fabric over Forge's eyes, blindfolding him.

He can sense the metal in my costume.

Can he sense the iron in my blood?

Mother's and Arum's warnings resurfaced. Would Forge target me and excuse it as an unfortunate accident? If he did puncture my flesh, would I be able to heal myself? I imagined ribs to be delicate things, simple to heal. But a wound to the heart... could anyone fully recover from that?

They spun the wheel again and I tried to fight the panic that surged through my blood. I whirled around, tendrils of my hair dangling and then falling against my cheeks, only to dangle again. I watched Forge as best I could. The sure way he handled the knife, the way he bent one knee toward me. He knew exactly where I was. Knew me by heart, he said.

A knife landed at my jaw, the handle wobbling for a second before snapping into place.

Another found its mark above my forehead. Then, in rapid succession, blades flew, glinting silver in the torchlight. When the wheel stopped and I looked left, right, and down, I found a perfect outline of my body tattooed on the death wheel. Forge ripped off his blindfold and bowed as Arum gestured to him and then me.

The men unbound my ankles and wrists and helped me step out of the pattern of knives, each taking a hand. Forge jogged to me with a beaming smile and together we bowed as the audience roared louder than Sarabi.

It wasn't until we reached the tent flap and the fresh air hit me that I began to shake uncontrollably. He grabbed my hands and then abandoned them to wrap his arms around me. "I'm sorry," he apologized.

"You didn't hurt me."

His eyes held mine. "I told you about Arum and led you here. I put you in this position."

I shook my head. He was giving himself far too much credit and feeling far too guilty over our predicament

– however fortunate or perilous it would wind up being in the end. "I chose to go with you. I could've left Cauldron on my own and blazed my own path. If I didn't want you with me, I could've kept you from following me."

"It's less lonely and far more interesting with me in tow," he asserted with a slight grin. Forge ran his hands up and down my arms. "Arum is your coven mate. Perhaps he'll act like it now that he knows...."

We waited outside in the inky darkness until the final acts were through, until the crowd stood and clapped and cheered, and then slowly filtered out of the stands to retrace the well-trodden paths back to town.

Arum burst outside moments later. He removed his hat and tossed it to me, then peeled off his thick moustache and barked at us to follow him, his tone leaving no room for argument.

Arum did not reside in a wagon. Not surprisingly, he lived in an impressive, forest green tent hidden within a thin copse of pines. The tent was distant enough from the wagons his troupe resided in to afford them and himself some privacy, but close enough he could keep his eye on everyone in case there was trouble.

He pushed through the tent's heavy draped door and waved us in after him. The interior was sparsely decorated, as if Arum refused to accumulate more than he could carry at a moment's notice. There was a small, scarred desk with a wooden chair pushed beneath it far across the room. A few candles burned on its tidy surface.

A hammock was strung between two of the four broad poles holding the tent's roof up to our right, and to the left were a few scattered tables that held water, bowls of fruit, papers, and more vials in varying sizes than I could count. I scanned them to see if any held thorns or briars, but all held liquid. Could he have distilled the very thing we needed?

Without preamble, Arum asked, "Am I to assume you've run away from Cauldron? Is that why you cloaked yourself?"

I shook my head. "No, I haven't run away."

Arum stopped pacing and glared at Forge, then me. "You told me a Silverthorn was injured and that was why you needed to know how to find a gravebriar bush, but you lied to me. I want to know why. I want to know why you're here... I need to know everything." The threat in his voice was as plain as the scent of pine in the air. "You've endangered every member of my troupe, *my* coven. And I will protect them with my life. Trouble can't be far behind the pair of you. I'm just not sure if it will emerge from Cauldron, the hunters, or both."

The only way out of this was to tell Arum the truth and hope he would still honor his word. Forge flashed a sliver of metal in his palm. He was willing to do *whatever* it took to keep us safe. But violence wasn't the answer here. Arum wasn't threatening us. He just wanted to protect those he loved. No one could fault a person for that.

I shook my head ever so slightly and Forge tucked the sliver back into his pocket.

"A member of *our* coven was poisoned at a revel my parents hosted. I was accused of harming him and was given a chance to find the gravebriar and bring it back to heal him. My parents have no gravebriar left. It's been many years since one of our coven mates died, and it's my understanding that the only way the gravebriar grows is from the soil of a freshly dug grave of a Gravebriar witch."

He nodded once. "My only hope was to find the ancient graveyard of our ancestors, hidden somewhere in the forest. Mother said that it might still have the bushes growing there. Without the gravebriar, my coven mate will die. Like you, I'm willing to go to great lengths to protect him and prevent his death." I hoped he would understand my deception and that I hadn't done it to harm him or his troupe, but to save mine. "I'm sorry if I put you and your family in jeopardy."

Arum relaxed a fraction. "It truly is a family. I'm glad you understand and can appreciate that fact, Castor." He paused as if another thought struck him. "You." He pointed to Forge, narrowing his dark eyes. "Why are you with her?"

Forge stood taller as he explained the mandate he'd received.

Arum didn't appear to be upset. He was quiet, which made me nervous.

A flap in the back of the tent raised before a familiar face emerged from the shadows. Ecriver, the Spellsweet Power Parler's son, nodded to Arum and then to me and Forge. He was my parents' age, dark-haired with caramel eyes, and as gifted with the written word as his father was the spoken.

"She speaks the truth. A Gravebriar witch fell ill from poison the night of the revel. He still lies weakened in their Estate. The Diviners say he only has days to live."

"Days?" I breathed. "But Mother said she would keep him alive until I returned..." My stomach dropped. "Oh, no." I felt sick.

"What?" Arum asked, taking a step toward me. "What did she say?"

"She wanted me to hide in the forest, then circle around and sneak back into our home. She didn't expect me to actually do as the Council asked. She didn't expect me to be gone so long." Either that, or she'd once again lied to me. I pondered that as Ecriver told Arum how the Council had spent hours bickering about how best to handle the situation, of their decision, and what Forge's father Sterling had secretly ordered him to do.

Forge tensed beside me as Arum silently fumed, like a scab had once again been picked off a wound I didn't see him suffer. "Why are you here, Ecriver?" Forge asked, narrowing his eyes.

Ecriver stood a fraction taller. "Arum is a friend of mine and my father's. We visit often when he's nearby, as he doesn't travel this way often."

Forge didn't question him further, but the tension didn't bleed from his shoulders, either. He crossed his arms and stared at Ecriver as if he was a puzzle piece that didn't quite fit in the scene he was revealing.

"Your covens are at war," Ecriver carefully announced, wagging a finger between us. "The others are choosing sides. I actually wanted to ask you, Arum, if things get worse, would you take in a small number who wish to flee?"

Arum sighed, pinching the bridge of his nose. "Of course."

"War?" I breathed, still unable to grasp what that meant for our covens and Cauldron as a whole. "What happened?"

"It started with the pair of you, then the altercation between Valerian and Nickel. Someone retaliated against Nickel and put one of his eyes out. The Silverthorns accused the Gravebriars, of course, who denied the accusation. Now, the Gravebriars are refusing to heal him, which means he'll be partially blinded indefinitely. The Silverthorns have built a metal wall around the land of their Estate.

"Because of the violence and turmoil, each Estate has ordered the witches in their covens to stay within their grounds. Most of the covens have taken one side or the other. Only one remains neutral now." Ecriver pulled out the chair behind the desk, sat in it, and rubbed his temples.

"It's not even safe to walk through town. All the shoppes and restaurants are closed for the foreseeable future."

My heart ached at the thought of the lovely shoppes being boarded up, the galleries closed and paint-covered brushes stilled, the vibrant Diviner tents hollow and rotting in the elements, and the magic in the streets dead.

"Yours is the neutral coven," I observed.

He bobbed his once head to affirm.

Arum crossed his arms over his chest. "I'm afraid your mother sent you on a fool's errand, Castor. There is no ancient Gravebriar graveyard. No such thing exists. Gravebriars are buried in and return to the forest from which they draw their power, and the briar sprouts from the recently deceased's grave. It lives for one full day, twenty-four hours, and swiftly dies away. Gravebriar witches' graves are never marked. There is no magical place with rows of our dead and briars galore. We've never buried our dead the way humans do."

Disappointment and anger roiled through my chest. Mother lied. To me. To the Council.

Ecriver pushed a hand through his dark hair. "My father and I knew it was a lie. We did not tell the other Council members."

I raked my lip with my teeth. "Why would you do that? Why cover for her lie?"

"Because we didn't agree that you should be banished or killed. If someone in our coven had a power as unique as yours, we would've made the decision to hide it, too. We also wanted time to speak with Arum about you."

"Why would you speak to him?" I asked Ecriver, staring at Arum's stern face.

"Because *he* is the rightful Gravebriar Power."

Arum chuckled darkly. "But that's not true now, is it, Ecriver? There is *one* whose magic is even stronger than mine."

Ecriver focused on me. As did Arum. As did Forge.

Enough. "What happened to you, Arum? I was told you were burned at the stake."

"I was," he said simply. He moved to a table and ladled water into a small wooden cup. He held it out for me, but when I shook my head, he quickly drained the glass. "You and I need to speak privately, Castor."

"No," Forge snapped. "I'm not comfortable with that."

"Your comfort is of no consequence. My *granddaughter* can decide for herself."

Breath escaped my chest in a whoosh. "Granddaughter?"

He nodded and pursed his lips. "You look so much like my Rose it's uncanny."

I looked to Ecriver, who nodded to confirm, then to Forge, who looked as taken aback as I felt. He hadn't known.

When I looked closer, I could see Mother in some of his features. I could see myself.

Arum spoke the truth, and the truth, once uncloaked, could never be hidden again.

FiFTEEN

Arum and Ecriver left Arum's tent to speak outside, but Arum promised we would have that chat when they finished their conversation. While they were gone, Forge paced, tearing at his hair. "I didn't know," he whispered. "I swear."

"I know that. You wouldn't have brought me here if you knew."

"Are you comfortable speaking to him alone?" he asked.

"He has information we need. That *I* need, Forge." Besides, what other choice was there? I had a feeling Arum wouldn't take no for an answer. And then there was the little fact that he was my grandfather. A man who should be much, much older than he appears.

He nodded once, and that was all the time we had before Arum ducked his head back inside and asked Forge for a favor. He waved us outside the tent and the four of us stood in an inky darkness unbroken by stars or torches. My eyes slowly adjusted as Arum laid out his plan.

"My troupe has learned of hunters in the woods between Falling Waters and Southmist. I worry for Ecriver's safety, so if there's anything you can do, Forge… and if you can see him to the forest's edge just to be vigilant, I would appreciate it."

Forge nodded, then agreed to escort Ecriver through Westbrook to the forest's edge. I realized it was a ploy to keep Forge busy so Arum and I could speak, but I couldn't help but think it might be more when Ecriver swallowed a cloaking spell that transformed him into a middle-aged man with dirty clothes and stringy, thin hair. His belly protruded, sinking his belt. His stained shirt was unbuttoned, revealing a thick carpet of hair on his chest. There were bits of food stuck in that carpet and, to top it off, he smelled of sour ale with a hint of manure – which appeared to be clopped onto his boots.

With coppers, Forge fashioned three knives. "I made these, so I can sense them and know where they are... I'll be able to tell when you pass through the hedge and are safe."

He looked pointedly at me and I thought of the knife he'd made me. If I'd have kept it with me, he would know where I was. But at present, it was in my bag, hidden in our borrowed wagon.

I darted my eyes toward the wagon village.

He handed two of the three blades to Ecriver and extended the other one to me. I held it next to my thigh as Forge and Ecriver left. Forge gave one last grim look over his shoulder before disappearing into the night over a small knoll.

Arum told me he'd be right back, then entered the tent, rustled around doing something inside, and returned carrying a hand towel and copper kettle. "Do you still like tea?" he asked.

"I love it."

He nodded toward the knife Forge had given me. "I'm assuming your touch is much more lethal than that thing."

I stabbed the blade into the earth, burying several inches of it.

"You trust me enough not to carry it? You don't think I'd carry you away from that boy if I thought it'd do you any good? Forge Silverthorn's reputation is not admirable in the least."

"I don't want to talk about Forge. I want answers," I told him.

He harrumphed. "Of course you do."

In a small ring of stones filled with ash and old coals, he began to build a fire. I helped him carry wood from a meager pile stacked against a nearby pine. With nimble hands that should not belong to a grandfather, he drilled into a piece of wood until the quick motion produced smoke, then an ember. Carefully, as one might carry something very precious, he moved the ember to the kindling and waved air onto it with his hands. The kindling caught, followed by the dried, split wood. When the tall flames calmed themselves, he nestled the kettle onto the stacked wood and waited.

The waiting made me antsy. And I couldn't help but wonder how he could stand to make fire when it had once burned him.

"Why were you burned?" How could he even stomach flame after being scorched by it? Did he wear a Spellsweet disguise to cover up his true form?

"I was never burned. It only looked that way," he answered. "Your mother made me swallow a very powerful potion, concocted by Parler himself. It protected my body, even as the flames surrounded me. And it made everyone watching see my flesh melt away, down to the scent and sounds of sizzling. Admittedly, the smoke did get to me and I lost consciousness. While I was out, Rose declared me dead and asked an Elementine to extinguish the flames before she and your father took me to the forest where they were to bury me. Instead, the two woke me there."

"They helped you escape?"

His eyes burned like two dark coals. "Don't think of them as heroes, Castor. It was their ambitions that tied me to the stake to begin with. With me out of the way, your mother claimed the Power position within the coven. She just couldn't stomach actually killing me."

"Are you saying she wasn't more powerful than you?"

"She wasn't, and never will be. It drove her mad when she realized it," he said bitterly. "Knowing she'd never usurp me as long as I lived, or as long as I lived in Cauldron, she hatched a different plan. She told the Council I'd poisoned you – with gravebriar." He laughed bitterly. "You'd just taken your first steps when your mother stole the entire coven's supply of gravebriar, ground it up, and made you drink it. You liked sweet teas even then, and gravebriar is known for its sugary sweet taste."

"How many gravebriars did I consume?" I croaked, my throat constricting as if the serpent still lay coiled around it.

"Thirteen," he said, pushing on his knees to stand. He stepped into the tent and emerged with two matching copper mugs, each cradling a small tea bag at the bottom, each with a silver spoon swirling around its rim.

Tears pricked at my eyes. Arum's throat bobbed when he saw them. If he was right, if what he said was true, then the greatest guilt and fear I'd felt throughout my life *wasn't*. But a worse truth had been thrust into the light.

I didn't poison my mother's womb. She poisoned *me*.

Did she make me this way?

Arum wrapped a towel around the kettle's handle and poured the steaming water into our cups. As the tea steeped, its sweet fragrance filling the air, I realized he'd made my favorite: jasmine and chamomile with a pinch of lavender and a slice of orange.

"How can you possibly be so young? Are you cloaked?"

"Ecriver and his father are capable of many things, and their spell work has slowed my aging." He held the mug out for me and I wrapped my fingers around its handle, reveling in the warmth and aroma. It was a familiar comfort, something from home. He gave me a grandfatherly smile, something I had no idea he was capable of before this moment.

"Why doesn't Parler use the Spellsweet magic to prevent his own aging?"

He laughed. "Parler doesn't want the burden of such a long life's worth of decisions. He wants to live a natural one and be done with it."

There seemed to be a surreal, but severe divide in my life. The life and lies I lived before leaving Cauldron, and the new beginning I'd claimed since stepping out of the city's boundary. As much as I didn't fit in here, I wasn't sure Cauldron was home anymore.

I'd been prepared to tell the Councilwitches everything, then pack my things and leave before they could toss me out. Maybe that was my mind recognizing the divide and wanting desperately to cross it on my own terms.

"What are the limits of my body's ability to heal itself?" I whispered.

His lips went thin. "I'm not sure there *are* limits, Castor."

I blew over the tea's surface. "One cannot live forever."

He quirked a challenging brow. "There are a few words I find it prudent to avoid. Most are absolutes. Never, always... *cannot*." He sipped his tea, blowing over the surface to cool it. "Where is your grimoire?"

"It's safe."

He took another sip and stared into the fire.

I squirmed. "Can I ask one more question?"

"You seem to have a never-ending supply," he teased.

"Why don't you care for Forge?"

211

His eyes slid to me, narrowing a touch. "He is reputed to be worse than his father. Much crueler. Much hungrier for power. He's used others to advance himself. I believe he's using you to do just that. He will claim victory before you can open your mouth to address the Council upon your return."

I bristled. That sounded nothing like Forge. "You don't know him."

"Are you sure you truly do know him? I trust Ecriver and Parler with my life because they've cared for it. Their actions have never betrayed their words, and they've both informed me of truths regarding Forge that concern me. I don't want *his* past negatively impacting *your* future – in or out of Cauldron."

I opened my mouth to ask another question when he stopped me by holding out his hand. "We're no longer alone." I searched the darkness and came up empty, which bothered me. Sensing the danger in the darkness was the only way to survive it. "I'd appreciate it if you kept our conversation private," he said, sipping more of the tea.

The fire sent tiny sparks into the air as one of the logs collapsed, crumbling into coals.

"Your mother wanted you to come home alive – likely to advance her own agenda – but still. If she warned you away from that boy, there is a reason, and likely a valid one. Your mother is sly and cunning, but she recognizes a threat to her goals when she sees one."

He searched the darkness and I stared where he did until a form emerged with a familiar gait. Forge.

"What about the gravebriar?" I asked. "Ecriver said that Arbor is deteriorating."

Arum dumped his remaining tea over the fire, fragrant steam rushing into the air and vanishing. "A deal's a deal. I've explained that my business, and taking care of my family, is paramount. That said, you owe me one more show."

My fingers flexed toward him. "Do not consider using your magic against me. I am spelled in more ways than you can comprehend." He fumed for a silent moment. "The two of you should rest while you can."

I stood and pulled Forge's knife from the soil before giving Arum a weary goodnight.

He entered his tent and Forge and I left to find the dirt paths back to the borrowed wagon. At the edge of the pine forest, Nocturn kept watch over the wagon village, crouching on a limb like an owl would clasp it. His shoes raked across the bark as he shifted his weight, watching us as we entered its boundary.

The group of Elementines, the largest in Arum's troupe, held a small revel. Fire witches controlled a large blaze in the yard. They'd invited Bloodlings and the few Silverthorns of the troupe. Shadow sat on the porch among them, laughing, clearly intoxicated. We didn't linger, but I could feel their eyes following us. No one invited us to join in. Not that we would want to given the evening's revelations.

Forge peered into our borrowed wagon to be sure it was safe, then waved me in. He lit the candle on the table. I would've said he was being paranoid, but given everything that had happened to us thus far, I wasn't sure one could be cautious enough.

I removed the invisibility spell and took our things out of their hiding place; a small cubby that I'd found in the floor of the wagon. If anyone snuck inside while we were busy and peered into the space, they'd see nothing. If they raked their hand through the chamber, they would feel nothing. It was fortunate that I'd grabbed my grimoire before storming out after Mother to face the inquisition.

Distracted, I handed Forge his bag. When he stepped outside, I realized I couldn't change without some assistance. Shadow had knotted the corset so tightly I couldn't get a grip on the satin lacing. I gave up and sat on the bed, reaching in to find Bog.

My heart seized when I remembered he wasn't with me anymore. He was free.

He was free, but I felt a terrible pang of regret.

I hoped I'd done the right thing.

I hoped he was okay.

Thoughts tumbled through my mind like the swirling wheel of death – dizzying, disconcerting.

Taking out my grimoire, I flipped to a page empty of pressed leaves or flowers. The page dedicated to the gravebriars I'd yet to find. It was only a hasty sketch of the leaves, stalk, and briars, but I wondered if Arum really had them or was deceiving us. The fact that he was my grandfather still seemed so strange to me. And what he'd said about Mother...

How could she make me drink *thirteen* of them? Did she know I was poisonous before and was desperate to heal me? Maybe she tried one or two and they didn't take away my toxic nature. Maybe she thought thirteen would be enough to heal me of the magic that made me dangerous.

Unless Arum was right and her ambition was the reason she fed me the coven's entire supply of gravebriar. Unless she *wanted* me to be like this.

Or had tried to kill me.

That notion didn't ring true to me. My mother was capable of a great many things, but if she couldn't burn her own father, it didn't make sense that she could poison me.

Gravebriar was a healing balm to our coven. If its properties somehow became trapped in my body or in my magic, could I heal my coven mates, or only myself?

Forge came back in wearing a pair of plain brown trousers the color of rich soil. He didn't bother with a shirt and I didn't bother hiding the fact that I couldn't look away. I snapped my grimoire closed as he laid the clothes he'd borrowed to perform in on the table and crossed the space separating us. "Gearing up just in case?" he asked, not a teasing tone to be found in his voice.

I shook my head.

"Do you need help with the laces?"

"I do."

I stood and slowly turned my back to him. His fingers began working the knot at the base of the ties. When I felt it come loose, I held the corset against my chest as he tugged the satin ribbons – the only thing he hadn't turned to silver. I tried to ignore the feel of his warm fingers accidentally brushing my skin.

It wasn't that I'd never been touched. I wasn't poisonous in that respect, but no one had gone out of their way to get close to me. I couldn't blame anyone for being cautious and protecting themselves.

The night of the revel, Arbor held my hand confidently. He danced with me. But he did so because he was ordered to, because he thought it would garner my parents' favor, or maybe even mine.

I could hear Forge swallow as he finished loosening the top rung. "There you go," he rasped.

"Thank you," I told him.

He ran a finger down my spine, a whisper of a touch but not an accidental one. A touch that meant everything.

"I'll be outside." He lingered behind me for a moment, and just as I was about to turn around, I heard the swishing of fabric as he walked away. The floorboards of the wagon creaked, each of his steps making the wagon wobble ever so slightly. I dressed in the same long shirt I'd worn to bed the night before and with a wet rag, dragged the crimson lipstick from my lips and the liner from my eyes.

I slid my grimoire in my bag, tucked it beneath the single pillow, and lay down with my face turned to the door.

A few agonizingly long moments later, Forge ducked back inside and quietly lay down beside me. The candle flickered as he stared at the ceiling. I watched the golden flame play over his long lashes. He would probably ask what Arum and I had discussed, and Arum had asked me to keep our conversation private. As much as I wanted to trust Forge completely, my mother and grandfather's warnings clanged through my bones.

"Do you miss Bog?" he asked out of nowhere, closing his eyes, the dark lashes fanning onto his cheeks.

The swirl of heartache and regret emerged again. "I do, though I haven't had time to properly mourn him yet."

He rolled his head toward me. "He's not dead."

"No, but he's missing from my life and I feel the loss of him. I… when I grabbed my bag just now, I searched for him like I always do and then remembered that I'd abandoned him in the woods."

"You didn't abandon him," he quietly argued.

"It feels like it. I mean, I set him free. I know that. But I also left him behind and walked away. That's the definition of abandonment."

"I was never allowed a pet, or even a familiar," he said. "None in our coven are. That's one of the first things I'd change if I ever decided to claim the Power position. After making peace with the Gravebriar coven and those who align with them and melting the ridiculous wall my father has erected."

"What animal would you choose as a pet?"

He smiled. "A dog."

"I thought cats were a witch's best friend."

He chuckled. "Cats are moody."

"One tried to eat Bog once."

He gave a curious look. "What happened?"

"Once was all it took. She spat him out, but enough of the toxin had entered her bloodstream that she died.

She was the familiar of my coven mate, Zinnia, an older woman who took the matter all the way to my parents. They, of course, took up for me and quickly dismissed her demand that I buy her another."

"But you did," he guessed.

"But I did. The very next morning, I went into town to a pet shoppe and replaced her companion. I couldn't replace the bond they shared, but it was the best I could do. It wasn't my fault any more than it was Bog's that her cat died, but I saw the grief in Hazel's eyes. I wanted to try to ease it the only way I could."

"Your heart is golden," he whispered.

I laughed. "My heart is like the rest of me: poisonous."

He shook his head. "I know metal, Gravebriar. Yours is formed of solid gold, pliant enough to beat."

"And yours? What's yours made of?" I teased with a grin.

"Titanium," he answered, his tone strange and flat. I wasn't sure if he truly believed it or if he merely wanted it to be true.

"So it's impenetrable?"

"Nearly," he said almost curiously. "But apparently not entirely." He nestled further into the bed and folded his hands beneath his head. "Get some rest, Gravebriar."

He didn't kiss me. Didn't call me Castor. But I still felt the echoes of the pad of his finger drifting along my spine and remembered the timbre of his voice when he said my heart was golden.

It took me a long time to fall asleep, and Forge lay awake with me until I finally settled.

SIXTEEN

I woke while darkness still surrounded the wagon. Forge lay beside me. When I shifted, his eyes snapped to mine. "Princess, you woke before noon!" he cooed, booping my nose.

A growl tore from my throat.

Forge grinned widely, then drew his lips into a pout. "Aww, does someone need breakfast pastries?"

I perked up a bit.

He sat up on his elbow. "Want to go visit your favorite bakerie and take our breakfast to the beach? We can watch the sunrise."

"Yeah," was all I could muster. How did he look so perfect fresh from sleep, when I was sure I looked positively haggard? He laughed and threw the covers back. While he tugged his arms through a shirt and buttoned it, I padded to the water basin and splashed water on my face. On my wrist, something rattled and cool metal slid along my skin. A small, silver bracelet with two dainty charms — one forming an S and the other of Bog, right down to his suctioning toes and the dark spots that decorated his back.

"Thank you," I told him.

He shrugged. "Thought you needed something to remind you that he's in your heart, even if he's not with you."

Tears stung my eyes for a moment before I could speak around the knot in my throat. "And the S?"

"Silverthorn, obviously," he guffawed.

My smile turned watery. "Thank you, Forge. It's perfect."

I toyed with the charms while he finished dressing.

Last night was emotionally exhausting, but this morning, I felt better. Free, even. Arum knew who I was. Arum, my grandfather. Tonight, we would perform another show for him, and then he would give us the information he had. I thought back to the vials in his tent, wondering if one might contain what we needed.

Why wouldn't he just give it to us and send us home? If he cared at all, he would.

"Are you thinking about the gravebriar?" Forge intuited.

I nodded. "Ecriver said Arbor is dying. We need to go home."

"With gravebriar," he added. "Otherwise, our arrival will be unwelcome."

I debated the merits of marching to Arum's tent and dragging the information out of him.

"Hey," Forge interrupted my thoughts. "Let's go get breakfast and we'll talk about what to do next while we eat. If we're leaving, we'll need to gather a few supplies anyway."

He was right. When I turned around, I saw his eyes raking up my bare legs. I remembered his hands clamped on my waist, the look of longing in his eyes, and the tension in the balmy night air. "See something you like?"

"Yes," he answered without pause. "But I suppose you'll cover them to spite me." His lips formed a pout.

I shook my head playfully. "I'll cover them so as not to scandalize you, or myself."

"I don't worry for *my* reputation, Gravebriar. Feel free to scandalize me," he said, a touch of dare in his tone.

I rolled my eyes and crossed the room to rummage for a pair of trousers, coming up empty-handed. I sighed when I remembered where they were. "They're outside on the line. Shadow said she'd hang them out there to dry."

Forge beat me to the door and a second later tossed the mostly dry pants across the room. He lingered on the bottom step. "We should buy some clothes today."

"I have plenty at home," I said, tugging the pants over my hips.

"We're not there, though."

No, we certainly weren't. I hid our bags away, sprinkled the contents of another potion over them to conceal them, and jogged down the steps. We took the trodden pathway that led to town. I only startled a little when his pinky brushed mine. A little less when he made it clear he did it on purpose by doing it again. And when he took my hand and gave a questioning look, I smiled.

"Is this still okay?" he asked.

The beehive came alive in my stomach, their busy feet tickling. "It's more than okay."

"We don't have to pretend now that Arum knows," he baited, watching for my reaction to his statement. If there wasn't a vulnerable sheen in his eyes, I might not have been brave enough to tell him the truth swimming in my heart. But that sheen was so bright, I couldn't deny him.

"I don't want to pretend anymore."

Forge gave my hand a squeeze. "I don't want to pretend anymore either."

The owners of the bakerie brightened when we stepped inside. Forge ordered another round of everything and asked if they could possibly pack our food to be taken away. He gave them another full pouch of coppers and asked nicely if we could take their glass pitcher of juice with us.

They obliged happily, packed our breakfast, and handed the pitcher to Forge, again thanking him and me profusely for returning and for being so generous. He told them that he wasn't sure if we'd be able to return the pitcher, but they said they'd be able to buy tenfold with the extra we'd paid.

Now we were sitting on the shore, close enough to see the docks but far enough where we enjoyed a bit of privacy.

"I should've bought a blanket," Forge apologized.

"I like the sand."

"It's damp."

"I like the *damp* sand," I amended with a smile.

We ate quietly and listened to the gentle, rolling waves lap against the shore. Once again, the pastries were delicious and I ate until my belly was painfully tight.

"I like you, Gravebriar," Forge said out of nowhere.

I smiled and swallowed a mouthful of cinnamon bread. "I like you, too, Silverthorn."

He locked eyes with me. "What if I told you that I *more* than liked you? What if I said I care about you? That I worry for you and not just myself anymore. What if I told you I have no idea how you've done it in just a matter of days, but you're all I can think about?"

"What if I replied that I was glad I occupy your thoughts, and that I have no plan to release my hold on them?" My tone was haughty, playful, though a swarm of bees buzzed happily through my stomach at his admission.

The corner of his lips lifted. "What if I countered your reply by saying I'm not sure how to go about this? My entire life has been a falsehood."

I shrugged a shoulder. "What if I tell you mine has been, too? So, maybe the answer is to navigate the uncharted waters together."

"What if the waters are dangerous?" He scooted closer, swiping a crumb from my lip. His hand lingered, settling on my jaw.

I leaned in, melting into his touch, then ran my fingers over the back of his hand and brought his palm to my lips, placing a slow kiss in its middle. He swallowed thickly and closed his eyes for a moment. When he opened them, he breathed out, "Damn, Gravebriar."

Grinning, I reminded, "You keep saying that."

Instead of answering, Forge captured my lips with his. With his every kiss. Every small touch. Every gesture that showed me he wasn't afraid... he captured a piece of my heart.

We should have bought supplies: food, clothes, perhaps canvas and rope with which to make a makeshift shelter. Perhaps, we should have left, but decided to stay and make another plea to Arum for the information we needed. We walked back to Arum's tent, only to find it, and him, missing.

So, Forge and I decided that we would stay for the evening, complete our act, and try to hold Arum to his word afterward.

We went back to the beach and spent the day learning one another, enjoying each other's company as if the weight of Cauldron wasn't pressing us both into the earth. We stole a few hours and didn't regret our thievery in the least.

It was the best few hours of my life.

We swam in the sea, dried in the sun, laughed, and asked shallow and deep questions that rivaled the sea before us. We waded back into the ocean as the midday hour came and went, the sun drifting west. "I wish time could stand still for everyone but us," I said wistfully, trailing my fingers lazily through the water.

Especially for Arbor.

Forge floated on the waves until a larger one tumbled him. He burst from the water, coughing. I tried not to giggle and failed miserably.

"I have poison in my blood and almost got taken out by something as insignificant as a wave. One of millions of others just like it. That's not even a dignified way to die!" he sputtered.

"Does it matter if one dies a dignified death? The end result is the same," I laughed.

"It absolutely matters. Or it does to me," he answered seriously. "If I'm to die young, I want it to be for a great cause."

Not because of a wave.

Not because of me… my poison still sang through his blood.

My brows kissed. Did I trust him enough to dissolve the poison and remove it from him entirely? I wasn't sure why, but a scene kept playing through my head; one where I was being bashed in the head, struggling to see clearly through rivers of wet, sticky blood, my limp, broken body being tossed into a hole. Of cool dirt being piled on top of me, all the while someone waited above my grave for what he wanted most – a sprout to emerge and unfurl, bristling with briars along its stem as it matured. I could see fingers tearing each briar away, tucking them into a small pouch for safekeeping.

I told myself Forge would never hurt me. He'd said that so many times. Still, I wasn't ready to remove what I'd surged into his skin for safekeeping. It wouldn't hurt him for the toxin to stay in his blood indefinitely, and if I died, my magic would leave along with my essence, like water evaporates in the brilliant rays of the sun.

Another thought: If I learned that Mother and Arum were right to warn me against Forge, I'd have a way to defend myself against him. I tamped that thought down, deep into the dark heart of me. I hated that it even surfaced, hated I still couldn't trust him despite how desperately I wanted to. Would I always be this frightened of letting someone in?

"Forge, would you tell me more about the hunters? What do you know about them? How have you come to know so much about them?"

Forge nodded as if he'd anticipated my question. "There are a few humans who harbor prejudice against witches in every town, but they still tolerate them for the most part. Those who aren't tolerant form small packs and attempt to disturb a witch if they know he or she lives among them, hoping that if they disrupt her enough, she'll move along to someplace quieter. Some packs are formed as an opposition to our beliefs and how they contradict their own. Religion can play a large role for human packs. Many acolytes are taught and later believe that witches are evil." He paused for a moment. "Some religious packs are more violent. More determined. They're zealots who think they have a divine duty to rid the world of us."

"Is the pack who's trying to bring down the hedge driven by such beliefs?

He shook his head. "No. Religion doesn't drive them."

"How large is this pack?"

He shrugged. "It's hard to say exactly, but they have numbers enough that if our hedge came down, we would have a serious fight on our hands." Waves swelled over us and tugged us toward the shore. "Their leader is a man named Artemis. He hates Cauldron." Forge sighed. "Or so I've been told. I've never met him, but I've done business with one who knows him well."

"Does Arum know him?"

Forge chuckled. "I can't say for sure, but I'll tell you that Arum makes it his business to know everyone. Friends, witches, allies, and especially threats."

The sun sank steadily west, and while on any normal day it happened so subtly one wouldn't notice it until it had moved a considerable distance, this wasn't a usual day. My eyes tracked it across the sky as it ticked down the minutes I had left with Forge.

"Gravebriar," Forge said softly, taking both my hands. Waist deep in the waves, he stared at our clasped fingers. A tumult of emotions played over his expression.

"What's wrong?"

His lashes were wet, separated and thick. Beautiful fanned frames for the metallic swirl of colors I loved. "Once we get the information regarding the gravebriar... what then?"

"We go back to Cauldron when we have it," I answered confidently.

He leaned his head back defiantly, lifting his chin. "What if the Council doesn't welcome us back?"

"If we bring the cure, they will."

He shook his head. "They don't have to be anything but what they are."

"Which is?"

"Self-serving. Malicious. Power-hungry. Devious..." he squeezed my hands as if they anchored him. He could've gone on, I could tell.

"I want to take the briar to Arbor. After that, we'll see how we're received. If we aren't welcome, we can always leave."

"And if my father brings the charge of treason?"

"He'd be a fool. The Councilwitches would know he tried to circumvent their ruling and impose his own instead. If we bring back the briar, you've done what they asked. You'll tell them we found an old grave marker just before dark, and couldn't see well at night, so you made the decision to spend another day looking. You would've followed through with the order if we hadn't found it."

"And if they want to charge you with Arbor's poisoning despite you bringing back the briar for him?" he posed.

"They announced publicly that I could return with it – and that all charges would be dropped." They wouldn't dare risk public ridicule... I hoped. They did care about appearances and reputation.

Forge had good reason to be nervous, and to be honest, I had asked myself these questions. Maybe that's why I was ready with their answers. He'd revealed many things, trusting me with information I was sure he hadn't told anyone else.

"I always thought that I'd poisoned my mother's womb, causing her to be barren after I was born. In a way, my magic poisoned my coven. They never should have been asked to lie for me." I forced myself to meet Forge's eyes. "I'm not sure what will happen when we return – if we return – but I believe that if I walk back into Cauldron, my parents will defend me. I believe my coven will, too. Even if your father stands against you, would your coven not support you?"

"I'm not sure I want to be accepted back, especially by those who would stand behind someone like my father. When he told me to kill you, it wasn't to save Arbor. It was so he could claim the victory and take control over the gravebriar, and thus have power over the Gravebriar coven he hates so much," he admitted.

"What happened between our ancestors?"

"I'm not sure if it was one thing or many small ones, but I don't think anyone knows or remembers what actually happened between us at this point. And anything not worth remembering certainly isn't worth fighting over. But it's not just my father or coven I'm worried about. If

Cauldron's covens are at war, it won't matter which one we're from. Only whose allegiances align with ours at any given moment. There will be those whose Power chooses a side and whose witches take another. War isn't just coven against coven. It will pit brother against brother, mother against daughter, father against son, because both will feel that their reasoning is sound and justified, that they're right and those opposed to them are wrong."

"This battle has been a long time in the making," I whispered.

"It has," he agreed. "It began before we were born, but like the waves, turmoil builds until it can't anymore, then it crashes, dragging under anything in its way. And while our covens have been the most vocal about their disdain for one another, they aren't the only ones who hold grudges that simmer below the surface."

I swallowed thickly, imagining a wave taller than the clouds, angry, churning, and deadly coming for us. "You're not planning to stay in Cauldron, are you?"

"I'll see you home," he replied resolutely.

"And then?"

His eyes met mine. He hadn't voiced his reply, but I could feel it as clearly as I felt the water I stood in, the soft, sand shifting beneath me.

"Lovebirds!" someone yelled. I turned to find Shadow kicking sand up as she walked toward us. "Time to get dressed."

We waded from the water with too much left unsaid between us. Too many questions and too few answers.

Forge took our bags and boots and waved me on. "Go get ready. I'll meet you after."

"Arum has arranged a farewell feast for us all to enjoy before the show," she revealed, hooking her arm through mine and guiding me back in the direction that led toward the circus. Her dark hair lay in sleek waves that spiraled like kite strings in the wind. "I suppose you know we're packing up and leaving Westbrook after the show."

"Yes." I tried to memorize the feeling of sand between my toes. The way the sky bled red into the sea. The plaintive sound of the gulls crying as they caught the wind overhead.

"You could come with us," she said as we walked.

"I have an obligation," I answered carefully, "but once that's resolved, perhaps I can find you."

She gave a broad smile. "Perhaps."

We left the sand behind us and traded it for soil and sparse grass that thickened the farther we walked. "How do you manage to evade the hunters as you bounce from town to town?"

Shadow nodded. "Arum is usually aware or made aware if a pack makes itself known. He places a few witches in key areas around the town, letting out rooms for them so they can keep watch for the bulk of us. But he's also made a broad network of friends in his travels from place to place. Those friends warn us, too."

"They know what you are and still help?" I asked, surprised.

She nodded once. "All are witches, and they know Arum would defend them and their towns if it came down to it. They know that because we have. Once in Romena, a pack of particularly determined hunters began searching homes for witches. They didn't realize Arum had a troupe full. Let's just say their search didn't last long, and it didn't end well for them." She smiled breezily.

Our feet found a trampled path. We walked down the row of wagons that led to Shadow's. She squeezed my arm. "I have the perfect outfit for you..."

"I can wear the same one I wore last night."

"No," she boldly protested. "That won't do. Your act might be similar, but you cannot look the same. Besides, tonight is our grand farewell, and Arum wants this show to be something his patrons will never forget."

I remembered Arum mentioning that. He and Shadow seemed excited by the prospect, but I didn't care who sat in the audience. I just wanted this all over with and for Arum to spill his secrets.

"Forge is wearing the same costume," I argued.

She winked. "Forge isn't who the crowd will focus on, dear."

We stopped outside her wagon, lingering at the base of the steps. "Shadow, I killed the snake..." I said guiltily. "Am I only to perform with Forge?"

She laughed, deep and husky. "Oh, no... You're pre-show again. Arum has something fun planned for you. Don't tell me he hasn't spoken to you about it?"

My stomach dropped and the phantom weight of the constrictor settled on my neck and shoulders once more. "What does he have planned?"

Her eyes sparkled. "He'll have to tell you himself."

After I bathed, salt melting from my skin and hair, Shadow and I dumped the water from the wash tub and waited as Brook, the pale Water witch, slipped in and filled it with fresh, warm water for her bath.

I sat on the step, letting the breeze wring the dampness from my hair. From within her home, Shadow chattered about what things she'd need to secure before the wagon would be ready, telling me all about the vast variety of food Arum usually provided them as a farewell-slash-job-well-done to celebrate the end of one adventure and the beginning of another.

When she was finished and dressed to match me in a plush towel, she called for me to come inside and watched again in wonder as I slowly braided my hair into a swirl, explaining what I was doing and how.

"This will take practice if you want to learn, but for tonight, would you like me to style your hair?" I offered.

Her eyes lit up. "You wouldn't mind?"

"Of course not." She sat and I stood and brushed, separated, and braided her hair on either side, then down the center, binding all the braids at the nape of her neck. Showing her the final result in a hand mirror, Shadow couldn't contain her giddiness as she raved about it.

I painted my lips red with a delicate brush as she pulled a rose gold bodysuit from her armoire with a cheeky grin on her face, wagging her brows. "This will be perfect. I saw how Forge appreciated last night's outfit. This covers more, but it will show your every curve. It'll drive him crazy."

It *was* lovely. My fingers slid over the soft fabric, encrusted in golden and crystalline beads that glittered even in the scant amount of warm light leaking in from outside.

"I have shimmering powder for your cheeks," she said, dismissing me and telling me to dress quickly.

I pulled the silken fabric up my legs and let it envelope my arms. The bodysuit extended up my neck to my jaw, stretching to each wrist, clinging to each ankle. Shadow swiftly tugged the zipper up the back. "I knew it! Utter perfection," she said with a wink in the mirror. She swiped a soft brush over my cheekbones and looked proud at the end result. "Now, it's perfect."

Shadow turned and donned a fuchsia number with sequins on the bodice and feathers over her hips. Perching a hair clip with matching feathers into her tresses, she tugged it to make sure it was secure and then quickly applied bold makeup with angular strokes. Her vivid eye paint matched her ensemble.

"You look beautiful," I told her.

She smiled over her shoulder, her excitement palpable and contagious.

"Does the troupe travel to large cities?" I asked.

She shook her head. "Cities have large churches, and churches have guards who watch for our kind, so Arum keeps to smaller towns and villages. A single guard could take a seat at the show and know in a heartbeat that what they were witnessing was witch magic." She spritzed herself with a floral perfume, holding the bottle out for me to take a sample. "Arum made it."

The warning Forge gave before we entered the circus about not accepting anything from Arum or his witches rang through my mind. "No, thank you."

She shrugged and replaced the bottle. Her eyes flicked to mine. "Things look pretty steamy between you and Forge." It was my turn to shrug. "Have you been lovers for long?"

"It's fairly new." Not a lie at all.

"That's the best kind of love. When it's fresh and exciting and you can't get enough of one another." She turned on the stool and plucked a pair of shoes for each of us from her armoire. Rose gold flats for me, and fuchsia heels for her.

"What about you?" I asked. "Do you have your eye on anyone?"

"Goddess, no," she answered with a laugh. "I've had my heart stepped on and ground into the dirt enough times to know not to fall in love ever again. Not that the occasional tryst doesn't happen. I'm not averse to making love, just… being in it."

"Magic is real. Perhaps love is, too," I offered.

She pursed her lips and tried to smile. "If it is, I've never seen it."

SEVENTEEN

Shadow and I walked to Arum's tent together. Much of the troupe was already gathered inside, hovering in small groups around the counters and desktop where Arum had piles of steaming bread, meats, cheeses, and bottles of wine uncorked and already being poured.

This get-together was no grandiose revel hosting clusters of familiar strangers. It was so much better. An intimate dinner among those who valued one another. If our coven survived this storm, would this be the new norm for us, too?

Forge wasn't in the tent or outside it. I double-checked the faces to be sure. Just as I was about to leave Shadow's side to search for him, Arum crossed the space and met us, inclining his head to Shadow.

"Thank you once more for looking after her. I'll compensate you well."

The knowledge that she'd only helped me for a fistful of coppers stung.

"Save it," she said. "First of all, it's been fun having someone to dress with, and secondly, I owe you more than I'll ever be able to repay."

233

He huffed a laugh. "You never know what I might ask of you in the future."

"As long as it's not during her resting hours, it'll be fine," I teased, chiming in.

She groaned but didn't disagree. Arum laughed heartily, wagging a finger at me. "You've already learned her habits, and in such a short time."

Forge ducked beneath the tent flap just as Arum invited me to eat with him. His gaze found me immediately, the apple in his throat bobbing as he took me in. "Someone likes what he sees," Shadow giggled into my ear before threading her arm through Arum's and leading him toward the feast.

Forge was quiet as he approached, wearing the same borrowed clothes as he'd donned last night. As he reached me, his brows met and the muscle in his jaw worked. He looked over my head, scanning everything and everyone but me.

"What is it?" I asked, wondering what was wrong.

He leaned in so no one else could hear. "I'm trying really hard not to say, '*Damn, Gravebriar*'."

I laughed. "I think you just did." He hung his head as if in shame, his smile on full display. "I'm glad you like it."

"Understatement," he replied, placing a soft kiss in my hair. His hand curled around my waist and he began to sway, as if the musicians were playing something soft and sweet and he couldn't help but dance with me.

I swayed with him, completely intoxicated. Completely entranced.

"Are you hungry?" he asked.

"Is that even a question? You said not to accept food or drink…"

"They're all eating it, so it should be safe enough. Plus, I have my own poison tester with me today." I shook my head and huffed a laugh I couldn't suppress. He grinned. "Did you hide our things?"

"Yes," I replied, clasping his hand.

We walked to the tables, taking enough to sate our hunger. Arum met us at his desk, holding two copper cups of wine. We accepted them, of course, but while he turned to lead us to where he sat, I placed a finger in each to make sure they were free of poisons. They were.

Arum settled on the floor next to a Bloodling and a few fire Elementines. I felt warmth pour off them as we joined them and I sat between Forge and Shadow. Arum muttered something to Shadow. She laughed huskily in response. "Oh, no. *You* tell them."

Arum's eyes glittered as he turned to look at me and Forge. "I was hoping I'd entice the two of you to help with a little pre-show entertainment."

Forge did not smile. "If it involves the lion, the answer is no."

"It involves no lions, but instead requires your particular skillset, Forge Silverthorn," Arum answered, sipping his wine. "I'd like to resurrect the crossbow."

Forge stopped chewing mid-bite, then chewed until it was gone. "You want to make her a human arrow," he deadpanned.

"Arrow?" I butted in.

Forge's steely eyes never left Arum's as he explained, "The crossbow is an enormous version of its namesake and shoots witches as arrows."

"What catches me?" I asked, my curiosity thoroughly piqued. The two men stared at one another as if no one and nothing else existed, a battle of wills raging between them. But it wasn't their decision. It was mine. "Arum, what would catch me if I chose to be shot?" I asked pointedly.

He slid his attention to me, a sly smile tugging at his lips. "Forge would."

I laughed. "He can't catch me! The impact alone..."

Arum looked to Forge. "That's not true now, is it, Mr. Silverthorn?"

Beside me, Forge was like stone. He flicked a sideways glance at me. "I can do it. You wouldn't get hurt."

"And you?"

"I wouldn't be injured either."

"Then let's do it," I said, excitement flooding my veins and making my heart skip. I wanted to know what it felt like to fly. To taste true freedom. Just once.

We were about to head back to Cauldron, and the very thought made me feel like a firefly trapped in the solarium for aesthetic purposes.

I silently pleaded with Forge until he gave the slightest nod, pursing his lips tightly together.

Arum seemed pleased. He stood to give a toast to his troupe for all their excellent performances and for being so resilient, and raised his glass to new adventures and prosperity.

Some left after his speech. Others lingered. Forge tugged me outside. "I can't turn this suit to actual gold. Gold isn't a heavy metal, but it's heavier than this fabric. I can turn the beads to gold if you'll allow it, though."

"Of course."

He placed his hands on my upper arms where clusters of beads trailed down my biceps. A warmth slid from his palms, oozed down my arms, spread across my collar bones and shoulder blades, and radiated down my body, turning each crystalline bead heavier. "I'll know where you are. I'll catch you."

I nodded.

"After you fly, I'll turn your suit golden before you take to the wheel."

"Are you worried you'll make a mistake? Why bother with this?"

"I'm confident in my power, Gravebriar, but I'd rather not chance even the slightest mistake. Besides, you look amazing in metals..." He kissed the corner of my mouth.

My fingers drifted up his chest and my thumbs raked his unshaven jaw, the short whiskers rough against my skin. The sun had set, and again, we stood in the twilight wanting more. More time. More touch. More of us, and less of the world and all its demands. "Why does it feel like we're stuck in an hourglass with sand draining away beneath our feet and time tugging us toward the bottom?"

"Because there will never be enough time for us to spend together," he said softly into my ear, tickling the hair on my neck. I tilted my head to meet his eyes and inched toward him, slowly... "An eternity wouldn't be enough."

My heart leaped toward him, clearly agreeing with the sentiment.

"The show is about to begin," announced the surly conjoined twin. "We'll show you where to stand and the two of us will fire the crossbow." He jerked a thumb toward the tent and to Forge said, "You need to wait on the other side."

Forge squeezed my waist once. "I've got you. I promise."

He left to walk to the other side. Inside, the musicians' song danced from their instruments, lively and enchanting. Perhaps Arum took spelled instruments from Cauldron before he left, or maybe Ecriver smuggled them to him.

The brothers held up the tent flap and the three of us ducked inside. The smell of smoke and popped corn and ale filled the space. From the smaller tent, we watched the tightrope walker traverse the entire length of her rope by walking on her hands, then return across the ceiling in a series of jumps and flips. This was her grand finale; her farewell and a chance to showcase what she was really capable of. Gone were the fake flubs and missteps. She knew the rope like she knew her own skin. It was as much a part of her as she was part of the air that enveloped her.

Nearby, the enormous crossbow was already in position, aimed to shoot me into the tip top of the tent. The great contraption was made of thick wood and metal. I wondered which Silverthorn had constructed its firing mechanism and hoped it was someone with great skill.

The audience's applause made me look up and away from the bow.

The Elementine girl was magnificent, taking her time and pushing the limits of what might be considered natural. My eyes drifted over the audience. The torchlight and shadow mixture somehow seemed harsher this evening. If Crow had been allowed to come back, I didn't see him seated where he was yesterday. I couldn't find his face anywhere among those seated, their attention wrapped around the aerialist's little finger.

The conjoined brothers, Merc and Ury, from what I'd overheard – they never bothered to introduce themselves and hadn't seemed interested in conversing with me while we waited – chatted amongst themselves in a language I didn't recognize. I wondered if it was from some faraway place or if they'd made their own language.

When the tightrope walking Elementine finished, she gave sweet bows, soaking up all the praise she could with a delighted smile on her face, her chest rising and crashing. She deftly descended the rope ladder, and someone unclipped her rope from the top and climbed down a ladder propped precariously against the tent's side wall, a coil of rope between her feet. A swirl of Bloodlings collected and wound the rope, placing the pile behind the stands.

"Arum doesn't want you to hit that," the friendlier brother Merc, teased, elbowing me.

"Come on," Ury grunted, jerking his head toward the bow.

It was much larger and taller, much more intimidating, when one stood beside it. Arum was already waiting there. "Are you ready?"

"As ready as I'm going to be."

"Remain calm, Lilith," he enunciated. "I wouldn't endanger you, and surprisingly, neither would Forge. I'm still not sure how you tamed that beast. Must be the Shade magic in you."

The conjoined brothers snorted simultaneously. "No kidding," Merc agreed.

Ury added. "Not sure how you put up with someone like him."

Arum tutted at his men. "He's been perfectly well-mannered during this visit. Surely, you aren't insinuating that he's putting on a show for our sweet Lilith, boys."

The surly one gave him a knowing look, then shot me one of warning.

Forge waited across the tent, standing between two sets of bleachers. He met my eyes and smiled confidently. "I'll catch you," he mouthed, holding his hands out to emphasize it.

I nodded once and tried to smile. Sucking in a deep breath, I tried to calm my racing heart and slid my sweaty palms down the clingy fabric of my bodysuit.

Shadow stood far behind Forge with an encouraging smile on her face. She gave me two thumbs up.

"Is this tied to one of your stories?" I asked Arum.

He chuckled. "Of course it is. You've inspired many, my dear." Arum waited as the musicians' song ended and waltzed to the tent's middle. "Good evening, ladies and gentlemen! I'll be your ringmaster on this fine evening. Tell me, are you having a marvelous time?"

The crowd clapped, whistled, and shouted their excitement.

Arum smiled graciously, holding his arms out at his sides and spinning in a circle so all could see him. Tonight, he wore a dark green hat and suit, so dark they could almost be mistaken for black in this lighting, but I could see the telltale hue refusing to be swallowed by the darkness. "This is our last night in Westbrook, I'm afraid. So, how about we go out with a bang!"

Again, they cheered. And when he lowered his hands to his sides, the audience quieted.

"There once was a girl who wanted, desperately to touch the stars.

She set her thoughts on nothing near, but only looked afar..."

He gestured to me.

I gave a wave and a smile as the brothers escorted me up a small set of steps and told me where to stand on a metal platform. "Lie on your stomach on the metal chute," Merc whispered. I lowered myself onto my stomach. "Arms plastered to your side. Imagine yourself an arrow," he instructed. "And try to stay in this position in the air."

"Her beau knew deep within his heart, with the heavens he could never compete.

So he helped her build a crossbow, her dream she then could seek."

He swept a hand to Forge, who stepped into the ring, looking daring and bold in the firelight made brighter by the Elementine controlling the flames.

Our eyes met across the space and I could almost hear him plead for me to trust him. I took a deep breath as the brothers moved behind the firing mechanism and waited for Arum's signal.

"The girl took a deep breath, and readied her empty hands.

Then fired herself into the sky, to catch a starlight strand."

One moment I was lying in the chute, my heart thundering, balmy palms pressed against my thighs, staring up at the tent's ceiling. The next, a loud *thwang* came from behind and I was launched upward.

I ripped through the air, soaring so high I could almost reach the tent's top. I couldn't help but smile and reach out. My fingers came so, so close to the canvas.

But like everything that goes up, my momentum slowed and I began to fall. My stomach, which had soared thus far, dropped and sheer terror crept into my bones. My heart tore at her cage. I tried to remain straight, like an arrow, but it didn't matter my form when I began to plummet. I searched for Forge but only saw the blur of the crowd and the rich earthen circle under me.

Panic set in.

Arum's words barely registered.

"Her beau kept watch as she pierced a cloud, dragged her fingers through a star.

And when she fell to earth again, he caught her in his arms."

The impact rattled my bones. Trembling so hard my teeth clattered, I looked up to see Forge's face hovering over mine. His hands readjusted so he could hold me better. "You're okay. I've got you," he promised. But I heard the strain in his voice and the tight breaths he heaved, his heart beating a terrible staccato that matched mine.

The crowd stood and applauded. Their shrill whistles cut through the air.

Forge placed my feet on the ground and made sure I could hold myself upright before we began to bow. "So?" he said, his metallic eyes glittering.

My knees were water, my teeth chattered. I couldn't control my shaking hands.

"So what?" I asked.

"What was it like to fly?"

"Flying was everything I thought it might be. It was the fall that frightened me."

EiGHTEEN

Outside, Forge wrapped me in his arms and kissed my forehead, cheek, lips. His fingers trembled against my sides. I squeezed the blades of his shoulders and kissed his jaw. "One more act," I told him.

"One more act."

He used his magic to turn my suit into gold. It wasn't solid, but malleable, like he'd infused the element into every strand that knit the bodysuit together. I wondered if that was how he felt me, as a gridwork of threads. Delicately spun chain mail. I wondered if he questioned whether I might unravel. After the last act, I wondered the same thing.

"Arum won't goad me like he did last night. He'll want something grander. It's the final show in Westbrook, and he and his troupe won't come back for quite some time." As much as I'd wished time would stand still for us at the beach, I now wished it would speed ahead. I wanted this night to be over with.

"Are we up soon?" I asked as he picked up the harness of throwing knives and strapped it on.

"We're last. Arum wanted to give us time to 'collect ourselves,'" he mimicked in Arum's slick tone.

"Do you want to go watch Shadow and the others?" I asked. "It might distract me from the panic rattling my bones."

He took my hand, and together we walked back into the small tent and stood among the others. As Arum introduced Shadow and Sarabi, the lion let out a great roar when they entered the ring, the young witch riding on the beast's back as if he were one of her horses.

A swell of laughter bubbled from my chest. "She's amazing!"

"Quite a powerful Shade," he added, assessing her as she guided Sarabi around the ring and dismounted.

She took the great cat through a series of tricks where it leaped over her as she crouched low on the ground, then as she only crouched a little, then Sarabi bounded over her head as she stood straight, not bending at all.

Suddenly, Forge's hand clenched mine.

He went still, his face pale. "We need to speak to Arum. *Now.*"

Arum was waiting for Shadow to finish her performance, lingering on the other side of the tent, just outside the ring itself.

He clasped my hand and pulled me outside, and we ran around the tent, carefully avoiding the staked ropes. "What's wrong? Why now?"

"It's urgent." Our feet pounded the ground and we were around the tent in no time.

"What is?" I asked as he pulled me through a tent flap. We pushed through a few Elementines gathered to watch the show and came up behind Arum. He turned with his arms crossed, looking annoyed until he saw Forge's expression. I could almost see his hackles raise.

"Were you expecting Ecriver to return?" Forge asked.

"No," Arum replied gravely. "Not unless something happened and he wanted to catch me before I left again."

"He's at the edge of the forest. Stopped. He isn't moving. Hunters are near him..."

Arum considered what Forge had revealed. He waved over a Bloodling and told him to find Crow and ask Crow to search the edge of the forest in the direction of Cauldron. The Bloodling nodded and scurried out of the tent.

Arum questioned Forge, "Have you seen anyone you know, Forge? And before you lie, you know exactly what I mean."

He shook his head. "No one."

"Well, at least there's that."

"If they attack during a show..." Forge led.

Arum's eyes flicked to me. "It'll be a blood bath, and all of Westbrook will know what we are. Word will spread faster than plagues and wildfire combined. There will be no place safe for us. And the circus will die along with us."

Sarabi roared again, drawing our attention as Shadow rode him out of the ring. Arum looked to Merc and Ury, whom I hadn't realized were standing behind us. "Don't let her out of your sight."

They nodded succinctly.

Arum stepped into the ring and a swarm of Elementines breathing, twirling, and spinning fire stepped in, surrounding him. He met my eyes. Held them. Then spoke.

"Long ago, there was a Rose, she bloomed with beauty and grace..."

I knew he meant my mother.

"She cared not for anything as shallow, as her lovely and pretty face.

"The rose knew that she would be plucked, by a hand who might toss her away," he intoned.

The fire spinners used their magic to form fiery roses as the crowd gasped and clapped. Ooohs and aahs came from all around.

"So she lined her stem with briars, sharp as glass, to keep the hand at bay."

The tent went dark; all the torches along the wall and the Elementines' flames were extinguished at once, tendrils of acrid smoke filling the air.

Then, from the ground in the center of the ring, a red rose grew as Arum used his power. The fire Elementines lit the ring again and shadows danced across Arum's face.

"The tiny briars, the poison and cure, pricked the hand of those who loved her.

"But the Rose cared not and passed the briars on to her buddling, for the Rose was to be a mother…"

The scent of roses filled the air as petals in every natural color rained from the ceiling. No one questioned how. They just lifted hands to catch the them, bringing full hands to their noses. Some threw their bounty while others tucked them away to take home with them.

My bones felt like stone. I replayed Arum's verses. They made no sense…

Forge turned from the scene to face me with an incredulous look. "Do you know where to find it? Have you known all along?"

I shook my head. *How could he ask me that after all we've been through?* "I don't know anything!"

"That's not what Arum just insinuated," he accused.

I shook my head. "I don't know where to find it, Forge. I swear."

He nodded once, but in his eyes, there was distrust. I'd seen it many times before in the faces of those I knew, but never before in Forge's. He had walked into the forest believing in my innocence.

My stomach turned at the sight.

Shadow came to stand with us. Merc and Ury still hovered close by, each searching the crowd, for whom I wasn't sure. "Did you see Sarabi?" she beamed, but her giddiness bled away when she saw our tense faces. "What's wrong?" She looked between me and Forge.

"Nothing," I told her gently.

The concerned look she gave me said she didn't believe me, but she didn't press. "You're almost up. The two of you should go stand near the wheel," she said, cupping my elbow.

I walked past her into the cool night air, but an oppressive weight pressed down on my chest and I didn't feel like I could breathe. The brothers did as Arum instructed and followed me and Forge to the smaller tent where the wheel sat poised, ready for its performance. Old scars randomly cast upon the wheel sat next to the fresh ones received last night. My body had been outlined and the scars still bore my likeness. With a finger, I traced one of them.

I looked to Forge. "I know you're upset, but please don't—"

"Don't say that," he pleaded, hurt lacing his voice. "Please, don't ever think it. I could and would never hurt you, Castor."

Merc and Ury each sucked in a breath upon hearing my name. They looked at one another and clamped their mouths shut.

Forge's eyes were wide when he realized his gaffe. He cursed, pressed his eyes closed, then turned to me. *I'm sorry*, he mouthed.

I grabbed his hand and squeezed, letting him know it was okay. We would finish our act, speak with Arum, and be on our way either with gravebriar, or with the information to find it. After his little rhyme during the pre-show, I knew he had knowledge of where to get it. I hoped he wasn't insinuating that Mother had it all along, or that she'd given it to me, because she hadn't.

"And now…" Arum's voice boomed throughout the tent, "the final event. I give you… the wheel of death." He gestured toward us.

The brothers carried the wheel into the ring and attached the legs to stabilize it again. Forge took my hand and escorted me to it. I stepped onto the foot pads and took hold of the pegs. As the brothers each strapped an ankle and wrist, Forge's metallic eyes met mine. In them swam the promise he'd made to me again and again. He wouldn't hurt me.

He stepped away, removed the first knife from his harness, and bowed. I waved my hands as much as I could as the audience cheered.

Arum watched us from ringside.

Lightning fast, Forge flung a knife. It lodged in the wood far from me. He smiled and walked to the wheel and plucked it off, pretending to warm up, practicing for more dangerous flings. "Breathe, Castor," he whispered.

He returned to where he'd stood and threw it again, came back to collect it, and stepped far across the ring. The crowd was so silent, I could hear the words a girl in the front row whispered to her Mother behind her hand. She wondered if he might accidentally hit me.

Forge took another two knives from his harness and flung them so quickly I could only count the *thunks* as they landed in the wood around me and splinters flew.

Forge's attention was stolen away for a second, but when he looked at me once more, something had changed. He launched knife after knife at me, peppering the board. The brothers whispered a warning that they would spin the wheel and then they set me in motion. I closed my eyes and pretended I was flying, catching the tail of a star as a splinters of wood struck my temple, nose, hair. Sharp blade edges lined my fingers. Feet, toes, face. They wedged in the soft spot between my neck and shoulder, between my thighs, knees, at either side, under my arms. Dizziness set in when I opened them again, and I immediately regretted eating before the show. The brothers slowed the wheel and then stopped it, but the earth kept spinning as they unstrapped my wrists and ankles.

Forge lifted me from the wheel because I had no room to move. Every inch of the board was covered in knives except for where I'd been.

"We have to go. Now," he said as we paused to bow, turning in a circle to face all directions. The ring flooded with performers, everyone bowing as Arum thanked the fine people of Westbrook for hosting them for so long. Forge tugged me through the crowd to the tent's edge. "We need to leave *now*." He stabbed his fingers through his hair. Merc and Ury were already searching for us.

"We can't without talking to Arum first!" I whispered. "I want to know what that little rhyme was about."

"Forget Arum. He's playing games. We have worse things to worry about."

"What?" I asked, my brows kissing.

"We're in danger. I can't explain everything now, but if we remain here, we might not see home again. Let's fall in with the others like nothing is wrong and pretend we're going to meet with Arum as planned. Then we grab our things, rush into the forest, and make for home." He saw my hesitation. "You promised that we would leave when we got in too deep. Well, I'm telling you we're both drowning, Gravebriar. If we don't leave now, we won't make it out of Westbrook alive."

"Okay," I agreed, my heart in my throat. "I'm with you."

As the crowd cheered, Arum slipped out of the tent on the other side, no doubt heading toward his own. I could hear him on the other side, barking orders to make sure everything was secured in their wagons and to begin tearing down the tents the moment they were empty. Sarabi rumbled from the small tent as Shadow led him back to his cage.

Forge and I slid in among the crowded troupe heeding Arum's instructions, but as we were jostled, I lost Forge's hand and then lost him. I walked to our borrowed wagon, collected our things, and waited, but he never came. The troupe thinned until no one walked past.

I jogged to Shadow's wagon and found her checking the knots in the rope around her armoire. The light of a single tapered candle lit the room. She'd changed into trousers and a shirt. "Hey," she said, giving the knot a jerk. Satisfied with it, she took up a bag larger than mine, stuffed to the brim, and walked across the floor. "You haven't changed yet." Her eyes lit. "Are you coming with us?"

"Have you seen Forge?"

She shook her head slowly. "No, why would he be here?"

"I don't know. I can't find him anywhere. We got separated in the crowd."

NiNTEEN

Forge burst into Shadow's wagon, startling us both. "Shhh," he warned, his eyes wild. "I need you both to be very quiet."

"What's wrong?" I asked fearfully. He didn't answer. "Forge, what's happening?"

He pressed a finger to his lips before pinching the wick of the candle and plunging the wagon into darkness. I slung my bag on and took his up as well, then I padded across the wagon where my hand found his shoulder. Shadow was just behind me.

"Hunters," he whispered. "A large pack of hunters is in Westbrook harbor."

Shadow's brows sharpened. "How do you know that?" He pressed his lips closed and refused to answer. "Forge, how do you know about the hunters?" she repeated.

He turned to me and grabbed my arms. "I need you to trust me." He kissed my temple and looked between me and Shadow. "I need you two to slip out and crawl under the stairs, under the wagon to the back. When it's clear, run to the next row, crawl under that wagon, and the next and the next until you reach the pines. Go tell Arum about the hunters. Do you have the knife I gave you last night?"

"Yes, in my bag," I whispered. "But –"

"Keep it on you at all times." He kissed my lips. Hard. His arm was a steel band around my back, drawing me closer. "You have to go." Without hesitation, Shadow and I rushed across the wagon and scrambled down the steps, tucking ourselves beneath them. Her worried eyes met mine. "Make sure it's clear," he reminded us.

We crawled to the rear of the wagon and looked. There was no movement. No candlelight or lanterns. Only cricket song and the sky leeching from pitch to blue again. Shadow and I rushed across the path and crawled beneath another wagon. Each pathway revealed nothing. I saw no one; there was no obvious danger lurking in the darkness.

Finally, the pines appeared and we dashed into them, running through the needle-covered ground to Arum's tent. As soon as I opened the flap and entered his space, something cold and sharp pressed against my neck. "Arum!" I whispered.

He took the blade away, tucking it into a sheath on his belt. "Castor? Shadow? What are you doing?"

Surprised, Shadow breathed my name. "Castor…. Castor Gravebriar?"

I ignored her and the fear contorting her features. "Forge said there is a large pack of hunters in the harbor."

Arum rushed to the other side of the tent where a tiny silver bell sat. "Only *my* witches can hear the toll. They won't do anything rash, but this will tell them to be on high alert." He rang it once. I couldn't hear its toll, but Shadow clapped her hands over her ears, wincing at the sound.

"Where exactly did Forge sneak off to?" he asked derisively. "And how convenient his timing…"

I bristled and purposely ignored his question. I didn't know where Forge went, only that he meant to keep me safe. I also realized that no matter my answer, Arum wouldn't like it because he didn't like Forge.

Outside the tent, Arum, Shadow, and I began searching the camp, careful not to alarm those who were packing or draw attention to the fact that we knew the hunters were nearby. Shadow's eyes were wide and reflective, her pupils swollen and taking in everything. "See anything?" Arum whispered.

"No," she replied.

She might have taken her magic from her mother, but her Nocturn father did contribute some advantages.

"Can you run ahead and scout for us?" He handed her the tiny bell. "Toll this if you see even a single threat." Shadow clutched the bell in her palm and ran into the night, zigging and zagging through the wagons. "I'm not sure how much Forge has told you, but hunters are pack animals. Once you see one, you're already surrounded."

Where the circus wagons ended and the path veered toward the sea, someone ran toward us. When Arum stopped, I paused with him.

"Arum?" someone called out.

"Crow." He walked purposefully toward his sailor. "What word of the ship?"

Crow jogged to meet us on the sand. Panting, he answered, "Last I was with her, she was fine, sir, but Ecriver is not. Forge is guarding him."

In all the commotion, I'd forgotten Arum had sent Crow to find Ecriver in the woods.

"Is Ecriver okay?" I asked.

He shook his head and flicked a dire glance at Arum. "He's just inside the forest."

We crossed the unfinished brick street near the bakerie and ran toward the tree line. At the edge where Westbrook ended and the forest took over, Crow told us where we would find Ecriver. Arum ordered Crow to stay just outside the wood and keep watch for us. If anything moved or made a sound, he was to alert us immediately.

I sensed his reluctance to be left behind, but he followed Arum's orders, pausing and turning to watch out for us. Arum and I slipped just inside the tree line, where we found Forge pacing. His shirt and face were smeared with something dark.

"Where's Ecr—" My words died in my throat, choking me. I covered my mouth and nose, tears pricking at my eyes. *No.*

Thick rope bound Ecriver's torso to a thick pine, and his arms were stretched to reach the lowest branches of the tree to which he was bound. A glinting copper knife handle protruded from each wrist. The hunters had staked him to the tree with the knives Forge made him. No wonder he could sense him here. His magical cloak was gone. All I could see was Ecriver's dark hair as his head slumped against his chest.

Arum cursed and trudged forward, reaching out to grab the handle of one of the knives Forge had made and with which he'd armed Ecriver.

"Don't," Forge hissed. Arum wheeled to face Forge. "*I'll* remove the metal. You use your magic to heal him."

A mirthless laugh punched from Arum's chest. "My boy, I am skilled at healing wounds, but I'm no miracle worker. Ecriver is dead."

There was blood below him on either side. Great puddles of it. The leaves were all drenched.

Ecriver's chest did not rise or fall.

His legs, hands, and head were limp as he hung there. He was dead.

Forge wrapped his palm around the handle and jerked one of the knives free of Ecriver's hand, easing the appendage down to his side before plucking the other blade free. With it, he eviscerated the rope that bound our friend to the tree's trunk and caught his body as it toppled, then eased him to the ground.

Ecriver's head lolled. His eyes were fractionally opened. His lashes didn't flutter, his pupils didn't roll.

"Get over here," Forge snapped at Arum.

"I cannot help him," Arum argued, exasperated.

But then Ecriver sucked in a deep, dry breath, hacking coughs barking from his lungs. His eyes popped open and his chest rose and fell.

He coughed. Wheezed.

Cried until tears streamed into his hair.

Forge held Ecriver's head up off the ground and gently told him to calm down. Ecriver tucked his hands into his chest as if to protect his wrists. He rolled from left to right, then back again, his feet squirming against the ground.

Arum rushed forward and fell on his knees, using his magic to heal the knife wounds and replenish his blood. Ghastly green light poured from his palms. "Who did this?" Arum asked, not even giving him a moment to appreciate that he was among the living again. I wasn't sure if he was worried he'd die again and this time not be able to come back, or if we were still in danger. I kept watch around us. If the hunters had known Ecriver was a witch through the cloaking spell he wore, they might attack Crow for guarding us as we helped him.

"Who, Ecriver? Who did this to you?" Arum tried again.

The Spellsweet coughed until his face turned red. I took a few steps toward him and gently clasped his ankle, infusing him with an herb to calm him down.

Arum's eyes snapped to mine with a glaring look of warning.

"It will only calm him," I soothed. "He's in shock."

"I know that," he gritted, holding tight to Ecriver's biceps. "You should probably put him to sleep."

That was drastic. Ecriver would be fine once he relaxed.

Ecriver calmed as mine and Arum's magic flowed into him. His breathing steadied and his pallor returned to normal. He looked from me to Arum, then to Forge.

"Who attacked you?" Arum sternly demanded.

I took my hand off Ecriver's ankle. Minutes ago, he'd been dead, and though it was Arum's magic that was restarting his body and closing the wounds on his wrists, it wasn't Arum's magic that revived him. Forge's had.

My grandfather came to that conclusion at the same moment I did, turning to the Silverthorn. "There seems to be much we need to discuss, Mr. Silverthorn. I'd heard rumor of you spelling the weapons you made, but never imagined them capable of so much."

Forge nodded once. "We aren't discussing anything here. It isn't safe."

I was very aware of how unsafe we were. How vulnerable. Were the hunters still at the harbor, or could they be watching? Would they follow us back to the tents and wagons, or had their pack withdrawn into the forest? Could Forge and I even get back to Cauldron at this point?

When Ecriver felt well enough, Forge and Arum helped him sit up. When he felt he could stand, they helped him do so. And when he felt he could walk, he limped forward using the men as his crutches on either side.

We collected Crow and made fast tracks back to the safety of the troupe's small city of wagons and tents, carving a path to Arum's in particular. Arum's family was all safe – all on edge, but intact – and gathered outside Arum's tent. They parted to let us pass through. Arum pushed open a flap and shouted for everyone to follow us inside. His troupe members followed him like a queen into her hive.

"Light the torches and candles," he yelled. The fire Elementines wasted no time and firelight suddenly drowned the space.

I hurried ahead to pull the desk chair out for Ecriver.

Arum met my eye while the troupe came near. "Drop the cloak. My family needs to know who you are. They deserve to decide whether to go on with me or part ways now."

Forge let out a soft curse.

Crow tilted his head. "You're cloaked?"

Surrounded by witches hailing from every coven, some from multiple covens, witches Arum loved and protected, I let the cloak magic fall away. Arum's family reacted as if we were in the ring where Arum had woven one of his intricate stories and we'd somehow brought it to life in a fantastical, daring way. Only this wasn't pretend anymore. This was real.

Crow's dark brows met, his lips parting as he looked to Arum, then me again. He blinked. "Your name isn't Lilith, I take it."

I hated the way people looked at me when they realized I'd lied to them. It was a terrible mix of confusion, disbelief, and something akin to disgust. "It's Castor."

His lips pressed into a thin line as he looked between me and the man he trusted with his life, and who trusted him in return with his livelihood. "Not *the* Castor?"

A murmur rolled through the tent.

Arum nodded. "My one and only granddaughter."

Shadow's lips were still sour. I shot her an apologetic look. Then a weighty thought hit me square in the chest. "You've told everyone about me?"

Head held high, he answered, "I've had my eye on you from afar for many years, Castor. Just because I was removed from your life didn't mean I removed you from mine."

Ecriver didn't bother with the desk chair my white-knuckled fingers still curled around. Instead, he pushed the men on toward the hammock. Forge and Arum, with some assistance from Elementine witches, helped him down into the cradling fabric. Ecriver's palms were almost healed when he curled them into his chest.

Arum quickly finished his work to seal the wounds entirely, knitting bone and sinew along with it. "If you wish to leave and not be a part of this fight, now is the time for you to depart," Arum told his troupe.

A Bloodling with warm brown skin, tattoos peeking from his collar and extending onto the backs of his hands, brought over a rag and a basin of cool water. He scrubbed Ecriver's hands, arms, and the skin of his neck and face until it was free of crusted blood.

Crow moved to stand close to me. He cleared his throat, then bent and whispered, "I didn't realize…"

"I know."

"Then you must know how very off-limits you are. Your grandfather is going to kill me."

"For escorting her around my ship?" Arum spoke up. "Unless something untoward has happened that I'm unaware of, I appreciate your attentiveness toward Castor. If, however, something has transpired that I wouldn't approve of, I might consider it."

Crow tugged at his collar. "No, sir."

"You're attracted to her, cloak or none," Arum observed.

Crow swallowed thickly, the firelight shimmering over his skin. Forge had bent to rinse the knives in the basin of blood-tinged water. His back slowly tightened, his shoulders turning to steel, as if they bore heavy, deadly wings again. When he rose, his eyes met mine with an I-told-you-so fire burning in their depths. He'd told me Crow was enamored, but now I wasn't sure he appreciated it. His taunting smirk was nowhere to be found.

Ecriver let out an agonized moan. The hammock he lay in gently swayed from the attention of the Bloodling and Arum's continued healing power, which made the Spellsweet look a sickly green.

Arum glanced around at his troupe, his family. "I need to speak to my granddaughter. Please go take the show tents down – and be quick about it. We leave within the hour."

His troupe immediately obeyed, quickly filing out of the flaps. Soon, quiet chatter could be heard outside, along with the sound of hammers striking metal, of canvas flapping in the breeze.

Shadow slipped in, her pants soaked from hem to knee and smelling of the salty brine she detested. "You searched the harbor?" he asked. "What did you find?"

She bent to whisper something in Arum's ear, then shot me a worried look before exiting as quickly as she'd come.

Arum waited quietly, focusing on Ecriver for several minutes. Only when he was satisfied did he step away and rinse the mixture of drying and still-wet blood from his hands. He stood and wiped them on a white towel, then strangled the fabric as he gestured to Forge. "Explain."

Forge stood up straighter, squarer. "Explain what exactly?"

"All of it!" Arum shouted. He took a moment to compose himself, took a deep breath, and cracked his neck. "Every bit of it, Forge. I know you've been providing weapons to the only pack of hunters capable of tracking Castor. How could you put her in such danger?"

Forge took a step toward Arum before stopping himself, but not before Crow wrapped his hand around the handle of his sword. Metal raked against metal as he began to draw it. Only my hand on his stopped him.

"I had no idea they would be near. I haven't heard anything from them in months."

"But you admit that you've provided him and his pack with weapons."

Forge's eyes flicked guiltily to mine and my stomach dropped.

What has he done?

Holding my gaze, he confessed, "I told you that I hunted hunters, but I didn't elaborate on why. I provide them with weaponry."

Crow growled beside me, "A traitor to your own kind."

"Not at all," Forge countered. "In case you didn't notice, my weapons are spelled. No witch can die from a wound they inflict."

"It sure feels like it when you're being run through," Ecriver noted in an exhausted voice. "And when you die, it feels like death. Only reviving feels unnatural."

Forge pinched the bridge of his nose. "It was the only way I could get them to trust me. I know their whereabouts because I can sense the metal I make."

"Then where are they, the great horde who was at the harbor just this evening?" Arum demanded. "Did they just vanish? There is no group gathered there."

"I don't know," Forge gritted. "The metal is at the harbor."

"About that you're right. Shadow searched the harbor. There is no horde of hunters, but there is a cache of weapons washing up onto the shore. Daggers and knives and swords litter the sand like shells, boy. Am I to assume Artemis knows of your trickery and that he dumped the weapons? Or that his pack only attacked Ecriver because they saw him carrying your signature blade? They wouldn't have seen through his cloak, but they might have recognized the daggers you gave him."

Forge growled and tore at his hair. "None of it makes sense! Why would Artemis use the spelled knives if he was aware of the spell and knew Ecriver would reanimate?"

The room was quiet for several minutes until I spoke. "Because he wanted to send you a message. He wants you to know that he knows."

Forge looked to Ecriver. "Was it Artemis? Do you remember his face?"

Ecriver let out a sigh. "I don't remember anything, but judging by the boulder-sized knot on the back of my head, someone hit me pretty hard."

Arum went still. "Did you give him the words?"

"I... I don't think so. I remember walking through the forest and then, pain," Ecriver answered. "Everything went black and cold, and then I woke again with you three standing over me."

"What words?" I demanded.

Arum shook his head and bitterly laughed. "Why do I feel like we're going to have to fight our way out of Westbrook?" He turned to Crow. "Ready the ship. And be on your guard as you return."

"Aye, sir." Crow gave me another apologetic look before ducking outside.

"Where will you go?" I asked my grandfather.

"For now, we'll stick to the sea."

The sea? Its fathomless weight and depth were more than I could grasp, along with all the life it carried within it. It was the fastest route out of Westbrook and likely the safest, given that he had at least one Tempest witch in his troupe, but surely, he couldn't abandon the circus and the life he'd built around it. "What about all the wagons?"

He smiled. "My dear, all things can be made and unmade, or made much, much smaller, in the blink of an eye."

I looked at Ecriver, who was blinking lazily in the now-still hammock. How quickly he'd been unmade, then made again. I couldn't imagine how painful it was, or how haunting the experience would be until he was unmade for good. "Arum, what words were you referring to?"

TWENTY

Arum asked to speak to me outside, alone. He asked Forge to stay with Ecriver, who weakly protested that he was fine but didn't move a muscle beyond speaking the words.

We walked outside Arum's tent just as the sun broke the horizon and shone orange over the land. "Will Ecriver recover?"

"His body is functioning perfectly, but exhaustion has set in. He'll be okay soon enough."

I nodded, glad to hear it. "Castor," Arum began, "I'd like for you to come with us – to leave with us on the ship." I shook my head and Arum raised his hand. "Before you list all the reasons you can't, I already know them and have weighed their importance against the value of your safety."

Arcana's fateful words resurfaced, spilling from my mouth like dripping pearls. She was right, so very right. "I'm not safe anywhere, Arum. Safety is a figment of the imagination; a pretty illusion we create to comfort our-selves. As I live and breathe, I'm never truly safe. No one is."

"Many packs of hunters are dogged in their attempts to hunt witches, but Artemis in particular, is ruthless. Look

263

what he did to Ecriver!" Arum argued. "That pack leader's sole focus is on breaching Cauldron's hedge. Many say that Artemis is… without conscience."

"You're afraid of him," I noted.

"I'm afraid *for you*. Someone in Cauldron is feeding information to him. He knows about you. He knows about all the Powers." He shook his head. "I bet he was told the moment you were sent away." His eyes flicked to the tent meaningfully.

"You think it's Forge."

"He's been doing business with him, selling our enemy weapons. What else should I think?"

"Forge can sense every piece of metal he makes, and he spelled the weapons so they couldn't harm—"

"Yet, they *did* harm Ecriver, didn't they? We revived him, but what if they had left him pinned to the tree like a moth for days, weeks? How long does his magic extend? What if he revived and then they stuck him with a weapon Forge *hadn't* made?" Arum threaded his hands behind his back and began to pace. "I insist you come with us."

I shook my head. "I need to take a gravebriar back to Arbor, Arum. I won't let him die."

"Arbor Gravebriar doesn't matter. You owe him *nothing*," he insisted, his head high.

"You're wrong. He does matter. Every member of my coven does. I owe them a warning if they're in danger. They've spent much of their lives lying for me. Protecting me. I just need you to tell me where to find the gravebriar or give me some if you have it. We held up our end of the bargain," I insisted stubbornly.

He snapped his fingers in front of me and laughed darkly. "Wake up, Castor. You. Are. Gravebriar."

I shook my head. "I don't understand. I'm *not* gravebriar."

He crouched and pointed to the soil. "Put your hand on this earth." I matched his position and did as he instructed. "You can grow gravebriar."

I shook my head. "I can't. I've never been able to make *anything* grow." My power had nothing to do with growth. Mother could take a seed, make it sprout, encourage its roots to stretch and push, and for leaves to develop and unfold. She could make flowers bloom or make them wilt.

"You are not the rightful Gravebriar coven Power because you have the ability to leech poison from poisonous things and transfer them to other things... *You are the Gravebriar Power because you hold the magic of our namesake in your blood.*"

I shook my head again. That wasn't true!

"Beneath the surface where you can hear poison's song... is there something else? Something deep and slumbering and far more powerful?"

The pit of my stomach became restless as the heavy, dark, secret thing I held within began to squirm. "Yes."

His voice dropped to a whisper. "Before they took me and bound me to the stake, I trapped it within you so your mother could not tap into it and use it against the other covens, or use you to harm them. I can unmake the magic that restrains you, Castor. But you have to promise me to use restraint with it. And no matter what, you must promise never to give a briar to Forge Silverthorn."

I swallowed, nodded, waited.

He crouched beside me and let his hand fall over mine. The warmth of his energy and magic poured into my fingers, heating my bones and blood as it whooshed back up my arm. Watching me carefully, he let my hand go.

His warmth was replaced by something else. Something foreign but familiar. Something that could kill *or* heal. A juxtaposition of things that should not be, but were. Like warm waves in the middle of a frigid sea.

Poison and cure.

I was both.

I released the restless feeling and felt its cool, velvety smooth texture travel up from my stomach, course through my heart, pour down my arm, and spill into the ground. The ground beneath the pads of my fingers trembled, and soon, something pushed at my palm. A small bush sprouted and grew. Even after I removed my hand from the soil. Even when I leaned back. On every limb were thorns, pale green at the stem – the color of my hair – fading to the toxic yellow shade trapped in my eyes.

Arum slipped something from his waist – one of the copper knives that Forge had given Ecriver. "I took this blade to show you…"

I quickly plucked the precious briars from the stems and cupped them in my palm. When there were no more to pick, Arum cut the bush to the ground where it died, withering in an instant.

"Not even magic can kill the gravebriar bush before it naturally dies away. The only thing that can *instantly* kill a gravebriar… is a blade forged by a Silverthorn. That duplicitous boy will be the death of you."

"What if the blade is spelled not to kill witches?" I breathed.

Arum leveled me with a pointed look. "Is that a risk you're willing to take? For Artemis to break the protective hedge built around Cauldron, he needs something from each coven who made it. Nine things. He has seven. Guess what the two final items are that will shred the hedge for good?"

I remembered Arum's question to Ecriver in the forest… *Did you give him the words?*

Ecriver's spell words.

And gravebriar.

Forge stepped out from behind a tree. "Don't listen to him, Castor. What did I tell you he'd do? He's trying to drive a wedge between us."

"How coincidental, Forge Silverthorn, that you led her to the only one who could release the lock on her power, and that you've garnered her trust so that she would give you the briar *you* seek for Artemis?"

I looked to Forge, his brows curving indignantly. "He's lying. He's manipulating you. I warned you he would. I don't even know Artemis. I know one of the members of his pack, and have done business with him through that person, but I've never met him. I would never do anything to help them bring down the hedge. My every effort was in attempt to keep us safe from his schemes."

My heart felt heavy, my stomach like lead as I squeezed my palm tight around the briars, imagining them as nothing but dust particles. Before any pierced my skin, they turned feather soft. Opening my palm, I saw a fine, yellow-green powder inside. I blew it away and when my breath hit it, and I imagined it ash, it turned gray brown. I didn't know who to trust, but I couldn't risk *anyone* else taking it and giving it to the ruthless hunter who sought to destroy us.

"Castor?" Forge said, a question in his voice. I knew what he was asking because it was the same thing I'd asked so many times: *Don't you trust me? Whose story do you believe?*

The bare truth was that I didn't trust anyone but myself. My entire life and every experience and person in it taught me that. Arum was accusing Forge. Forge claimed Arum was lying. I had no idea what the truth actually was.

Arum gave a haughty gesture. "I believe Arbor's poisoning was just a means of getting you out of Cauldron. Why settle for a few gravebriars when you can control the one who can grow them at will? Tell me, Forge, did you use castor beans to poison Arbor and frame Castor?"

The crop of castor plants in the forest's heart... it was grown by a Gravebriar, but that didn't mean a member of my coven wasn't working with someone else.

Forge bristled. "Don't listen to him."

"Is that why you were in the solarium?" I asked Forge. "Were you meeting someone? Had you met them already?"

His expression turned steely, save for the muscle jumping in his jaw. He lifted his head proudly. "Why did I tell you I was there?"

"You said you were there merely to admire your grandfather's ironwork and see the famed Gravebriar foliage." I pinched my bottom lip, released it. "Yet you're depraved enough to align yourself with Artemis, the wily witch hunter who wants nothing more than to destroy all witches. Even *you* must admit it sounds far-fetched."

Forge gritted his teeth and shook his head. "You gave me your word, Castor."

"Did you poison Arbor?" I choked out, my throat clogging with tears.

He shook his head. "No, I did not poison Arbor."

"Are you working with *Rose* Gravebriar, Forge?" Arum asked quietly, folding his hands in front of him and waiting for an answer.

Forge didn't answer at first, his jaw working. "No," he finally said.

Arum smiled smugly at Forge. He clearly thought he was lying.

Could my mother be at the root of this parasitic plot? Mother loved being Power of the Gravebriar witch coven. The night of the revel, before Arbor fell ill, she practically glowed. But Arbor's ascension would have jeopardized all that. As would I.

I couldn't imagine her being so ruthless, but framing me for his poisoning, and perhaps his death, would remove her only two known threats...

"I implore you to come with me, Castor," Arum pleaded.

"Don't," Forge urgently begged. "Please don't trust him. We left Cauldron together. We can leave this place now and return the same way. You said you were with me."

I felt like a rope pulled between two foes, tugged one way and then the other. I was fraying. I grabbed my temples. "I need time to think," I told them both.

Hands behind his back, Arum shifted his weight forward and back on the balls of his feet, settling them again. "Very well. I can respect that. I'm afraid there isn't much time left, though."

Forge was quiet, though I could tell there was much he wanted to say.

Ecriver called out from inside, "I need help. I can't get out of this thing."

Arum excused himself to go help our friend.

Forge reached out for me, but I backed out of his reach, my eyes welling when a painful expression flitted over his features. It was gone in an instant, his face steeling. "You promised me, Gravebriar. You said we were in this together."

But how could I trust him now? And not only him… How could I trust anyone? I couldn't trust my own mother, my own grandfather.

Could he see what I was planning? In just a matter of days, he'd become close enough to me to recognize it. He said he knew me by heart.

A tear fell, streaking down my cheek and splashing onto my shirt.

"Don't cry," Forge said so softly it broke my heart. Was he still acting?

"I need a few minutes…"

He nodded, swallowing thickly. I left him in the pines and jogged to the wagon, where I took our bags out of hiding and slung both over my shoulder.

Forge had been true to his word so far, I realized, knees digging into the wooden wagon floor. Besides that, my poison was still in his heart.

It came down to this: I now had the gravebriar. I had to get it back to Arbor before it was too late.

I needed to find Forge.

The two smaller tents had been taken down, the poles lying in a neat pile with their ropes coiled. The alternating green fabric was being carefully folded. A small group had begun to take down the big top, working the knots from the ropes that held the top up. Shadow waved me over. "Cas... hey! You just missed loverboy. He and Arum just walked by."

My heart pounded. "Forge and Arum?" And they'd been civil?

Standing beside her was the petite tightrope performer. Shadow ticked her head toward the wind Elementine. "This is Zephyr. Help us with these knots? They're stubborn."

I nodded to Zephyr. "Where did Forge and Arum go?"

She grinned. "I knew you weren't a Shade witch," Shadow said conspiratorially, punctuating the statement with a husky laugh. She shook her head slowly. "But Castor Gravebriar... I never would have guessed."

"Do you know where they went, Shadow?" I asked a second time, wringing my hands.

"Arum was not happy. Not that anyone could blame him. Forge is nothing but trouble, always has been. He is such a pretty liar, though, isn't he? Such a shame he's aligned himself with such dark creatures. Hunters are not to be trifled with. I have a feeling he'll soon learn that lesson the hard way. He said something to Arum about going after Artemis. Hunting *him*." My heart thundered. "Not that I believe that for one second. Forge has done business with Artemis for years. Arum told us all some time ago to stay away from Forge Silverthorn." She cursed. "I should've told you the first night while we were dressing. I just... I didn't know who you truly were. I figured if you were fool enough to be with him, you might be working alongside him, too. Birds of a feather, right?"

"Right," I said absently, wandering away from her. I didn't make it ten feet. Arum and Ecriver met me. Ecriver leaned against one of the still-upright poles, still ashen and weak.

"Where is Forge?"

Arum let out a long breath. "I kept him from chasing you to the wagon, escorted him from my borrowed sliver of land, and spelled it so he couldn't step back on it until we vacate it entirely. He did *claim* that he would find Artemis and kill him. But Castor, I believe he knows who Artemis is and that he's luring you into a well-crafted plan. You go after him, he tells Artemis where you'll be, and Artemis seizes you and takes the gravebriar."

"I would never let the hunter have it."

"I think I would have, if I hadn't passed out," Ecriver admitted tiredly. The sheen of sweat on his brow concerned me.

I looked at the Spellsweet. "You and I need to go back to Cauldron – but not together," I told them. We were safest within the hedge no matter what lay outside of it.

Ecriver shook his head. "I'll never make it."

"Yes, you will." I glanced at Arum, who nodded once, affirming my decision. I could make a gravebriar to restore him. I bent to the ground and placed my hand on the earth. Since I could grow it, I assumed I could control how much gravebriar emerged. I focused my power into a tiny spot in the soil. Ecriver watched hungrily as I made the gravebriar grow.

I plucked it and then used the knife Forge made me to kill the plant immediately. Standing, I put the briar in Ecriver's hand. "Chew it now, or I'll turn it to dust."

Without hesitation, he popped the briar in his mouth and chewed. A sugary scent filled the space between us. Within seconds, the sheen of sweat on his brow dried, the weariness bled from his muscles, and his pallor looked far healthier. "Thank you," he said in a strong voice, not the slightest wheeze or strain to it.

"If you sail him around to Southmist, Arum, it may divert Artemis's attention away long enough for me to make it to Cauldron."

Arum's eyes hardened. "A diversion isn't a terrible idea, but I don't like the thought of you traveling through the same woods where Ecriver was just attacked."

"I know the forest. Beyond that, I'm fast. *And* deadly."

He shook his head. "It doesn't matter how fast a fly is flying when it gets caught up in a spider's web. Only the intricacy of those sticky strands..."

"I'll melt anything that ensnares me," I argued. "You've seen what I can do with the gravebriar, but you haven't seen me with poisons yet."

"I want to send a crew with you," he countered. "People I trust with my own life, and thus can trust with yours."

I tipped up my chin. "I don't need your permission, Arum."

He chuckled. "Unless you plan to poison, incapacitate, or kill me, you certainly do."

"Because *you're* the rightful Gravebriar Power?" I smarted.

"Because I am your grandfather, Castor. If you leave here, my crew will be on your heels and will surround you to keep you safe. How close you allow them is your choice, but I will send a crew of people I implicitly trust, witches with varying powers. Or you can march onto my ship with Ecriver and I'll sail both of you to Southmist. It's a short journey to Cauldron on foot from their shores, and frankly, a far safer option."

My eyes narrowed. I considered putting him to sleep, but in the end, decided that making an enemy out of an ally might be a bad decision.

TWENTY-ONE

The final knots that held the big top together were unbound and the troupe efficiently lowered the poles, then painstakingly folded and secured the mound of canvas fabric. Artemis – the man whom everyone feared but no one could describe – needed two things to breach our hedge. I knew he didn't have what I possessed, but was it possible he had one of the other missing ingredients? Would the gravebriar restore his memory as well as his body?

"Ecriver, are you certain you didn't say anything of value to Artemis?" I asked. "Did you mutter any spell words to him?"

He stood up straighter. "I don't remember anything."

A great deal of things might be forgotten in the midst of trauma. Torture had a way of making the inconsequential imbed in our minds while erasing things of great consequence. My coven mate Holly fell into a fire once. She remembered a white cat scurrying across the yard at the sound of her screams, but not being pulled from the flames, or my mother healing her blistered, charred palms.

The gravebriar had healed him to a point, but hadn't returned what was missing from his mind. It was possible he was right and that he'd been dashed on the head and then pinned to the tree, but what gave me pause was how he said that when Forge's knives were used against him, it felt like he was dying. I couldn't help but think there were patches of memory missing.

"We need to be sure, Ecriver. Would you let me try something? I promise not to cause you harm."

My fingers drifted into the space between us and he glanced at Arum before lifting his hand to meet mine. "Okay," he agreed, albeit somewhat reluctantly.

I pushed a mild hallucinogen into his blood. He began to laugh, his head lolling as if it alternated between feeling light as a cloud and heavy as a stone.

Arum ground his teeth. "What did you do?"

I ignored him. "Ecriver?"

The Spellsweet's head bobbed to me with a silly, drunken grin stretched over his lips. "Castor Gravebriar. The poison of Cauldron."

My ribcage tightened. *Was that what everyone called me in secret?*

"Ecriver, I need you to think back to when you were attacked in the forest."

The drunken grin fell away. "It was terrible," he said, shaking away a shiver.

"Did you give your attacker any words? Did you write anything for him?"

He leaned forward. "The hedge of protection is only as good as the people it guards, Castor," he whispered.

"Did you give Artemis or his men the Spellsweet words he needs to take the hedge down?"

"I had no pen." He grinned triumphantly. His father's power lay in the spoken words; Ecriver's magic lay in the written.

"What does Artemis look like? Did you see him?"

He shook his head. "I don't know Artemis. I've never seen him before."

Artemis's reputation was renowned, but the man was a mystery. Did no one know what he looked like? Could he have watched Arum's show tonight and no one be the wiser?

My head tilted as his drifted down, down... "Did you see your attacker?"

His eyes tried to focus on mine, his pupils flaring then contracting again. "Yes. I saw Forge Silverthorn."

My heart stopped.

My lashes fluttered as I tried to absorb the name he'd just uttered.

"Forge Silverthorn?"

"Mhmm," he said. "That's who pinned me to that tree. Like a silver moth who fluttered 'round a flame... So taken by the light it threw, he never saw *him* aim." Those were the words Arum used during our first wheel of death performance.

He looked to Arum and erupted in a short fit of high-pitched giggles. A moment later, he went quiet. Completely still. Ecriver's chin fell onto his chest. He began to snore even as he stood beside me. His body relaxed and began to slump. "Help me lie him down?" Arum asked.

We eased him to the sandy, grass-spotted soil. I looked at his healed palms, remembering how he looked pinned to the tree...

"I believe his brain was rattled with the blow Forge delivered him. I healed the welt, but it was like he could feel it anyway. And though you fed him a gravebriar, the injury must be deeper than we thought."

"Wouldn't the briar have completely healed him?" I asked.

"It would heal a great deal, but he is not a Gravebriar witch. The same rules that apply to us do not apply to Spellsweets. His father's words would do him much good. Every coven has a very potent magic to tend to their own with, but there are limits to each kind – as you've learned." Arum was quiet as we regarded our friend.

I pulled the hallucinogen from Ecriver's blood, still thinking about what he'd just claimed. When would Forge have had the time to hurt him? He snuck away for a short time after we performed, but not until just before Crow came to get us. And some of Ecriver's blood was dried by then, which meant he'd been there for more than just a few minutes. Did he attack him before he changed clothes and came to find me, just before the dinner Arum provided? Was there ample time? It didn't seem like it…

Could someone have cloaked themselves to look like Forge?

"I'm sorry, Castor," Arum finally said, breaking the horrible silence. "I could tell your heart was attached to the boy, but he's nothing but trouble. Always has been. I can't help but feel relieved that he left you."

He left me.

I tried to wrap my mind around every experience I'd had with Forge to compare it with the profile of someone capable of such horrible things. I couldn't reconcile the two, no matter how much I tried.

None of this made sense.

Arum looked upon Ecriver, still snoring on the ground, and turned to me. "As the rightful Gravebriar coven Power, I will honor your decision on this matter. I know I was forceful earlier, speaking from a place of concern within my heart and as your grandfather. If you choose to go it alone, I will support you. If you'd like for me to send a crew to guard you, I would be happy to contribute any of my resources to keep you safe and chime in on any scheming your plan might require. Either way, I'd like to work together to enshroud whatever path you choose."

Just as a butterfly from a chrysalis first stretched and fluttered its wings, a plan unfolded in my mind.

"Take Ecriver to Southmist. I want to travel alone."

His eyes sharpened a fraction, but he inclined his head. "Very well."

Arum planned to cloak one of his witches with my image. She would walk to the ship flanked by the entire troupe in a grand effort to divert attention from the green-haired girl racing through the forest.

As we waited for his chosen decoy to find her way through the crowd of gathered witches and find us in the pines, Ecriver's words kept ringing through my mind, constantly pummeling me from within.

Forge Silverthorn…

Ecriver couldn't have lied to me under the influence of such a powerful hallucinogen. He saw Forge Silverthorn attack him. But was it truly Forge? I wanted to believe that someone had cloaked themselves, worn his handsome face, and that it wasn't Forge at all. I wanted to think it wasn't possible for Forge to hurt someone like that.

He was out there in the wood, though not close enough that I could hear my poison sing from within his veins.

"Don't dwell on him any longer," Arum advised.

"I'm not," I lied.

He raised a brow. "He's not worth it."

Maybe Arum was right, but my heart refused his words. She wanted to give him the chance to defend himself before condemning him. After all, I was given a chance to clear my name.

A feather, a shell, and the stub of a ticket were tucked into my grimoire. I still hoped that in the end, whenever the dust from this confusing implosion settled, they would remain tokens from my time here, reminders of fond memories. I hoped they'd be warnings, reminding me of how foolish I'd been.

Then again, if the allegations were true, in all fairness, he'd warned me from the beginning that he was a hunter. I just never thought I would become his prey.

The fire Elementine Arum chose for the task of pretending to be me arrived, and I studied her fiery hair and amber eyes. Fearlessly, she swallowed the potion Arum handed to her, and in seconds, she'd disappeared and my skin lay over hers. My hair, eyes, the rose gold bodysuit I still wore. "When the others leave, Flicker, you leave with them," Arum told her. "Don't breathe a word of this to anyone."

She agreed and took her place among the troupe, standing next to Shadow, who immediately started chattering between Flicker and Zephyr as she would if I stood beside her instead. I would miss her. She'd become a fast friend of mine and those weren't something I had in spades.

The tents and wagons were ready. Arum's troupe clustered at the edge of their makeshift village as he used a Spellsweet powder to shrink everything – wagons, tents, equipment – down to the size of dice. The witches spread to pick up each small piece, which they brought to Arum.

The ringmaster laid each in a box lined in green velvet that had no leftover space once he was finished arranging them inside. He handed the box to Crow, who waited with the others. Crow vowed to keep it safe. His eyes slid to me as Arum cupped his hands. "To the ship!"

He hurried ahead of the troupe, most likely to ready the ship they'd soon be sailing.

Flicker, the girl wearing my likeness, kept to the center of the crowd of witches, exactly how one might expect I would leave. Protected on every side, from every angle.

Her pale green hair flapped like a pennant in the stiff, warm sea breeze. I couldn't help but think of Forge and whether he had the girl in sight already. She was in danger just because she pretended to be me, and I wondered if life would ever settle enough so that no one had to pretend anything anymore.

Forge told me more than once that he knew me by heart. If what Arum said of him was true, would he take one glance and know she wasn't me?

Arum handed me a nondescript hat into which I quickly tucked my hair. "I wish you luck, granddaughter. I have a feeling you'll need it."

"Thank you. For everything."

"Our paths will no doubt meet again one day now that we've been reacquainted." He offered a respectful nod before striding away with his family. "Goddess bless you with speed."

I watched them for a moment until they disappeared over the knoll. The only evidence they'd even been in Westbook were the tracks and trails of foot-worn paths.

Then... I ran like hell.

Ignoring beaten paths and wide wagon trails, I pounded through the underbrush and pushed through saplings whose branches lashed my face. Instead of making a bee-line to Cauldron, I carved a crescent path. It was ironic that I rushed back to my city in the same fashion I'd left it, harried and terrified of Forge Silverthorn's intentions.

My legs burned and my heart screamed, unwilling to believe Forge had used me or that Mother was behind me being sent out of Cauldron. If that was the case, then why would she warn me and beg me to circle around and return?

Unless she wanted me to burn.

No. When she warned me away from Forge, she meant it. I heard her heart in her words. She didn't want to see me hurt or killed. Did she know more about Forge than just why he was being sent with me? How much did the Councilwitches know about his dealings with Artemis and his pack?

My heart raged, circling back to Forge. Was he a masterful player at the game of deceit, or did he mean it when he said he would never hurt me? That he liked me? That he didn't want to pretend any longer?

Every rustle behind me set my teeth on edge. I wasn't Nocturn, so I could barely see more than a few feet in front of me. I was painfully aware that darkness this deep could conceal many dangers.

As I was running through a broad stream, splashing water left and right, I turned my ankle on a stone, wincing and hobbling to a boulder to sit on. Sharp pain lanced through me, but seconds later, it abated. Another moment and it was gone. I'd healed once more.

I resumed my sprint, clambering up the side of an embankment.

The stream and boulder reminded me of Forge again, of the swim we took together. The frustrating part was that every mundane thing reminded me of the Silverthorn. Every burr that lodged in my shoe, every spider web I clawed off my face. I remembered his smirk, the quirk of his brow, his laugh. The feel of his hand, warm in mine, clutching it tightly, him carrying me further into the sea as he kissed me so feverishly it couldn't have been fake.

Just as dawn painted the sky its gentle shade of blue and crowned her with golden clouds, I spotted something enormous creeping through the wood. Something that shouldn't be there. Some*one* who shouldn't.

Shadow was supposed to have sailed away with Arum. Arum had lied. Had he sent his crew after all?

Sarabi shook his head and fluffed his thick mane. He carried Shadow on his muscled, tawny back as he padded through the forest, quieter than a beast his size should be able. She held a dark longbow and on her hip hung a quiver with matching fletchings.

Either she was here to see me home, or she intended to prevent me from reaching it. I wasn't sure which, so I kept still. Ducked behind a very old, large oak, I hoped Sarabi's sense of smell wouldn't hone in on me as I watched them. Shadow searched to their right, Sarabi to their left, step by quiet step.

I peeked again, my fingernails digging into the bark of the great tree I hid behind as Sarabi stalked, his back curved and his tail swishing. Shadow had changed from her simple clothes into a dark fitted bodysuit and matching boots. The perfect outfit to hide oneself within darkness.

A noise caught their attention and Sarabi darted toward it, Shadow guiding him.

Gently turning on my heels, I rested my back and head against the bark of the ancient tree, my hair tangling in its roughness. I had no idea what to do now, or how to avoid them, which was what I wanted.

Even if they were here to protect me from Artemis, I couldn't afford to slow down or be distracted. A meeting with Shadow and Sarabi, even if friendly, would attract attention from anyone nearby.

Then... movement. Just in front of me, Crow hid behind a thick green bush. I swallowed, my heart stuttering for a second. He had me. One yell, and Sarabi and Shadow would come. Even if I used my power, he could alert them to where I was.

I gritted my teeth.

Crow pressed his finger to his lips and with his eyes pleaded for me not to make a sound. A familiar-style knife winked from his belt. Forge had made it.

When Sarabi and Shadow were out of sight, he moved, easing toward me and keeping low to the ground. Into my ear, he spoke lower than a whisper. "You have to listen to me... Arum lied to you. Ecriver lied, too. Forge didn't hurt him. They wanted to separate the two of you to make it easier to hunt you," he breathed.

My stomach dropped and I instinctively knew what he was going to say before he said it.

"Arum *is* Artemis. The weapons Forge made and sold him are on the ship. Arum cloaked them and then removed the cloak to disturb Forge and draw him away from you. Arum knows now that he'll never be able to control you, so he told us all to hunt you, kill you, and alert him once the deed is done so he can bury you and harvest the gravebriar he needs to obliterate Cauldron's hedge. All of the pack carry witch bells to ring when you're spotted. Forge didn't leave you, Castor. Merc and Ury attacked him and dragged him onto the ship where they locked him in the brig."

"I thought you were on the ship!" I exclaimed softly.

"I was, but just before we arrived in Southmist harbor, I freed Forge and escaped with him... barely. He's hurt, Castor."

"How badly?"

Crow winced. "He's pretty roughed up. The twins made sure he had no metal to use against them, but they didn't mortally wound him. Arum forbade that, at least. If you made it to Cauldron, Arum was going to use him against you as a backup plan – Forge, in exchange for a single gravebriar."

I pressed my eyes closed, heart clenching. I would've given it to him for Forge.

284

"Who among the troupe hunts us?"

"Everyone. The troupe *is* Arum's pack. He nicknamed himself Artemis and spun stories about this fearsome hunter so those in Cauldron wouldn't suspect him. Arum said that a few know he escaped, but that your Councilwitches, to save face, forbade anyone from talking about it publicly. He said Forge tried to warn his father." Sterling Silverthorn was officially one of my least favorite witches. "Arum didn't dump the weapons in the harbor either, like he led you to believe. Shadow lied. Arum figured out that Forge had spelled the weapons he sold him when he tried to kill a witch and the witch resurrected. This entire time, he's been playing both of you, but you need to be careful now especially. He distributed the weapons Forge made to his pack. They are the only things that can kill you, Castor."

This kept getting worse.

"But Forge knows where they all are! He can track them."

Crow nodded once. "Unless Arum cloaks them individually."

How clever Arum was with his concealing magic... A witch who can cloak weapons can likely cloak poisons as well... which means Artemis –Arum – likely engineered this entire thing, beginning with poisoning Arbor. But who inside our hedge was his accomplice, or were there many?

"Thank you, Crow. For everything." He gave a firm nod. "Where is Forge? I need to find him. They'll capture him to use him as bait, or kill him."

"We were walking together when we saw Shadow. He sensed the metal you have that he made and sent me to find you, and said he would draw them away," he said, gesturing in the direction Sarabi and Shadow had just diverted. I reached out for my magic and felt the dullest hum from farther into the forest.

"Why are you helping us?" I asked, standing up.

"Because if Arum can order us to kill his own grand-daughter, he's capable of anything and loyal to nothing but himself. I thought he would only ask you to grow the gravebriar he needed... not... I'm so sorry, Castor."

I clapped his shoulder. "You've helped more than you know."

He ticked his head in the direction we needed to run. "We should find Forge and avoid the lion."

Definitely both of those things.

He peeked around the tree.

"See anything?"

He shook his head. "What do you say we make it a little more difficult for the pack? It would be somewhat hard on you, though..."

"How?"

"I'll make a storm," he grinned playfully.

I laughed, fitting him into the piece of Arum's intri-cate puzzle. "Of course! Who better to sail Arum's precious things across the sea than a Tempest?"

Crow nodded. "He keeps one on every ship."

"Exactly how many ships does he have?"

"An entire fleet of trade vessels," he admitted.

"He's made an empire, yet he seeks to destroy a single city."

"Hatred fuels many a fire, and seeks to consume the one who set it. It would make for a nice inheritance for his only granddaughter, though." Crow winked. He looked to the sky. The dainty, gold-laced clouds from dawn had long since dimmed, but he thickened them, making them churn like waves in an angry sea, pluming like thick smoke.

They darkened.

Built.

Turned my favorite shade of green.

Wind gusted through the forest, ripping leaves from the canopy and flattening saplings so they bent flush with the ground.

Nothing could hide here. Crow was the storm and could feel everything it touched.

The hat Arum had given me was torn off my head. I laughed as the dark swell inside my stomach woke, antsy to be unleashed.

TWENTY-TWO

"C auldron's hedge is surrounded," Crow warned as we left our hiding spot. "Every Bloodling and Elementine is positioned just outside it."

Strands of hair blew across my vision, my now-stretched bodysuit flapped in the powerful gusts coming from behind us, raging toward home. "Why didn't he just attack me in Westbrook?" I shouted above the storm, running toward Forge.

Crow shook his head. "Arum is afraid of your power. He knew you'd fight him if he tried to take the gravebriar forcefully, so he let you think he was on your side and set you free. He's confident that if his pack doesn't find you before you reach the hedge, his witches will prevent you from crossing it. There are far more of them than you and he's there, too. Waiting."

We rushed through the roaring forest, the storm absorbing the noise we made. Here and there, Crow pointed out evidence of Sarabi's tracks in the soil and the heavy indentions he'd left in the moss growing.

From just ahead on the other side of a rolling hill came Sarabi's thunderous growl.

The wind tore at my back. Saplings clawed at my skin and clothes. Crow hauled me up when I stumbled over a log, my heart panicking to reach him. When I crested the hill, I saw Forge caught against a rock wall with Sarabi, controlled by Shadow, stalking forward. The great cat roared again. He had no way out. If Forge ran left, right, or tried to scale it, Sarabi would catch him.

Fury poured through my veins, the dark piece of me roaring back at the lion, who sensed us at his back. He backed sideways, keeping us and Forge in his sights. Shadow saw me first, then her gaze latched onto Crow. She tilted her head and narrowed her eyes as she curled a disgusted lip. "After all he's done for you?" she shrieked.

"She's his blood. If he'll do this to her, what would he do to you, Shadow?" Crow asked, pointing at me to punctuate his argument.

"He would never betray us," she argued, but it sounded weak to my ears. I wondered if she heard herself. If she even believed it.

"Arum serves himself and uses whom and whatever he can to do so. This isn't right, Shadow! You know Castor's heart," Crow argued.

She shook her head. "I know she's a liar. She wore a cloak and crept among us for a time. She means to deceive, not make friends. Friends don't lie to one another. Arum has always been honest with us."

I'd hurt her by concealing who I was. To her, I'd proved once more that no one could be trusted. That not only did love not exist to her, but neither did true friendship. I was sorry she couldn't see that I had to keep hidden. For her safety, and ours.

But the fact that I'd hurt her didn't give her the right to hunt me down, or worse.

While they argued, my heart cracked as I studied Forge from afar, knowing he would look infinitely worse the closer I moved toward him. Both eyes were blackened. One was swollen shut. His bottom lip was split in the middle. Bruises marred his jaw and cheeks, even his temple. More likely lay beneath his blood-stained clothing. The white shirt plastered against his skin as the winds rolled down and struck him, then the rock wall, rattling the vines creeping down it. He was barefoot, chest heaving, his one good eye flicking between me and the great beast Shadow hadn't yet guided to either of us. "Castor, run!" he yelled.

I shook my head. "I won't leave you again."

"You didn't leave me. And I didn't leave you either. I was detained."

I crouched to the ground, then looked up and asked Crow, "Can you make the storm stronger?"

Crow nodded resolutely. Staring up into the heavens, he intensified the storm. Lightning crackled over the green-gray sky, causing the hair on my forearms to rise.

The wind roared relentlessly, harder and harsher. Tall pines bent sideways and deciduous leaves turned silver, each flapping like a ship's flag in a gale. Beside me, Crow luxuriated in the storm. He stared into the sky like he'd finally met with a dear friend after a long time spent apart. As the Tempest on Arum's ship, he had to chase storms away to keep the ship safe from sinking. Now, he could embrace the tumult. Now, there was nothing keeping him from stretching the wings of his power.

Through the howling wind, the thrashing forest, and the flickering sky with its bolts that rained all around us, Crow stood calmly beside me, pleased with the work he'd done, completely at home with his magic. A small, serene smile graced his face.

Shadow's hair lashed her now-garish face; yesterday's makeup lay harshly underneath her eyes and streaked her lips. Strands of her hair tangled in her eyelashes, but she didn't seem bothered.

Of the two of them, only Sarabi seemed shaken by the weather. The beast took a few steps away before Shadow guided him back to his position. He shook his head and paced back and forth, wanting to make her happy but unsure how. Wanting to leave, but also to obey the one to whom his soul was bound.

I let the power that lumbered deep within flow from my palm into the ground and pushed it hard into the soil, arcing it toward Shadow. Then, in my mind, I drew a circle around her and the lion. From the ground coiled a massive tangle of bushes. Sleek, sharp briars erupted on their stalks, bright green fading to yellow. The stalks thickened, stretched, obeyed. So did the briars.

Sarabi roared, pawing at the thorny hedge surrounding them.

The pad of his paw was sliced. Shadow called him down, laughing in the husky voice I once thought had been friendly. "Just because you've trapped the two of us, doesn't mean you can stop us all. There's an entire pack hunting you, Castor. You won't make it back to Cauldron alive."

I asked the bushes to fully to cage them in, closing the hedge over their heads. "We'll see about that."

She reached into her pocket and withdrew something small, smiling cruelly, then flicked the witch bell. Crow covered his ears and shot me a worried glance.

I ran toward Forge; Crow ran alongside.

Forge limped toward me. He hissed when my hands found his upper arms. "I'm so sorry," I breathed.

His hands threaded around my back and held tight. One hand moved so that his fingers threaded into my hair. He kissed my temple, my cheek, the corner of my lips.

A tear fell from my eye. My fingers shook as I tried not to hurt him, but longed to touch him, so thankful he was alive. "I'm so glad you're okay. I'm sorry for ever doubting you."

He shook his head. "Don't. You had every right. I should've told you everything from the beginning."

Crow cleared his throat. "Castor, you might want to heal and then arm him. Arum and the rest of his pack will descend on us soon because of that bell."

Shadow laughed from her briary cage. She was crouched and using her dagger to slice the stalk of briar closest to her. It withered and died, a section of her cage rendered useless. She moved on to the next bush.

I walked to her cage of briars and pinched a small gravebriar off the vine, handing it to Forge. As he chewed it, and as the bruises mottling his skin evaporated, I clasped a section of the gravebriar bush. I poured poison into the stalks and surged it to every sharp tip. I felt my poison move through the roots, to the next bush, and the next, until the entire cage was filled. If Arum wanted to snap one off... let him. If he touched this gravebriar, he'd be dead before his legs crumpled beneath him. "What are you doing to it?" Shadow demanded.

I smirked. "You're loyal to him, willing to kill for him. But let me ask you this, Shadow: are you willing to die for him?"

She gave Arum's bell another shake.

"That's enough racket from you," Forge warned. He raised his arm from beside me, and the metal bell and dagger in her hands melted. She shrieked when the molten silver touched her fingertips, coating them. She pulled them to her chest as the remainder of what had once been her bell splashed onto the leaves at her feet. Sarabi tried to find some room, but there was barely enough room for Shadow and the lion to stand without one of them accidentally brushing the poisonous briar tips.

"Easy," she comforted. "Don't push me into the thorns."

I handed Forge's bag to him and he withdrew two slivers of steel. In a second, he had a long, curved sword in each hand. I held his forearm. His brow furrowed. But then he breathed easier as I leached my poison from his blood. "You don't have to…"

"I know," I nodded. "I want to."

He bit his top lip and nodded back. "Thank you."

He clasped my hand, thanked Crow, and together the three of us ran in the direction of Cauldron. We didn't make it over the next knoll before Merc and Ury were upon us.

Zephyr was with them, staying back and hiding behind a broad tree. She used her wind magic to occupy Crow as Merc and Ury took in Forge's healed face and body… then his swords. "There's a price on your head, and Crow's," Ury continued. "*We* intend to claim both." He pulled a dagger from his waist I recognized as Forge's design.

Forge raked his sharp blades together, a metallic hiss ringing despite the storm that still raged. The men weren't deterred in the least.

"Forge," I called out, grinning. "Remember the vagrants?"

"How could I forget them?" He smiled back before raising his hand and melting the blade in Ury's clenched fist, then did the same to Merc's, still sheathed at his side. He cried out when the metal streaked down his trousers, jumping wildly to cool the hot metal, dragging Ury with him. The two tumbled backward, until they righted one another and together, turned to fight us, balling their boulder-sized fists.

I saw red when I thought of them using those fists against Forge.

He and I split to circle them.

Crow called down a bolt of lightning, arcing it around Zephyr's throat and pinning her to the tree's bark. It charred and burned, smoke swirling in his wind around us. "You're better than this, Zephyr. Better than him."

She hissed, trying to bury the back of her head into the tree's bark to avoid the bolts threatening her. "You're disloyal," she gritted in her tiny voice. She pulled her bell out, but it barely tolled before Forge melted it, too.

Merc and Ury looked a little nervous. "Can you not handle the three of us without reinforcements?" I taunted.

Ury let out a growl and the two charged as one. I side-stepped but Ury grabbed *my* wrist. I smiled. That was all I needed. He realized his mistake in an instant. With wide eyes, his breaths became shallow before his torso flopped forward and his leg went limp. Merc dragged his brother's half backward, trying to hold his chest up and hugging Ury's limp form to his side. "Ury! Ur –" He strangled on the word, his brother's labored heartbeat pushing the toxin into him. The two men fell forward onto the forest floor.

I loosed a breath.

"Are they only sleeping? Like the vagrants?" Forge asked, panting as he crouched and divesting them of the twin daggers they hadn't bothered using.

"They hurt you!" I cried dramatically before hugging him. Whispering into his ear, I told him, "They're sleeping."

Forge gave me a grateful smile before pursing his lips tight and wrapping both my hands in his. "Their weapons are mine, Gravebriar. They're going to try to kill you."

"I know," I told him. "Crow told me everything."

Forge stood, spotting one of his blades tucked into Zephyr's boot. He walked to her and took it back, crumbling the metal in his hands like a giant would crush rock.

Zephyr whimpered when I started toward her.

Crow stepped between us, raising a hand, stopping me the way I'd stopped him from drawing his sword against

Forge. "She's young. Her sister is a flyer. Her brother is my crewmate. Arum gave them a home when their parents abandoned them. They believe they are indebted..." He turned to the young girl. "But you've more than repaid him for what he's provided, and you don't have to do what he says anymore."

Tiny tears streaked down Zephyr's cheeks. She was young and easily manipulated. She was Arum's prey. They all were. He took those who needed much, gave them little, told them they owed him the world, and they believed him, thankful for any crumb that fell from his table. "If I let you go, will you return to help Arum?"

She shook her head as best she could, her blue eyes flooding again. "I won't. I'll go find Gale, I swear." Her tears splashed onto the forked bolt twitching around her throat, small plumes of smoke rising when the lightning's heat consumed them.

"Swears and promises mean nothing to me," I replied.

"Please?" Crow quietly pleaded. "Zephyr, give *me* your word that you'll go straight to the ship. You'll have a spot on my crew."

"But the ship belongs to –"

"It's Crow's ship now." I didn't want to hurt her. I hadn't hurt Merc and Ury either, but she didn't know that. "Know that if you help Arum in any way, if I see you in the forest or among the pack, I will end you. Regardless of how powerful he is, he's not as powerful as I am and he knows it. He can't stop me now that he unbound my power."

She sniffled and nodded profusely as more tears fell from her lashes. "What about Breeze?" Her sister, I assumed. The little flying girl who wowed the audience from her trapeze perch.

"If she cooperates, your captain will send her to the ship as well," I acquiesced. I nodded to Crow, who released his bolt.

"Zephyr, straight to the ship. And don't touch any gravebriar you see along the way!" he shouted after her as she fled. She turned and met his eye but never stopped, quickly disappearing over the hill.

"Will she listen?" I asked him.

Crow pursed his lips. "I hope so. She and her siblings are good kids. They needed a break and Arum was there to provide it."

"Is that what he did to you?" I asked gently.

"That's what he did to all of us. They just can't see it yet."

I gestured to Merc and Ury. "They will wake at dawn."

Crow's lips parted. "They're not…?"

I shook my head. "I wanted to scare Zephyr into leaving Arum and his ill-fated goals behind."

"That and she can't stomach hurting someone," Forge said, a hint of both pride and care in his voice. He hugged me to his side.

I really couldn't. I wasn't going to ask him to give them coin, though. They *did* try to kill me, and that was far ruder than petty theft.

Crow kept the storm near but allowed the winds to die and calmed the lightning, though I could still feel the electricity buzzing in the air. We needed to be able to hear anyone coming close. "How did Arum move his troupe so close to the hedge so quickly? It's almost sunset, and we've walked all day and are just now drawing near. Southmist is close, but they still should've had trek to the hedge."

"Ecriver. The Spellsweet is powerful. He wrote a spell to carry them there," Crow admitted.

"I'll destroy all the blades, Castor," Forge promised.

"Not yet," I told him. "We need to know where they are. You feel the bulk of them near the hedge?"

Forge gave a tight nod.

"Ecriver is Arum's true weapon," Crow warned. "You need to incapacitate him. His hands *and* his tongue."

"He said you attacked and pinned him to that tree," I told Forge, who looked taken aback.

"Arum cloaked himself as Forge," Crow confirmed. I'd considered that, but hearing it didn't take the sting of the blow away.

He looked at me pleadingly. "Castor, if something happens, don't worry for me or Crow. Surround yourself with poisoned gravebriar if you must."

I shook my head, knowing it wouldn't work. "If they managed to incapacitate you and have Silverthorn blades, they could just cut down anything I conjure."

"Then keep making them. Replace what they destroy faster than they can cut them down. Make every bit of the bush poison; push your magic up the metal and into the hands of those who would kill you!" Crow suggested.

It seemed a paltry bandage for a severe wound, but I could do it. I just wouldn't if it meant that Forge or Crow was left to fight Arum or his pack alone. Merc and Ury said there was a price on their heads. Arum wanted them dead. He was done negotiating.

The farther we walked, the closer we came to Arum and his pack, his troupe, the family he made loyal to only him. Forge thought each of them would forsake themselves for their leader's approval. I wondered if he was wrong and that more of them were like Zephyr. In the end, she valued her siblings over Arum, or at least she pretended to. If she circled around to rejoin him, we'd know soon enough.

A thought entered my mind. We weren't walking toward a pack of wolves, loyal to their alpha. We were marching toward a pride of lions ready to defend their king. Some animals attacked the weakest in their midst, establishing a pecking order, slowly building toward the fight with their greatest opponent. Each fight bolstered them, building their skills and preparing them for the next fight, concluding with the final opponent they would face. They would learn from each battle, every scar, every defeat and victory.

Lions were different. Lions attacked their greatest threat first.

If a lion wanted to lead, he went straight for the king's jugular.

And if he wasn't successful, he was forced out by the pride who remained steadfastly loyal to their king. After all, it was the king who kept them safe, made sure they found food, and led them to water.

The king of a pride ruled because he was strongest... but with my arrival, that wasn't true of Arum any longer. He was willing to battle to retain his crown. And he would attack me first, because I was the greatest threat among the three of us. I had to be ready, and I couldn't do this alone...

"I have a plan, but it'll put your acting skills to the test again," I teased.

Forge smiled. "You know how much I *love* acting."

I grinned. "With me."

"With you," he heartily agreed, grinning before pecking a kiss on my lips.

Crow groaned. "Why do I get the feeling you two aren't really talking about acting?"

Forge and I laughed.

TWENTY-THREE

The hedge was so close I could almost taste the varying powers blending within it. One flavor was stronger than all the others: gravebriar. It was the only ingredient Arum didn't have, the only force keeping the hedge from fracturing and falling completely apart.

Forge suddenly stopped short, holding out a hand to stop us. The three of us went still, searching between tree trunks for threats. Forge cursed. "We're surrounded." I turned in a circle. There was nothing visible, but I knew that a powerful Spellsweet such as Ecriver could hide much. The hedge lay beyond us, its pulse constant and stable. We were so close… yet I knew without seeing them who and what lay between us and it.

Ecriver appeared, his arms raised. His short, inky hair didn't even look mussed. It took little effort for him to use his magic, but for us to combat it would take everything. I was comforted by the fact that no Power from any coven was stronger than the next. If he was more powerful than his father, and I was more powerful than my mother, then he and I were equals at the very least. The dragon in my bones spit fire, claiming that she was his better. She wanted to make sure he knew it. She wanted to singe him for his treachery.

When he lowered his arms, palms floating down, Arum's pride appeared, each holding a Silverthorn blade.

Forge quickly disintegrated every blade.

Ecriver spoke and regenerated them.

Forge used his power again. Ecriver resurrected the metal.

Around us was a small army. They inched toward us, closing in all around... Elementines, holding water, fire, rock, and palm-sized twisters. Muscled, tattooed Bloodlings. The sword-swallowing Silverthorn woman. I recognized them all now.

Crow flicked a glance to me as if asking what he should do.

"I'm disappointed in you, Crow," Arum chastised as he emerged from between two Bloodlings whose forearms were thicker than my thighs. "I thought you embraced my vision."

"Your vision is distorted," he boldly countered. "What sort of man seeks to kill his own granddaughter? Not one I want to follow, and certainly none I'd trust with my life if he can so quickly devalue hers."

"She's got you twisted around her little finger, doesn't she?" he mused. "Her mother was skilled at that. Weren't you, Rose?" Arum turned to look behind him as two more Bloodlings walked my mother forward. Fabric was tied around her mouth and her wrists were bound behind her back. Her hair was pinned away from her face, but she was not the wilting, crumbling flower I'd left behind. She wore battle leathers and an enraged expression. She worked her jaw and the fabric loose until her mouth was free.

Her eyes locked with mine. "End this, Cas—"

Ecriver flicked his wrist and her voice died.

She tried to speak again. Her lips and jaw moved, but not even a squeak emerged from her throat.

Low enough that only Crow could hear me, I asked if he saw Zephyr among their number. He scanned the faces of those who were supposed to be his family, finally shaking his head. If she wasn't here, she had listened and hadn't somehow found Arum and told him that Crow warned her away from the briars.

I toed off my flats and stretched my bare feet over the ground. If my magic could flow from my palms, it could flow from my soles. I imagined roots beneath the ground, vibrant and green, pushing their way through the dark soil toward Ecriver. When it reached him, I urged the root to grow a stem, and that stem to grow thorns, and the thorns to wrap around his leg. Infusing the thorns with a paralytic. The stalk burst from the soil, vined around his ankle, stuck his flesh. He fell with a muffled thump.

None of Arum's pack noticed because their eyes were trained on me and Arum. Ecriver had been standing away from the group, keeping near the hedge, ready to dart inside to what he imagined was safety, no doubt.

Forge nudged my arm and shot me an approving smirk. "That was too easy for you," he whispered. "Didn't you know he was to be the Spellsweet Power?"

Crow cleared his throat to stifle a laugh, tucking his smile away again.

Arum brought Mother closer. "I can let her go, Castor. I will release her to you, *if* you give me what I need. An even exchange."

Mother shook her head, her eyes warning me to say no. She would rather die than let her father back into Cauldron.

Arum's head swiveled to where Ecriver had been standing. Through the crowd, I wasn't sure if he could see him lying on the ground or assumed he'd run away, but he knew

Ecriver was going to be no further help. If it rattled him, he gave no indication. His attention returned. "What do you say, Castor? A Rose for a briar?"

"Such a skilled negotiator you've become, Arum." I raised my chin defiantly. "If I were to take your bargain, what would you do in Cauldron once you gain access?"

"Seal the four of you out and take back the position of Gravebriar Power," he said easily.

"As Power, you would be duty-bound to heal Arbor, who was nearly as powerful as Mother. He'd already surpassed Father's abilities."

Arum scoffed. "Why would it benefit me to restore a threat?"

"What did I tell you about safety, Arum? As you live and breathe, you are never truly safe."

"You are the one in danger, my dear. You can save your lecture about safety."

"What if I say no, and that I won't give you a gravebriar in exchange for my mother?" I baited.

"Then I will cleave it from your grave," he hissed, taking an aggressive step toward me. Mother stumbled as he brought her forward with him. His patience with me was growing thin. After so many years, he could almost touch the hedge and I was his only obstacle, the one who could give him the briar he needed to break the magical barrier separating him from the life he created and the one he'd been forced out of.

Mother looked at Arum like he was the vilest creature she'd ever encountered. If she had my power, she would have poisoned him the moment he touched her. Still, he was her father. If she'd saved him from burning, sparing him a traitor's death, it would be no different than what I'd done with the vagrants, Shadow, Merc and Ury, Zephyr, and even Ecriver, the Spellsweet traitor whose chest still gently rose and fell.

"Well?" he demanded. "Your decision, girl?"

"I'll give you what you seek," I answered. "What other choice do I have?"

Forge protested, just as we'd planned. "Please don't. There has to be another way," he pleaded.

"Trust me," I answered, locking eyes with Forge Silverthorn and hoping my plan didn't fail. The futures of my mother, Crow, Forge, and my own depended on it.

His brow furrowed. "Are you sure? We should think about this."

"We're out of time," I answered.

Crow cringed as I crouched and held a hand to the ground. "You'll want a briar for each of your family members, too, right?" I asked as if to clarify. Arum frowned in response to my question. "To protect them in case something happens when you breach the hedge and encounter witches that don't want you to tear their city apart?"

Arum tensed for only a second, then smoothed a hand down his tailored jacket.

"Of course," he said, glancing around at his pack and rocking back on his heels. "One for each of them – one for the hedge, *and* a cache for our coven."

I lifted my hand and could almost hear him grit his teeth. "If I give you all of those, we'll have to amend our original agreement where you wanted a briar in exchange for Rose – my mother. If I give you all of those briars, do you agree that you and your pack won't hurt my mother, Forge, Crow, or me?"

"I give you my word." He gave a slight bow as if he was still playing the part of ringmaster – a role I was about to steal from him.

"Your word is meaningless!" Crow spat. He looked to me. "Don't trust him, Castor."

I raised my hand from the earth. "Send my mother to me first."

Arum shook his head. "No. If you want to exchange her fairly, you'll give me one gravebriar as proof that you'll conjure the rest. I will send your mother to you at the same time you place the briar in my palm."

"Are you sure it's an actual briar that you need to break the hedge? Or do you need *me* to shatter it?"

"Whether it's you or your briar, it doesn't matter. You will help me, or I will help myself."

I felt sorry for him in that moment. He'd taken a chance at another life and squandered it. He found people who loved and respected him and took them for granted. He let hatred and self-righteousness reign in a world where he was king and didn't even know it. He held the scepter, sat on the throne, and wore the crown, but to him – as long as it was outside this hedge – they meant nothing.

I eased my palm back to the ground. "Are you sure this is what you want, Arum?"

"Of course I'm sure."

"Is it what you *need*? There is a difference. Needs are things one cannot survive without. You've built an amazing life without it. It's a shame you appreciate none of it."

The members of his troupe shifted uncomfortably. Could they see that he didn't value them? That the only thing that mattered to him was his status within Cauldron? He cared for nothing outside its borders.

He narrowed his eyes and gritted, "Give me the gravebriar."

I pushed my magic into the soil, and a breath later the first stalk of a gravebriar bush ricocheted against my palm. I urged a single, tiny briar to burst from the stem, plucked it, and stood to face him, holding it between my two fingers.

I leeched a deadly concoction into it and bound it with my intentions. If Arum used the briar to attempt to break the hedge, the poison would seep into his skin. If he ingested it, the poison would leech into his body. If he harmed anyone I loved, he'd never draw another breath.

His was a death I wouldn't regret. I could feel it in my bones. Arum was a plague eating its way across the flesh, inch by inch, until there was nothing left for him to feed upon. The safety of those I loved, and of Cauldron and everyone within its hedge depended on him not breaking it and preying upon them.

I remembered facing Forge in the forest after Mother told me he was going to try to kill me; how my hands shook, my very soul vibrating from fear of using my power to harm. I felt none of that anxiety as I extended my hand toward my grandfather. "A briar in exchange for a Rose."

He shoved Mother forward as he accepted my offering. She stumbled, but Forge caught her and quickly cut the rope binding her hands.

Abrasions circled her wrists.

Arum shot me a smug smile before pushing his way through his pack, heading straight for the hedge.

"What about us, Arum?" a Bloodling shouted after him. "You said we'd all be given a gravebriar as protection. Have her make our briars before you shatter the hedge. If something goes wrong, we won't have our briars!"

The witch's plea didn't stop Arum's feet, didn't even slow him down.

"Isn't it obvious?" I shouted. "He doesn't care what happens to you. He didn't suggest that you each receive a briar for protection. I did. If you fought and died, he wouldn't mourn you," I announced. "Pinched between his fingers is what he's always wanted, and he used you all to help him get it. You were just a means to the end."

Pain flashed across the faces of all who had dedicated themselves to his every whim, who thought he loved them and cherished them.

I knew that look well, because I'd worn it often of late. It was the look one wore when finding out everything you thought you knew was a lie.

I let my voice ring loud and clear through the wood.

"Once there was a clever man, the best liar of them all.

He hid away his shriveled heart, within its bony wall…"

Arum's steps sputtered and then stopped. His shoulders tensed…

"He took in the outcasts, the orphans, the poor, and made himself, a king of lore.

Within his tent, his witches thrilled.

Their fantastical feats, kept his coffers filled."

Arum turned on his heel and flicked a hate-filled glance toward me.

"But in the end, the clever man, was the greatest fool of all,

For his eyes weren't set on the wonderment, but fixed on a magical wall."

Arum started forward again, his troupe now refusing to move out of his way to make his path easier.

"He forsook his family, the witch troupe that he'd built.

When they realized how he really felt, they all began to wilt."

They were too hurt to be enraged. They were also too hurt to defend or aid him further.

When I followed after him, his pack parted, granting *me* passage. Forge, Crow, and Mother trailed a step behind.

"The thorn was sharp and pretty, vital green and vibrant yellow.

But you know what they say about beautiful things, and what they do to foolish fellows…"

His troupe fell in step behind our smaller one, watching angrily as Arum approached the hedge. The air around it distorted, like heat wafting from scorched earth. The hedge rose far above the canopy, and if he dug a thousand years, he'd never reach its bottom for it had none. No beginning or end; it just was. Solid and infinite magic.

He hesitated, then pinched the briar and held it out to the magical barrier.

"He eased her toward the combined spell, that kept fools like him at bay."

My intention spread from the briar into his fingers, filling the whorls on the tips, the lines that came from his age despite Ecriver's clever spell work.

"And didn't know it was too late, till on the ground he lay."

One of Arum's knees buckled and he grunted as the poison seized his heart. He somehow managed to stay upright for a breath, then fell dead just shy of our hedge and the forest's dark heart. The briar tumbled from his fingers and landed nearby, glowing brightly on the dull, dark floor.

I picked it up and turned to offer it to anyone else who chose to continue Arum's insane quest, to follow him unto their deaths.

No one accepted my offer.

"You have a decision to make. To follow Arum's tutelage and the path of hatred, or to carve out a life for yourself, in or outside of Cauldron."

The tiny flying girl, Zephyr's sister, Breeze stepped out from behind a larger boy I recognized as her partner. "You... you'd invite us in after what we've done?"

She and Zephyr shared a nose, had the same bow to their lips. "Conditionally, yes. To step through the hedge, you'll have to take my magic into your blood along with my intention to kill any one of you who threatens my home or anyone in it. Time and action will prove whether you can be trusted."

"Do you have the authority to make that decision?" the Silverthorn sword-swallower questioned, brushing her pewter-streaked hair over her shoulder.

"Cauldron is a sanctuary for witches, and she belongs to you as much as any other witch."

Some immediately walked away, carving paths through the forest toward Westbrook. Others went toward Southmist. Those who remained huddled together, quietly conversing.

They were a coven. Some whispered, wondering if they would they be split apart once inside the hedge? If they'd be allowed to leave if they decided it wasn't for them? Could they trust me not to kill them?

"This isn't a decision to make lightly, so I know you need time, but I can't stay while you consider my offer. One of my coven mates lays dying and I need to go help him. What I can do is return later today to take in anyone who wants to seek refuge in Cauldron."

The troupe looked to one another, agreeing to wait near the hedge for me to return. "I'll be back as soon as I can."

I looked to Crow. "Will you come with us now? You've more than proven yourself trustworthy."

He looked torn, then fixed his gaze in the direction of Southmist. "My ship is docked in Southmist Harbor, and my crew will be waiting there…" He smiled. "I'm afraid I don't belong on land. The sea is my home."

I stepped away from Forge and Mother. "May I hug you?"

"Of course," he assented.

I wrapped my arms around his neck. "Thank you, Crow. Thank you for seeing."

"Seeing?" he asked as I pulled away.

"Seeing that *I* wasn't the poison who sickened your troupe."

He ducked his head, his cheeks blushing furiously, and folded his hands behind him. "Thank you for breaking Arum's hold on me. On *us*… I hope." Again, his gaze trailed toward those of his troupe who'd remained with us, ready to enter Cauldron when I allowed them through the hedge. "And for the hug," he winked.

He looked to Southmist at the backs of a few of troupe members who didn't want to enter the hedge. "If I'm to claim that ship, I need to beat the others to it."

"A storm might slow the others down," Forge suggested, clapping him on the arm.

Crow nodded and shook his hand, then bowed to Mother, telling her it was nice to have met her. He stood awkwardly before me, smiled, and bent to whisper in my ear. "May I write to you?"

"I certainly hope you will. We're friends, and beyond that, we're allies now."

He inclined his head. "Then await the first of many messages." He cheekily grinned. He pulled a wooden box out of his pocket and placed it in my palm. It was the box that contained the wagons, the tents... everything one might need for a circus of witches.

We watched him jog away, the wind already gusting in his wake.

Forge carried Ecriver through the hedge, and Mother and I stepped through side by side. He laid the traitorous Spellsweet on the forest floor just inside the boundary's safety far gentler than I would've dumped him.

Mother surprised me by almost tackling me to the ground. She crushed me in her arms and cried, her body heaving as she sobbed into my ear. Her hands shook when she drew my face to her lips, kissing my cheeks and head.

"You didn't come back!" she croaked, pulling me in for another hug.

"I couldn't do that to Arbor. How is he?"

She pursed her lips, her eyes flooding with tears.

My heart dropped. "Is he dead?"

She sniffled and blinked more tears away. "No, no... he's not dead. But he's not recovering, either. He has grown very weak despite our most valiant efforts."

"Then why are you *here*? Why aren't you there helping him?"

"You needed my help," she explained. "When Bog returned without you, I knew something terrible had happened. You would never leave him behind."

My mouth fell open. This time, tears filled *my* eyes. Around the frog-sized knot in my throat, I confirmed, "Bog came home?"

She nodded frantically. "I found him on the terrace this morning, and I have never been so scared. You... I don't tell you enough, Castor, but I love you so much. If something had happened to you, I never would have forgiven myself."

Forge locked eyes with me, his pressed lips curled on one side. I felt a twinge of guilt that his reception home wouldn't be as warm as mine. Though admittedly, mine was far warmer than expected.

Still crying, she held me away from her. "What are you wearing?" She toyed with a strand of my hair. "What happened to you?"

My bodysuit no longer looked pristine and pretty. The rose gold was more of a sad, pale brown. It was torn in places, soaked with my sweat, as was my hair. There were twigs caught in it and again, I'd lost the hat Arum gave me at some point, so I'd caught more spider webs than Forge had on our way to Westbrook. But what I wore didn't matter...

I hated doing it, but as she clutched my fingers, I surged a tiny amount of hallucinogen into her hands. Her pupils dilated and her tears dried. Her hiccoughing chest calmed. "Castor?" she said, dazed but somehow still poised. Ever the elegant rose.

"Tell me about your father, Arum," I entreated.

A despondent, sorrowful look fell over her face. "He was not a good man. He was the Gravebriar Power when I was young."

"Did you feed me gravebriar?"

Her delicately arched brows pulled together. "No, I most certainly did not feed you gravebriar. My father did and I saw that he paid for his crime – or so I thought." Her pupils flared. "My father used to make you tea every afternoon when you were just a toddler. You loved the flavors and the sweetness. One day, your eyes looked yellow instead of their crystalline amber hue. Your hair looked a little green instead of golden. I didn't realize why until you told me about your grandfather's special tea and how it was green and yellow instead of warm brown. I panicked then and found our supply – thirteen briars – emptied. I bound him immediately and called for the Councilwitches."

That liar. He'd blamed it all on Mother.

"Why would he have me consume the gravebriar?"

"To a witch of our lineage, a single gravebriar is healing. The Goddess discourages greed, and for that reason, if a Gravebriar witch consumes more than one briar, it is poisonous to her blood. My father tried to kill you, Castor, because a Diviner told him you would be more powerful than I, more powerful than he. What he didn't know was that you already were more powerful, and that your power was different than ours. He didn't poison you at all. If anything, he made you stronger."

I watched her pupils swell and contract as she fought to focus on my face. "Did you know he cloaked my true power? Did you know that I could grow gravebriar?"

"No," she said, brows kissing, words slow. "I didn't know you could do that... Arum never confessed, never spoke even to defend himself when he was accused of poisoning you. You told us what he'd done, that he'd taken yellow and green briars and ground them up. He had you help him, even made it fun for you." She pursed her lips, emotional even as she was under the influence of my magic. "You told me he'd taken your magic and hid it away, and until we realized what your magic was, I thought he was right. I truly did think you were powerless for a time. That changed later, of course, when you learned what you were capable of.

"So, no. I had no idea you could grow gravebriar... until just now. I knew you could heal yourself. You fell on the terrace one afternoon and cut the skin of your knee to ribbons. Blood was pouring down your shin, so I sat you on a table to get a better look so I could heal you without leaving a scar, and when I did, the wound was already closed. All I had to do was wipe the blood away. But I didn't know you could grow gravebriar until you grew it for Arum outside the hedge... I'm glad he's finally gone. A daughter should never have to feel that way, but I do."

I held her hands a little tighter, slowly withdrawing the hallucinogen, and she began to perk up. "Mother, how did Arum escape being burnt at the stake?"

"I suspect Parler saved him, but have no evidence. It was the Spellsweet power, or a strong Fire witch."

I looked to Ecriver – lying on the ground, chest rising and falling. It seemed there were many secrets that needed to be revealed this day, and that the Gravebriars and Silverthorns weren't the only ones keeping things from the Council.

I gave a mirthless laugh. "No wonder Parler believed in my innocence! He knew I hadn't poisoned Arbor. And if I had never shown up – if Arum would've succeeded in his dark task – everyone would have assumed I had chosen not to return. They would think I'm a coward, that I ran."

"Speaking of Arbor," Forge nudged. "We need to hurry home."

Mother sharpened, emerging completely from the hallucinogenic fog I'd poured over her. Her hand clamped onto my arm. Unafraid. "Did you just… did you use your magic on me?"

"I had no choice." I defended. "Arum accused you of many things and I had to be sure."

Mother gestured in the direction of home. "The two of you should know that Cauldron isn't the same as you left it. The Gravebriars and Silverthorns are openly at war."

At least Ecriver hadn't lied about that.

Forge's metallic eyes fell on me. Dread swam within their depths, but also resolution. "Then we should probably put an end to it as soon as Arbor is well. Are you with me, Gravebriar?" he asked, a hint of a dare in his voice as he held out his hand.

I placed mine in it and he curled his warm fingers around my skin. "I'm with you, Silverthorn. Always."

He pulled me in for a quick kiss.

Mother's lips parted. "I'm very glad you didn't heed the wishes of the Council, Forge." She turned to me. "It appears much happened on your journey." A single brow arched. She gestured to Ecriver. "This traitor should face the Council."

"Will they burn him at the stake?" I asked.

She nodded once. "Along with his father and any others conspiring with them against Cauldron."

The thought of seeing, or even hearing or smelling anyone being burnt at the stake turned my stomach. Despite all they'd done. Despite the fact that they were traitors who almost got me and Forge killed, whose scheme hopefully hadn't led to Arbor's death.

Forge's hand tightened around mine before he let it go. "I can bind him with what's left of the rope they used on you, Rose," he offered.

She gave a nod. "Bind him and then wake him, Castor. Let him walk in with us." Mother's tone had hardened as her gaze drifted to her father laying just beyond the hedge. "That leaves the task of burying Arum, once and for all. Forge, can you drag him in?" Forge crossed the boundary and took Arum's ankles, dragging him through the hedge. His troupe watched as the body of the man they once trusted was left beyond their reach. Whatever gravebriar grew from his grave would be poisonous, like him.

"I'll send some from our coven to handle his burial, and equip them with one of your blades, Forge," I told him. Whatever he produced had to be destroyed.

TWENTY-FOUR

Forge guarded Ecriver, the traitor's hands bound tightly behind him. The cloth he'd helped Arum gag my mother with, now gagged *him*. Crow had warned us to silence him and still his hands. Now, he could neither speak nor write.

"Who is the current Gravebriar Power?" I asked Mother, walking beside her.

"That honor lies with Zinnia." Zinnia was Mother's age. They were once friends, once close. I wondered if the recent tumult had quelled her affection for our family.

As the four of us walked into the back lawn of the Diviner Estate, our presence did not go unnoticed. A curtain was jerked open in an upstairs room, followed by a flood of commotion as the Diviners rushed to fill the windows.

Mother and I led the way into the Gravebriar yard, jogged the steps to our home's terrace, and together pushed open the double doors.

"Zinnia!" one of my coven mates shouted into the house.

Heels hurriedly clacked down the hall before Zinnia turned the corner in a plain, sage day dress, stopping abruptly in front of us. Her eyes widened. She opened her mouth, but didn't speak. Her shoulders deflated at the sight of us – mother and daughter. Both Powers in our own right. Both far more powerful than her. Her lashes fluttered as she tucked a curly red strand of hair behind her ear. "Rose, you're back. And, I see you found Castor."

She took in Ecriver's state and pressed a hand to her chest, clearing her throat.

"More correctly, she found me, but yes," Mother answered.

"How?" she choked, darting a look between us all, leaving the question open for us to fill the void of confusion. "Why is Ecriver bound?"

"We'll explain later, but right now, Castor has the gravebriar Arbor needs and she must see him right away."

Zinnia swallowed thickly. "Of course. I'm so happy she found it."

Zinnia's voice did not sound joyful at all.

"I can stay down here with him," Forge offered, nodding to Ecriver.

I shook my head. "We stay together."

I didn't trust anyone. Not even Zinnia. And I wouldn't until we were safe and things were made right and settled once again.

She led the four of us upstairs to Arbor's room. He lay where I last saw him, but in the six days I'd been gone, his condition had deteriorated greatly. He was wane, his face gaunt and too thin. The room was dark, with only a single candle flickering on his bedside table, almost at its wick's end. Just like Arbor.

His chest rose and fell slowly, his eyes unmoving behind his lids.

He looked peaceful, but so, so tired. Like his body was weary from too long a battle.

If Arum had taught me anything, it was that magic had no limit other than stifled imagination. If he could cloak my magic, if a poison could be hidden so I couldn't detect it, then I didn't need soil to grow the gravebriar...

"Where is the briar?" Zinnia asked.

Arbor's lashes fluttered.

I reached deep within and imagined myself the gravebriar bush, my body its stem, my arms a stalk emerging from it, then briars spreading over its surface like sharp teeth... Something tingled along my forearm and Zinnia gasped, covering her mouth. My forearm was lined with gravebriars, but I only needed one with which to heal him. I plucked a single briar and urged the others to sink back into my skin.

"Mortar and pestle?" I asked Zinnia over my shoulder. Forge kept Ecriver upright in the room's corner. He tried to speak around the gag, but said nothing coherent. Forge told him to be quiet more than once, but the more time we spent in the room with Arbor, the more agitated and combative he became.

Zinnia listened to see if she could make out his ravings, but eventually turned away, shouting my request into the hall where plenty of our coven mates hovered to see what was happening. "Mortar and pestle, please!"

A moment later, Laurel, the closest thing I had to a friend before the revel, appeared in the doorway with what I needed. She handed the mortar and pestle to Zinnia, who brought them to me. I sat next to Arbor on the side of the bed like I had before leaving Cauldron and carefully ground the green and yellow briar into dust.

She handed me a spoon and a small cup of water Laurel had returned with, and I made a paste, scraped it up with the spoon, and asked Arbor to open his mouth. Laurel watched from the doorway as Arbor parted his chapped lips and let me insert the spoon. I held his eyes as the gravebriar paste settled on his tongue. "I did not poison you, Arbor."

He closed his eyes and I wondered if he believed me.

Ecriver raged behind me. Forge kept him still as best he could, but he was trying to wrench himself from Forge's grip. I'd had enough and walked to him. His eyes went wide when I lifted my hand. "You're being disruptive," I tutted, grazing his cheek. Ecriver settled as the concoction I fed him, not at all different from the one I tried to first calm the constrictor with, entered his system.

I turned back to Arbor and watched as the gravebriar quickly took effect. He held out his hand. I clasped it and helped him sit up, then went to pull away when he clasped my hand tighter. "I believe you," he rasped.

"I will find who did this to you," I vowed.

He nodded. "Thank you for saving me."

His dull eyes brightened to their freshly disturbed mud-puddle color and his pallor improved. He looked to the corner where Forge and Ecriver stood, his eyes widening when he saw the Spellsweet was bound. "What happened to Ecriver?"

I stood and faced Zinnia. "I'd like for you to call a Council meeting. Most already know we're back. I'm sure they won't mind coming to the Estate."

The lines on Zinnia's forehead deepened. She crossed her arms. "I'd like for you to tell me what's going on before I go to them."

"Zinnia," I began, "what I have to say, I will only say once – to, and in front of the Council."

She flicked a wary glance at Mother, who stood on the other side of the bed. "Please, Zinnia. We aren't disrespecting your position within the coven, but asking you to have faith that what we are about to reveal is important enough to warrant the Council's advice, and that the matter is one of great urgency. Please, I ask you as a friend and coven mate."

Zinnia waited a long moment, then finally bobbed her head. She regarded Forge. "Very well. The Silverthorns may decline the invitation, though."

Forge laughed. "Just tell my father I'm here. He'll come."

Zinnia barely made it out of the room before my father entered it. He paused as if he wasn't sure whether to go to Mother or me first. Relieving his indecision, we both walked to him, each of us tucking ourselves under one of his outstretched arms.

"Goddess, if either of you leave Cauldron again, I don't know what I'll do, but don't leave without telling me. I'd at least like the chance to go with you."

I looked to Mother. She'd left without him?

She pulled away, placing enough space between them that might as well have been a deep chasm. Did the absence of their careful lies mean they had little in common now? Or was it the loss of the statuses they loved that stretched between them?

On the back lawn of the Gravebriar Estate, the nine Council members gathered. This time, I wasn't the subject of their disdain, but of their intrigue. I faced them with Zinnia, Mother, and Father at my side. From the back door, Forge brought Ecriver out, the Silverthorn prodding along the stumbling Spellsweet. They traversed the terrace, and I moved to touch Ecriver's cheek, removing my calming concoction.

He sobered immediately, taking in our party before moving his eyes to the Council. His lips parted when he looked at his father.

"Parler," I addressed the Spellsweet Power, "shall I speak on your behalf, or would you prefer to confess?"

The older man looked to his feet. His long, white hair seemed thinner, the bow in his back more severe. Even his baggy clothes couldn't hide that he was withering away.

Parler slowly raised his head, straightened his back as much as he could. "Arum Gravebriar is and always will be the rightful Gravebriar coven Power!"

"Arum Gravebriar is dead," I told him, watching his proud expression crash like a wave upon a rock. I'd once highly esteemed Parler, admired his steady leadership, but had no idea his foundation wasn't of stone, but sand.

"Arum was burned at the stake years ago..." the Bloodling Power, Sanguine casually intoned. "Of course, he's dead."

"No, he wasn't," I said sharply. "The Silverthorns and Gravebriars are hardly the only covens with secrets. Some worse than the others... Parler, I believe, cast a powerful spell that preserved Arum from the flame. He and Ecriver volunteered to carry him into the forest, beyond the barrier, where they set him free. For years, the Spellsweets have been conspiring with Arum to decimate the hedge that our covens built to protect one another, and they almost succeeded. They had all but one ingredient left to break the binding magic." I've never heard the Council so still as they took in the gravity of my allegations. "I don't believe the Spellsweets were alone in their treachery. I believe others within Cauldron readily helped Arum Gravebriar in his attempt to ruin us all." I let my eyes travel over the assembled witches, leaders most considered above reproach, and wondered who else among them had pushed for my death.

"I did not poison Arbor Gravebriar, but whoever framed me knew the secret of my magic. They had to have learned it from Arum as he's the only one who knew the extent of my power. And they knew the only way Arum could succeed was if I was removed from Cauldron so that Arum and his witches could hunt me down and kill me. To plant me in the ground and harvest the briar from my grave. If he'd have succeeded, there wouldn't be a Council. Arum said he wanted to reclaim his position, but he wouldn't have stopped there. He'd have killed any who opposed him and taken full control. If you think differently, that he was altruistic when he told you his plan, you're a fool."

Crystabal swallowed thickly, haughtily brushing her curled coral hair away from her face. Was she upset that she wasn't made aware, or had she known the whole time?

"You say Arum is dead now?" Sterling Silverthorn bit, his steely gaze fixed on his son.

"Together, your son and I protected ourselves, Cauldron, and its hedge, and therefore, all of you. So, whatever insignificant squabble exists between our covens needs to end here and now."

Forge shifted control of Ecriver to my father and moved to stand at my side. We clasped hands. To them, it was likely a show of solidarity. Two young people had fought a formidable adversary and emerged from the battle victoriously. They didn't know how close we'd become. But in time, if Forge was willing, we could make that as clear as the solarium glass.

"So... you found the gravebriar in the cemetery Rose told us about?" Sterling asked. If I was right, he knew there was no such place...

"Arum revealed a truth neither I nor my parents knew. When you burned him for treason, for feeding me the coven's entire supply of the briar... *that* was what I became. The overdose of gravebriar didn't poison me, because poisons were where my magic already lay. But it *did* make me stronger and gave me the ability to grow our namesake at will."

"What are you saying?" Crystabal asked.

"I'm saying... *I am the gravebriar.* Or could you not *divine* that?"

323

Seething, she watched carefully as I raised an arm, pushing the briars from my skin so they could see. Many heads reared back at the sight.

"I did not poison Arbor, but I will find out who was involved in this plot to usurp my family."

"You have no authority here!" Sterling blustered, jerking on the lapels of his finely tailored jacket.

"No, Father," Forge said coldly. "*You* have no authority here. I formally challenge you for the title of Silverthorn Power."

His father looked as shocked as the rest of us, myself included. I turned to Forge with a question in my eyes, remembering all the times he said he didn't want the responsibility.

He leaned in to my ear and softly said, "There's only one way to have a say, Castor. Only one way to set things right and that's to lead. We were given great power for a reason." He squeezed my hand. "I stand with you no matter what you decide you want to do."

Parler blustered. "You and your family have no right –"

"Let her speak," Wraith, the Nocturn Power barked. He'd likely just woken up to come here. The sun was setting again, dusk stretching her cool fingers over the Estates. "It is you who have no right to speak on matters that involve the Council or Cauldron anymore, Parler Spellsweet."

Forge had challenged his Father so bravely, so surely. And he was so right. So, so right. I looked to the Council. "I am the most powerful Gravebriar witch. I know it was wrong to hide my magic from the Council. I admit my mistake. But a Council is only as strong as the witches who occupy its seats. I'd like the opportunity to challenge Zinnia for the title of Gravebriar Power as well."

Zinnia clutched her chest, her eyes shining. I thought she would protest, but instead, she burst out laughing. "If the Councilwitches accept you, I would proudly concede.

As you've said, a Council is only as strong as the witches on it. And by extension, a coven is only as strong as its leader. Your magic makes mine seem miniscule. I would concede and give you my full support, Castor. In my opinion, you've proven your loyalty and love of this coven and this city."

I thanked her and accepted the hug she proffered, then turned back to the Council. "We need to know who was part of this treachery," I told them. "Questioning everyone won't work, as many would lie to conceal their part of this coup. I need you to trust me that I can reveal who was involved. I just need you to call your covens to the yard."

Sterling was deadly quiet as he glared at Forge, at our still-clasped hands, at me.

Parler raged like he was part Tempest until Sanguine decided his words were dangerous and asked me to quiet him.

The Powers called for their covens, and the witches of Cauldron divided among the back lawn, although this time, they weren't arrayed along fine tables. This time, they weren't being kept apart, but separated themselves.

Eyes flicked quizzically from Councilwitch to Councilwitch, to Forge and me, and to Ecriver – still bound and gagged. To Parler, strangely quiet beside his son, and Arbor, who'd felt well enough to dress in a finely tailored suit and stand with the Gravebriars in a show of solidarity.

He looked strong and solid, despite his brush with death. He looked angry.

I didn't blame him. If someone had poisoned me and considered my life expendable, I'd want to know who it was. Likewise, I wanted to know who falsely accused me, managed to get me banished and almost burnt at the stake. Who had pointed me toward Arum's sticky web?

The Council members, as we'd discussed privately, moved to stand with their covens. Forge moved Parler and Ecriver to stand with theirs, then joined his father in front of his own, while Arbor and I stood with the Gravebriars, Zinnia nodding to me to indicate she was behind me.

Gust, Power of the Elementines, cleared his throat, waiting for everyone to stop fidgeting, stop whispering. He was tall and thin, like a pine that had survived many a storm. His kind, sparkling eyes reminded me of Crow's, and I hoped he'd beat the others to the ship that was rightfully his, that he'd gathered his crew and set sail on the ocean he loved too much to part with. "We gather today to honor Castor Gravebriar and Forge Silverthorn, as they have saved our great city from one who would have seen her destroyed." Soft murmurs began. "Their covens have caused great strife in our community since the pair left and even before that their turmoil touched us all at one point or another, but like all wounds, the actions of these two brave and determined witches will allow us to begin healing and forgiving one another for past grievances."

An Elementine girl whose magic lay in water stood near the back of her coven. Gust had pulled her aside the moment he saw her enter the yard and asked her for her help. He'd also asked for Scribe's, the young Spellsweet who would likely take Parler's place.

Obeying her Power, she flooded the grass, carrying Scribe's truth spell to the skin of every witch standing on the lawn. Some stood, confused about the water, unable to focus on anything else. They lifted one foot, then the other. Others gently splashed, laughing and wondering what was happening, confusion fusing with their smiles.

Gust allowed his booming voice to carry over the lawn. "Would the person or persons who poisoned Arbor Gravebriar please step forward?"

Everyone who was splashing, stopped splashing.

Those who chattered, stopped speaking.

Those who stared at the water, lifted their heads.

I focused on Arcana, but she did not move.

The only person who moved, the only person who stepped forward, was Arbor himself.

My mouth gaped and feelings of betrayal and hurt swirled through my gut. My eyes found Forge's waiting, but I turned back to Arbor. "Why?"

"How was I ever going to be better than you?" he winced. "*You* are the true Power."

"Did you know Arum was alive? Did you know of his plan?" I asked, struggling to keep my tone smooth, even as my thoughts roiled.

He nodded. "Yes. I helped get you out of Cauldron. They said you'd heal me right away and then be banished. I could claim the Power role and you'd be gone."

"Did they tell you Arum intended to return as Power?"

"His intentions didn't matter," he said. "I'm stronger than Rose, who was stronger than him. He would have come back, but he wouldn't have bested me."

No, Arum planned to let Arbor die. I bet he didn't know that.

"If you conspired with Arum in any way, small or large, step forward," Gust instructed.

Again, Arcana did not move.

But Crystabal did, as did a few of Parler's confidantes in the Spellsweet Coven. But what surprised me the most, and what painted a look of hurt and distress on Forge's face, was that his father stepped forward as well.

Gust kindly turned to me. "Are you satisfied, Castor? Is there any other question you'd like to ask?"

"I think that's all." He motioned for the water Elementine to drain the grass. Crystabal, the Spellsweet conspirators, and Sterling Silverthorn stood apart from their covens, every eye fixed on them.

"You," the Silverthorn Power growled, starting toward me.

Forge stepped in front of me protectively. "Touch her and you'll die by my hand. I swear I'll cut you down right here – if she doesn't kill you first."

Sterling's chest rose and fell rapidly, a vendetta brewing in his eyes. He didn't look at his son. He refused to. He kept his cold stare focused on me, and I was glad looks could not cut, because the Silverthorn's former Power would have sliced me to the root and I'd shrivel and dry and crumble to dust.

"The penalty for treason is death," Gust noted.

"I propose something far worse than that," I told him. "Far more punishing."

"What could be worse?" Gust's gray brows drew in.

"Being rendered magicless."

His lips parted. "You can take their magic?"

"I can't take it, but I can poison their magic. I can kill it." The crowd was completely still. "I think we should let the traitors choose: death or banishment and a life devoid of magic."

Sterling turned to stone, as did Crystabal, Parler, Ecriver, and their compatriots.

Gust nodded slowly. He called forth who was left of the Council, and they were unanimous in their support of giving their former peers the choice I'd offered.

Gust went down the line, calling the conspirators by name and offering their choice. I expected them to fight, to rage, but in the end think they knew they would not get out of this without choosing and each wanted to make their own choice.

None chose death.

Forge armed himself and accompanied me as I approached them one by one. I touched their skin and poured my poisonous power and intention into each of their magics, beginning with Parler and followed by Ecriver, then the few coven mates they'd likely dragged into the matter. Crystabal glared at me while I killed her divination abilities, gasping and clutching her stomach when she reached out for that part of her she knew by heart and found it empty.

Sterling stared accusingly at Forge standing resolutely beside me, my protector against his coven, the only who could cut me down... I melted away his metal magic before he changed his mind and lashed out.

Forced to empty their pockets, the traitors were escorted through the parted covens, then from Cauldron by a horde of volunteers comprised of witches from every coven who served as witnesses that the banished traitors had been pushed through the hedge they'd tried to help Arum destroy.

Mother and Zinnia sent Gravebriars to see to Arum's burial and the destruction of the vine he produced – if his evil heart pushed anything through the soil.

I hoped this somehow was a beginning to the end of the unrest churning in Cauldron, and that Forge wouldn't one day hate me for robbing him of his father. His voice tugged me out of dark thoughts.

"The feud between our coven and the Gravebriars ends here and now," Forge announced, sweeping his molten eyes over the witches who remained. "The Gravebriars are not our enemy. None of the covens should consider another their enemy. If we want to better Cauldron, we have to put our differences aside and rule this place with the same ambition as the ones who founded it. We must work *together* to make their vision come to life." With the power of his words still ringing in the air, Gust dismissed everyone.

As the witches funneled from the soaked grass, and as the sun fully set to the west behind the gray clouds that had somehow packed the sky without me noticing, Forge turned to me. He gathered me in his arms and squeezed me tight as I locked mine around his neck and held on. I shook my head, still trying to come to terms with the tumultuous events of the past day. "I can't believe it was Arbor all along."

"Not only him. I'm sorry my Father was involved, though looking back, he did know a lot about Arum. I should've known, should've questioned him, but I made the mistake of trusting him," he said. A mistake I'd made, too, and had endured the consequences of. "Tomorrow?"

My brows kissed. "Tomorrow?"

He leaned back. Mischief glimmered in his eyes. "Yeah. I mean, after you sleep until noon, can I see you tomorrow? There's this delicious little bakerie on the main avenue…" He leaned in and captured my mouth, hands finding my sides and squeezing as he deepened our kiss. Goddess, I would miss him. The butterflies he always woke swirled around my stomach, a delicate, violent tornado.

And when we parted, I realized how grateful I was he'd come into my life. That I cared for him. And that my heart had spoken and meant her words when I told him I had no intention of releasing my hold on him.

"If you think that our claiming the Power roles means we won't have free time, think again. We just need to straighten things out and then learn to delegate. A lot. That way, we'll have time to perfect our acting skills. Often."

"You're incorrigible," I noted, smiling at him.

"You love it." He kissed me again.

I did love it.

I didn't notice it until that moment, but my parents stood awkwardly waiting for us to finish our 'conversation.'

Father was clearly struck by the fact that his daughter was in love with a Silverthorn, perhaps even a bit uncomfortable with our public display of affection, but Mother's eyes twinkled with approval when she glanced between us.

I was her child. I was happy. I was alive, and home, and no secrets lay between us and anyone else now. We were free.

The truth was freedom, I realized. Lies were what bound a person.

Forge didn't care that we had an audience. He was quite the skilled performer, after all. He kissed me again, slightly more chastely, then spoke into my ear. "It still has to be you and me against them all. Not because anyone is our enemy now, I hope, but because we are stronger together than we are apart. The near future is going to be fraught with difficulties, but… if you're with me, I know it'll be okay."

"I'm with you," I promised.

"No matter what happens…" he led.

"No matter what."

TWENTY-FIVE

F orge." I froze, my hand on his forearm. "The troupe is
still waiting for me."

"You have to speak to the Council before bringing
them inside. Acting alone will damage any trust we've garnered today," he warned.

The two of us jogged to gather the Councilwitches once
more before they trailed back to their respective Estates, to
their homes. Many gathered to answer questions and calm
fears. We explained what we knew of Arum's troupe, how
he'd manipulated and abused them, our feelings that they
were entitled to a life here – as much as any of us were, and
what I'd planned to ensure the safety of our sanctuary.

A few dissented, but the remaining Councilwitches
gave their consent to bring Arum's troupe inside the hedge
predicated on the conditions I'd already insisted upon.
They would take my poison and intention into their blood
and flesh, and if they tried to harm Cauldron or any witch
within its walls, they would suffer Arum's fate.

He and I arrived at the hedge as darkness made its
debut to escort what was left of Arum's troupe inside, each
shaking my hand and receiving their dose of my magic.

Each looking completely emotionally and physically wrung out. I gave Forge the box Crow entrusted me with and asked that he seek out Scribe for a spell to counteract the one that shrank their wagon homes. He promised to have things settled by the time I got back.

I still had two beasts to deal with…

Sarabi grunted when he heard my footsteps. Without my torch, I wouldn't have seen even one step ahead, but Wraith guided me through the darkness with ease. The orange fire-light flickered over their vibrant, briary cage, still intact. Neither of them had touched the sharp thorns, a testament to Shadow's patience, and her love for Sarabi.

Face draped in darkness, highlighted by my torch's warm glow, Shadow stayed close to the lion. She kept one hand on the great cat's back. "What do you want?"

"I've come to set you free."

"You've come to kill us." She stroked Sarabi's mane as if to calm him, or perhaps to calm herself. It was something my mother did, something I recognized. It happened when fear was too great to contain and contact was the only thing that could solve it. Contact with your beast. Mother used it when raking her hands down her fine clothing…

"I've only killed one person today and won't add to that number unless you force me to. Would you prefer we leave you out here indefinitely?"

She glanced at Wraith, studied his Nocturn eyes, so much like hers. "I'd prefer it over whatever you intend to do to me."

I walked the circumference of the briars surrounding them, and she and Sarabi followed, turning a tight circle to keep me in sight.

In my fist was a paper with a spell written in beautiful swirling letters. Scribe had given it to me. As the acting Spellsweet Power, he was more than willing to help, and promised to try to counteract any ill-doing his predecessors and coven mates had done. Wraith held my torch while I unfurled the note.

"Sarabi… *resilio felis, non nocere et cunctis diebus vitae tuae.*"

The great lion, so ferocious, felt the magical words wrap around him, tightening, tightening until his bones shrank, then followed his skin and sinew, fur and teeth and claws. Until he was reduced to a yellow house cat. The words shrank him. The words made him harmless.

Shadow gasped and fell to her knees, picking him up. "Why?" she cried, holding Sarabi to her chest.

I pushed the thorns close to her, even as she shrank away, huddled her body around the little kitty's… until I felt a thorn pierce the skin of her back. She cried out and I let my intention sink into her skin. I poisoned her magic, too, but not her.

My briar bushes died, turned to gray dust and crumbled all around her, and fell down on her where they'd caged her in.

She felt her chest. "My magic…" Her eyes shone with tears.

"You deserve worse. You're lucky I didn't treat you as you treated me in the end."

She cried, holding Sarabi and rocking back and forth.

Wraith nudged my arm. He ticked his head back toward Cauldron, and the two of us left Shadow and Sarabi in the forest.

When we stepped back in the hedge, Forge was there with Gust and Arcana, the acting Diviner Power. She met me with a smirk before I could reach Forge. Wraith saw someone he recognized in Arum's troupe and raised hand, blending in with the darkness as he made his way over to their wagon.

Arcana pushed her pastel purple hair back as she stopped in front of me, wearing a pale pink dress not unlike the one I'd worn while making deliveries just before the revel. "You proved my vision wrong."

I wasn't about to apologize for it. "Did you know he poisoned himself?"

"No," she said breezily. "But I saw him die days later. The poison, to me, looked like a constrictor slowly clenching his heart until it could no longer beat, like it would its prey."

"Your vision revealed more than you know," I admitted to her. "I thought you were involved. I'm sorry to have accused you."

"You were also falsely accused," she replied with a shrug.

"Then I apologize again, because it was the worst thing in the world – having no one believe in my innocence."

"Even your parents," she mused. "That surprised me."

"It hurt."

She looked over her shoulder at the rows of wagons arranged side-by-side stretching around the back lawns of the Estates like a great wooden fence. "I'm glad you were strong enough to defeat my vision, and I wanted to let you know that I've received another that involves you and Forge."

My heart skipped as I watched him smile at one of his coven mates. A female Silverthorn, far more of a compatible match than I would make for him.

Arcana twisted a lock of hair. "Do you wish to hear it?"

I shook my head. "No. I want to be surprised…"

TWENTY-SIX

Bog suctioned to my shoulder as I followed the walkway to the front door of the Silverthorn Estate, the host of this morning's Council meeting – the first since we came back home.

Our coven hosted all the others as often as Mother could conjure a new party theme, but it wasn't until now that I realized that the other covens had never invited us to their Estates before. I'd walked past them a thousand times, but had never been inside any Estate but ours.

I suddenly realized Forge's awe while looking at the inside of the Solarium instead of just admiring it from the outside.

I slid my balmy hands down my white dress as a young boy with a few missing teeth met me at the door. "Won't you come inside?" He shyly brushed his too-long dark hair out of his eyes. "The meeting will take place just down the hall, Miss Gravebriar," he said politely.

Wraith and Gust were already seated at a round, silver table. They nodded to me as I took one of the empty seats beside them. I would've listened in on their conversation, but a moment later, Forge strode into the room wearing a fine, dark gray suit reminiscent of the one he wore to the revel. His easy demeanor was a comfort. Forge made his way around the table, nodding to Wraith and Gust before sliding into the chair beside mine. "Gravebriar," he greeted with a smirk.

"Silverthorn."

He scooted closer, closer. Until the arms of our chairs were the only things separating us. The bees in my belly began to buzz at his proximity, at his brazenness. At the fact that no matter where we were or who was around, Forge was just Forge and he wanted me. "Miss me?" he asked.

"Duh," I playfully answered, rolling my eyes, trying hard to keep my smile at bay. In truth, I'd missed him terribly. The past week, he and I spent every moment together – waking and sleeping. I didn't realize how reclusive I'd attempted to make my life before he entered it, and how completely his steadfast presence filled what once was empty.

Forge chuckled, then leaned in to steal a lingering kiss before gesturing to Bog, his face still so close to mine it hurt not to kiss him again. "How is this little guy?"

He wanted to pet him. His finger inched out. Brushed the skin on my shoulder, leaving a trail of goosebumps.

I sighed, straining to see my yellow friend – my familiar – but Bog turned his head away. I could almost hear his huff of aggravation. "He's still mad at me."

I can't believe I didn't recognize the bond we shared as being the deep pairing of witch and familiar. In my defense, it was rare for any witch other than a Shade to soul-bind with a creature, but then again, my coven mate Hazel had bound her soul with the cat that tried to eat Bog...

But Bog was right about my ignorance. I should have known he was more than just a pet when a piece of my heart tore away when I left him in the forest. I brushed my finger down his back.

Forge looked closer at my sticky friend. "Nah. He's forgiven you. Just look at that face."

I looked at Bog again, who had swiveled to see Forge better, but quickly turned his head and avoided my stare. He let me carry him and allowed me to stroke his back, but still refused to look at me, even though I promised never to leave him behind again. Even though I relented and let him come to the meeting so he could hear for himself what was going to happen with the Council.

So far, I'd been unable to convince the amphibian that I'd done it out of a misguided sense of protectiveness for him. Forge seemed confident that he'd come around, but the longer he gave me the cold shoulder, the more I wondered if he might never forgive me.

We were reunited, but still, it felt like a forest lay between us.

The Silverthorn boy who'd led me to the meeting room returned with Arcana and Storm, the Tempest Power. Arcana looked nice in a dark purple pantsuit, while Storm wore lightweight robes, the darkest gray I'd seen clouds become before spilling the heavy rain they carried. They suited him.

Zinnia flitted in wearing a billowing bright green chiffon dress, giving me a wink as she rounded the table and took a chair along the wall behind me. "Do you want to pull your seat up here?"

She waved me off. "Seconds sit behind their Powers – a symbolic show of support, but also so we're kept informed of matters in case we need to fill in for our Powers."

I imagined Father in this room, seated behind Mother. Having her back.

She, Mother, Father, and I spoke on the terrace as the sun rose this morning. Zinnia pointed out that Mother was still qualified to be Second, but Mother was adamant that she did not want to push the Council on the issue. She wanted them to accept me and felt her presence would create animosity that wouldn't foster community, but divide once again.

It's time for me to enjoy your leadership, Castor, and yours, Zinnia, she'd graciously conceded. She was right. Pushing her into a leadership role again would send the wrong message, push a bit too hard, too fast, too far.

The seats slowly filled, Seconds seating themselves behind their Powers, two circles of focused strength, one inside the other.

Forge's Second, Steel, a tall, quiet man with wise eyes settled behind him and greeted Zinnia. Bolt sat behind Storm, forming the Tempest seats. Fox took a seat behind Wraith to form the Nocturn portion of the circle. Mystic sat behind Arcana. Scribe arrived, nodding as he sat beside Forge and his Second, Lilt, gracefully claimed the seat behind him a moment later.

Bloodlings Sanguine and Crimson filed in behind Flame, Gusts's Second. Finally, the Shades Umbra and Blear arrived, the last pieces of our circular puzzle.

Once everyone was seated, Scribe spoke words that sealed the room and prevented the walls from absorbing or repeating what was discussed privately.

In the end, Arcana, Scribe, Forge, and I were presented by our Seconds, who swore that we were the most powerful among our covens, and the Council voted to confirm each of us. The new Seconds present were also accepted.

We discussed the difficulties that the Council's integrity faced in light of the complete upheaval in its seats, the challenges we would face moving forward as one, and as individuals, and agreed that we had to present ourselves as a unified front if we expected our witches to move on from such recent wounds – wounds that were still open and raw. If we were to foster healing, we had to lead by example.

Forge garnered permission to form a team to gather intelligence on and combat any other packs of hunters. His request was quickly and unanimously supported. Arum posed a threat because he came from within, but he explained there were plenty of threats outside of Cauldron's hedge, too. Ones we needed to be aware of, because awareness would allow us to combat any attack someone tried to blindside us with.

We also agreed to reform the hedge, to strengthen it and put into place some sort of failsafe that would protect us even if someone managed to get as far as Arum had, gathering the things he needed to shatter it. We would each come up with ideas and discuss them later.

We also agreed that now that Arum's plan had been spoiled, and our city purged of those who would cause her harm, everyone could begin anew with a clean slate. Even Arum's former troupe, as Sanguine referred to them.

There was unease about them. I could feel it radiating from the Powers. But I knew in my heart that I'd guarded the city against them, and beyond that, knew that the troupe had been purged, too. Those who stayed took as great a risk in coming into Cauldron as we had by allowing them in. I didn't think they would take that for granted.

"I'm glad you brought up the troupe. I don't want them to be identified as Arum's. They are Cauldron's now. They're a family as much as any of our covens are a family. And associating them with Arum, I believe, will lead witches from the other covens to segregate instead of embrace them. They'll associate them with danger and consider their presence threatening."

"How would you suggest we move forward inclusively?" Umbra asked, fingers threaded over his stomach as he sank back into his seat.

341

"We could offer to allow them to split and join the other covens according to their heritage if they wish," Sanguine suggested, rapping his knuckles gently on the table.

Everyone looked to me and Forge. We knew them best. "It would show our willingness to include them, but I don't think they'd want to be parted. Things are unfamiliar. Some might not be sure if they want to stay or leave," I answered.

"You have an idea," Arcana intuited.

"Perhaps we could add a tenth coven to our ranks. They could elect a Power and Second and receive equal representation on the Council. If they decide to disband or leave, we can remove their standing within the Council." The room went still. "If you need time to consider…"

"Yes," Forge quickly agreed. "It's only fair."

We hadn't spoken about this. We hadn't had time to. But he was with me, just as he promised.

"I vote yes," Arcana said, nodding to me. "We chose to allow them inside the hedge; it's only fair that they're represented, assuming they want to stay together instead of split apart."

Sanguine suggested all weigh in, and that anyone who wished for more time to consider it to please simply state it. No one would judge anyone for wanting time to carefully form a decision.

Some things needed consideration. Some issues needed considerable debate. But on this matter, no one hesitated. Every Power voted for inclusion, and I'd never been more proud to call myself a citizen of Cauldron.

"There is one final matter I'd like to ask for your help with," Forge announced. "My late cousin's wife, Jenny, will give birth to his child soon if she hasn't already. The child will have magical blood, even though Jenny doesn't. I'd like to offer them a home here amongst the witches, to protect the babe."

Wraith slowly nodded. "It would be safer for the child here. We could teach the witchling how to master his or her power as it matures."

Again, everyone assented, and none refused her sanctuary within the hedge. This group of witches truly wanted to move forward, to restore, to better. And it made it easy to breathe, even easier to hope.

When the meeting ended, I remained at the table with Forge, Bog still refusing to look at me. "Any word from Crow?" he tested.

"Not yet." I'd sent him a letter in a bottle. Scribe gave me words that should've magicked the note directly to him, but I hadn't heard back. It wasn't urgent. I'd just written to see if he'd made it to the ship, if his crew was happy, and if he was safe on the sea.

I just wanted to know he was okay.

Forge took hold of my charm bracelet, pressed his thumb into the metal, and left a new charm on the chain.

I smiled, taking the small charm in my fingers. It was a golden charm, imprinted with the head of a house cat. It was Sarabi. When I came back to Cauldron last night, he had arranged the wagon village as he promised, and he and Scribe were helping everyone settle. I'd told him then what became of Shadow and her lion...

"You need something to remind you of the day you faced a lion and reduced him into a house cat."

"That was Scribe's doing."

"Scribe wasn't with you and you didn't need his words to defend yourself." He gestured to the round table. "What you did here this morning had nothing to do with anyone but you. You spoke from your heart, even though you were nervous to ask for anything for the troupe, but you convinced them. You probably felt the Council was another lion today, and your heart, your love reduced them into kittens." He smiled. "Whomever called you the poison of Cauldron did not know you at all."

That… that meant everything to me. I didn't only want to be destruction.

"Thank you for backing me up when I broached the subject. You didn't hesitate or question me at all."

He brushed a hand down my cheek, leaned in close. "If you're the briar, I wish to be the stem strong enough to support you, to see you grow."

If my heart had arms, she would have reached out for him. The moment he stepped into the forest and told me he believed I was innocent, she was his. Every moment after just solidified it. I should never have let Arum's slick lies cloud what she was telling me all along.

"What's this?" he asked, smoothing his thumb at the space between my brows that was no doubt scrunched.

I shook my head.

"Wish you would let me in."

"I just wish I hadn't doubted you, hadn't let Arum get inside my head."

He shook his head. "I'd worry more if you had blindly trusted me, Gravebriar. You had every right to question everyone and everything around you." He pulled me up and wrapped his arms around me. "You have to heal, too, Castor. So do I. We all do."

Mother waited for me on the terrace, her pale pink gown draped elegantly over her chair. She rose when she saw me. "Zinnia told me to ask you what they'd decided."

I would explain everything in time. But first… I walked to her and hugged her neck. "Thank you for coming to find me, for putting yourself at risk. For trying so long and hard to protect me."

Her breath stilled along with her hand on the back of my hair. "You're my daughter, Castor."

That was the only thing she knew. The only thing that mattered and reason enough to justify everything.

"Did you notice that there wasn't a single Gravebriar witch who left with Arum and joined him outside of Cauldron?"

I shook my head. "I hadn't noticed, but you're right."

"Do you know why?"

"Why?"

"Because we all knew he was guilty and not one would stand up for him. Not one would come to his defense. We wanted him to burn for what he did to you. We all cared for and loved you. We all stood with *you*, Castor. Against him."

"Why did the others follow him?"

"I don't know if you noticed, but my father was a smooth talker. He convinced many that it was I who poisoned you and that I'd framed him for it."

I had considered that for a time, because she was right, Arum was charismatic.

"Arbor supported him."

She pressed prim hands over her thighs. "Arbor supported himself, darling. Never anyone else."

She was right again. I wondered what he would do now that he had been thrust out. Would he use his dimple and charm to survive now, or would that only take him so far?

She hugged me again. "Mother..." When she pulled away, I smiled. "I was hoping you might assist me with planning a grand revel. I'd like to involve the troupe..."

Excitement blossomed across her face. "I would love to. Just tell me what you need."

TWENTY-SEVEN

On the eve that Coven Troupe – who had elected to remain together, an unbroken family – was voted into Cauldron as its tenth represented coven, the Gravebriars and Troupe joined together to host a great revel, one to rival all the Gravebriars had hosted before, one to rival all past performances.

An enormous tent had been erected on the back lawn of the Gravebriar Estate, striped in alternating bright moss and forest green. Inside, along the tent's canvas walls, torchlight flickered and winked, looking like fireflies had been trapped within.

I lingered at the window, remembering the last time I'd done this, the dread in my belly at the thought of walking downstairs, of meeting Arbor, and of lying once more. I felt none of that now. Because no secrets had to be kept now. And I knew who would be waiting for me this time… Butterflies flitted through my stomach, eager to see him. Eager to feel his hand on mine, his unashamed lips.

Mother and Zinnia, dressed in whimsical, glittering floral gowns chatted on the lawn, just below the terrace, ready to greet our guests. Mother's was a fuschia rose number that hugged her petite frame, while Zinnia's was a brighter red-orange with a broad skirt that swished when she walked.

Mother had asked our coven to help her arrange great tables, draping them with neutral linen and plain white settings, simple crystal flutes at each seat. There were more tables at this revel because there were more witches in Cauldron now.

She'd arranged long banquet tables, but another coven had volunteered to fill them.

More of my coven mates filtered onto the grass, mingling with Coven Troupe whose members were making a grand effort tonight to introduce themselves to witches from the other covens. The Gravebriars shimmered in elegant dresses that skimmed the blades of grass in the yard. Mother had seen to every detail, putting her personal stamp on the evening's décor, our coven's attire, and the ambiance in general.

The Troupe dressed in vibrant costumes that allowed for mobility and played up their beauty at the same time. The witches seemed eager to make an impression upon Cauldron. What better way for them to do it than to showcase their magics the best way they knew how: a spectacular show curated for witches, and performed by witches. Unencumbered. Unbridled. Unleashed.

If the citizens of Cauldron weren't enchanted by the troupe tonight, they might be unenchantable.

I'd unearthed and potted the orchid Forge had touched before he knew I watched him in the solarium, touched its silken petals and asked them to spread over my skin to form a gown that was equal parts Gravebriar Power and honorary troupe member. The fitted strapless gown stretched almost to the knee, a bustle of sparkling petals streaming down behind me to the planks of my bedroom floor. If my coven mates glittered, I wanted to, too.

Around my neck, I wore a necklace Father had had delivered this afternoon with a note telling me how proud he was of me. He requested I save one dance for him tonight. The delicate necklace, purchased from an Earth witch and carefully set in silver crafted by a Silverthorn, was adorned with alternating emeralds and diamonds whose facets reflected any light they caught.

Clasped on my wrist was the bracelet Forge had given me. Another charm had shown up as I walked into my room to get ready. This one, a trio of tents, all with alternating stripes.

I'd braided my hair into a mint green swirl, exactly as I'd worn it in the circus shows with Forge. No one knew it, but tonight, he and I were part of the show.

I'd dusted a small amount of shimmering dust onto my cheeks and collarbones. I'd painted my lips a dazzling red.

The only thing left was...

I walked to my dark room where Bog clung to the moss-covered log. A beetle scuttled by but he didn't eat it. He'd eaten earlier today when he thought I wasn't paying attention.

"Would you like to go to the revel with me?" I asked, crouching in front of him, though my heels made my ankles teeter.

He stared at the wall. "Bog. Please. Please, forgive me. You can feel my heart and know how sorry I am. I know I can never make it up to you, but let me try."

Slowly, he swiveled his head, his obsidian eyes meeting mine for the first time since he leaped home to find someone to help me.

"You were so brave," I told him, tears clouding my vision. "You came so far all alone, and I'm sorry I put you in that position. I just love you so much, and I didn't want you to be hurt because of me and I didn't want to rob you of a life you could live in the forest. I plucked you out of

349

it when you were so young… and I'm so, so stupid for not having known what you truly were to me. What you are to me. I love you, Bog."

His throat inflated a bit and he let out a tiny ribbit, then turned to me, reaching out one of his hands, his little fingers

I smiled and put out my finger and he climbed on. I put him on my shoulder so he could see everything I saw, swiping tears of relief.

We left my rooms and strode down the hallway, my eyes still stinging.

Forge waited at the bottom of the staircase, looking handsome as ever. I almost leaped over the balustrade. I knew he'd catch me if I did. But when I saw his heated gaze, I thought it best to torture him just a bit. Forge wore a black suit, black shirt, glittering silver vest neatly tucked beneath. He'd shed the jacket soon enough, but for now, I would enjoy the way it hugged his shoulders and trimmed his waist.

He smiled, possessively locking one hand on my side, bent so that he could whisper in my ear. "Damn, Gravebriar."

I grinned. "Silverthorn. You look nice."

His brow quirked. "Nice?"

I nodded, suppressing a smile. "It's a compliment."

"You look delectable," he said, the rasp to his tone sliding over my skin.

Swallowing thickly, I brought my lips just shy of his, hooking an arm around his neck. "Don't mess up my lip paint," I warned.

He plastered himself to me, his stomach shaking with laughter that held a warning. "Someone wise once told me crimson lips aren't the only kissable place a woman possesses."

His lips found my jaw, the side of my neck, my… Bog.

My familiar let out a huffy ribbit.

Forge grinned. "Look who finally forgave his enchanting mistress." He kissed my temple. "Are you ready to go outside? Your mother has asked me when you planned to show up no fewer than four times."

I laughed and took hold of his arm, this time excited to attend the revel and for everyone in Cauldron to see us and know that our feelings were very, very real and not an act at all.

With Bog perched on my shoulder, Forge and I walked out the tall double-doors and stepped into the warm, summer night. A breeze slid over the lawn and for a second, I swore I could smell the sea again. Like we weren't at the Estate but were walking along the docks, my hand drifting over the wet, wooden hulls.

Lively music filtered from the big top that took up nearly the entire back lawn.

Mother saw us and made her way across the lawn. She hugged my neck, nodding knowingly to Bog and smiling. "You look lovely, Castor."

"As do you, Mother."

She pressed her lips together, tears shimmering in her eyes. "I'm so glad you're home and that *you're* fixing what has been broken for so long. Things I was not strong enough to fix."

"Thank you," I croaked, emotion clogging my throat. Without all the worry and lies swirling around and between us, Mother was much freer with her feelings, and her praise.

"Your father is inside. He saved seats for you both in the front row, as you requested. Along with the thing you sent for, Forge."

My brows met. *What thing?* But more importantly, had Father saved a seat for her as well? "Mother, what is happening with you and Father?"

She tried to smile, shook her head, then pressed her chignon to make sure it hadn't fallen. "That's a conversation best kept for another time. Let's enjoy the evening and the magic it promises."

She'd said enough with those two sentences that no conversation was necessary. Father and Mother were not Shades; they had never soul-bound. They were free to pursue other people at any time. I just hadn't imagined they would, or maybe I just hadn't *wanted* to think about it.

Mother left us to buzz about the yard, glittering in her fitted fuchsia dress, shoulders back, head held high, a sad but genuine smile on her matching lips. She urged those lingering in the yard to step inside and find a seat.

Forge tugged me toward the buffet tables, where a divine and familiar scent filled my nose. Cauldron's bakers were talented, but this was not from Cauldron.

My mouth fell open. "How did you...?"

"Coppers get you pretty far in Westbrook. Good thing I can make plenty. I'm happy to report that, once again, the old married pair was much happier when I left than when I walked in," he winked.

He'd traveled to our bakerie.

There were carafes of freshly squeezed orange juice, petite cakes, honey bread, chocolate breads, cinnamon buns, apple and blueberry and strawberry tarts. "Thank you," I breathed, hugging him.

"When did you find time?"

"Scribe can do many things. I told him how you said your power was only limited by the bounds of your imagination, and he has imagined a great many things no one realized was possible. The trip to Westbrook took mere seconds with his help."

"That would've been nice," I laughed.

"Yes, but then you wouldn't have been able to ogle me from behind."

He had a point there.

"Or watch you inhale spider webs," I teased.

"Or watch me inhale spider webs," he grinned.

The skin on my wrist warmed as he pressed a new charm into existence. A petite cake. "To always remember our time outside of Cauldron and that we can go wherever we'd like. Our adventure is not limited to within the hedge. If you want to go to our bakerie, we'll go. If you want to see great cities, we'll see them. Together."

"Together," I agreed.

I pushed up on my toes, angling my crimson-painted mouth toward his when Mother primly announced that the show would soon begin.

Forge laughed. As the stragglers filed inside the tent, Forge grabbed a few things for us to share while I stole a carafe for us to split. We rushed across the yard, both smiling and in love.

"I'd thought about finding puffed corn and ale, but thought you might like this for a treat at first."

"It's perfect."

354

TWENTY-EIGHT

We ducked inside the tent and closed the doors, the last to enter the space, then made our way to where Father had saved our seats. Four were empty beside us. We claimed two and waited for Mother.

Forge slid a hand around my waist and turned my silver-colored dress to a network of delicate, malleable threads made of pure silver. Mother sat down with us, noticing the difference in my gown. Her brow rose, but she didn't voice her question.

"Will you hold Bog for me?" I asked, taking my little friend off my shoulder.

Her expression was part horror and part acceptance. Mother was afraid to touch Bog. I laid him on a honey bun and passed him to her. She awkwardly took it as Forge stood and offered me a hand. "Ready?"

"I am."

The flyers climbed the ladders into the ceiling and then... they began to soar. The girl dove forward, swung back and forth until she was going as high as she could. She let go of the bar and her partner swung down to catch her.

He twisted her in the air and tossed her like she weighed nothing at all.

As they performed, Mother watched in awe. So did Bog.

I looked to Father, who held a similar expression of wonder on his face, then to all of our peers, who mirrored my parents' expressions.

"Good evening," a familiar voice boomed as none other than Crow stepped into the center ring wearing a glittering black suit. My mouth fell open. I swatted Forge playfully. He'd kept this secret. This was the thing he'd ordered... or invited, rather.

Crow's dazzling eyes fell on me and he flashed a brilliant smile, mouthing the word, *Surprise.*

"Welcome, welcome, to a city where witches roam, where any amount of magic means a witch can make a home. We at Coven Troupe would like for you to kick back and enjoy the show, but if you feel like performing, then we invite you to showcase your talents with us!"

Applause and roars filled the tent. The people of Westbrook could probably hear the joyous uproar. At least, I hoped they could.

Fire Elementines poured from the smaller tents, enshrouded in flame, twirling in acrobatic stunts and tricks that defied gravity. They tossed one another into the air, formed great pyramids of fire and flesh.

Water Elementines extinguished their flames. Even shy, pale Breeze laughed as she flung water from her palm to drench an incandescent Fire witch. The Wind witches, hot on their heels, sent warm gusts swirling to dry everyone and everything off, while the witches of Earth conjured giants made of rock that pushed against the tent's top and helped the flyers to the ground. The two stepped into a giant's palm and he gently eased it back to the lawn. They stepped off and bowed and waved as the gathered crowd cheered and applauded.

"We're up," Forge eagerly announced as the Elementines cleared the space, and a familiar nicked wheel with swirling shades of green paint was rolled in, the legs set by a pair of Bloodlings. I did not miss Merc and Ury. Not one little bit.

Forge took my hand and led me to the center of the ring to Crow. I threw my arms around my seafaring friend's neck. "I'm so glad you're okay. I wrote to you."

"So did Forge. He invited me here. He wanted it to be a surprise," he said.

He and Forge helped me onto the wheel and fastened the buckles to keep me from falling off it. I smiled at Mother who was not smiling at all. She covered her mouth with her hands as she took in the amount of silver knives along Forge's belt. She slowly shook her head.

I raised my thumb to her as best I could while restrained and turned back to Forge as Laurel and one of her new friends approached. He looked enamored with my coven mate, but she didn't seem to notice.

"The wheel of life is a puzzling thing, sometimes she's steady and sometimes she spins..." Crow's voice echoed. "But it's much easier to face each day, when you've got a steadfast friend."

"Ready, Castor?" my friend Laurel said from beside me.

"Ready."

She and the lovestruck Bloodling boy took hold of the wheel and gave it a spin.

Forge knew me by heart, I reminded myself. Instead of fearing he might hurt me, I laughed, enjoying the ride as his knives fell around me.

"But you can withstand almost anything when you have family, and you have friends..." he finished.

Laurel and her friend steadied the wheel, and though it took a moment for my vision to stop spiraling, I couldn't stop laughing. They unstrapped my arms and ankles and helped me down. I turned to look at the wheel and saw Forge hadn't outlined me on the wood. He'd written something. Letters arched from one shoulder to the other.

Pinned into the wood... *Gravebriar*.

The witches of Cauldron roared as Laurel and her friend freed my wrists and ankles.

Forge grabbed my waist and spun me around, kissing me soundly, crimson lips and all, grinning like a fool in love. I did, too. In fact, I couldn't stop smiling.

"Castor Gravebriar, tonight, we honor your valor, your steadfast heart, and your resolve to see Cauldron become the city you imagine she might one day be," Crow proudly said, taking my hand and raising it into the air.

I laugh-cried as my peers cheered, this time for me.

"I wasn't alone. If Forge Silverthorn hadn't seen a truth in me that no one else did, I wouldn't be standing here today."

That night, beneath the tent, the City of Cauldron celebrated. I danced with Father, and he told me how proud he was, how scared he'd been, and how hopeful he was for the future. He also told me that he approved of Forge Silverthorn, and that many a witch would have done as he was told and never questioned the Council's instruction.

I danced with Crow for a few songs and learned he had taken the ship, that his crew was happy, that he was facilitating trade among the cities, that he was at peace with his decision even as he was happy to visit us for a time.

I didn't miss the charm that appeared on my wrist as he and I swayed: a crow to remind me of my friend.

Crow didn't protest when Forge asked to cut in as one song ended and another began. Forge's warm hand found the small of my back, the other holding my hand up to the stars.

"I've had ample time to think as you've spent the majority of the evening with Crow instead of me."

I tilted my head. "I danced with him for three songs and he's leaving at dawn. Besides, he's not you, Forge. Green is most certainly not a Silverthorn's color. You have nothing to be jealous of..."

He was quiet for a moment, but I could see orneriness swirling in his molten metal eyes. "Speaking of green and silver, do you think we should merge covens?"

My mouth gaped. I barked a laugh. "What?"

"I mean, if it's you and me against the world, maybe we should merge covens. I think the Silverbriars has a great ring to it."

"I think you've lost your mind," I laughed. "First, you're delusional – and jealous – about me dancing with Crow when you invited him, might I add, and now, you want to merge our covens into the Silverbriars."

My cheeks hurt from smiling at him so often tonight.

"Number one, I have every right to be jealous anytime I don't have your full and complete attention. If I'd danced with ticket booth girl for that long, you'd have clawed her face off. Number two, those were the three longest songs, and therefore slow dances, in the history of music. Even longer than *all* the dances you had with Arbor at the last revel. I thought they might never end."

"You're being dramatic. They're no longer than the next three, which I intend to hold you hostage for," I said as we swayed.

"Then the next three will feel far too short."

I tilted my head at him. How could he know that?

Bog moved on my shoulder as if he wanted to see Forge better. As if he didn't understand either.

"There will never be a song long enough for me to dance with you to. There will never be a day, year, or lifetime long enough to spend with you, Castor Gravebriar. When you love someone..." His eyes flicked to mine as he searched for more words. But they weren't necessary.

My heart raced toward him. The beetles in my stomach took flight. "I'm glad you feel that way. I made a promise to you, Forge Silverthorn, and I intend to keep it."

"What's that?" he grinned.

"You and me against the world. I love you, too, and I promise I'm with you, Forge."

"And, I'm with you, Princess."

I narrowed my eyes and kissed him silly for the use of that pet name, until the only thing he could utter was, "Damn, Gravebriar." He kissed me again, then his eyes glittered and I knew I was in trouble... "I'm going to use that pet name much more often."

ODE TO BOG

Your toes cling to my finger,
As if you'll never let go.
Until you see a beetle,
Then after it you throw.
Your tongue is long and grabby,
And like me, you can be crabby.
You know I am no poet,
But you listen to my tries.
You listen to my laughter,
And listen when I cry.
Your skin is cool and calming,
Your form of matchless grace.
It makes me want to kiss,
Your familiar froggy face.

ACKNOWLEDGEMENTS

I'm ever thankful to God for His mercy and blessings in my life. I have to thank my family for their constant love and encouragement (no matter what), my friends for their support, and fans for loving my characters and stories as much as I do.

Thank you, Melissa Stevens, for designing the perfect book cover, interior, map, tarot card and every other thing related to bringing this book to life visually. And thanks to Stacy Sanford for waving her magic red pen over my manuscript and polishing it beautifully. Thanks to Kendra Gaither for proofreading the final product.

Special thanks to Cristie Alleman, Amber Garcia, C.L. Cannon, Christy Sloat, & Heather Lyons.

ABOUT THE AUTHOR

Casey Bond lives in West Virginia with her husband and their two beautiful daughters. She likes goats and yoga, but hasn't tried goat yoga because the family goat is so big he might break her back. Seriously, he's the size of a pony. Her favorite books are the ones that contain magical worlds and flawed characters she would want to hang out with. Most days of the week, she writes young adult fantasy books, letting her imaginary friends spill onto the blank page.

Casey is the award-winning author of When Wishes Bleed, The Omen of Stones, Things That Should Stay Buried, and With Shield and Ink and Bone. Learn more about her work at www.authorcaseybond.com.

Find her online @authorcaseybond.

ALSO BY CASEY L. BOND

When Wishes Bleed & The Omen of Stones
Things That Should Stay Buried
With Shield and Ink and Bone
The Fairy Tales
Riches to Rags, Savage Beauty, Unlocked, & Brutal Curse
Glamour of Midnight
The High Stakes Saga
High Stakes, High Seas, High Society, High Noon, &
High Treason
The Harvest Saga
Reap, Resist, & Reclaim
The Keeper of Crows Duology
Keeper of Crows & Keeper of Souls
The Frenzy Series
Frenzy, Frantic, Frequency, Friction, Fraud, & Forever
Frenzy

CPSIA information can be obtained
at www.ICGtesting.com
Printed in the USA
LVHW090840250421
685470LV00020B/218/J